TIME OF DEPARTURE

TIME OF DEPARTURE

DOUGLAS SCHOFIELD

MINOTAUR BOOKS NEW YORK

TIME OF DEPARTURE. Copyright © 2015 by Douglas Schofield. All rights reserved. Printed in the United States of America. For information, address St. Martin's Press, 175 Fifth Avenue, New York, N.Y. 10010.

www.minotaurbooks.com

Designed by Omar Chapa

Library of Congress Cataloging-in-Publication Data

Schofield, Douglas.
  Time of departure / Douglas Schofield. — First edition.
      pages ; cm
  ISBN 978-1-250-07275-7 (hardcover)
  ISBN 978-1-4668-8461-8 (e-book)
  1. Women lawyers—Fiction.   2. Public prosecutors—Florida—Fiction.
  3. Cold cases (Criminal investigation)—Fiction.   I. Title.
  PR9275.C393S36 2015
  813'.6—dc23

                                                        2015022092

Our books may be purchased in bulk for promotional, educational, or business use. Please contact your local bookseller or the Macmillan Corporate and Premium Sales Department at (800) 221-7945, extension 5442, or by e-mail at MacmillanSpecialMarkets@macmillan.com.

First Edition: December 2015

10 9 8 7 6 5 4 3 2 1

FOR MARIA AND LAZARO FERNANDEZ, WITH LOVE

ACKNOWLEDGMENTS

Various versions of this story have been kicking around in my head since the 1980s, but offbeat ideas do not become published novels without the assistance of many willing hands. I wish to express my gratitude to the following friends and colleagues for their encouragement and support.

In the Cayman Islands: Alister Ayres, Karen Myren, Carol Rouse, David Dinner, and Janet Morse, all of who provided invaluable help by reading early drafts and by refusing to forbear when critical comments were required. I also pay tribute to Janet's husband, author Graham Morse, who is not only a loyal friend, but also a man of impeccable timing.

In Florida: I must first thank respected Miami author Les Standiford. Based on a brief synopsis of this novel, and without us ever having personally met, Les opened an important door for me. My profound thanks go, as well, to my old friend Lee Peters Jr., former ATF agent, former Florida State prosecutor, and recently retired Florida public defender; and to Frank and Lorna Nolin, who introduced me to the matchless charms of Mexico Beach on the Florida Panhandle. Finally, I thank our dear Miami friends, Lazaro and Maria Fernandez, for their constant and unswerving support. This novel is gratefully dedicated to them.

In Washington State: My profound gratitude goes to Dr. Greg Hoeksema, USN (retired), who provided medical advice in language that even an attorney could understand.

In New York: I would like to thank my agents at InkWell Management,

Kim Witherspoon and Lena Yarbrough, for their enthusiasm, for their energy, and—most important—for their exceptional instincts. They knew just where to take my manuscript. So, thank you again, Kim and Lena, for introducing me to a lady I have come to admire greatly: my editor, Daniela Rapp, at St. Martin's Press.

Daniela, thank you.

Last, first, and always, I thank my beloved wife, Melody, for her strength, her guidance, and her unfailingly wise advice. I am a very lucky man.

We shall not cease from exploration
And the end of all our exploring
Will be to arrive where we started
And know the place for the first time.

—T. S. Eliot
Four Quartets,
"Little Gidding" (V)

TIME OF DEPARTURE

My darling daughter,

This is your mother's story. The knowledge that I must some-day draw you into this circle of hell has weighed sorely on me for thirty years. But it is a promise I made to her. She wanted you to know her story. She held nothing back. She wanted you to know everything.

I have faith, as she did, that you are strong enough.

Now it is up to us. The end of your mom's story is back at the beginning. So that is where you and I must go . . . together.

Dad

CLAIRE

1

My new corner office wasn't much different from my last one—battleship gray walls, faux-wood furniture, patternless nylon carpet—but at least it was brighter. It had been empty for almost a month, yet I was still picking up whiffs of the previous owner's cologne. It was one of those vintage brands—Bay Rum, maybe, or Bacchus. I couldn't tell. My talents didn't extend to discriminating between specific brands, just between out of date and up to date. All I knew was that I'd have to figure out a way to eliminate the lingering odor. I didn't look forward to putting in fifteen-hour days under the olfactory pall of Roy Wells's ghost.

Wells had been a reasonably competent prosecutor, but he'd never made me feel very welcome in the Florida Eighth Circuit State Attorney's Office. Not just because I was another female interloper in what his right-wing mentality firmly believed should have remained a male preserve, but also because I'd been breathing down his professional neck ever since Sam Grayson had hired me. Sam had fifty prosecutors across six counties to choose from, but he'd made me Felony Division Chief two days after my thirty-first birthday. One notable result of that announcement was the thin-lipped silence I now endured whenever I passed a colleague in the hallway.

Maybe it was the stress of this new order that had dropped Roy Wells in his tracks. Forty-six was a bit young for a fatal heart attack.

I slotted a nail through a metal picture hook.

Thump!

I laid the hammer on my desk and hung my diploma:

The President and Fellows of Harvard College . . . in solemn council assembled, have admitted
        CLAIRE ALEXANDRA TALBOT   . . .

I was straightening the frame on the wall when I heard Sam's voice behind me.

"Claire! What are you doing here? It's after ten!"

Sam Grayson filled my doorway, all 230 pounds of him, with his suit jacket slung over one shoulder and a look of concern on his broad face.

"I guess I could ask you the same question," I responded. "What does it look like? I'm moving my ego wall to its impressive new abode."

"Impressive?"

"Well . . . it's a little bigger than my last closet."

Actually, it was only about thirty square feet bigger.

"Go home, girl! Freddie can do that for you tomorrow."

I let the "girl" thing pass. Sam was in his mid-fifties, and he'd retained a few old-school habits, but he always backed me to the hilt when it came to the job.

"I've started now. Might as well finish." I stooped and picked up another framed document.

"It's a career, Claire." Sam peered at me over his glasses. "Sometimes you act like it's a race against time."

"Sometimes it feels that way."

Sam watched while I marked another spot on the wall. I fished a hook-and-nail combo out of the packet on my desk.

"Claire?"

"Mmm?"

"Just out of curiosity . . . what *is* your plan?"

I turned to him. "Plan?"

"Your career plan. You know . . . the female attorney 'I can have it all' plan."

I stared at him. "Has someone been leaving women's magazines in the men's room?"

"No. But my girls leave them all over the house," he replied, referring to his wife, Diana, and their adult daughter, Suzanne. "Listen, I might be old, but I'm not deaf and blind. Over fifty percent of law school graduates are female, but the way this damned society works, any ambitious girl like you—"

"Woman?"

"—*woman* like you has two choices. You work your ass off, never marry, and spend your nights alone eating takeout, or—"

"—or," I finished, "I work like crazy, marry late, take a couple of years off to have kids, and then hire a nanny and climb back on board. It's called 'You can have it all; you just can't have it all at once.'"

"Sounds cheerful, but there's a downside."

"Being . . . ?"

"Being, when you climb back on board, all the attorneys who stayed in the game have left you behind." He paused, watching me. "So, which is it?"

"Keep working and wait to see where life takes me." I lifted the hammer.

He smiled as if he'd just won a bet with himself. "Tell me you've eaten since lunch."

I grinned at him. "No, Dad. I'll grab some Chinese on the way home to my empty house."

He gave me another of his funny little smiles and surrendered. "Okay. Don't forget to set the alarm when you leave."

"Will do."

He shook his head indulgently and left.

It was pushing midnight when I finished. I'd hung the remaining certificates and retrieved a couple more from a box in the footwell of my desk. I had my reasons. When you've been a qualified attorney for only seven years *and* you've just been appointed head of a division *and* you're female, you need all the framed evidence of professional gravitas you can bring to bear.

I'd run an errand earlier in the evening, and when I returned, I'd left my car in the Chief Investigator's space next to the main entrance. As I walked toward it, I thought I caught a ripple of movement across the street. I stopped. In my job, you have to be alert. "Situational awareness," the cops call it.

Several mature laurel oaks were spaced along the sidewalk on the opposite side of University Avenue, and the glow from a streetlight at the end of the block had transformed their trunks into a colonnade of dark pillars.

But there was nothing else to see.

I unlocked my car, got in, and started the engine. I pulled out of the lot and headed west on University. As I accelerated, a set of headlights flashed across my mirrors. A vehicle swung an arcing U-turn behind me and then sped away in the opposite direction. I hadn't seen or heard it approaching, and the maneuver startled me. I watched in my rearview mirror as the vehicle's Euro-style LED taillights flared at the Main Street intersection. Their odd pattern resembled a railroad symbol on a map legend.

The vehicle turned the corner and disappeared.

Feeling slightly uneasy, I drove home.

Home was a rented town house exactly 9.4 miles from my office.

I'd almost gotten caught up in that crazy real estate bubble in the run-up to its collapse. In July 2008, I'd been considering buying a loft in a new development not far from the office. The location had definite appeal, mainly because it was a short walk from work. But then something happened. On the third Friday of the month, I happened to watch *Bill Moyers Journal* on PBS. I learned that millions of subprime mortgages were resetting, that the foreclosure rate was climbing fast, and that property prices were forecast to crater. On Monday afternoon, I walked into my bank and told the mortgage manager I wanted to reconsider.

"No problem, Claire," he said. "I got your message."

"What message?"

"That you'd changed your mind."

I must have appeared confused because he shuffled through one of the piles on his desk, extracted a folder, opened it, and handed me a typed form.

It was a phone message.

*Ms. Talbot's accountant called. She'll be in later to cancel her request
for mortgage preapproval. Please do not process further.*

I handed the message back. "Interesting . . . since I don't have an accountant."

His eyebrows notched up. He rechecked the document. "Hmm . . . maybe Mrs. Tierney misheard the customer's name. Good thing, though . . ."

"Why?"

"Because I was about to register your file in the system. Cancellation would have cost you a seventy-five-dollar fee."

"I thought preapprovals were free!"

"New bank policy. They're calling it a 'commitment fee.'"

"A commitment fee for a *pre*approval? That makes no sense!"

"The real estate business is booming, and—"

"Not for long, from what I'm hearing!"

"Maybe. But right now a lot of people are going from bank to bank, making multiple applications. Our loan officers are working flat out, and management says we can't afford to have them wasting time on people who aren't serious, so it's seventy-five dollars for bank customers and a hundred dollars, payable up front, for noncustomers."

"You didn't mention this fee when I first spoke to you."

"Oh? Didn't I?" He didn't seem too concerned. His mind had moved on. His eyes swept the stacks of paper on his desk. He grimaced, tapped the phone message slip, and said, "Now I'll have to figure out which file this call was about. There's no return number."

I left him to his confusion. The next day I changed banks. Fees for preapproval?

Bankers!

As it turned out, I had actually benefited from the housing crisis because my rent payments were now ridiculously low. A year after I walked out of that bank, I became the proud tenant of a recently renovated two-bed, two-and-a-half-bath end unit in a quiet complex on Magnolia Walk in Haile Plantation. It came with all the features Realtors had been happy to extol when they were seducing the chronically underemployed into signing subprime mortgages: hardwood floors, plantation blinds, blue granite counters, solid mahogany cabinets, and . . . wait for it . . . genuine wood-burning fireplaces in both the living room and master bedroom. True townhome luxury at 100 percent financing! How could a buyer lose?

Let me count the ways.

I stepped under the cute little clamshell awning that hung over my front door and slid the key into the top lock.

It was already unlocked.

I always lock the dead bolt when I leave the house.

I put my hand on the knob and twisted. It didn't budge. The bottom lock was still engaged. I used my key and quietly stepped inside.

The house was silent. I flashed on Sam Grayson's advice to me during a particularly tense gang prosecution a few months earlier. "Get a permit, girl," he'd said. "Buy yourself a gun, and learn how to use it."

Advice I had ignored.

I slipped the machete out of the decorative umbrella stand my mother had given me. I searched both floors, room by room, closet by closet. There was no one there. I set the machete on my bed and started searching cupboards and drawers. I'm not a shopper, and I'm not an accumulator, so the search didn't take long.

Nothing was missing.

As far as I could tell, nothing was even disturbed.

I descended the stairs and I slid the machete back into the stand. I wandered into the living room. I stood in the middle of the room, thinking . . . trying to remember my exact movements as I left for work that morning. I was beginning to doubt myself: Did I forget to lock that dead bolt?

Then I noticed it.

It was very faint. Just a whiff that barely registered, and then it was gone.

It was perfume.

I stood at the bathroom mirror for ten seconds or so before going to bed, just staring at myself.

Here I was, doing it again.

Here I was wondering why the hell I was here . . . in this place, in this time. Why hadn't I been born centuries ago? Why now? Why had I been born in 1979 and not in 1479? Why was my name Claire and not some other name? Why was I born in Florida, and not, say, Nairobi or Brisbane or Kiev?

Why do I have this lopsided, watercolor face and not some other face? Why didn't I have a face that was more . . . conventional?

I was fairly sure most people would not consider me beautiful, at least not in any classical sense. In fact, not in any sense for which a descriptive word exists in English. In a world obsessed with youthful, gorgeous—

and symmetrical—faces, the one looking back at me from the mirror was more likely to be described as "intriguing." It was a bit narrow, which actually worked for the cheekbone thing, but not so much for the chin. My lips were standard issue, but my smile was wider on the right side than the left. On top of that, I was probably a bit too thin. I'd always figured I had to stay in tight shape if I was going to endure the debilitating grind of jury work without ruining my health.

Bottom line was, for whatever reason—my looks, my manner, my pushiness—after my first few months on the prosecution staff, my male colleagues stopped including me in their Friday-night plans.

It didn't matter what the lawyers at the office thought about me. I wasn't looking for a relationship with any of them. The problem was . . . I had no relationship outside the office, either. It's not as if a female prosecuting attorney can cruise the happy hours or start dating a defense attorney.

Close observation of my mother had taught me, from a young age, not to expect a romance-novel version of life when I grew up, but for reasons I hadn't yet plumbed, the only men who ever came on to me were invariably already married.

I sighed, switched off the bathroom light, and took my intriguing self to bed.

2

"Okay, folks. That's it for this week."

Sam Grayson was sitting at the head of our boardroom table; I was on his right. Prosecutors gathered papers and began to drift out.

I started to get up. Sam stopped me.

"Wait, Claire." Sam called out to one retreating figure, "Perry!"

I settled back into my chair.

Assistant State Attorney Perry Standish was about to exit the room. He turned around. Sam pointed at the chair on his left. Perry reversed course and walked stiff-backed toward us. He was dressed in his usual foppish style, complete with boutonniere. I'd never seen him work in shirtsleeves, except on those rare occasions when he came in on a weekend to prepare a case.

I wasn't the only one who had observed that the man's unshakable self-regard was hardly justified by his conviction rate.

I felt cold eyes sweep over me as he took his seat.

"If this is about the grievance I filed—"

"No. It's about the Whitman trial. Claire hired a jury consultant. You dismissed her!"

Cold eyes switched back to me. "I guess I've been around long enough to know how to pick a jury."

Sam paused for a second, studying the man's expression. "You think I don't hear the talk, Perry? Defense lawyers calling you Prince Catch-'n-Release?"

"Prince? Really?"

Sam stared at him in straight-faced disbelief. He leaned forward. "They're laughing at you, Perry! Watch my lips! *No plea bargains on Whitman!* This is a full-contact prosecution! It's not just the press who are watching this case. People in positions far above your pay grade and mine are watching. Do your job, and do it well!"

Cold eyes slid back and forth between us. "You're the boss."

"Yes, I am. And so is Claire."

Standish stood. He shot me a quick sulfurous look that Sam didn't see, and walked away. My eyes followed him out the door.

"I know what you're thinking," Sam said quietly.

"What am I thinking?"

"That maybe he'll resign when he loses on that grievance."

"Will he?"

Sam shook his head. "He'll never resign. He lost his shirt in the market."

"You'd never know it from the way he dresses," I said.

Sam chuckled. "That's the thing about mediocrities, Claire. They're always at their best."

"You could push him out," I suggested.

"I could. But I'd just be making trouble for both of us."

"How?"

"His family is well connected in Tallahassee."

"Then why isn't he in the Attorney General's office? Why is he here?"

"You can go only so far on connections."

"I get it." I stood up to go.

"Hang on," Sam said. "As a matter of interest . . ."

"What?"

"Why the jury consultant?"

"Groupthink."

Sam looked puzzled.

"The fastest way to a unanimous verdict is to encourage groupthink," I explained. "To get that working, it helps to have the right mix of personalities."

"You're talking about packing the jury with conformists."

"In a sense. But I've read the studies. It doesn't mean they'll necessarily conform to convict; they can just as easily conform to acquit."

"Still . . . it sounds a bit cynical."

"I know. But like it or not, the defense bar have started doing this. Wade Garrison hired a psychologist from Seattle to help him pick the Capelin jury. It's a question of equality of arms, Sam. If they're doing it, we have to do it."

"I thought Whitman was a special case. If we start hiring jury consultants for every trial, it's going to become a budget issue."

"I'm not saying every case. But definitely the big ones. Look at it this way: What we spend on experts, we could save on hung juries and retrials."

"I don't know." Sam sighed. "Maybe I'm just getting too old for this job."

I squeezed his arm. "Come on, now. Don't you quit on me!"

I suppose I could have warned Stirling McCandless about what I was planning to do before he got up on his hind legs and made that big tear-jerking pitch to Judge O'Connor. But one of the first things Sam Grayson had taught me was never to interrupt my opponent when he was making a mistake. And . . . I wanted to hear McCandless say it. I wanted to hear him repeat the lies his client, Barbara Hauser—former jewelry chain owner and now convicted felon on her own plea—had told him.

So when we entered the courtroom earlier, I'd just nodded to McCandless and taken my seat.

"—and so, Your Honor," he was saying as he wrapped up a thirty-minute waterspout of distortions, "the regrettable facts are clear: My client is deeply remorseful for the financial loss she has caused to each and every one of her former employees. Although she would dearly wish to make good on those very substantial losses, her grave physical condition makes it virtually impossible for her to pay restitution in the near term, and as the medical reports we have filed with the Court show, she is in no position to serve a custodial sentence of any length, or at all." He took a long overdue breath and then resumed his bleat. "The traffic accident was not her fault and, coming on the heels of her arrest and public humiliation, can only be viewed today—in these proceedings—as a substantial mitigating factor."

Stirling laid a theatrically comforting hand on his client's shoulder.

"Judge, in these highly regrettable circumstances, a suspended sentence, with a lengthy probationary period, is really the Court's only viable option."

Stirling's client sat slumped in her wheelchair, dabbing at her eyes with a tissue. She looked utterly pathetic. From the moment her daughter rolled her into the courtroom, her posture of defeat and hollow-eyed despair had been on constant display for all to see.

The judge gazed down at the defendant. Plainly, he was affected by what he had heard. The defense had drawn the best judge in the circuit for their case. Evan O'Connor was every inch a gentleman jurist: quietly spoken, even tempered, and scrupulously fair. He was also inclined to err on the low side when it came to sentencing in cases of nonviolent crime. Stirling McCandless knew that, and so did I.

But I knew something else about Judge O'Connor.

He could not tolerate a liar.

The judge's blue eyes turned to me. "Does the State have a reply?"

"Yes, Your Honor. In fact, we have a witness to call."

McCandless leapt to his feet. "We object, Your Honor! We've had no notice of any witnesses to be called at this hearing!"

"That is correct, Your Honor. I will explain."

"Who is this witness?" O'Connor asked.

"Your Honor is familiar with Mr. Edward Carlyle, from our office." I gestured toward the tall, heavyset man who was sitting behind me. One of the first African-Americans to head up an ATF Field Division, Eddie had joined our office after his retirement from the Bureau. He worked just as tirelessly for us as he had for the feds.

"Why should I agree to hear evidence from the State Attorney's Chief Investigator at this stage of the proceedings?"

Eddie reached into an inner pocket of his jacket, removed two DVDs, and passed them to me. I checked the labels, selected one, and held it up for the judge to see.

"The witness will be tendering this surveillance footage of the defendant, showing her working in her backyard, mowing her lawn, moving garden furniture, and weeding her flower beds. This footage was shot over a forty-eight-hour period—" I paused for effect. "—last weekend."

I heard a general intake of breath and a few muttered expletives from the gallery rows directly behind me, where a number of the defendant's former employees had been hanging on every word. For several years prior to her arrest, their employer had been embezzling from their pension plan contributions. Some had lost thousands of dollars.

I glanced over at Stirling McCandless. His face had gone pale under his health-spa tan, and he looked genuinely stunned. I realized that he had been completely taken in by his client. I shifted my gaze to the woman in the wheelchair. She was glowering at me, obviously torn between maintaining her tragic pose and leaping out of her chair to go for my throat. I placed the second DVD on the corner of my counsel table. "I have a copy of the exhibit for Mr. McCandless."

At my comment, McCandless seemed to recover. He came out fighting. "Your Honor, these tactics are an outrage! My client—!"

"—had already entered her guilty pleas when this surveillance took place. Her status before the Court had changed. Ms. Talbot's conduct would be open to criticism only if it were unlawful. Tell me how it was unlawful."

"She's had this evidence for a week! We have had no notice—none!—and therefore we have had no opportunity to study it, or to obtain medical evidence to . . . to assist the Court."

I waited quietly. I knew the judge would come back to me.

He did.

"Ms. Talbot, Counsel does have a point. Am I to understand that you arranged for your investigator to place the defendant under intrusive surveillance in her own backyard, that you obtained the proffered evidence one week ago, and that you have been sitting on it until today?"

"No, Your Honor."

"No to what?

"No to each of your questions."

Judge O'Connor leaned forward. "Ms. Talbot, please don't play word games with the Court."

"Permit me to explain, Your Honor. Our office did not arrange for this surveillance. We first learned it had taken place at six o'clock last evening, when an insurance adjuster attended at our offices and briefed Mr. Carlyle. The surveillance on this DVD was conducted by a private investigator retained by the insurer of the other driver involved in the defendant's automobile accident. The attorney representing Mrs. Hauser in that action—not Mr. McCandless—has submitted a very substantial claim. The surveillance was conducted from a neighbor's property. The neighbor, we have been told, was only too ready to assist. Therefore, as a result of Mrs. Hauser's own actions in separate proceedings, the State is today in a position to refute her claim that her 'disability' should exempt her from a prison sentence."

McCandless interjected. "Your Honor, the prosecutor told us she wants to call Mr. Carlyle to the stand. In light of what we just heard, clearly he is not a proper witness to place the DVD into evidence. For all we know, this footage is a year old and entirely unrelated to my client's civil claim! Only the investigator who recorded the footage could prove otherwise. Why isn't he here?"

The judge looked at me.

"The investigator is currently working on a foreign assignment. We understand he is in Germany. His firm expects him back by the end of the month." I held up the DVD. "The identity of the subject of this footage is self-evident, and every frame is date stamped."

McCandless protested. "Date stamping can be faked, Your Honor!"

"I think we can deal with that remote possibility, Mr. McCandless," Judge O'Connor responded. He turned back to me. "Ms. Talbot, I expect the defendant's accommodating neighbor can cast some light on this. How much time would you require to secure that person's appearance?"

"A moment, please, Your Honor . . ." I conferred quickly with Eddie and then addressed the judge. "I am told that her workplace is only a few blocks from this building. May I have thirty minutes?"

"Make it an hour. Have Mr. Carlyle contact the witness. In the meantime, I want to see you and Mr. McCandless in my chambers. And bring that DVD with you."

Three hours later, while her daughter quietly wept, Barbara Hauser was escorted from the courtroom to begin serving a ten-year sentence. Pointedly, the judge ordered her to leave her wheelchair behind.

I delayed packing up, allowing time for McCandless to beat his dejected retreat and for the gallery to clear. I chatted with Eddie and then began loading my briefcase.

As I turned to exit the now-empty courtroom, I saw an older gentleman sitting in the back row, watching me. I'd noticed him enter earlier, just before the court reconvened to hear evidence from Mrs. Hauser's neighbor. The witness—a widow, we'd learned—had lived in the adjoining property for five years. She'd been only too willing to certify that the footage on the DVD had been shot the previous weekend from a guest room on the second floor of her residence. She must have had a specific reason to dislike Barbara Hauser, because she took pleasure in recounting how she came to be recruited by the insurance investigator, and how she had kept him supplied with food and drink during his two-day "stakeout," as she called it. As I listened to her, I caught myself wondering what other services she might have volunteered.

When the older man saw me looking at him, he rose from his seat. He was quite handsome, and he possessed something you don't see often on men of a certain age—a flat stomach. He gave me a strange smile and then exited through the double doors to the lobby. I followed.

I was immediately approached by a married couple I had interviewed when I was preparing the Hauser case. The wife was one of the defendant's bilked former employees. They were both effusive with their thanks. Even though they were unlikely ever to recover their money, they seemed to derive some gratification from the stiff sentence the defendant had received. But as soon as I heard the husband utter the word "closure" for the second time, I decided it was time to end the conversation.

The older man who had left the courtroom ahead of me was standing several feet away, watching.

"Thank you," I said to the yammering couple. "But you'll have to excuse me now. There's something I need to deal with." I shook their hands and then walked over to the man. He was clearly a few decades older than me, but I couldn't tell if he was in his fifties or his sixties. The lines on his face seemed to speak more of tumultuous life events than the simple grace of aging. As I approached, I noticed that his eyes were a startling shade of blue, and disconcertingly, they were showing more than a glint of male interest.

I couldn't help smiling inwardly. *Good for you, old man,* I thought.

"Very neatly done," he said.

"What?"

He nodded toward the courtroom. "The way you wrapped that up."

"Thank you. Are you connected to the Hauser case?"

"No."

"Okay. Did you want to speak to me?"

"Not yet." There was an odd catch in his voice.

"Not yet?"

"That's right. But soon."

His cryptic replies were faintly irritating. I decided I didn't need this conversation. "Fine. Let me know."

"I will."

I started for the elevator.

"By the way, you're very beautiful."

I stopped and turned. "Don't you mean 'intriguing'?"

"Definitely. *And* beautiful."

I smiled and walked away.

How about that? A man who thinks I'm beautiful.

Too bad he was twice my age.

As I was leaving the building, an attractive young woman stopped me to ask if there was a Starbucks nearby. While I gave directions, I noticed male heads swiveling as they passed us.

One thing was certain: They weren't looking at me.

The woman didn't seem to notice. She listened intently, touched my arm to thank me, and went on her way.

Oh, to be that oblivious.

As I was walking away, something nagged at my memory. The woman had reminded me of someone.

Or . . . something.

Then I had it.

The scent she was wearing.

I had smelled it in my living room.

I turned to look for her, but she was gone.

There were only four treadmills at the small second-floor fitness center where I held a membership. When I arrived that evening, two were in use and a third was out of service. That left the fourth one, which was positioned a few feet from the floor-to-ceiling bank of windows that overlooked the street. I had never been too keen about using that machine because it made me feel like I was exercising in a fishbowl. But I'd missed a few sessions lately, so I programmed it for random speeds and inclines and climbed aboard.

My membership at the gym kept me fit and kept me off the streets at night. I preferred running outdoors, but only in daylight—something my work hours didn't always permit. A female jogger always needs to be careful, but one who is routinely instrumental in sending people to prison needs to be vigilant. Most convicted prisoners have at least one pissed-off relative.

The treadmill was set up parallel to the window, so at least I wasn't staring out into the night while I ran off the day's frustrations. But my continuing unease about being a brightly lit target for any passing wacko with a grudge and a gun caused my eyes to drift to the left from time to time. Despite the reflected glare of the gym's lighting, the angle from my vantage point afforded me a degraded image of the street and sidewalk below.

Twenty minutes into my run, I caught movement. A steady crowd was filing along the sidewalk from left to right. There was a multiplex just around the corner, so I assumed a movie had just finished. Then I noticed one particular male figure in the crowd. All I could make out was a ball cap, a white shirt, and dark-colored pants. What drew him to my attention, although for only a second, was his trajectory against the flow of pedestrians. He was striding determinedly forward in a straight line, forcing a path through the oncoming flood of humanity.

I fixed my gaze on the wall in front of me, and concentrated on my running and my pain.

I glanced down at the sidewalk a few minutes later. The crowd had dispersed, but Ball Cap Man was still there. He was standing perfectly still next to a parked car.

He appeared to be watching someone.

Me.

I couldn't be certain, but he sure as hell looked like that older guy I'd met at the courthouse. I'd been slightly charmed the first time, but if that was him, he was getting under my skin. I launched myself off the treadmill, leaving it running, and sprinted for the stairs.

When I reached the street, he was gone.

Down the street, a set of taillights brightened. I had seen that LED pattern before. The car turned at the corner and passed under a streetlight before it disappeared.

It was a white SUV.

That night, I had the dream again.

It was always the same. I was back in the playground, across the street from our house in Archer. I don't know how old I was, but the playmates who kept popping into my field of view didn't seem much older than first-graders. I say "field of view" because the dream always made me feel as if I were watching the action through a telescope. I could never see any part of myself, not even my arms or legs. It was as if I were a disembodied observer. All I saw were kids on swings . . . kids on the teeter-totter . . . kids on our beaten-up old carousel that squealed when it turned . . . and a man sitting motionless on a bench, watching us.

Watching me.

And, always, my mother calling from the porch of our house. "*Cat! Come now, please! Now, Cat! Now!*"

. . . and me running and running and running on invisible legs . . . and the freeze-frame sequence of me racing up the steps of our porch, and my mother holding me tight against her thigh, and the man getting into a car, and the car's taillights disappearing at the end of our street.

There was something wrong with my life.

It had been lurking behind the tree line of my consciousness for a very long time.

3

"What's going on with Martínez?"

"His inventory's down, so we should get some action soon. The taps are in place." The cop sounded confident.

"Good. I want daily transcripts."

"Daily?"

"Is that a problem, Detective?"

He waited a beat before he answered. Just so I'd get the message. "No, ma'am."

"Thanks." I hung up.

Roberto Martínez ran a local auto wrecking yard out on NE Fifty-third. It turned out his business was devoted to more than just offering a highway towing service and salvaging cars that insurance companies had written off. The man was making his real money by operating a steal-to-order auto theft ring.

Wreckers tend to form unofficial networks. If one yard doesn't have a particular part for a particular model, the owner will contact wreckers in neighboring communities to see if they have the part or know where to find it. Martínez always seemed to have hard-to-find parts in stock. In the rare cases when he didn't, he would have the part within a day or two. Eventually some of his competitors got together and compared notes. Being good citizens—and prudent businessmen—they reported him to the authorities. After the detectives assigned to the case had exhausted the usual investigative techniques, I was able to secure an ex parte interception order from a judge. For the past two weeks, the squad had been running a wiretap on the phones at the wrecking yard and Martínez's residence.

But if the cops working the case appreciated my help, they weren't ready to show it. Roy Wells had been the Felony Division Chief for eight years. He'd been their tame attorney and their drinking buddy. They clearly weren't ready to transfer their allegiance to a successor who was not male, not tame, and mostly kept to herself.

There was a knock, and my door opened. Annie Morrison entered. Annie was ten years older than me, a single mom, a bit overweight, and an absolute star of a secretary.

She was carrying a thick package. "A man left this for you." She set the package on my desk.

It was addressed in neat printing that looked like it had been done with a Sharpie.

FOR DELIVERY TO CLAIRE TALBOT—CONFIDENTIAL

"What man?"

"Older guy. He wouldn't leave his name."

Older guy? Oh hell!

"Describe him!"

"Harrison Ford."

"What?"

"I mean, he kinda reminded me of him." Annie smiled, more to herself than to me. "Maybe not as old, but he was fit like him, you know? Joan called me out to reception, and he was standing there, and my first thought was that he was probably pretty hot when he was younger."

"Your first thought, huh? Maybe you should get out there more, Annie."

She looked a bit sheepish. "Yeah. Maybe."

She left.

Harrison Ford? Hmm, now that she mentioned it . . .

I pushed the stupid thought away.

I eyed the envelope suspiciously. I already had the uneasy feeling that I was being stalked, and it crossed my mind that I should send the package to the police lab for fingerprinting and a controlled opening.

I flipped it over. It was neatly sealed with packing tape.

Should I or shouldn't I?

My curiosity overcame my paranoia. I opened a drawer and took out a pair of scissors. I cut the envelope open at both ends. Then I slit it lengthwise and carefully folded back the flaps.

I breathed a sigh.

No wiring. No detonator. No suspicious-looking granular material.

Just photocopied documents and a map of Alachua County.

I unfolded the map. The area in and around Gainesville was marked with eight black circles. Next to each circle a female name appeared, printed in black ink. Each circle contained a thin, hand-drawn line traced in red ink, one end marked *S* and the other marked *F*. I puzzled over it for a moment and then set it aside.

The next document was a photocopy of a magazine article.

GAINESVILLE'S "DISAPPEARED"

A decade later, eight unsolved cases still haunt this Florida city—

The date on the top of the page was May 1, 1988.

Embedded in the text of the story was a photo array of eight smiling young women, seven brunettes—six Caucasian, one Asian—and one blonde, with names printed underneath. I checked the names against the ones written on the map. They matched.

I flipped through the rest of the documents: eight stapled photocopies of missing person reports, all filed with the Gainesville Police Department or the Alachua County Sheriff's Department and all on outdated official stationery. Each report bore a black-and-white photograph, and each matched a photo in the magazine article.

I went back to the text.

Gainesville, Florida, is home to the University of Florida and its famously successful "Gator Nation" athletic program, one of the best in the country. In the late 1970s, Gainesville had a population of around 80,000, swelled by several thousand students every

September, but still a community of fairly modest size by college-town standards.

But despite the many undoubted attractions that Gainesville's boosters will be only too pleased to extol for the inquiring visitor, it is a city suffering under the dark cloud of a haunting memory.

As far as is known, it all began late on the afternoon of April 2, 1977. Ina Castaño, 21, put on her freshly laundered uniform, kissed her mother good-bye, and set off to report for her scheduled shift at the local Denny's. The restaurant was located just a few blocks from her mother's home on NW Fourth Avenue, so during daylight hours, Ina normally walked to work. When the evening shift ended, a fellow staff member was usually available to drive her home.

Ina had worked at Denny's for just over two years, where her energy, cheerfulness, and ready smile made her popular with her workmates and memorable to her customers.

But Ina didn't report for work that night.

She walked out of her mother's house, shut the door behind her . . . and disappeared.

Over the next 13 months, seven other women vanished without a trace. Six of them, like Ina Castaño, were Gainesville residents. The other was a reporter from *The Miami Herald*. Pia Ostergaard, 30, was in the city on an assignment to investigate the disappearances. She left her hotel one evening to meet a colleague at a local restaurant and was never seen again.

Apart from Pia Ostergaard, all of the women were in their 20s and—again with the exception of the newspaper reporter—all were brunettes. In each case, a missing person report was filed; in each case, the police conducted a thorough investigation; and in each case, the investigation came up empty.

Completely empty.

As could be expected, the abduction of an investigative reporter resulted in a frenzy of media attention—both national and international. Despite this firestorm of publicity, two more women vanished during the two months following Ms. Ostergaard's disappearance. Four different law enforcement agencies sweated over these cases: the Gainesville Police Department, the Alachua County Sheriff's Department, the Florida Department of Law Enforcement, and the Federal Bureau of Investigation. At times they worked separately and at times together in multiagency task forces, but none of them ever found a single trace of any of these young women.

No trace of them alive.

And no trace of them dead.

Amanda Jordan, 24, was the last of the eight to disappear. She left her home in Newberry, a small Alachua County community located 17 miles west of Gainesville, on April 22, 1978, to attend her bridal shower—she was due to marry during the following month—and was never seen again.

Then, as abruptly as they had begun, the disappearances ended.

It is not difficult to conclude that a serial killer was at work in the Gainesville area during those years. A serial killer who—for whatever twisted reasons—was fixated on young, attractive women with dark hair. The sole exception to that victim profile was Ms. Ostergaard, a blonde. Law enforcement investigators are convinced she was targeted for a different reason. The most prevalent theory is that, following leads she had developed herself, she unwittingly crossed paths with the killer and paid the ultimate price. If she had committed her suspicions to paper, she must have been carrying those notes with her on the evening she disappeared because—according to the *Miami Herald*'s own intense follow-up coverage—nothing the reporter left behind in her hotel room was of any assistance to the investigation.

Experienced homicide investigators say that it is almost unprecedented for a killer to operate for such a lengthy period of time and not leave a single witness, a single clue, or—in the words of one retired officer who worked the case—"a single molecule of physical evidence."

"The only thing we're pretty sure of is that these poor women weren't victims of Ted Bundy," the ex-detective added. "Although Bundy remains a prime suspect in several unsolved disappearances of young women across the country, he was already in custody before the last four Gainesville women were taken."

Bundy, by many accounts the world's most notorious serial killer, was apprehended by a Pensacola police officer near the Alabama state line on February 12, 1978, just one day before Victim No. 5, María Ruiz, disappeared, and ten weeks before the final victim, Amanda Jordan, went missing. Bundy was later convicted of murdering two coeds in Tallahassee in January 1978 and a 12-year-old schoolgirl in Lake City a few days before his arrest. He was executed last year at the Florida State Prison in Starke.

The article meandered through interviews with two retired cops, the mother of one of the missing girls, and a pointless quote from a long-dead city councilman. As I read on, I began to perspire. I dabbed at my forehead with my hand. I felt an odd sensation ripple down the skin of my back . . . odd at first, but then uncomfortable. It reminded me of an attack of prickly heat I'd suffered one summer as a young child. The sensation seemed to subside as I finished the article.

Ten years have passed since Amanda Jordan walked out into the Florida night and disappeared. Today, the authorities know no more about her whereabouts than they did on that fateful evening.

Whatever happened to the eight young women you see pictured here remains a mystery—a mystery that may forever haunt this quiet college town.

I set the news story aside and started reading the missing person reports.

Ten minutes later, I was bent over a toilet, retching.

For no damned reason.

The missing person reports were as bland as anyone would expect, carefully pecked out on a typewriter a generation ago in the stilted syntax of police operational language. In my short but eventful career as a prosecuting attorney, I'd spent hours poring over crime scene photographs of torture and murder. I'd attended autopsies. I'd once stood, horrified, over the body of a decapitated child. The staggering depravity of some so-called human beings had often made me sick at heart and, yes, nauseated, but it had never made me vomit.

I'd been halfway through the file on Amanda Jordan when a wave of nausea hit me like a tsunami. As I raced for the bathroom, the fear struck me that there really had been some toxic substance mixed in with the photocopies. That I should never have opened that envelope. That now I was going to die because I was an idiot.

I straightened and leaned against the partition, bracing for another wave of nausea.

It didn't come.

Relieved, I left the cubicle and tottered to the sink. I stared into the mirror. My pallid face stared back.

What was that?

I rinsed my mouth, returned to my office, bundled up the papers, and shoved them into a drawer.

4

The patio at Sam and Diana Grayson's seemed almost as big as their indoor living space, but that was just an illusion, since the four-thousand-square-foot penthouse was on two levels. Sam had started his career doing personal injury and class action work, and he'd scored a gigantic judgment against a Fortune 500 company while he was still a relatively young man. "A very big judgment, with an embarrassingly big fee," as he sometimes described it, with demonstrable justification. A framed copy of the payout check hung over the desk in Sam's study.

For the last twenty years, Sam had devoted himself to "giving back through public service," as he liked to put it—although he could usually be counted upon to add: "Not that anybody seems to notice. All they remember is that damned judgment!"

It was early evening. Sam and Diana had invited about forty people to this semiannual get-together. Well-dressed men and women sat or stood in groups, some in deep conversation, others talking animatedly or guffawing over someone's recounted antics. A trio of gas barbecues smoked away in one corner of the patio, tended by a uniformed chef from a catering company.

I was standing near the fringes of the crowd, champagne glass in hand, making idle conversation with a middle-aged couple whose names I had already forgotten. I heard Sam's voice.

"She's over here, Ernie!"

I turned to see Sam heading my way, accompanied by District 14's balding, barrel-chested chief bloviator, State Senator Ernie Spotts. I groaned inwardly, but managed to fix a welcoming expression on my face as they approached. The couple I'd been speaking with evidently knew a thing or two about Mr. Spotts, because the lady touched my arm, whispered, "We'll talk to you later," and beat a hasty retreat, taking her husband with her.

Cowards, I thought.

Sam stopped a civilized distance from me, but the senator washed into my personal space like an overeager porpoise. Eyes bright with habitual insincerity showed an immediate and undisguised interest in my physical presence. I immediately regretted leaving my hair down and wearing the most revealing summer dress in my closet.

I took a step back and came hard up against the railing. Sam, missing nothing, eased himself partially into the space between me and my suitor, under the guise of introducing their mission.

"Claire, Senator Spotts just wanted to extend his—"

The senator grabbed my hand. "Ah wanted to personally congratulate ya, is all, young lady! Damn smart move on Sam's part! After ya put those Smoochie twins away last year, Ah said to myself—"

"Pouchie," I said, retrieving my hand from the senator's fleshy grip.

"What's that?"

"The twins . . . their name was Pouchie."

Daniel and David Pouchie had run a smart little crime wave. They always dressed in matching clothes, and they took turns committing armed robberies. They were quite brazen about it. Apart from wearing Minnesota Twins ball caps, they seldom took precautions to hide their faces—even though they knew there were security cameras. In fact, in a few cases they had looked directly at the camera, as if to taunt the police. After their arrest, they had coolly defied us to produce a single witness who could say which one had committed which robbery. They were so eerily identical that we knew no victim would ever be able to positively identify the correct offender. I was pretty sure we had them cold on conspiracy, but I wanted a complete indictment. That's when I decided to enlist the services of a forensic videographic analyst with a fortuitous subspecialty: facial mapping. He went through every frame of every CCTV capture of every incident. He soon discovered that there was one infinitesimal but defining difference between the two men: David had a condition known as aponeurotic ptosis—in other words, a drooping eyelid—in his case, the upper left. The difference was tiny, less than a millimeter, but it enabled my expert to take the stand and identify which twin had committed which robbery. The Pouchie boys were both sentenced to life in prison.

"Rahht," the senator responded. "Ah said, 'That's one smart girl! Sam'd better hang on to her!' Phoned and told ya so, didn't Ah, Sam? Anyway, young lady, Ahm really sorry Ah wasn't in town when the Attorney General made the announcement. Ah woulda been happy to call a press conference!"

"I wasn't aware she'd made an announcement," I said.

Sam looked discomfited. "I figured it was best not to tell you. The press hounds were so busy baying over those corrupt drug squad cops in Miami that the announcement ended up buried on a back page."

"Youngest prosecutor in the state to head up a Felony Unit!" the senator effused. "Yer a credit to Sam's office, girlie, and a credit to the State!"

I concede that my expression may have frozen during the second or two before I fixed Mr. Spotts with a level stare and repeated: "Girlie?"

Sam knew what was coming next. He shot me an imploring look. I pretended to relent. I forced myself to smile broadly, and before the senator's tortoise-paced wits could digest my initial reaction, I unleashed a bit of mischief on both of them.

"Thank you, sir. I really appreciate your confidence." I moved pointedly closer to Sam and leaned into his big comfortable frame. My move forced him to drop an arm around my shoulders. "But, you know," I continued, injecting a hint of Marlene Dietrich throatiness into my delivery, "I couldn't have done it without Sam. He's the best mentor any young attorney could ever ask for."

Senator Spotts opened his mouth, and then closed it. One of his eyebrows notched upward.

I noticed a few nearby guests were looking at us strangely.

Sam must have noticed, too, because he quickly disengaged his arm and clapped the senator on the shoulder. "Ernie, I almost forgot! My daughter made one of those Pavlova desserts you're always raving about! She wants your opinion. She's in the kitchen."

Sam's daughter, Suzanne, was twenty-two, highly intelligent . . . and gorgeous.

"Sure." The senator tore his eyes away from my cleavage. "How is she, anyway? Your daughter . . . uh . . . ?

"Suzanne."

"Suzanne. What's she doing these days?"

"Senior year at UF."

As they were leaving, Sam bent close and whispered to me. "Thanks, Claire. Now please explain that last little move to my wife!"

I looked around. Diana was standing inside, watching us through the sliding glass door.

After an apology to Diana that had her choked with laughter, an excellent meal, and several utterly forgettable conversations, I was ready to head home. Sam walked me to the door.

"Thanks, boss. It was a great evening."

"Until a certain senator showed up."

"A minor blip," I replied. "I had a good time, really."

That was mostly true. I've never really felt comfortable making small talk in forced social environments. I also despised the way certain untalented people tried to take advantage of Sam's hospitality to grin their way to prominence. "Self-pimping," as one observant journalist had labeled it. I'd been watching a few operators working the group tonight.

I glanced past Sam toward the living room, where Ernie Spotts was holding forth to a captive audience.

"You might be in for a late night."

Sam looked resigned. "Never fails. If it wasn't Ernie, it'd be some other gasbag." He checked to make sure no one was watching, and then gave me a hug. "You'd better hope that fool doesn't start spreading stories about us, young lady!"

"Are you afraid of Diana?" I was smiling.

"You can wipe the smile off. That kind of gossip would only fortify the opinions of certain office dinosaurs. We both know who they are."

"Sam. I can handle—"

"I'm not just talking about prosecutors. There are more than a few Neanderthals in the police as well. Ask me. How do you think they feel about reporting to an Indian?"

Sam was full-blooded Seminole.

"This isn't exactly the Land of Enlightenment, Claire. In some ways, not much has changed since I started practicing back in the '80s. You're young . . . you're female . . . you're good looking . . . and you're giving directions to men who are years older than you. You need to watch your back."

There was a moment of silence between us, and then I grinned.

"I'm good looking?"

He laughed. "Get out of here!"

5

As I rode the elevator down to the lobby, it hit me.

That uncomfortable feeling that I was walking along the edge of a precipice.

I'd been experiencing the feeling off and on all my life. It was always the same . . . a tightening in my stomach, a strange vibration in my body, increased pulse, and—I sometimes suspected—increased blood pressure.

And, always, an uneasy feeling that something was about to happen.

I had never told anyone about it. Not even my mother. Not even on my worst day. I imagined that if I'd said anything, she'd have told me it was just an attack of nerves. I might have come to the same conclusion long ago if it were not for one nagging problem: For me, the feeling never came before a court appearance, or before a jury address, or—during my college days—before a make-or-break final exam.

For me, it came only when there was no apparent reason for it. I just kept getting this feeling that something was about to happen . . . and then it didn't.

It was damned exhausting.

I exited the elevator, crossed the lobby, and left the building. My car was in the visitors' lot. I keyed the remote on my key chain. The parking lights blinked their usual welcome. I opened the driver's door, got in, and put the key in the ignition.

As I reached for my seat belt, my front passenger door jerked open and a beefy thug with a shaved head leapt at me. I had a glimpse of a vicious-looking knife in his right hand just before I made a panicked grab for my door handle. I got the door open a few inches before he lunged across and yanked it shut.

"Not smart, lady!" His voice was a gunmetal rasp, and his breath stank of beer. He eased back, holding the point of the knife against my throat. "Drive!"

"If it's money you want—!"

"Money? . . . Fucking bitch! Don't even recognize me, do ya?" Thick fingers grabbed my chin and twisted my face toward him. He pushed close, breathing his fumes straight up my nostrils. "Look at me!" he yelled. "*Look at me!*"

"I think I recognize you." I forced calm into my voice. "I don't remember your name. I'm sorry. I get a lot of cases."

He released my face. "Bitch!" The point of the knife pressed harder against the skin of my throat. "Five years in Starke, fighting off the cornholers, and all I am is some fucking number to you?" He switched the knife to his left hand. He twisted my ignition key. The engine started. "Now . . . *drive!*"

I put my left hand on the wheel. He relaxed slightly but kept the knife in position. I shifted my right hand toward the gearshift, moving slowly so he wouldn't cut my throat, but also trying to delay while my mind raced, attempting to work out what to do. I was pretty strong for my size, and I'd taken some self-defense training, but I knew I was no match for this brute in such a small space. He outweighed me by a good seventy-five pounds.

My right hand collided with his thigh. "You'll have to move if you want me to put the car in gear," I said, using as reasonable a tone as I could muster.

He shifted his leg.

At that instant, there was a flash of movement in my side-view mirror, and the passenger door flew open. Strong hands seized my attacker and yanked him violently out of the car.

I kicked my own door open and dived for the pavement. As I gathered myself to get up and run, I heard the impact of a blow hitting flesh. Peering under my car, I saw two pairs of feet facing each other. There was a cracking sound, a grunt of pain, and my attacker's knife dropped to the ground.

I lurched to my feet, ready to sprint for the lobby of the apartment building, just in time to see the same older man who'd been watching me in the courtroom drive my assailant's head into the tailgate of a nearby pickup. There was a sickening crunch, and the man disappeared from view.

I inched around my car. My assailant was lying on the pavement. The older man was kneeling next to him. He seemed to be checking his vitals.

Evidently satisfied with his investigations, my rescuer stood up. "You're okay?"

I felt my throat and examined my fingers. No blood. "Yeah," I said shakily.

He yanked a cell phone out of his pocket. He thumbed a number, listened, and then started talking. "My name is Marc Hastings. I'm standing in the parking lot at Collingwood Towers. Some creep just attacked Claire Talbot . . . that's right, your prosecutor." He listened, his eyes locked on mine. "No, she's fine. Just a bit shaken up. But her attacker's going to need an ambulance. . . . Yes, of course. Thank you." He disconnected.

I looked at him. Harrison Ford, Annie had called him. Maybe. This old guy sure had the moves. Then I was struck by another thought:

This time, when my body had told me something was going to happen . . . *it did.*

I sat in the front passenger seat of the squad car as Detective Sergeant Jeff Geiger made his notes. My savior, Marc Hastings, whose name I had first learned when he made the 911 call, was sitting behind me.

I'd met Geiger several times over the years. He was in his late thirties, fresh faced, and dress-down cool . . . or so he thought. I still hadn't made up my mind about the man. My senses always told me to be wary of him, but I'd never worked out why.

A uniformed officer sauntered toward us. Behind him, paramedics were loading my assailant into the ambulance. The officer passed a card to Geiger through the open driver's-side window. "Guy's a parolee."

Geiger studied the card. He looked at me. "Daniel James Calder. Know him?"

I recalled a sordid trial, an audio recording of a rage-filled voice mail message, and the partly reconstructed face of a weeping, terrified woman on the witness stand. It seemed like a lifetime ago. I nodded wearily.

"I got him the full five for breaking his ex-wife's face."

Geiger sighed. "Another dissatisfied customer." He made a show of checking his ultracool TAG Heuer Monaco watch, flipped his book closed, and said, "Okay, Ms. Talbot, you know the drill. Come in tomorrow and we'll take a statement. I'm on at four."

I thought the "Ms. Talbot" formality was a bit odd, but then there was a stranger in the car.

Geiger shifted his attention to the man sitting behind me. "You, too, Mr. Hastings. Can you drop by our office tomorrow?"

"Sure."

Geiger passed his business card over the seat. "Pretty gutsy, by the way. Taking on the guy like that." The words "at your age" were implied but unspoken.

"I used to be on the job."

"Yeah? Guess you haven't lost your touch. How did you happen to be here? Just right time, right place?"

"Something like that." I sensed from my rescuer's tone that he wanted to end this conversation. He confirmed that impression with: "Are you done with us?"

"Yes, sir. For now."

"Mind letting me out?" he asked.

Geiger pressed the security button under the dash, and the rear locks gave an audible click. "Times have changed since your day, Mr. Hastings. Everything's electronic."

"I suppose that's good in some ways," Hastings replied. "Not in others." He opened the door and got out.

I followed suit. "I'll speak to you tomorrow," I said to Geiger as I stepped out of the car.

Hastings stood waiting. "I'd better walk you back to your car."

I decided to let him. "Thank you for coming to the rescue."

"My pleasure, Miss—"

"Claire is fine."

"Marc. *Marcus*, actually, but no one's called me that since grade school."

"So you're an ex-cop."

"Here in town. Before your time."

"Interesting."

We reached my car. I turned to face him. "When you made that 911 call, you knew my name and my job. That's not just from being in my courtroom that day, is it?"

He smiled faintly. "No, it isn't."

"I'm guessing it was no accident that you were in this parking lot tonight. Am I right?"

He was silent for a second. "I left you a file."

"I figured that was you. Why?" Uneasiness stalked my thoughts. I pressed him. "Why were you in this parking lot?"

"I wanted to talk to you."

"Have you heard of making an appointment?"

"Would you have given me one without knowing what it was about?"

He had me there. "Maybe . . . eventually."

"Eventually?"

"Yes, eventually. After I'd had you arrested, I might have dropped by the lockup to ask you why you've been stalking me."

"You would never have done that."

"What?"

"Had me arrested."

"You sound confident."

"I am."

I opened my car door. "I assume you want to talk to me about those missing women?"

"Yes." He held the door for me while I slid behind the wheel.

I looked up at him. "That file made me sick."

"It's made me sick for thirty years."

"No, I mean—"

"You mean physically. You read it, you started to perspire, and you had to run to the washroom."

My expression must have registered surprise and roiling suspicion, but he made no effort to explain. He just stood there . . . looking haunted.

I had a sudden, overwhelming feeling that I didn't want to hear any more. I had to get away from this man. I said, "Make an appointment," and pulled my door shut. I started my car and drove away. I checked my mirror as I drove out of the lot. He was still standing where I'd left him . . . watching.

I drove two blocks and then, on an impulse, I took a right and circled back. I decided that if I could spot him getting into a car, I was going to follow him. When I reached a corner where I could observe the parking lot I'd just left, I saw him. He was standing on the far side of the lot, at least two hundred yards away, but I could see he was looking in my direction.

He waved.

I felt like a fool. For some reason, he had expected me to double back, and he'd been standing there, waiting.

He walked to a vehicle and got in. As it drove off, I saw that it was a white SUV.

Something about the man's movements nagged at me, but at first I was too distracted by what had just happened. After a few seconds, it dawned on me.

He had entered the vehicle on the passenger side.

6

Two days later, I set my alarm for five, got up, and drove to the UF campus for a morning run in the open air. The Lake Alice loop was only three and a half miles—shorter than my usual five-mile treadmill run—but at least the time and place had the advantage of being randomly chosen. I'd spent the last thirty-six hours brooding over the events outside Sam Grayson's building. I didn't like the feeling that I was being watched, even if it was by a man who had helpfully broken cover to save me from being maimed or killed.

More than that, I didn't like the idea that the man seemed to know what I was going to do before I knew it myself.

The parking lot at the Baughman Center on Museum Road was deserted. I drove through the lot and parked in an unpaved area under some trees. I went through my usual stretching routine, set my watch, and headed off. The run was flat and easy, but it still felt good. Somewhere in the final mile, I passed another runner—a big guy, built like a linebacker, wearing heavy boots, moving slowly and wheezing like a steam train. Despite my precautions, I half expected to see Marc Hastings leaning against my car when I loped off the Ficke Gardens path and back into the parking area.

But the lot was still empty and I was still alone.

I was walking in circles, cooling down, when I heard the faint sound of my phone ringing. I quickly unlocked my car and retrieved the phone from under the seat. I checked the call display.

Sam Grayson

I answered. "Sam?"

I was still breathing hard and Sam must have picked up on it. "Is this a bad time?"

"No. I just finished the Alice Lake loop. Just catching my breath."

"You just finished a run?"

"Yeah."

"Girl, it's six thirty in the morning! I don't know where you get the juice!"

"Yeah . . . well, along the same lines, I could ask what's so important that you're calling me at this hour."

"I called to tell you not to come to the office."

"What?"

"I want you to go to the morgue. Speak to Terry Snead."

"Why?"

"I'm not sure we've ever talked about this . . . it's a cold case . . . happened back in the '70s. There was this string of missing women. They were all from around here, all young, in their twenties—"

My breath stopped in my throat.

"—but there were never any bodies."

The sweat from my run went cold on my body. I heard myself ask a question. My voice seemed unconnected and far away. "What's at the morgue?"

"Damnedest thing, Claire! You know the road-widening project they're doing down near Bronson? It's part of that bypass the DOT's planning."

I was vaguely aware of it. "Yeah."

"Some workmen on the site uncovered a grave. Two bodies. Snead thinks they're from that case!"

I felt faint. I closed my eyes. "Can't be . . ."

"Well, let's find out! I've got meetings all morning. Go see what Terry's got. You can brief me this afternoon."

I was struggling for words. A few seconds passed.

"Claire?"

"I'm here. I'll go." My mind was in turmoil.

"Great. See you later." He disconnected.

I slid behind the wheel of my car. I was feeling light-headed. I sat there for a minute, taking deep breaths. Finally, I started the engine.

I took exaggerated care on the drive home, the way people do when they've had too much to drink.

7

"Claire Talbot! Always a pleasure!"

Associate Chief Medical Examiner Terry Snead didn't climb to his feet when I entered his small office in the basement of the UF Pathology Department. Instead, he rolled his chair back from his desk and relaxed into a half recline so he could look me up and down. I knew Terry had a crush on me, and I'll admit to exploiting his feelings occasionally over the years when I'd needed to squeeze an extra bit of investigative work out of him.

Terry didn't really know how to flirt creatively. Twenty years of adult life might have pruned away most of the awkward mannerisms of the congenital nerd, but behavioral artifacts remained. It was still possible to detect the brilliant but guilelessly uncool college kid of an earlier time. For me, one of the main indicators was the gape of undisguised admiration that I was being greeted with at that very instant.

"You know," Terry said, "you should come around here more often."

"Yeah, I know." I finished the tired joke for him. "The place is dead—needs livening up."

"Hey, I heard a new one! A mortician and a blonde walk into a bar—"

"Terry!" After the events of the past week, I was in no mood for this.

"Okay, okay! It's great to see you."

The office had a single guest chair. I sat. I was wearing a dress, so I didn't cross my legs, because I wanted Terry's full attention.

"I'm guessing you're here about that find down at Bronson."

"Sam asked me to come. Is this for real? Two bodies from that old case?"

"As I told your boss, everything's just preliminary. We'll need a lot more to be certain, but one of them looks pretty promising. Since they were both found in a single grave." He gave a little open palm gesture, as if to say, *ergo*.

"Who found them?"

"The way I heard it, a work party was clearing brush and a survey crew was following behind, shooting in a line of stakes to guide the excavators. You've probably seen them yourself on road projects—those flagged stakes that are marked for 'cut' or 'fill.' "

I hadn't, but I nodded knowingly so he wouldn't launch into a mini-lecture on civil engineering. My tactic almost failed, because he stared off into space and muttered, "I wonder why they were doing it the old way."

Here we go, I thought. I decided to play along for a second. "What do you mean?"

"Shooting line and using a level to mark the stakes. Nowadays, they can use GPS for everything, even the z-value." I held my tongue while he thought it through. Finally, he gave me a eureka look and said, "That must be it!"

I took the plunge. "What?"

"Poor communication with the satellites. Maybe a solar flare. I should check that." He made a move toward his computer.

"Terry! Could you do that later?"

"Okay, sorry. So, at one point, the survey guys were skirting along the top edge of an embankment. One of the chainmen pounded in a stake, and the ground on the face of the embankment subsided a bit. The guy didn't pay much attention, but when his crew chief moved forward for the next setup, he spotted a foot sticking out of the dirt."

"A foot?"

"Well, as in . . . the skeletal remains of. They stopped work and called it in. That was in the morning. We spent the rest of yesterday and most of last night doing the archaeology. Got the remains moved here about three hours ago. A couple of crime techs are still out there, working the excavation. There was some through-and-through root growth. They're taking photos and measurements, and taking samples. I've lined up one of our botany profs to identify the plants, examine the growth rings, whatever it is they do, to see if he can give us a time line. Not that you're going to need that evidence."

"Because?"

"Because . . . well, first, we're bringing in a forensic anthropologist to give us something more definitive, but I can tell you right now they're both female—the subpubic angle of the pelvises pretty much gives it away, and the skull indicators are consistent. One was in her twenties and the other . . . late twenties, early thirties."

"Okay. And, second?"

He pointed at a box of surgical gloves on his desk. I plucked out a pair and snapped them on while he rolled his chair to a small exhibit safe. He spun a combination, opened the door, and reached in. He brought out a pair of plastic cups. Each was covered with a paper lid like the ones provided by expensive hotels for their bathroom glasses. Each bore an exhibit sticker. He set the cups in front of him on his desk.

"I was too tired last night for logging and bagging." He removed the lid from one of the cups. "Hold out your hand."

I complied. He upended the cup, and a white gold ring rolled out onto my palm.

"The younger one was wearing that. So obviously robbery wasn't the motive."

It was a woman's ring—a blue gemstone, accented with small diamonds, in a partial bezel setting. I actually recognized the shape of the stone. It was what jewelers referred to as a cushion cut.

"I think it's a topaz," Terry said. "There's an inscription inside the band."

I located the inscription.

BD TO AJ 12/25/77

I looked at Terry.

"'Billie Decker to Amanda Jordan.' She was one of the missing girls. Decker was her fiancé."

"You work fast."

"Not me. The cops. Lipinski came out to the site. He and that detective who wears those cargo pants—"

"Geiger."

"That's the one. They arrived just after we found the ring. They wrote down the inscription. Lipinski called me last night. He said the ring was mentioned in an old crime report. So I guess Lipinski gets the credit for working fast."

"That's not exactly his reputation."

He smirked. "Hear ya."

I dropped the ring back in the cup. I was thoughtful. "Eight girls disappeared. Amanda Jordan was the last one."

Terry looked surprised. "You know about this old case?"

I thought of the eight missing person reports stored in my desk. "Not in great detail, but I've read a bit about it."

"We can't be certain it's the Jordan girl. But the ring was still on her finger, so it's probably her. We'll confirm with a dental match or DNA."

"Any ideas on the identity of the other body?"

"Not yet. But this was also found in the grave. It wasn't clear which body it belonged to." He passed me the other cup.

Inside was an enamel locket on a gold chain. I poured it out into my hand. The locket's face had an exquisite white Tudor rose embossed on the rich cobalt blue enamel background. The enamel itself had an intricate repetitive pattern etched into it.

"This looks like something from an estate sale."

"It's a Victorian mourning locket. That background pattern is what they call guilloche engraving. It's a French technique."

"You seem to know a lot about jewelry, Terry."

"My mother was a collector. That chain's more modern—what they call a spiga weave. Pretty common and probably harder to trace."

"You didn't happen to find a nice mystery-solving portrait in the locket, did you?" I had already guessed the answer.

"No such luck. Just a seed."

"A seed?"

"Yeah. Small and red with a black spot. At first I thought it was some kind of handicraft bead—you know, like you'd see on one of those Caribbean tourist necklaces—but I'm sure it's a seed. I'll get the botany guy to identify it."

"Can I see it?"

"It's locked up in the botany lab upstairs. The prof's away at a conference. He'll be back tonight."

I was quiet for a moment as I mulled over what I'd heard. Then I said, "I'd like to see the remains."

"You'll have to gown up."

8

The university's autopsy suite was state of the art, engineered to maintain negative pressure during examinations and equipped with three stainless steel pedestal-style downdraft autopsy tables with built-in sinks. The downdraft ventilation feature operated through perforated grid plates on the table's surface. It was designed to eliminate fumes and bone dust during examinations. Two of the tables were full sized, and they'd certainly seen their share of postmortem gore over the years, but it was the sight of the third table that always wrenched at my heart. It was a shortened version designed for the dissection of children.

A door in the far wall led to the cold unit, a long room lined along one side by those iconic storage drawers—Terry called them "cabins"— that I'd only seen in a few movies and on television crime shows until I joined the State Attorney's Office. Since then, I'd visited this facility several times, and even managed to keep down my lunch during the two autopsies—including the one involving the decapitated child—that I'd been dispatched to witness.

There was no compelling reason for a prosecutor to personally witness a postmortem, but soon after I joined the office, I learned that attendance was viewed as a rite of passage for junior prosecutors in the same way it was for rookie police officers. And, of course, sadistic throwbacks like Perry Standish and my now-deceased predecessor, Roy Wells, had happily anticipated hearing that I'd fainted at the sound of a Stryker saw biting through some departed soul's skull.

The bastards had been disappointed.

Gowned and gloved and wearing a surgical cap, I followed Terry Snead across the suite to a pair of cadaver lifts parked side by side near the door to the cold unit. Each lift was covered by a surgical drape. On the wall just above them was another exemplar of Terry's outré sense of humor—a sign that read NO LOITERING.

Terry pulled the drape off the lift on the left. "This one was wearing the ring. Until disproven, I'm calling her Amanda."

Meticulously arranged on the lift tray was what appeared to be a complete set of human skeletal remains. The image that immediately came to my mind was that of an archaeological excavation I had visited in Nova Scotia. I'd been a college kid on a summer bicycle trip with two friends, and we were touring an old British colonial fort. A summer dig was under way near the fort's original sally port, and the archaeologists had just exposed the skeleton of an eighteenth-century soldier. What struck me at the time was the man's diminutive stature. He couldn't have been more than five feet tall, and his bones looked too fragile to have carried the musculature necessary for a fighting man. His skull was so delicate it made me think I was looking not at a soldier, but at a long-dead scullery maid.

Amanda Jordan's bones—if these were indeed those of that unfortunate woman—were not nearly so discolored as those of the buried soldier, but to my untrained eye, the two skeletons were otherwise indistinguishable.

"She was quite tiny, wasn't she?"

"I ran the regression equation on her femur and tibia. I make her just over five feet. Lipinski says that calculation fits the Jordan girl's height that was provided in the missing person report."

"I missed that."

I was too busy getting sick to my stomach.

"You've read that report?"

"Someone left a copy in my office."

He gave me an appraising look. "You took over from Roy Wells, didn't you?"

"Yeah."

"Congratulations."

"Thanks." I bent closer, examining the remains on the tray. "Did you find anything indicating a cause of death?"

"No visible trauma. But there's no doubt about this one. . . ." He tugged back the drape on the neighboring lift, exposing another neatly arranged skeleton that appeared to be five or six inches longer than the Jordan remains. "This one's still a Jane Doe. But as you know, they were found in a common grave. Jane here was on top." He rolled the skull. I found myself staring at a half-dollar-sized hole high on the left side of the cranium.

"Looks like a bullet exit." I'd seen photos of headshot exits in other cases.

"Correct." He rolled the skull the other way, exposing a small circular perforation near the right temple. "Entry here. I found microscopic traces of powder residue embedded in the bone. She was shot from close range."

Heat prickled on the back of my neck. "An execution?"

"Maybe . . . or judging by the angle—" He lifted the skull and indicated the slight upward angle from entry to exit. "—it could have been self-inflicted."

I felt the perspiration start. To distract myself, I kept the conversation going. "You said this one's older?"

"I'd say late twenties to early thirties."

"How can you tell?"

"The medial end of the clavicle is almost completely fused to the sternum." He pointed. "See, here. That usually happens around the age of thirty. But I'm not the expert on age calculation. We'll bring in an anthropologist to take a read. They can sometimes peg age within two or three years."

"I was just thinking . . . this girl's older, and she was shot through the head. She might be the reporter. She was investigating the disappearances, and then she went missing herself."

"You mean the one with the Scandinavian name?"

"Yeah. I mean, I read that she was blonde—which fits with the name, I guess—and that she was older than the others, so she didn't fit the victim profile."

"Are you thinking he just killed the reporter because she was getting close?"

"Something like that." I looked at him. "What about hair? In the grave, I mean."

"We found a hair mat under Amanda's skull. The color looks right. But there was no hair with this one."

"That means—"

"Right. Her body was moved after significant decomposition." He paused. "There were other disappearances after the reporter, weren't there?"

"One other, and then Amanda Jordan. Over about two months."

"Then you have to wonder why he would keep the reporter's body for two months, and then bury her with the last victim."

I stood there, staring at the trays of bones. I was being stalked by that same weird sensation I'd had in my office. I concentrated, trying to stave it off.

"There is one other thing. . . ." Terry's tone carried a faint air of mystery.

"What?"

"It's over here." He led me to a portable instrument table that was parked against the wall. The only object on the table was a stainless steel tray with a metal cover. "This was located with the remains." Terry lifted the cover and set it aside.

I found myself looking at a scattered arrangement of tiny bones, or— more accurately—what appeared to be tiny bone fragments. Their shapes were unrecognizable. I bent to examine them. "It looks like some kind of small animal. Or a bird." I straightened. "These were in the grave?"

"Yes. Some of the smaller fragments didn't show up until the crew started sifting the soil removed from the grave."

"Okay. So . . . what is it?"

Terry let my question hang for a second. "A fetus," he said quietly.

I blinked. "You mean a human fetus?"

"Yes."

"One of them was pregnant?"

"Jane Doe."

"You're sure it was her and not Amanda?"

"Positive. The fetal remains were found in her pelvic region."

"You said she was significantly decomposed."

"In female bodies, the uterus is the last to go." He looked away. "I wonder if there's a divine message in that."

I ignored his tone-deaf afterthought and asked, "How far along was she?"

"I couldn't even begin to tell you. Despite a lot of puffed-up claims in the literature, determining gestational age of fetal *skeletal* remains—as opposed to dating an intact deceased fetus—is still not an exact science." Terry pointed at a tiny bone artifact that for all I knew could have been part of a sparrow. "This could be the skull. If so, the fetus was maybe eight to ten weeks old. We've got a forensic osteologist coming from Atlanta. We'll have a better idea after she examines it."

I went quiet, thinking. "Assuming Jane Doe was the reporter—"

"—someone in her family might have known she was pregnant," Terry finished. "That would be a pointer, but DNA will tell the tale."

As I stared down at the collection of tiny bones, a wave of nausea washed over me.

Terry was watching me. "Seen enough?"

I nodded, maybe a bit too quickly. "Yeah."

We returned to the anteroom, stripped off our protective gear, and dumped it in the bins. Out in the hallway, I walked beside Terry as we headed back to his office. At least, I started out walking beside him. After a few steps, my knees felt weak. I stopped and leaned against the wall.

Terry turned. "What's wrong?"

I pinched the bridge of my nose. I knew what was coming. "Just give me a minute." I lurched toward the ladies' restroom.

Fifteen seconds later, I lost my breakfast.

When I returned to Terry's office, he was standing at his light box, examining an X-ray. He swung around when I entered, took one look at me, and hastened to my side. "Claire! What's wrong?"

I really must have looked like hell. I let him help me to his guest chair. I could feel the perspiration beading on my forehead. He pulled a handful of tissues out of a dispenser and passed them to me. He watched as I dabbed at my forehead and upper lip. "You should see a doctor. It looks like you're getting a fever."

"I think this will pass. It did last time."

"Last time? All the more reason to see an MD!"

"You're an MD."

"Yeah, but if you end up on *my* examining table, it'll be pretty clear you didn't follow my advice." He grinned. "Of course, I'd get to see you naked."

I managed a wan smile. "You'd like that, wouldn't you?"

His face flushed. "Of course not, like . . . you know, under those circumstances." He stumbled over the words.

I took pity on him and didn't come back with the obvious response. I took a few deep breaths while he watched me nervously.

As I expected, I was starting to feel better.

"Terry," I asked casually, "have you ever heard the name Marc Hastings?"

In exaggerated slow motion, his eyes widened. "He was a cop . . . twenty-five, thirty years ago. Before my time, but I've heard he worked on this case—the missing girls—and then one day he just up and quit the department. Moved away up north somewhere." He fixed an eye on me. "Funny you'd ask."

"Why?"

"Because Hastings walked in here this morning and asked to see the remains."

My head snapped up. "What?"

"Yeah. Just showed up out of the blue and demanded to see them. Left about a half hour before you got here."

"You let him?"

He shrugged. "I figured, you know, why not? He'd worked the case for years. From what I've heard, the whole thing got to him—girls vanishing, no bodies, no clues—screwed up his head and basically ended his career. I told him we had nothing firm on the IDs. He said he understood but he just wanted to take a look. Put his mind at rest, he said." Terry stopped. He seemed to be pondering something. "Another funny thing . . ."

"What?"

"When I showed him the locket, he got sick. Just like you."

9

"Do you know how spooky this is?"

I guess I was yelling, because Annie appeared in my doorway, looking alarmed. I waved her off.

Sam was still in meetings, and I hadn't had a chance to report to him on my visit to the morgue. I'd been sitting at my desk for more than an hour, staring at a stack of pending files, all marked URGENT. I hadn't touched them. I'd been too busy mulling over my series of recent encounters with Marc Hastings, turning them over and over in my mind. Suffice it to say, I was pretty wound up when my phone rang and Annie told me Harrison Ford was on the line.

"I suppose it might seem that way," Hastings replied. His voice was calm, and he was speaking so quietly, I had to press the receiver to my ear to hear him.

"*Might?* You leave me eight missing person reports from a case that's been gathering dust for thirty years, and less than a week later, two of the bodies show up! Some creep attacks me in my car, and guess who conveniently happens to be standing nearby, ready to come to the rescue? I go to the morgue this morning to discuss a case that the press hasn't even been told about, and discover that you've already been there, snooping around. Who the hell are you, Mr. Hastings, and what are you up to?"

"Just a citizen trying to help you, Claire. I know you can break this case."

"Break this case? That's the police's job! I'm just the lawyer! You were a cop . . . you know how it works! Look, I understand! I do! You worked this case, you never broke it, it eats at you! But if you've got some information that will help, stop following me around and talk to CID!"

"You mean, talk to *Lieutenant* Lipinski? Excuse the language, my dear, but you and I both know the man couldn't find his ass in a locked room!"

"I'm not your 'dear'!" I snapped. I wasn't giving him an inch.

"Fair enough." His voice changed, as if I'd touched a nerve. "Please listen carefully, Claire. I'll talk to you, and only you. Call me when you're ready."

"Call you when I'm ready? Have you heard a single word I said?"

"Yes, I have," he replied. "Now you need to think about what I've said."

He ended the call.

At that second, Annie reappeared in my doorway. She caught the furious expression on my face as I slammed down the phone. "Please don't kill the messenger," she said.

"I won't. Just do not—repeat, do not!—put any more calls through from our movie star friend! Now, what do you want?"

"*I* don't want anything," she sniffed, "except maybe a substantial raise for hazard duty. Mr. Grayson, on the other hand, wants you in his office."

I took a few seconds to collect myself and then headed for Sam's office. As I walked in, he was just ending a phone call. "Yes, I'm well acquainted with the principle of two plus two," he said. "Thanks for the call." He hung up his phone. He looked at me.

"What's this I hear about you getting mugged?"

"Oh, that."

"Yes, that! Right outside my apartment building! Why didn't you tell me?"

I dropped into a chair. "I wasn't hurt, so no harm done. The guy's in custody, or in the hospital under guard. I'm not sure which. You're busy. You don't need to worry about things that might have happened."

He studied my face. "But I do need to worry if one of my prosecutors is being stalked."

"You've been talking to Annie."

"She's only assigned to you, Claire. She works for me."

I sighed and told Sam everything. Well . . . almost everything. I left out the part where I got sick twice. He was silent after I finished. He leaned back in his chair and stared out the window. Finally, he said, "Of course you're grateful that he saved your ass that night—I sure as hell am!—but my advice is to stay clear of him."

"I'm trying to." I had already explained about directing Hastings to the police and instructing Annie to block his calls.

"We can always arrange some coverage for you."

"Are you talking about police protection?"

"Something less visible. See if he's still following you."

"I don't know . . . it's not like he's dangerous. At least to me," I added, remembering how efficiently Hastings had dealt with my assailant.

"Don't be so sure. Word is there's something strange about him. For a time, after the last girl disappeared in that old case, he was even a suspect. He was cleared, but not long after that, he resigned from the department and left town. He claimed he'd inherited some money."

"That was thirty years ago. How do you know all this?"

"Lipinski was transferred to CID a year after Hastings. They knew each other, but I'm not sure their relationship was that friendly."

When I was relating my experiences to Sam, I had elected not to mention Hastings's assessment of Lipinski's professional deficits. Apparently the discussion was running ahead of me.

I leaned forward. "Lipinski's been talking to you about Hastings, hasn't he?"

"That was him on the phone."

"Why did Hastings's name even come up?"

"Detective Geiger attended the scene outside my building, remember?"

I made the connection. "Right. Lipinski's Man Friday."

"The fact that Hastings resurfaced in Gainesville the same week those two girls were found at Bronson has generated some talk in the squad room. Cops always say they don't believe in coincidences, and I have to say, Claire, neither do I."

The old coincidence trap, I thought. Nobody ever bothers to break it down. There are different kinds of coincidences, and some of them are just that—coincidences, and nothing more. Others . . . okay, maybe not.

And, in this case, I had to admit—

Sam's phone rang. He answered, listened, and said, "Put him through." He handed the receiver to me. "It's Terry Snead, for you."

"Hi, Terry." I listened to him for maybe thirty seconds without saying a word. For the last fifteen of those seconds, I had my eyes locked on Sam's. When Terry finished, I said, "Thanks. . . . I'll call you. . . . Yes, I definitely will. I'm with him now," and hung up.

"What?" Sam asked.

"Do you want the latest development or the latest coincidence?"

"Use your discretion."

"Okay. The latest development is that Terry brought in a consultant dentist, and she identified the smaller skeleton using dental records. As he suspected, it's Amanda Jordan. But still no luck on Jane Doe."

"Okay." He waited.

"The latest coincidence is that Terry called CID twice, asking them to find the missing girls' dental records. While they were still searching through the boxes, Marc Hastings showed up at the morgue and handed him photocopies of the dental charts for six of the missing girls."

10

It was getting late and I still hadn't touched that stack of urgent messages and files on my desk. I'd been spending the past few hours re-reading the eight missing person files Marc Hastings had left for me. In fact, I had read each file twice and committed their dismal chronology to memory:

1. **Ina Castaño**—age 21—last seen on April 2, 1977. She left her mother's home to work an evening shift at Denny's and vanished.
2. **Constance Byrne**—age 20—last seen on July 8, 1977. Her roommate told the police that Ms. Byrne's car wouldn't start, so she had decided to hitchhike to Cedar Key, an hour's drive from Gainesville, to visit her mother. She never arrived.
3. **Catherine Brady**—age 25—last seen on October 28, 1977. The third-year veterinary medicine student left her apartment to visit her boyfriend, who had been hospitalized after a motorcycle accident. She never arrived at the hospital.
4. **Patricia Chapman**—age 24—last seen on December 24, 1977. The hospital phlebotomist disappeared after filling in for a coworker on a Christmas Eve 4 P.M. to midnight shift. Her car was still parked in the hospital's staff lot.

5. *María Ruiz*—age 23—last seen on February 13, 1978. The single mother of one lived in Hawthorne, but worked in a flower shop at a strip mall a few miles west of Gainesville's city center. She disappeared after locking up the shop just after 9 P.M.

6. *Pia Ostergaard*—age 30—last seen on March 1, 1978. The Miami journalist was in Gainesville to investigate the disappearances. She vanished on her way to meet a colleague for dinner at a restaurant near her hotel. The investigators suspected that she had been targeted for abduction because of her work.

7. *Victoria Chan*—age 22—last seen on March 19, 1978. The UF coed left her apartment early one morning for a regular morning run and was never seen again.

8. *Amanda Jordan*—age 24—last seen on April 22, 1978. Ms. Jordan worked as a bank teller. She vanished while walking a distance of three blocks from her mother's residence in Newberry to the home of a girlfriend who was holding a bridal shower in her honor.

I admit I choked a bit when I read the file on victim number 7. Victoria Chan had been jogging around Lake Alice, following, I imagined, the same route that I had retraced earlier that day.

I sat at my desk, twirling a strand of my hair. Despite my misgivings—despite my smoldering hostility toward the man—I couldn't stop thinking about the mysterious Mr. Hastings.

I felt a jolt of pain. I was so engrossed in my thoughts, I'd twisted the strand of hair right out of my scalp. I cursed aloud and picked up the phone. I dialed the number I'd found on a Post-it note stuck to the last page of the magazine article. At my request, Eddie Carlyle had already checked the number, so I knew I was calling a cell.

He answered on the first ring. "Hello, Claire. I've been expecting your call."

"I'm getting a little tired of being a foregone conclusion."

"Maybe it's fate."

"I doubt that." I sharpened my tone. "I've been strongly advised to stay away from you."

"By your boss."

"That's right."

"But you're calling me."

"Yes. I want you to explain to me why I should ignore his advice."

"It would be easier to show you."

The address was a loft apartment not far from the U of F campus. It was dark when I arrived. I parked on the street and locked my car. I walked to the building. There was a keypad console next to the main entrance. Before my finger could locate the correct button, the lock buzzed. I entered the lobby, took the elevator, and followed the numbers to his apartment door.

I was about to knock when the door swung open.

Hastings was standing there, wearing a Hawaiian shirt, pleated slacks, and a complacent expression.

Okay, maybe not complacent, but a bit too satisfied. I remained where I was and said, "This feels like a big mistake."

He smiled. "Life begins at the end of your comfort zone."

"Sounds like something you read on a bumper sticker."

"It is." He moved aside. I hesitated, and then I stepped into the apartment.

It was more spacious than I'd expected. Straight ahead was a modern kitchen, and to the right a stylish living room. A short corridor leading off the far end of the living room hinted at bedrooms beyond.

I followed Hastings into the living room. One entire wall was covered by bookshelves and an entertainment center. A curved nautical-style staircase led to the floor above.

"They said you moved away years ago."

"I did."

"And this?"

"I moved back."

"When was that?"

"Two months ago. Would you like a drink?"

"No, thank you."

"I have an '83 Margaux."

I blinked. "You have a what?"

"A bottle of Château Margaux, vintage 1983. I thought you might join me in savoring that noble year."

I felt my knees go weak. Memories washed over me. Second year at Harvard. The handsome constitutional law instructor I had fallen for during the fall term. The sparkling intellect and the lean body that seduced me. The passion for French wines that charmed me. The thrill I felt when I drained my meager savings to buy him a *Premier grand cru* birthday present . . . and the devastating pain and humiliation I felt when the snake accepted the wine, kissed my cheek, and dumped me for Rosalie Webb, one of my classmates—a slattern with cheerleader looks and sensational breasts who'd been pretending to be my friend.

I glared at Hastings. "Okay, what's your game?"

"There's no game, Claire."

I raised my voice. "Damned right there's a game! Who the hell are you?"

"I'm the best friend you'll ever have." He must have sensed that I was about to turn on my heel and leave, because he cleverly settled into a soft chair and said, in the kindest tone, "Do sit for a minute."

Fuming, I dropped onto the near end of the sofa.

"I'm very happy you came," he said, "and it is important that you stay."

"How could you know about the Margaux?" I demanded. My voice was shaking.

"Let's just say I spoke with someone from your Harvard class."

"Who?"

"I'd rather not say, but I was also told that you almost failed the year because of that particular swine." As he spoke, his eyes went hard, as if it were him and not me who had been betrayed.

I looked at him in wonder. What he said was true. Assistant Professor Robert Vance, the teacher I'd been so naively infatuated with, had ended our relationship two weeks before final exams. Instead of pushing the bastard out of my mind and bearing down on my work, I'd allowed my emotions to destroy my concentration. The result was predictable—I blew two finals. I'd spent the summer beating myself up for my stupidity and preparing for the rewrites. One thing the experience taught me was never to let up and never drop my guard. Some of my fellow students started referring to me as a "gunner"—college slang for someone who is obsessed with achievement and devoid of a meaningful social life. I didn't care. I scored a perfect GPA in my final year and graduated third in my class.

As it turned out, "gunner" pretty much described the habits of my working life ever since graduation.

I realized Hastings was still talking.

"What did you say?"

"I said I know something else about Professor Vance. Something you may not know."

"What?"

"Six months after you graduated, he dumped the Webb girl. Six months after that, he impregnated a first-year student. Unfortunately for him, she was not only the daughter of a federal appeals court judge, but her family was staunchly Catholic besides. The girl kept the baby and nailed Vance with a paternity suit. He lost the case, and his teaching position. I suppose the word went out, because not even a regional college would hire him. Right now he's practicing out of a storefront in Cleveland."

I was finding it difficult to sustain my anger. Improbably, this man's quirky company was strangely comforting. I heard myself saying, "Château Margaux 1983 . . . a bottle from that year would have to cost three or four hundred dollars."

"Double that. I was lucky . . . a friend owed me. I've been saving it for your visit."

That last comment got my attention. I leaned forward. "Let me get this straight. You've been studying me? Researching me?"

"Correct."

"And prying into my personal life?"

"To some degree. I'm sorry."

"You don't look sorry."

"Okay. I'm not. You're a fascinating woman."

"Thank you, but let's get that off the table right now. You're too old for me."

He blinked, and then gave an odd smile. "I accept that."

The smile had arrived a beat too late. Behind it was something else. Thinking back, I realize that it wasn't just pain that I'd detected in that fleeting instant. Most of us carry some level of pain—that accumulating burden of our misjudgments, our transgressions, and our regrets that seem to dog us throughout our days. This was something deeper.

But I wasn't paying attention. All I could think about was that the man sitting across from me wearing that silly Hawaiian shirt had been peering into the darkest corners of my life.

"Why are you doing this?"

"You showed extraordinarily good taste in your choice of wine, if not your choice of lover. You were a struggling student. You probably emptied your bank account to buy that bottle. When I heard the story, I decided you at least deserved a taste of the classic grape you had paid for."

"That's not an answer."

"I know."

My mind blanked on a comeback. The left side of my brain was still sounding the alarm. It was telling me to stand up and walk out the door. But some other part of me, something more than pure logic, something more complex, was telling me to stay.

After a few seconds, I heard myself say, "Open the bottle . . . and show me why I'm here."

11

"It's up here."

Marc Hastings mounted the curving staircase two steps at a time, carrying an uncorked bottle of vintage claret and two crystal wineglasses. Even though I had already witnessed him thrash a much younger man in the parking lot next to Sam Grayson's building, his speed and agility surprised me.

From the layout of the apartment, I expected to find one—or at the most, two—bedrooms on the upper floor. Although I was still wary of the man's manipulations, he'd given me no reason to suspect an imminent sexual assault, so I followed him up. There was a small landing at the top of the stairs and a single door. He waited for me, then opened the door, reached inside, and flicked on the lights. He stood aside to allow me to enter first.

I wasn't wrong about it being a bedroom. But I wasn't right, either.

What was once a master bedroom had been converted into an office. An office with a difference: the entire space was outfitted to replicate a law enforcement incident room. In the center was a long rectangular worktable with two chairs on rolling casters. One end of the table's surface was covered with photographic enlargements, most of them in color. To the left of the entrance was a solid-looking hardwood desk with a left-hand return. It was set up with a telephone, a laptop computer, and a laser printer. Heavy drapes covered what I assumed to be sliding glass doors allowing access to one of the balconies I had noticed from the street.

Glancing to the right, I spied a dry erase whiteboard sitting on a wheeled aluminum frame. Doorways led to an en suite bathroom and a walk-in closet.

On the opposite wall, straight across from where I stood, was a long bookshelf. Its shelves were almost completely filled with black binders. Without saying a word, I crossed the room. Behind me, I heard the clink of glasses, followed by the sound of the wine being poured. I ran my fingers along a row of binders, randomly reading the printed labels on their spines.

CATHERINE ANNE BRADY—VOL. 1

MARÍA ELENA RUIZ—VOL. 4

AMANDA MICHELLE JORDAN—VOL. 5A

Marc arrived at my side. He handed me a half-full glass of ruby dark wine. "To you," he said quietly, touching his glass lightly against mine. My eyes went to his face, back to the rows of binders, and then back to him. I couldn't think of a response, so I shrugged a sort of offhand acknowledgment and took a sip. Actually, it wasn't just a sip . . . it was more like a serious swallow. The effect was instant—a taste that was at once rich and dense and exotic. I felt a rush in my head, and for a second I thought he had drugged the wine. I must have taken an audible breath, because he set down his glass and rolled a chair over to me.

I sat. My mind was a turmoil wrapped in cotton.

He pulled up the other chair and sat beside me. He took a sip from his glass and said, "So, what do you think?"

"About what?"

"Start with the wine."

I felt my nostrils flare. The man was exasperating, and I wasn't ready to admit that I was already hooked. I replied by fluttering a hand at the rows of binders. "Does CID know about this?"

"No. But it's all photocopies. I created a mirror file of the entire investigation."

"You had photocopiers back then?"

"Yes, indeed." He flashed a smile. "And cars, and Quarter Pounders, and a lot of people even had indoor plumbing."

I ignored the remark and homed in. "That's a lot of three-ring binders. That's a lot of photocopying."

"Forty-one four-inch binders, to be exact. And they're not three-ring. They're Lever Arch."

"Lever what?"

"Lever Arch binders. It's a European two-ring design, finger-touch opening. I like them better than the ones we use over here. So will you."

"You assume a lot."

"Yes, I do. You and I are going to solve this case. You just need to believe it."

My eyes lasered into his. "Marc, you're not a cop anymore!" I was so intent on cross-examining him, I didn't notice that I'd addressed him by his first name.

"As far as I'm concerned, this is still my file. Nobody's bothered to look at the case in over twenty years. Nobody but me."

"They're bothering now! Terry Snead says CID is all over it!" His expression darkened, and I was reminded of his views on Lipinski. Views I shared. Views this man somehow knew I shared. I decided to change tack. "There were eight girls missing, but you left only six dental charts at the morgue."

"Ina and María were Cuban refugees. Their families didn't have the money to pay dentists."

"'Ina and María'? It's become that personal?"

"Nobody else has been looking for them, Claire. I'm their only friend." His jaw tightened. "Especially Mandy's."

"Amanda Jordan?"

He nodded.

"Why her?"

His eyes filled with sudden emotion. "Because I knew her."

I thought of the smiling girl in the photograph in the file, and the remains of her petite body laid out on the cadaver lift in the morgue. I started imagining the horrors she must have endured. I suppressed the train of thought and took another swallow of wine.

Marc blinked dampness from his eyes. He said, "This isn't really the way you're supposed to drink this stuff, but what the hell . . . ," and took a slug from his own glass.

I upended my glass and drained it. "So much for sipping and savoring a noble grape," I said, handing him the empty glass. "May I have some more?"

He stared at me for a second, and then he started to laugh.

It was a wonderful laugh.

He went to retrieve the bottle. We'd been sitting at the worktable, so I took advantage of his momentary absence to roll my chair a few feet along to the spread of photographs I'd seen when I entered the room. I picked one off the top of the nearest pile. It was an establishing shot, showing an area of broken vegetation and the stumps of freshly felled trees cut off almost flush with the ground. A shallow excavation could be seen in the center of the photo. The next picture was taken from the edge of the excavation. Intertwined human skeletons lay clearly exposed, in situ, at the bottom of the hole. Close-up shots followed, one featuring a distinctive ring on a skeletal finger—the ring I had seen in Terry Snead's office. Several more featured tiny anomalous bone fragments in Jane Doe's pelvic region.

These had to be the Forensic Crime Unit's photographs of the grave site next to the Bronson highway project.

Marc returned to my side, carrying refilled glasses.

I looked up at him reproachfully. "How did you get these?"

"I still know people. I kept in touch."

"It's been thirty years! There can't be anyone left at the Forensic Unit who was there when you were on CID!"

"There are still a few retired guys around. After twenty or thirty years struggling to pay off the mortgage, they tend to stay put."

Marc pulled his chair over to mine while I flipped through the rest of the photos. Other than replying to my occasional question, he said nothing and left me to it. Along with the recent shots taken at the grave site, there were eight groups of photographs, some in black-and-white, each collection clipped together and labeled with the abductee's name. Each started with a copy of the victim's photograph from her missing person file and went on to show, in stages, her point of departure (apartment, dormitory room, shop premises, hotel room, etc.), her known or presumed route on foot, and, incongruously, the destination she never reached, including a photograph of Constance Byrne's mother's home in Cedar Key.

When I was halfway through the last group—the Amanda Jordan photos—I stopped, puzzled. I flipped back to one I had just examined. It showed a paved sidewalk, a narrow grass verge, then the concrete curb and part of the asphalt-paved street. In the upper center of the photograph, in the middle distance, an unidentifiable object could be seen on the edge of the sidewalk.

The next shot was taken from a position much closer to the object. I could see it was a roll of something, possibly a carpet, seen mostly end-on, so its length was difficult to estimate.

The next shot was the one that had sent me back to the earlier photos. It showed a roll of carpet, about five feet in length and eight or ten inches in diameter, lying partly on the sidewalk and partly on the grass verge.

Later photos showed the same roll of carpet, taken from different angles.

I asked Marc, "What's the point of this?"

"Amanda would have walked along this sidewalk on her way to that bridal shower. It's where I believe she was taken."

"Why?"

"At the time, it was just a hunch I had. I decided to test it by bringing in a tracking dog. We used some clothing from the laundry hamper in Mandy's bedroom. We started the dog from the front door of her house. The track ended on the grass there"—he pointed to a mark on one of the photos—"just a few feet from the carpet roll. The dog reached that spot and just sat down and whined. Just to be sure, we ran the track again with a different dog. It led us to the same spot, sat down, and whined. It was eerie." He sipped from his glass. His mind seemed to drift off for a second. "You remember Ted Bundy." It wasn't a question.

I felt a chill. "Yes."

"Bundy would sometimes pretend to be disabled. He'd have his arm in a sling, or he'd use crutches, and persuade the victim to help him load something into his car. Something heavy, like a box of books."

"Or maybe . . . a roll of carpet."

"That's right. But we know this wasn't Bundy. He was already in jail, and he didn't start describing his abduction techniques to the FBI investigators until years later."

"So what's your theory?"

"My theory is that if great minds think alike, maybe sick ones do, too."

12

Hours later, the wine bottle was empty, the remains of our ordered-in pizza were congealing in the box over on the desk, and I was in the end stages of a running audit of the contents of the forty-one binders. After we finished the pizza, Marc had left me alone to concentrate. He checked in from time to time to bring me water and to answer questions, but mostly he stayed downstairs and out of the way. I took my bathroom breaks in the en suite, discovering a spectacular sanctuary featuring an antique claw-foot tub.

I had been only skimming the binders, trying to get an overview. Marc had been right—the Lever Arch files were easier to work with than the ones I was used to. But the reams of written material they contained had offered no real surprises.

Naturally, there were no autopsy reports. With one exception, there were no lab reports, since no one had ever pinpointed an exact location for any of the abductions. In Amanda Jordan's case, the area around the carpet roll had yielded virtually nothing of evidential value. A hair and fiber analysis of the carpet itself came up empty, revealing only that it was a recently manufactured area rug. The manufacturer's label was intact, leading the investigators to a company in Missouri. Based on the lot number, the company was able to tell them the month of manufacture— October 1977—but, critically, not where the carpet had been shipped. It could have been sent to any one of fifty-seven retail outlets spread across the eastern half of the United States. Detective Marc Hastings had

determined that a flooring company in Ocala, forty miles south of Gainesville, carried product from that particular manufacturer, but when he
showed a color photograph of the carpet to the purchasing manager, he
was told that the firm had never ordered from that particular line.

I came across a mostly unhelpful offender profile in the Patricia
Chapman volumes. It had been prepared by the FBI's Behavioral Science
Unit a few weeks after her disappearance. The report's conclusion
(". . . white male, 20–25 years, above average IQ, likely raised by either a
single parent, probably a mother, or by alcoholic parents or guardians,
likely sexually or physically abused from an early age, etc.") was so generic
that it could have applied to half a million men in the state of Florida
alone. The report had been written several years before the creation of the
FBI's Investigative Support Unit, later made famous by the writings of a
few retired profilers. I thought the predicted age range of the offender
seemed a bit amateurish. With these sorts of crimes, the basic rule—as I
had learned it—stated that the analysis should start at a notional age of
twenty-five and then add or subtract years depending on the sophistication
of the crimes. When this report was written, the unknown abductor had
already struck four times in just under nine months without leaving a single witness or a shred of physical evidence. I would have put the age range
much higher. But then, who was I? Just a seven-year lawyer.

Teams of detectives had canvassed all the known or projected routes
of each victim's walk from home to workplace, or from workplace to parked
car, or from home to social engagement. Roadways, footpaths, parks, and
landfills were combed again and again. The homes of known sex offenders
were searched—sometimes repeatedly, sometimes without a warrant. Not
a shred of usable evidence was uncovered, nor was a single witness identified
who recalled seeing the victim interacting with a potential abductor. Only
in the cases of the first and third victims—Ina Castaño and Catherine
Brady—did anyone recollect seeing the young woman during her final
journey. In each of those cases, the victim was said to be unaccompanied
and apparently in good spirits. Despite an advertising campaign, no one
came forward claiming to have seen Constance Byrne hitchhiking on
Route 24. In the case of Victoria Chan, a grad student from the College of
Engineering told the police that he had passed "a Chinese girl, or maybe
Vietnamese" when he was running the Alice Lake loop. Other than establishing that the young woman was still alive and unmolested at that ap-

proximate time and location, the man's statement provided no leads. Just to be safe, the investigators had run a complete background on him and cleared him as a possible suspect.

The investigators' continuation reports were arranged chronologically through each section of the binders. A tally of the investigators' names revealed fluctuating numbers, with the size of the teams expanding immediately after a disappearance—with the exception of the first two, when no one in authority seemed to be paying attention. After the journalist disappeared, the ranks assigned to what was by then a federal, state, and local task force swelled to more than twenty-five investigators. Despite the increasing effort, the mass of paper generated amounted to no more than a chronicle of investigative failure. There was a seemingly endless supply of leads that went nowhere or that led only to the clearance of unrelated crimes. There were pages and pages of anonymous tips sent over from the local police hotline—evidentiary will-o'-the-wisps that, out of desperation, had been doggedly pursued to their predictable conclusions, wasting precious investigative resources. As the list of missing women lengthened and the investigation continued to marinate in unrelenting failure, I felt the frustrations of the detectives seeping off the pages of their reports. Prominent among the later report writers was Marc himself, who had worked his way up from the missing persons squad after the second disappearance to a position on the local task force after the Christmas Eve disappearance of Patricia Chapman.

I was sitting at the desk, absorbed in one of the Amanda Jordan binders, when I heard Marc enter. It was a few seconds before I realized he wasn't moving. I lifted my head and caught him standing just inside the door, holding a coffee mug and watching me. There was something in his eyes . . . almost a look of longing, as if I reminded him of someone. Someone he had cared for deeply. The instant passed, veiled by his quick smile. He stepped to the desk and set down the mug.

"Black, no sugar."

I pushed back from the desk. "Thanks. Maybe I shouldn't. It'll keep me awake."

"I thought you were going for an all-nighter."

Startled, I checked my watch. It was after one in the morning. "Hell, I have to work tomorrow!"

"You can sleep in the guest room if you don't feel like driving."

I thought about the look I'd seen in his eyes a few moments earlier. "I don't think that's a good idea."

"Suit yourself." If he was disappointed, he didn't show it.

The aroma of the coffee enticed me. "Maybe a few sips," I said, and reached for the mug.

Marc rolled his chair over and sat across from me. He checked the label on the binder. "You've covered a lot of ground."

"Just scanning. I see thousands of words, but not many facts." I leaned forward. "Tell me the truth, Marc. I'm a seven-year lawyer. I have no deep experience in conducting criminal investigations, just criticizing them, which hasn't made me a lot of friends in the police. Why are you so sure I'm the one who can break this case?"

He thought for a moment. "Call it instinct. I've watched you . . . in court. You're good. You're thorough. And you're tough."

I eyed him. "I've seen you in my courtroom exactly once. There's something you're not telling me. Something important."

His silence told me I was right.

"What is it?" I demanded.

"Something you need to discover for yourself."

The man was exasperating. I flared. I waved a hand, taking in the room. "One word from me, and CID takes all this away! You know that, don't you?"

His facial expression shut down, closing me out. "That's up to you," he said stiffly. He got up from his chair and left the room.

13

Court was in session, and I was hating every minute of it.

Specifically, I despised the judge. He was tall and bony, with a narrow face, long nose, and a pair of small eyes embedded like raisins below his bushy eyebrows. He swept into his courtroom like a comic opera grandee, wearing his robe, a pair of god-awful oxblood dress shoes shined to a mirror finish, and a perpetually sour expression. Of course, his appearance would have been irrelevant had he been a man of evenness and courtesy. Regrettably, he was not. His angular presence came complete with an oversized affection for his own intellect. To some degree, that may have been the result of his election to the bench at a relatively young age, encouraging him to believe his own campaign propaganda. Whatever the reason, according to his haggard and much-harassed clerk, any reversal of his judgments invariably elicited a braying rehearsal of foulmouthed invective against "those pygmies squatting on the Court of Appeals."

Altogether, His Honor Judge Theodore P. Barlow was a thoroughly dislikable man.

But . . . the fact remained that, whatever the reasons behind the man's acerbic disposition, he was the judge and I was the lowly prosecuting attorney. I was obliged to veil my true opinion of the arrogant bastard behind the polite rituals of courtroom courtesy.

Today's hearing had been another example of Barlow's infamous dawn raids. We had convened at eight o'clock sharp. The judge took perverted pleasure in imposing early morning starts on attorneys—no doubt so he could ruin their days before they even got started.

I sat at the counsel table with Tracy Collins, our office's visibly confused young intern, studiously concealing my thoughts. Behind my bland expression, I was able to enjoy at least a moment of immature satisfaction. Because of me, Barlow was sitting straight-backed on his dais, presenting the packed courtroom with a spectacle of undisguised judicial rage.

At the other table, a rat-faced defense attorney from Live Oak named Morris Pascoe was whispering to a pockmarked lug in an orange jumpsuit. His client had beaten his own brother half to death with a crystal vase. Fortunately for the victim, the vase hadn't shattered. Unfortunately for him, he'd sustained a fractured skull and two cracked vertebrae in his neck.

"I'll give my ruling at eight o'clock tomorrow morning!" Barlow glared at me as he rapped his gavel. He slammed his bench book closed.

The bailiff stepped forward, nervously cleared his throat, and ordered, "All rise!" Barlow swept off the bench and vanished into his chambers.

As I started packing my briefcase, I noticed Marc standing near the back of the courtroom.

"What was that?" Tracy asked.

"He hates it when lawyers prove him wrong."

"He was badgering you! He was insulting."

"He hates it even more when female lawyers prove him wrong."

"It's not fair! It's like you had two defense lawyers against you! I thought the judge was supposed to be—!"

"This isn't law school, Tracy. If you want to practice in the criminal courts, you're going to need a thick skin. I'm afraid you'll have to get used to it."

The young woman subsided into offended silence.

I finished packing my briefcase. When I looked up, Marc was gone.

He wasn't waiting in the lobby, either.

I asked Tracy to take my briefcase back to the office.

"Where are you going?"

"I'm making a detour. It's time I paid a little visit to CID."

Lieutenant Ted Lipinski's office was located in a boxed-off corner on the CID floor. It had no outside windows, but two walls were paneled with tinted glass so he could survey the array of desks and cubicles in the squad room.

When I knocked and entered, I was presented with an interesting tableau.

Jeff Geiger was slouching in a chair with his gusseted loafers propped on his boss's cluttered desk. He was decked out in his customary micro-fiber cool duds, flipping through a glossy skin magazine and listening to what sounded like a ball game on a smartphone positioned on the desk near his feet.

Lipinski was standing in some kind of pose behind his desk. His sports jacket was a nauseating shade of green. He appeared to be admiring his reflection in the tinted glass. Quite apart from the ridiculous jacket, Lipinski's reflection was not one to admire. He was a doughy specimen in his late fifties, with just enough sagging skin and broken veins in his face to corroborate a lifetime of unhealthy habits. Considering the man was a contemporary of Marc Hastings, the contrast between the two could not have been more striking.

I noticed a tag dangling from one sleeve of his jacket. It bore a marked-down price notation in red.

"So, Lieutenant," I said as I shut the door behind me, "I see you're leaving the job."

Wary eyes studied me. "What are you talking about?"

"Judging from the jacket, you're going into real estate."

"Toldja, boss!" Geiger piped in as he lowered his feet from the desk and killed the game on his phone.

Lipinski looked affronted. "The woman at the store said it looked good." He aimed the response at me.

"This woman . . . would she happen to be the one who sold it to you?"

He scowled.

There was a metal-framed chair jammed against the wall to my right. I pulled it up and sat down. "Before you run off and join the Million Dollar Club, I'd like you to tell me what's going on with those two skeletons."

"Thought you were here to talk about your own case," Lipinski said. He dropped into the lopsided chair behind the desk. "That mugging. Or whatever it was."

This man really is an insect. . . .

"What it was," I replied mildly, "was something more than a mugging.

But I know perfectly well how to write a witness statement. I'll e-mail it to Jeff. Right now, I want to know where we are on this one."

"Where *we* are?" Lipinski's voice notched up as if I'd just issued a threat rather than merely asked a question. "It's not your case yet, Counselor! And it probably never will be!"

After today's session with Judge Barlow, I wasn't going to be fazed by Lipinski's saber rattling. I was about to highlight a few facts of life—for example, our relative positions in the food chain—when Geiger spoke up.

"We trolled through the Jordan file, looking for witnesses to reinterview," he said in a placating tone. "Almost everyone's either moved or dead. We think the guy she was planning to marry is living in Iowa. The state police up there are trying to track him down."

"Those bodies were found because of a road-widening project. The DOT's attorneys probably used their eminent domain authority to condemn that property and take it for public use. Have you tracked down the former owner?"

"Yes."

"Batty old broad!" Lipinski snorted.

I ignored Lipinski and focused on Geiger. "Tell me."

"Her name's Anna Fenwick. Lives down near Ocala. She told us she hadn't been near the property in over ten years. Sold it to the highways guys last year. Accepted their first offer."

Lipinski interjected. "Take it from us . . . the old woman's loopy!"

"What do you mean?"

"Because she's weird! Kept looking at me, calling me 'you poor dear,' saying I should be drinking some kind of herbal tea. 'Gabble' or something."

"GABA?"

"Yeah! What is it?"

"It's Japanese. They say it reduces the effects of alcohol."

"Alcohol?" His face reddened and his eyes slid away from mine.

I changed the subject. "What about the Jane Doe?"

"No match on the dentals," Geiger answered. "Snead's doing the DNA workups on both bodies, but it's not like the cops back then went around bagging victims' hairbrushes. No one was using DNA in 1978. We're going to have to track down family members and get blood samples."

"Considering where she was found, the odds are that Jane Doe was one of the eight."

"The dentals we have don't match," Geiger said. "So she'd have to be one of the Spanish girls."

"I don't know . . . those girls were both in their early twenties. Terry told me this girl was a lot older."

"He could be wrong on that," Geiger countered. "Said so himself."

"She's probably one that was never reported," Lipinski said. "A hooker nobody missed."

"Okay," I said, responding to Geiger. "Say Terry's wrong. Depending on whether she's Castaño or Ruiz, that would mean she was buried either two months, or more than a year, after she went missing. Either that or she was buried somewhere else and then dug up later and moved. None of which makes sense."

Lipinski eyed me suspiciously. "You seem to know a lot about this case." His expression darkened further. "What is this, Counselor? Some kind of test?"

My questions *were* some kind of test, but I wasn't going to tell Lipinski that. "I've just been doing my reading, Lieutenant."

"Reading what? The investigation files are all stored here."

I decided to understate the truth. "Our office has copies of all the old missing person reports."

"Why?" he badgered. "Who had them?"

I had to think quickly. "I guess Roy Wells. They were in his filing cabinet."

I was expecting more cross-examination from Lipinski, but Geiger spoke first.

"We do have one small problem: A box of reports is missing."

"Missing? As in . . . misplaced?"

"As in, gone. There were twenty-six boxes, all numbered. We can't find box eighteen. We've had three people searching the archives and the property room."

Lipinski's chair creaked as he rolled it forward and leaned his elbows on the desk. He growled, "Ya know what I think?"

"No. What do you think?"

"Hastings took it! I can feel it."

"Hastings?" I played dumb. "You mean——?"

"The guy who saved your ass the other night! Worked here in CID, back in the late '70s. Quit before his pension locked in. Moved up north somewhere." His lip curled. "I always thought there was something fishy about him. And now, right after we find the bodies, he shows up at the morgue! What does that tell ya?"

"That maybe this case has been bothering him all these years."

"Yeah? Then why resign when the investigation's still going on?"

"Maybe," I suggested, staring back at him, "because some of his colleagues started investigating *him*?"

"Who told you that?"

"Sam Grayson."

"Oh." He toned it down. "Well, there were some indicators. Nothing you could put your finger on. He knew the last girl. There was some talk, like maybe they'd dated at one time. All we know is the Jordan girl disappears and not long after, Hastings up and quits! He doesn't just transfer out of CID. He leaves the police department and then he leaves town. And after he quits . . . guess what? No more missing girls!"

"What does that prove? Sam told me Hastings was cleared."

"He had alibis. But I always thought there was something weird about the guy. And why, after thirty years, does he just happen to be in town, and why does he just happen to have copies of those girls' dental charts?"

"Were the original charts in that missing box?"

A pause.

"No."

"No?"

"We found ours later," Geiger said. "But by then, Snead didn't need them."

I almost laughed.

I stood up. I looked at Jeff Geiger—young, halfway intelligent, but exhibiting none of the drive of a man who wants to be all he can be. I took in his skin magazine, pointedly left open on the desk, displaying some anonymous temptress's crotch in all its high-def glory. I looked at Lipinski, squatting toadlike behind his desk, clad in that absurd jacket—an aging mediocrity, tired, defensive, and hostile.

I'm sure the expression on my face revealed my low opinion, but I couldn't resist driving the message home. "Maybe you boneheads should get off your butts and get to work before this Hastings guy completely shows you up!"

I turned on my heel and walked out, leaving the door ajar.

Lipinski called after me. "Just stick to yer lawyerin', girlie, and leave the police work to the professionals! *Ya hear me?*"

Girlie!

Detectives' heads swung as I stormed past desks in the squad room. I took the stairs so I could cool off before I reached the main floor lobby.

14

It was just after six when I left the office. Halfway home, I changed my mind, changed direction, and drove to Marc's building. I didn't call him to say I was coming. Two can play the surprise game.

But it didn't quite work out that way.

I found a parking space and was about to grab my purse when I spotted Marc standing near the curb in front of his building. He was facing away from me, talking on his cell and watching the street, as if he was waiting for a ride. I half expected the white SUV to appear, but instead a taxi drove up.

He got in and the taxi pulled away.

He hadn't once looked in my direction, so I was sure he hadn't seen me. I decided to follow him. He seemed to know a lot about me; it was time I learned something about him.

The cab navigated through the center of town and onto Route 20, heading east. I remained several cars back, keeping it in sight.

After seven or eight miles, it turned off onto County Road 325, heading south. I thought this was a bit strange. The next community was Cross Creek, a hammock-country backwater located on an isthmus between two lakes. The community's sole claim to fame was that Marjorie Kinnan Rawlings, a Pulitzer Prize–winning author, had once lived there.

The traffic had thinned, and there were no cars between mine and the taxi. It was getting dark. The road was dead straight, so I slowed down and followed the taxi's taillights from a half mile back. Miles of grassed road shoulders rolled by, punctuated by long tunnel-like stretches created by the immense trees intertwined overhead. Twice the cab's lights disappeared around a curve, and twice I pushed up my speed and reestablished contact.

But after the third bend, the road ahead was dark.

A sign read CROSS CREEK, but there was no sign of the settlement yet, just scattered homes and outbuildings. I caught a few glimpses of pastureland behind fences and screens of trees. I pulled to the shoulder and got out of my car. I scanned the geography behind me, searching for the telling flicker of a vehicle's lights on a side road or driveway.

Nothing.

I got back in the car and kept heading south. After a few minutes, I saw headlights approaching quickly from the other direction.

The taxi passed me, heading back to Gainesville.

Hell.

So much for spy games. Guess it's time to go home.

I looked for somewhere to turn around. As my tires whined across the concrete decking of a bridge, I spotted a clapboard-and-shake-sided building off to the right. A painted sign next to the road read: THE YEARLING. I pulled off the highway. There was a scattering of cars and pickups in the parking lot, but still plenty of room for me to turn around. I was about to do just that when a stray thought hit me.

I parked in the nearest open slot, got out, and walked toward the building. I could hear a country song playing—Lady Antebellum's "Our Kind of Love." A lopsided screen door led onto a porch that featured the main entrance on the left, an old-fashioned Coca-Cola sign with a bench seat below it, and a window on the right. I had planned to walk straight into the bar, but instead I altered course, stepped to the window, and looked in.

All I could see was a row of restaurant tables and a few scattered diners.

I left the porch and walked to another window farther along the building. When I looked in, I saw six or seven men sitting on padded stools at a bar and a few empty tables. But at the back, on the far left, I could see part of another table. Marc was sitting there. At first I thought he was alone, but then I noticed two drink glasses on the table in front of him.

Both drinks appeared untouched. I moved as far to the right as I could, but my view was blocked. I couldn't see the person he was sitting with.

I debated with myself: *Is this your business, Claire? Go home!*

No! I wanted to know more about this secretive man who had elbowed his way into my life. I retraced my steps to the main door and entered.

A short passage led to a reception podium, which was unattended. I took a left into the bar area. I immediately saw that Marc was alone at his table. He had his cell phone to his ear and he was staring fixedly at his watch. I steeled myself and started walking toward him. A few of the barflies stopped talking and turned to look. One let out a low whistle. When I was halfway across the room, an older, white-haired woman with a deeply lined face came out of a stockroom behind the bar. When she saw me, she froze.

None of that registered with me until much later, because in that compressed span of time, other things were engaging my attention.

I noticed that the second glass I'd seen on Marc's table was gone.

I noticed that his own glass was still full.

I noticed that a rear exit door located ten feet from his table was just clicking shut.

I noticed Marc lift his eyes from his watch, turn in his chair, and look straight at me. He snapped his phone shut. He rose from his seat and pulled out the other chair for me.

I sat, bewildered.

He resumed his seat.

"You knew I was following you," I said. It was a statement, not a question.

"I did."

"There was someone sitting here. In this chair."

"An old friend. I once lived near here . . . just down the road. She had to leave."

I glanced at the door that had just closed. "She, huh?"

"Yes."

"Short visit."

He didn't respond.

A short man with a dark tan and arms like rope appeared at our table. He was wearing a waiter's apron. I hadn't seen him when I entered. Behind him, the white-haired bar lady was edging hesitantly in our direction. She was staring fixedly at me. For some reason, she looked bewildered.

"Something for the lady?" the waiter asked.

Before I could answer, Marc shook his head. In that same instant, there was a bellow of rage from over near the bar, accompanied by the smash of breaking glass. All three of us turned to see a chair skittering sideways. It toppled with a bang as two men began scuffling and throwing punches.

The white-haired lady shouted, "Jimmy!" and hurried toward the melee.

The waiter rushed off, leaving his tray on our table. He waded straight into the brawl, attempting to separate the combatants—a gutsy move, considering both fighters were much bigger men. He was shoved aside, and the fight started in our direction. I looked at Marc and saw that he was gripping the waiter's tray with both hands.

"What are you doing?"

"Getting ready!"

"For what?"

"This!"

One of the drunks grabbed a broken beer glass and swung it at his opponent. Just in time, the scrawny waiter grabbed his arm. The weapon flew out of the man's fingers and spun away . . .

Straight at me.

In a blur, Marc lunged across the table and swung the tray up in front of my face, batting the glass away. It hit the floor and shattered.

The fight stopped. The room went quiet. I looked at Marc. He was checking his watch. There was an expression of wonder on his face. "It's eight fourteen," he said. I saw tears of relief in his eyes and the obvious question died in my throat. His hand dipped into his shirt pocket and brought out a twenty-dollar bill. He dropped it on the table and rose to his feet. "Mind giving me a lift home?"

I stood. Without a glance at the watching crowd, Marc took my arm and escorted me to the nearby rear exit.

As we left the building, I heard a woman's voice call out: "Marc?"

If he heard, he pretended not to. I looked back through the narrowing gap of the closing door. The bar lady was standing in the middle of the room, staring at us.

She seemed transfixed.

"What just happened?" I asked as Marc led me quickly around to the parking lot.

"I had a premonition. It's hard to explain. Please just trust me."

In that second, I decided that I would. "Do you mind driving?" I asked as I handed him my keys.

15

Four nights later, I was sitting at the worktable in Marc's improvised incident room. The Jordan binders were lined up in front of me and I was deep into one of the final volumes.

For the past three days—which had fortuitously included a weekend—I had followed up on my first scoping study of the documents by starting back at the beginning and reading every page. After all that work, it was frustrating to realize that I was not much wiser than I'd been after my initial high-speed tour. One area of inquiry that I had hoped might bear some fruit was what the gurus at the FBI referred to as "victimology." The victims in this case were attractive females in their twenties, and all but one was a brunette, but that wasn't going to take us very far without more information.

The question was this: What else did the victims have in common? Was there any correlation between them? Did their paths ever cross? Did they have any acquaintances, friends, relatives, or business contacts in common? If so, how many degrees of separation existed between each victim and that hypothetical common contact person? Had the investigators worked that angle, especially after the list began to lengthen? If so, had they properly documented their work?

Yes, they had.

Although the two Cuban girls had apparently never met, they had two friends in common. Both friends were Latina, and therefore about as likely to fit the profile for a serial killer as a five-year-old child. Nevertheless, each woman had been thoroughly investigated and cleared, along with all her family members and friends.

The only other connection was between the hospital employee, Patricia Chapman, and the *Miami Herald* journalist, Pia Ostergaard. They had attended the same high school in Fort Lauderdale, four years apart, and, amazingly, one of Chapman's male cousins turned out to be a former boyfriend of the journalist. The cousin also had an alibi. He'd been vacationing with his wife on the Caribbean island of Antigua on the date his ex-girlfriend disappeared. That, coupled with the fact that he had been on shift and hard at work as a police officer with the Miami-Dade PD when most of the abductions took place, pretty much put paid to any idea of his involvement.

Marc came in. He said something. It took a second for his voice to penetrate my deliberations.

"What was that?"

"I said I ordered Chinese."

"Oh good! I'm famished."

He joined me at the table. "We should start doing our own cooking. All this fast food is a bit hard on my vintage body."

"I make a pretty mean shrimp creole," I said.

"Oh yeah? Well, I make a pretty mean paella."

"We could stage a seafood cook-off, but who's going to judge it? No one knows we're working together, and we need to keep it that way."

"That will change."

I didn't argue the point. When it came to predictions, he had already proved himself. "Okay, I need to ask you something." I got up and retrieved one of the Ostergaard binders. I flipped to a page I'd marked with a paper clip. "Look at this. Each successive page is hand-numbered, and this section seems right at first—see?" I turned the page to show him that the sheets were in sequence and then turned back. "But this heading at the bottom is left hanging." I pointed.

PUTNAM COUNTY REPORT—WOMAN IN RIVER

I turned the page. "At the top of this page, there's a new heading and the text is unrelated. At least one page must be missing, maybe more. Whoever numbered the pages in the original file probably didn't notice."

Marc leaned close to examine the pages. I could feel the warmth of his body. A mischievous thought crossed my mind. I banished it.

"Put a flag on that." He didn't seem too concerned. "But I'm sure this wasn't related to the missing women. I would have remembered."

"I'd still like to read that report."

"I'll check to see if we have it."

"Check where?"

"There's a batch of miscellaneous papers in that box under the desk."

"While we're on the subject, there's something else." I looked him in the eye. "Geiger told me they're missing an entire box of reports."

Marc didn't blink. "Which one?"

"He said it was box number eighteen."

He didn't hesitate. "That was one of María's boxes. They must have misplaced it after I left the department. Probably during one of their moves."

"How could you know that?"

"Because we have the complete Ruiz file here, which means it was still there for me to photocopy."

"That reminds me," I said. "Lipinski said you left the police while the investigation was still ongoing. That would mean they have later investigative reports that we don't have."

"He said that?" Marc's mouth twisted into a scornful smile. "Claire, how many boxes did they tell you they have?"

"Twenty-six."

He nodded, obviously expecting that answer. "Lipinski's memory is playing tricks, or the man's lying. I left the department in April 1979, a year after Mandy Jordan went missing. Actually, I left in March because I had some accumulated leave. My last official act was to sign the complete file into the cold case archive. I boxed up all eight subfiles and labeled every box myself."

I saw where this conversation was going. "How many boxes?"

"Twenty-six. I kept a copy of the property room receipt. Would you like to see it?"

I felt my jaw tighten. Lipinski's memory hadn't faded. The bastard had played me. It wasn't difficult to reconstruct the likely scenario. Snead told Lipinski that Marc was in town. Lipinski called Sam Grayson, making sure to plant a seed of suspicion about Marc in the mind of the chief prosecutor.

During the phone call, Sam mentioned what Annie had told him about the sealed packet Marc had delivered to the office. When I met with Lipinski and Geiger, I told them that our copies of the missing person files came from Roy Wells's filing cabinet. Suspecting I was lying and that the files had actually come from Marc, Lipinski used our discussion about the missing box to try to undermine Marc's credibility in my mind.

Once you knew Lipinski for what he was, it all made a sick kind of sense.

"No," I replied. "I don't need to see it. Discussion over."

I leaned back in my chair and closed my eyes. I could feel Marc watching me.

I finally spoke, with my eyes still closed. "Eight girls. Four in 1977; four in 1978. But the frequency of disappearances was increasing. Three months apart, then two months apart, then varying from a few weeks to a month. Profilers say that's what they often see in these cases. The perp keeps getting away with it. He becomes more and more emboldened, and his cooling-off period gets shorter and shorter. Eventually, like Bundy, he becomes completely reckless and gets caught." I opened my eyes. "But not in this case. After Mandy Jordan, the guy just stops. Why?"

"Something happened. Something he never expected."

"Maybe he moved away and started somewhere else."

"The FBI were monitoring for that. Nowadays, they probably have computer programs that do it."

"He could have died."

"Maybe."

"Or he could have gone to prison for something unrelated, so no one made a connection."

"Possible."

"It sounds like you don't think it was any of those."

"I don't. I think he's still out there."

"Why do you think that?"

"Call it a hunch."

"So all this is here"—I waved my arm, taking in the cluttered room—"and *I'm* here, because of a hunch?"

"Do you want to back out?"

I guessed he knew what my answer would be, but I didn't want to give him the satisfaction. I unfolded the map he had sent to me with the missing person files. I had already concluded that the red lines traced within each black circle represented the likely walking route of each girl on the day she disappeared: *S* for "start," and *F* for his best guess as to "finish." The binders had contained plans of the same areas, each taken from the relevant municipal survey map, showing the routes in detail.

I tapped a finger on the map. "What were you doing here?"

"Not sure. Looking for a pattern."

I chewed on my lip, thinking. "Have you heard of geographic profiling?"

He shook his head.

"It's sort of new. Not really new, but probably after your time. I've never had a case that used it, but I've read about them. The police in Canada used it to track down a serial rapist. Then the FBI's Investigative Support Unit latched on to it. It's based on mapping criminal activity patterns. If you invert the data, it can sometimes point to the area where the offender lives."

"Or lived."

"These days, there are software programs that can do the analysis, but we'd need someone who's trained to use them," I said. "Or we'd need help from the FBI."

"Which means we'd have to go through Lipinski," Marc said, looking ill.

"Fuck that," I said.

"Nice language."

"I've got an idea."

Marc smiled. "So, I take it you're not backing out."

I must have fallen asleep. Somewhere beyond the horizons of my dream, I heard a phone. It sounded like my own phone's ringtone. I surfaced slowly. The ringing got louder. I woke up to find my face buried in my arms. I was still at the worktable. I sat up quickly, and paid for my haste with a sharp twinge in my neck. I discovered that a blanket had been draped around my shoulders.

Marc appeared in the doorway as I was fumbling for my phone. I answered groggily. "This is Claire."

"Claire, this is Terry."

"Hi, Terry. What's up?"

"Sorry, did I wake you?"

"No. Just dozing . . . on the couch."

"Okay. Listen, this is a bit unorthodox, but . . ."

"What is it?"

"I've discovered something about that old case that will interest you. Can we meet? I mean, off-reservation. There's something going on you should know about."

"Sure. When?"

"Tonight?"

I looked at my watch. "Okay."

"Another thing . . . you know Marc Hastings?"

I hesitated. "Yes." My eyes shifted to Marc, who was leaning on his desk, listening.

"He told me I could call you if I wanted to get a message to him."

"Oh, did he? When was that?"

"A while back. Can you contact him?"

"Maybe."

"Tell him he might want to come."

We arranged a time and place to meet and I hung up. "Why did you tell Terry Snead to call me if he wanted to reach you? Now he knows about our little alliance! If he talks to Sam . . ." I didn't need to finish.

"He won't."

"And you know that how?"

"I just know. Trust me."

I sighed.

16

The 1982 Bar on West University Avenue was an "all ages welcome" establishment that featured old video games like Sega and Nintendo
for retro-obsessed game nerds, stand-up comedy, costumed karaoke, and
other bumptious entertainments guaranteed to discourage off-duty CID
detectives from dropping in for a beer after their shift. In other words, it
was an inspired venue choice for our meeting with Terry Snead.

When we arrived, Terry was already there, slouched in a back booth
with a draft beer in front of him, playing *Super Mario Bros.* on a built-in
console. We slid in across from him. As he looked from Marc's face to mine
and back again, I thought I detected a glint of jealousy, as if Marc and I
were somehow now a couple and Terry resented losing his chance with me.

The look vanished as quickly as it had appeared. Terry dropped the
game remote back in its slot. "Claire . . . Marc . . . glad you came."

I thought I'd better clear something up right at the start. "Whatever
this is, have you already told CID? I don't want any problems."

"Yes. Everything I'm going to tell you, they already know."

"Okay."

"But I want to warn you. Lipinski's been talking to your boss. He
complained about your visit to his office the other day. He thinks you're
encroaching on his turf."

"Sam hasn't mentioned any complaint."

"Sam respects you too much to let Lipinski stir up trouble in his office.
But just be careful."

"I will."

"And, Marc, he came to the lab this morning and grilled me about your visits."

"Visits?" I turned to Marc. "As in, the plural?"

Marc looked sheepish.

"He's got some issue about you," Terry continued.

"I know he does. Thanks."

A waitress appeared. Marc gestured at Terry's beer and said, "I'll have one of those, please. And the lady will have a margarita, Casa Noble if you have it, on the rocks, no salt."

The waitress was gone before I could open my mouth. I frowned at Marc. "I don't remember telling you what I wanted to drink."

"Sorry. What would you have ordered?"

"Uh . . . that, probably, but . . ." Marc grinned, which pissed me off. "Please stop doing that!"

He played innocent. "Doing what?"

I sighed and turned back to Terry, who had been following our exchange with an expression of faint bewilderment. "Sorry," I said. "Just tell us what you've got."

He dipped a hand into his shirt pocket and pulled out a small ziplock bag. He opened it and removed a greenish-brown object. It appeared to be some kind of seedpod from a plant.

"I got this from a guy I know at the EPA." He looked at Marc. "Hold out your hand."

Marc complied. Terry split the pod open and four small red seeds dropped into Marc's palm. Each seed bore a black spot.

"The seed in the locket!" I exclaimed.

"Correct. These are crab's eye peas, also known as rosary peas. Latin name: *Abrus precatorius*. Their pulp contains a deadly toxin called abrin."

I picked one of the seeds off Marc's palm and rolled it between my fingers. It was ovoid, with a hard shell. It was deep red in color, except for the black spot, which covered one end of the ovoid shape. It looked exactly like a crab's eye.

"How deadly is the poison?" Marc asked.

Terry's expression turned somber. "You've heard of ricin?"

"Yeah," Marc replied, startled. "We've been hearing a lot about it since 9/11. It's made from castor beans, isn't it?"

"That's right. But this toxin is a hundred times more lethal than ricin. As you can see, the pea has a hard shell. You could swallow a dozen of those and they'd just pass through you. But if you cracked the shell before you swallowed—and I mean just the shell of one seed—you'd be dead in forty-eight hours. Pretty scary, considering how small they are."

The waitress arrived with our drinks. She glanced curiously at the seeds lying in Marc's upraised palm. We stopped talking while she set down our drinks.

"What about an antidote?" I asked after the girl left.

Terry shook his head.

Marc looked incredulous. "No antidote?"

"No antidote. The toxin blocks protein synthesis. It destroys your organs. You die from the inside out. And I'm told it isn't pretty!"

I sipped from my drink. "So, one of those girls had a locket and inside that locket was a poisonous pea. Where does that take us?"

"I'm not sure where it will take you, but it might take you further than Lipinski. When I told him what I'm about to tell you, he just gave me a blank look. That's one of the reasons I called you. I had a feeling you two would be more motivated." Terry took a swallow of beer. "Listen to this: We ran bone marrow assays on both skeletons, and what we discovered was that Amanda Jordan had ingested a lot of this toxin before she died. And when I say 'a lot,' I mean a *lethal* dose. But even weirder . . . it had to have been administered over time. To get levels that high in your bone marrow, you'd have to be given a series of tiny doses—nonlethal doses, but probably increasing over time."

"In other words, she was kept alive for a set period," Marc said. His expression darkened. "In other words . . ."

He trailed off, so I finished the thought. "In other words, he was probably a sexual sadist."

"Was . . . ?" Marc rejoined. Or, *is?*"

We were all silent for a second.

"What you've described would require some kind of expertise." I said. "Maybe we should be looking for someone who was a pharmacist, or a med lab tech—someone with specialized training."

"Not necessarily," Terry replied. "There was no Internet back then, but any reasonably intelligent person could learn enough from a textbook."

"Are there textbooks on poisons?"

"Yes, and that's a possibility, but books like that tend to be found in toxicology labs. They're not usually found in public libraries. A textbook on homeopathy would be more likely because it would explain systems of serial dilution that anyone could learn."

"Do you believe in that stuff?"

"No, but I've read a few papers on their dilution process. It's absolutely central to their treatment approach, and it's not difficult to follow."

"You haven't mentioned the results for Jane Doe."

"No toxin. Not a trace. But, then . . . she was shot."

"That's why I thought she was the journalist."

"The apparent age fits," Terry responded. "But her dental chart doesn't."

"Lipinski thinks she was someone who was never reported missing."

"He could be right."

Marc had been quiet through this exchange. Now he addressed Terry. "I've never heard of this crab's eye plant. Where does it grow?"

"Originally, India. It showed up on some of the Caribbean islands in the nineteenth century, and later it was brought here as an ornamental vine. But it ran wild . . . spread all over South Florida, choking out some of the indigenous species. Now it's banned. The state's had an eradication program in force for around thirty years."

My ears pricked up. "Thirty years? When exactly was it banned?"

"Nineteen eighty."

My mind started racing, making connections. "So . . . where was it growing in the '70s?"

17

One week to the day after our meeting with Terry, Marc and I were following the head of the UF's Geography Department along a locked corridor behind the department's lecture theaters. Professor Charles McNabb had taught a couple of my undergrad courses at Boston U, and we had maintained a casual friendship after both returning to Florida.

"As I told you, Claire, geographic profiling is not exactly my field," Professor McNabb said as he used a security card to unlock a heavy steel door. There was a metallic thunk as the lock cleared. "If you're hoping for a miracle, you'll have to get one of those FBI guys that do that stuff all the time."

He opened the door, revealing an impressive bank of computer processors.

"We will," I said as he led us through to a small office area, "but the FBI can't send anyone for another week. Anything you've come up with might help."

I think I surprised Marc with my smooth lie, because he gave me a quizzical look and rolled his eyes. I suppressed the urge to elbow him and responded with a bland smile.

The sole occupant of the room we now entered was an attractive—okay, beautiful—young woman. She was sitting in front of a wide-screen computer monitor. She seemed to be expecting us, because she rotated her chair and sat waiting as we approached.

Charlie introduced us. "This is my assistant, Jennifer Hilchey. Jenny . . . Claire Talbot, from the State Attorney's Office, and Mr. Hastings."

"Hi," Jenny said, taking our offered hands without getting up. She immediately swung her chair back to the computer, ready to get right to work.

"Jenny's a grad student in the department," Charlie went on. "Actually, she's our top grad student," he added, "and an absolute gem." Jenny's face colored slightly, and for a second I wondered . . .

None of your business, Claire!

I'd been there before myself—as Marc had easily discovered in his researches—although the dynamic here made me suspect the shoe was on the other foot and Charlie was the one who was headed for heartbreak down the road.

"Go ahead, Jen. Run it for them."

Jenny slid a CD into the console. "This will take a few seconds." She began working the keyboard.

Charlie took up the slack. "At a gut level, it's seems clear that there was a serial offender at work here. We had only the eight abduction locations to work with—not really locations, I guess, just likely local areas. The hitchhiking girl and the girl who vanished during her morning run were even more problematic, so those abduction areas were really just educated guesses. Plus, of course, we had the single burial site at Bronson, which at least can be pinpointed on a map. But, as I told you on the phone, without knowing the actual kill sites or burial sites for the other six girls, we're really out on a limb here."

We watched Jenny drill through dialogue boxes on the screen. Windows were opening and closing like magic. Or, more accurately, what I hoped was magic.

Charlie continued. "Combined with that limited data, we added what the EPA gave us, which was the rough northern limits for the spread of the crab's eye plant in the 1970s. We added data from the invasive species research facility here at UF, and even though the mapping is quite impressive, our scientists are the first to admit that they can't account for outliers."

The screen froze. Jenny sat back. "My mistake . . ."

"What's wrong?" Charlie leaned closer, alarmed.

She looked up at us. "First rule: Never let a computer know you're in a hurry. It'll just be a sec."

We hovered over her, watching the screen, as a multicolored map of northern Florida painted itself in graduated steps down the screen.

"There we go!" Charlie gave Jenny's shoulder a squeeze. "This is called an isopleth map. What Jenny did to get this result was to adapt certain software we have that . . . well, you go ahead and tell them, Jen."

Jenny took up the narrative. "A few years ago, the department developed a software program to analyze predator hunting patterns in the national parks. You probably want to ask, 'Are there even any predators left in the national parks?' The answer is yes. There are viable populations in the Rocky Mountains—Yellowstone and Glacier, as well as in the Canadian parks and in Alaska. We also have a mountain of data from Southern Africa. Without getting into the technical stuff, I took our program and plugged it into a software program developed by the Canadian police. They've been using it mainly to help them track down serial killers, although it's also been used to track down other types of serial offenders, such as arsonists. I used their program because it was the only one I could download at no cost to the university."

"Budget issues," Charlie interjected, looking chastened. "We all have our guidelines. Sorry."

"No need to apologize," I replied. This is really impressive."

Jenny continued. "The police program uses an algorithm they developed for using crime site geography to predict an offender's area of residence. It takes into account basic information such as where each victim was last seen, where the victim was attacked, where she was murdered, if known, and where the body was disposed of. It takes into account all kinds of variables with labels like 'comfort zone' and 'distance decay function,' et cetera, that we don't need to get into. The point is that their program incorporates several features that are equivalent to the ones deployed in our own program. In fact, the hunting-style categories have similar names: 'territorial killer,' 'nomadic killer,' 'game preserve killer,' and so forth." Jenny rolled her chair to one side so we could get a clear view of the monitor. "This is what I came up with."

The map on the screen was arranged in colored three-dimensional contours, lighter colors in the outer rings, darker farther in. The central zone was shaped like a teardrop and was colored bloodred.

"What you're looking at is called a probability surface," Charlie said. "The red zone has a probability of eighty percent."

"Meaning . . . ?" Marc asked.

"Meaning, there's an eighty percent probability that the predator's home is—that is, *was*—within that zone. This is a typical 'teardrop pattern.' It shows a directional bias toward a secondary anchor point, in this case, the Gainesville area. To use a simple analogy, if this were Africa, then Gainesville would be the equivalent of a watering hole or some other game-rich area, and this area here—" He reached past Jenny and tapped the screen. "—is where you would most likely find the predator's lair."

I leaned on the desk and studied the map. "Almost the entire red zone is in Levy County." I was astonished.

"That's right. Rural, low density. Mostly white cracker farmsteads. Only two towns of any size . . . Chiefland, in the north, and Cedar Key down on the Gulf Coast." He paused. "But you know, I've read some of the literature on these kinds of cases. If a body isn't found within one month of a person's disappearance, and if the disposal site is more than a mile from the place where the victim was last seen, the odds of solving the crime are less than five percent. These girls disappeared thirty years ago. Even if Jenny's work is absolutely dead-on, and even if your killer actually lived somewhere in that red zone, how the hell are you going to find him now?"

I turned to Jenny. "Can you make me a color copy of that?"

"Sure can."

I straightened and turned to Charlie. "We'll find him."

I felt Marc squeeze my hand.

I was conscientious about clearing my desk and locking my files away at the end of every day. I was doing just that when Sam Grayson appeared in my doorway.

"A few of us are heading for Harry's. Why don't you come? I promise I'll protect you from the chauvinists."

"Thanks, but I can't. I've sort of got a date."

He grinned. "A date? Like, with a man?"

"Yeah."

"Well, about time!"

"I've had dates!"

"Oh, yeah? When?"

"A few months back. I went out with—" I had to search my memory to recall the guy's name. "—Todd Bewley."

"The FBI guy from Jacksonville?"

"Yeah."

"You went out with him twice!"

"Okaaay! It was a drive-by."

He squinted at me. "A drive-by?"

"Yeah."

"Okay. And who was at the wheel?"

I didn't really want to get into that. It had taken me no time to realize that Bewley was one of those men who preyed on women who were drawn to the very traits that ran completely against their own best interests. In other words, desperate women. Be damned if that was me.

I deflected. "What are you doing, Sam? Keeping track?"

"No, but Diana is. She's worried about you. This guy tonight . . . anyone we know?"

"No." I answered quickly before my conscience could butt in.

"Okay. Will you be in the office over the weekend?"

"Probably not. I think I've got everything under control."

If only . . .

"Good. See you Monday. Have a good time, and stay out of trouble."

"Me? Trouble?"

"On the other hand, maybe you should get into a bit of trouble. You live a pretty boring life for a girl your age."

Sam, if you only knew . . .

He went off whistling while I sat there feeling guilty.

Since becoming aware of Lipinski's unhealthy obsession with Marc, I had taken to parking my car a few blocks past his building. Marc had given me a key to his apartment and another that opened the building's rear door, off the alleyway, and I had made a habit of using that entrance. As I crossed the street, one block up, I saw a white SUV parked, facing me, in the loading zone in front of Marc's building.

What first caught my attention was the driver's-side door swinging shut. The car looked familiar.

I stopped to watch as it pulled a U-turn and drove away.

An hour later, Marc and I were sitting at opposite ends of the long couch in his living room. The oddest thing was that after so short a time, we could just be silent together.

I was thinking about the FBI profile written after the Patricia Chapman disappearance. The report had rendered the unknown subject—the "unsub" in FBI parlance—in such general terms that I wondered why it had never been updated.

I said to Marc: "You know, the FBI telling you the unsub was obsessed with brunettes is hardly a brilliant insight. Telling you he would seem ordinary to others in appearance and personality, and that his acts were probably precipitated by some psychologically traumatic event that awakened long-suppressed desires, wasn't going to take you anywhere. Didn't anyone ask them to take another look at the case after there were more abductions?"

"We did," he replied. "They said they couldn't give us a better profile without better evidence . . . or unless we came up with a body or two."

"Eight girls had disappeared! I'd have thought they'd be all over this case!"

"There's something you need to understand. I don't know about today, but in those days, most of the FBI guys were still brainwashed by their own myth. Hoover was dead and gone, but the attitude was still there. They thought they could just roll into town in their black sedans and show the yokels how real professionals solve crime. Their standard procedure was to suck all the information out of your files, divert your detectives into support roles, take control of all press contacts, and make themselves look like the heroes. Even if some local investigator actually broke the case, by the time the news conferences were finished, his name would be a footnote." His mouth twisted into a sardonic smile. "But this time, their news-hogging routine backfired."

It dawned on me. "The Ostergaard case!"

"Correct. When the *Herald* reporter disappeared and the so-called 'FBI-led investigation'"—he pronounced the words with remembered bitterness—"came up completely empty, they took it on the chin. The next thing we knew, calls were coming in from D.C. saying their top people were needed on a major investigation up in Chicago. To us, it seemed like they were hoping the public would forget about their failure on that case back in Hicksville, Florida, if they could just grab the glory on a meatier one in a big city. They left a few agents behind to help us out and handle liaison. Actually, once the big guns were gone, the task force ran a lot more smoothly."

Marc unfolded a large-scale map of Levy County on the coffee table. I had shown him earlier how to pull up satellite pictures on my laptop, and he was methodically investigating the red zone on the probability map Jennifer Hilchey had printed for us. I wasn't sure what he expected to find, and I don't think he was sure, either.

I had a binder open on my lap, but I wasn't really focusing on it. As I watched Marc work, my thoughts shifted to the white SUV. My eyes swept his bookshelves.

"No pictures," I said.

Marc looked up from the laptop. "Mmm?"

I nodded at his shelves. "No family pictures."

He gave me a blank look.

"No wedding pictures. No kids' school pictures. No vacation cruise pictures." I leveled my gaze. "No proof of a life."

He didn't reply. He turned his attention back to the map.

"Were you ever married?" I persisted.

"Yes."

"Children?"

Another uncomfortable pause. "A daughter."

"What's her name?"

"Rebecca."

I waited for more. He picked up his beer, untouched since he'd opened it a half hour earlier, and took a big swallow. He set the bottle down and just stared at me. He didn't volunteer any more information.

I was perplexed. "Sorry. I didn't mean to—"

"Yes, you did." He looked at me. "It's okay. It's just not something I'm ready to talk about."

"I understand," I said. But I didn't. Why was he back here in Gainesville after all these years, dogging my footsteps, acting mysterious? Why wasn't he with his wife? Or his daughter? Was he estranged from them? If so, why? Or, had they died? If so, how?

Marc's voice intruded upon my roving imagination. "That grave site . . ."

"What?"

"You said the grave site was on land that had belonged to the same family for over a hundred years."

"The last survivor lives in Silver Springs, down near Ocala."

"The lady with the observant eye."

I recalled the welcome mental image of a sweet old lady unwittingly skewering Lipinski. "Her name is Anna Fenwick."

"Shouldn't we talk to her?"

"She told Lipinski and Geiger she hadn't been near the property in ten years."

"Mandy Jordan was buried on that property thirty years ago! Did those two buffoons actually spend any time with this lady? Ask her about the people she knew back then?"

"Somehow, I doubt it." I thought for a moment. "You know . . . she might just open up—"

"—to an older gentleman and a pleasant young woman. Stand up."

"What?"

"Stand up . . . please."

I stood. Marc cast an appraising eye over me. "Put your hair in a ponytail. And wear a summer dress."

"You didn't need me to stand up for that!"

He grinned. "No. But I like looking at you."

I felt my body get warm.

Damn this man!

I sat down quickly.

18

Anna Fenwick's tidy bungalow sat in comfortable seclusion on treed acreage abutting Ocala National Forest, just outside Silver Springs. Marc and I had arrived at exactly four o'clock in the afternoon, as previously arranged by telephone, and found our elderly hostess waiting for us on the veranda.

We were sitting on an ornate couch in the lady's living room. As instructed, I was wearing a brightly colored summer dress, with my hair in a ponytail. Today was the first time I had ever seen Marc in a suit. As clichéd as the phrase seemed when it first ran through my mind, there was no arguing that he looked very distinguished . . . like someone you'd meet at an embassy dinner. At this moment, however, the overall effect was somewhat degraded by the spectacle of the poor man sipping herbal tea from a china cup with a handle two sizes too small for his fingers.

Anna Fenwick occupied a straight-backed chair across from us. It was difficult to estimate her age. My best guess was late sixties. Her pale skin was free of age spots, which probably meant that she'd been careful about exposure to the sun throughout her life. Her most arresting features were her large blue eyes and her snowy white, perfectly executed 1930s-style finger wave hairdo. Her elegant attire appeared years out of date, yet not a whit out of place among the antique furnishings of her home.

A large crucifix hung on the wall behind her.

She was telling us about the property at Bronson.

"It was fifty-five acres. We lived near one corner of the property in an old farmhouse. The house was already old when my daddy bought it. Torn down now. Daddy tried growing tobacco, but he couldn't make it pay. My late husband and I sold off most of the property not long after Daddy passed away. We kept those last few acres 'for a rainy day,' as my husband used to say. Then those highways people came to see me last year." She paused. "I told all this to those two policemen who came here."

"Did the detectives ask you about family members or friends you had when you were growing up?" Marc asked.

"No. They just said a body had been found on that property. They wanted to know the last time I'd been there." Her face became animated. "The older man—the one with the reddish face . . ."

"Mr. Lipinski?" I asked.

"Yes. That one. He made it sound like he thought *I* had buried the body, for goodness' sake! He apologized for his tone later on, and so he should have!"

Marc nodded sympathetically. "Those officers told Miss Talbot that you hadn't visited that property for several years."

Nice touch, I thought. *Mrs. Fenwick is an old-fashioned lady, so he refers to me by "Miss."*

"The last time was probably ten or twelve years ago," she replied. "My husband showed one of those real estate persons around the property. At the time, we were considering selling it. It was a hot day, so I waited in the car." She looked at me. "The younger policeman asked if they'd noticed anything during their walk, which I thought was a perfectly silly question. I expect my husband would have said something if they'd found a dead body!"

I smiled and tried to redirect the discussion. "Mrs. Fenwick, do you, or did you, have any brothers or sisters?"

Her clear eyes studied me. "No, dear. I was an only child."

"In that case," Marc said, "Miss Talbot and I are wondering if you remember the names of any playmates you had while you lived there . . . any girlfriends, or perhaps boyfriends you might have had when you were in your teens."

She thought for a moment. "There was my best friend, Rosemary. We were inseparable from the age of seven. We stayed friends right up until she passed away last year—had the cancer, poor thing. And there were my cousins. They lived close by and were always visiting." She stopped. Her eyes had been on me while she was answering Marc. Now she seemed to lose her train of thought. She regarded me silently for a few seconds and then said, "You seem very young for this type of work, dear."

"I'm thirty-one."

She was thoughtful. "You must ready yourself."

"Ready myself?"

"Yes. For the sorrows to come."

An uneasy silence descended on us. I was about to ask the woman what she was talking about, but Marc quickly interjected.

"It would really help us if you could remember full names. And, also, the names of any of your neighbors."

Mrs. Fenwick hesitated. "Rosemary's last name was Roberts. Her married name was Henning. Then there was . . ." She trailed off, perplexed. "I have some photographs. They will help me remember."

Marc and I sat on either side of Anna Fenwick at her dining room table while she slowly turned the tattered pages in an old photograph album. Marc was taking notes as Anna identified the people in the photographs. Our agreement was that she would name as many people as she could and we would go back over the names with her later and find out what, if anything, she could tell us about where they lived then, and where they were now.

Assuming any of them were still alive, that is.

Many of the photos were in black-and-white, and a lot of them had been taken in and around the same two-story vernacular farmhouse. Apart from a scattering of scenery shots, mainly showing planted fields, most of the pictures were posed shots of men, women, and children of all ages, all of them white. A number had apparently been taken on some special occasion, or perhaps after church, because the subjects were dressed in what appeared to be their Sunday best.

Mrs. Fenwick tapped a photograph. "That's Charlie Baxter. His father used to beat him something terrible. . . . That's Benny White . . . and there's Cousin Harlan . . . and Cousin Doris . . . she was a bit strange . . . and, oh my goodness, that's Theresa McCall! I forgot all about her! She and her brother were playing with matches out in the barn and nearly burned it down. My daddy was pretty angry about that."

"What was the brother's name?" Marc asked, writing quickly.

"Uh . . . Alex, I think. He was older. He didn't come around much."

"Alex McCall?"

"Yes. I'm pretty sure it was Alex. Or . . . Alec."

She turned another page and pointed. "That's Rosemary. Always skinning her knees, that one! She was a real tomboy."

I had a sudden thought. "Mrs. Fenwick, would you mind if we photographed the pages of your album? Having the pictures might help us later."

"Of course not, dear! Did you bring a camera?"

"No. But my cell phone has a built-in camera."

"Oh, I think I read about those phones! What will they think of next?"

I got up to retrieve my phone from my purse. I returned to the table and stood next to Mrs. Fenwick, ready to start again on the first page she had shown us. I happened to glance down just as she leaned forward. Her high-necked blouse gaped slightly. I saw she was wearing a necklace that had been hidden from our view.

It wasn't exactly a necklace.

It was a rosary.

I knew it was a rosary because I could see a small silver cross and what looked like a Miraculous Medal. But that wasn't what froze my attention.

The rosary beads were crab's eye peas.

I lowered myself back onto my chair. "Forgive me, Mrs. Fenwick, but I just noticed your necklace."

Her hand went to her throat. "Not a necklace, dear. It's a rosary. When I look in the mirror, I'm reminded to pray."

I shifted my eyes to Marc, signaling, and then back to Mrs. Fenwick.

"I'd like to ask you about the beads," I said. "They're quite unusual."

She reached into the back of her blouse and undid the clasp. As she handed me the necklace, I saw Marc's eyes widen.

"They're called rosary peas, dear. They grow wild. And that is an original Miraculous Medal. It was struck in 1832!"

I laid out the necklace on the tablecloth. "Did you string this yourself?"

"Of course, dear. My mother taught me. It isn't difficult."

"Can you tell us where you found these peas?" Marc asked.

Anna Fenwick looked confused. "Where I found them?"

"Yes. Do you remember?"

"I didn't find them. Harlan gave them to me. He grew them."

Marc's body seemed to stiffen. He tapped the photo album. "Do you mean your cousin, in the photos?"

"Yes." She started turning pages.

"Do you remember when he gave these beads to you?"

"Oh, goodness! It must be twenty, twenty-five years." She pointed at a color photograph. "That's Harlan."

Marc and I both leaned close to look.

He was about thirty years of age. His long body was whipsaw thin and dressed in stovepipe slacks, a white dress shirt, and a narrow dark tie. He was leaning against a gray 1970s-era Plymouth. His teeth gleamed in a "say cheese" smile, but it was his eyes that caught my attention.

They stared blankly at the camera, conveying not the slightest glimmer of humanity.

I felt the skin prickle on the back of my neck.

19

"Harlan Richard Tribe, born June tenth, 1943. Never married. At one time, he owned a restaurant up on North Main. It was called The Lobster Pot."

We were sitting in our boardroom. Sam was holding the photograph of Tribe that we'd borrowed from Anna Fenwick, but he wasn't looking at it. He was staring straight at me while Marc continued the briefing.

"It's a Thai place now. Before that, he ran some waterfront dive over on Cedar Key."

"Cedar Key is in the red zone, Sam," I said, pointing at the jeopardy surface map on the table in front of him.

Sam didn't bother to look. His eyes stayed locked on mine. "Where is this man now?" he asked.

"He has a place on Northwest Thirty-second," Marc replied. "Small house on half an acre. As far as we can tell, he lives alone."

"Where did he live in the late '70s?"

Marc slid a packet of documents over to him. "I got those from the Levy County Records Clerk. Back in '71, Tribe bought twenty acres near the mouth of the Suwannee—also in the red zone. He lived there until the mid-'80s." Marc paused and then added, "The interesting thing is . . . he still owns the property."

We watched while Sam skimmed through the documents. When he was finished, he raised his head. He ignored Marc and fixed his gaze back on me. "Any record?"

I shook my head. "Annie ran his name. He's clean. The Cedar Key Police have him as a victim, back in '78. Apparently, he took a bullet during a robbery."

Sam cocked his head. "Seventy-eight?"

"Yeah. It was after all the abductions."

"Snead confirmed that the Jordan girl's bone marrow tested positive for this crab's eye toxin?"

"Yes . . . and that Jane Doe's was negative."

"Meaning no toxin? Not a trace?"

"That's right. She was killed with a gun. At first we thought she was the reporter who went missing."

"But no dental match."

"Right."

Sam pushed his chair back. "You might have something . . . or not. We'd need a lot more than this to get a warrant." He stood up. "Mr. Hastings . . . thank you. I'm sure you can find your way out. Claire . . . my office, please." He wheeled and left the room without a backward glance.

Marc looked at me. "That went well."

I didn't respond. My mind was already leaping ahead to the reaming I was about to get.

Marc started gathering up our papers. "Call me later and tell me how bad it was."

I was driving home. I had a pounding headache, probably because I'd been grinding my teeth for the last two hours. I sure as hell was in no mood to speak to anyone.

Especially Marc Hastings.

But I could feel him watching me. Reproaching me.

Damn him!

My cell phone rang. I didn't need to check the call display. I knew it was him. "What do you want?"

"Temper, temper," he said. As usual, his voice was infuriatingly calm.

"I'm risking my job! Have you considered that?"

"Yes, I have. But this is bigger than that."

I blew up. "Are you fucking kidding? I have a great job and I'm good at it! All your manipulations just about destroyed everything I've worked so hard to—!"

The blast of a car horn cut my rant short. I had been so busy yelling, I hadn't realized my car was angling into the next lane. I dropped the phone and swerved back. The other driver gave me the finger as he blew past. I signaled, pulled to the shoulder, and stopped.

I took a few deep breaths and picked up the phone. "You still there?"

"A problem with the neighbors?"

"I suppose you're going to tell me the make and model of that car!"

"I'm not that good. But I will tell you this: A time is coming when you will understand everything. On that day, you will remember my words."

"What words?"

"Ignorance *was* bliss."

He waited to see if I had a reply.

I didn't.

"Now, please tell me what Sam Grayson said."

"He made me promise that we would back off. He ordered me to give everything to CID and step back."

"Claire . . ."

"My job's on the line!"

"Not yet."

"Not yet? Where have I heard that before?"

"Claire! Listen to me! You're not done yet!"

My jaw tightened, and I could feel my headache getting worse.

I disconnected and dropped the phone on the passenger seat.

20

The night was exquisitely quiet.

My television and cell phone were off. The street outside was silent, and the couple next door had finally taken their argument off their patio and back inside.

I was sitting in semidarkness, sipping Chianti from a tumbler and thinking about how to go about explaining to CID what Marc Hastings and I had discovered. Specifically, I was thinking about how I was going to convince Ted Lipinski that the lead to Harlan Tribe was worth following. I was still groping toward a strategy when the enveloping silence was shattered by a ringing telephone.

I'd shut off my cell, but I'd forgotten to unplug the landline.

The annoying ringing derailed my train of thought. I'd been meaning to cancel the landline, since I relied mostly on my cell, but I just hadn't gotten around to it. I was still using one of those old-fashioned answering machines, so I just sat and waited for it to take care of the interruption. I figured the caller was Marc, and at that moment, I had no intention of speaking with him.

First I heard the computerized female voice give the generic greeting I had selected when I first set up the machine. "The party you are calling is not available. Please leave a message after the tone."

A second later, my living room reverberated with the din of bar chatter and the clink of glasses. I heard someone's breath on the mouthpiece of a phone and then a slurred voice yelled, "Got Grayson's message, girlie!"

Lipinski!

I leapt up, spilling wine down the front of my jeans. I stormed across the room.

"Okay, listen . . . great idea here! After we arrest some senile old man on, like . . . *no evidence,* ya call a press conference! Ya can tell CNN how you 'n' Sherlock Hastings solved The Amazing Case of the Rosary Pea Killer! The networks'll eat it up!"

His last few words were nearly drowned out by male guffaws. I pictured a band of off-duty detectives sloshing around a drink-covered table. As I fumbled to disconnect the answering machine from the phone, I heard Geiger ask, "What if she's right?"

I froze, amazed that Lipinski hadn't ended the call.

After a beat, I heard his incisive reply: "Naaaaw!"

The line went dead as I ripped the telephone cord out of the wall.

Seven A.M.

I called Marc from the car.

He answered on the second ring. "Good morning."

"You win," I said.

"What happened?"

"I'll tell you when I see you."

"When will that be?"

"In fifteen minutes. Feel like taking a drive?"

"The Suwannee property?"

"Yes."

"I'm ready."

"I thought you would be." I disconnected.

When I drove up, he was waiting outside. He got in, and I pulled away.

"Feel like breakfast first?" he asked.

"How about a drive-through? We can eat on the road."

"In a hurry, huh?"

"I am now."

He nodded and settled back. We stopped at the McDonald's on Route 24, just before the intersection with Interstate 75. We loaded up on Mc-Muffins, orange juice, and coffee, and then threaded under the interstate and set off for Cedar Key. Soon we were rolling down the straight stretch that would take us right past Archer, where I grew up.

Marc arranged some paper napkins across my lap, followed by an un-wrapped McMuffin. He settled back and started working on his own sand-wich. "Talk to me," he said.

"I called Anna Fenwick."

"Why?"

"To ask her about her cousin Doris."

"The one she said was a bit strange."

"Yes."

"Lots of people are a bit strange, Claire. And we're talking about a woman here. There aren't too many female serial killers."

"Point taken. But I still wanted to ask her what she meant by 'strange.' I learned two interesting things. First: Doris was Doris Tribe, Harlan's sister."

"Aaah . . . that *is* interesting."

"And, second: Anna thought she was strange because she got heavily involved in alternative medicines."

"Alternative medicines?"

"Yes."

"Was one of those homeopathy?"

"She thinks so. She said that every few years, Doris would abandon what she was doing and jump into a new study area. She was pretty sure homeopathy was one of them. So we can at least theorize that at some point she might have had a homeopathy textbook lying around the house."

"Where is she now?"

"Anna says she went to India to continue her studies and died of cholera."

"Damn!"

"Yeah."

Marc finished his sandwich. "So . . . what triggered the call to Anna Fenwick? Yesterday, you were swearing at me. You were ready to drop the whole thing."

I told him about Lipinski's drunken message. "That bastard will never follow up on this," I declared, staring glumly at the road ahead.

"He's not that stupid. Sam will expect him to investigate. On the other hand, you don't get to where Lipinski is without learning how to shape evidence. I'm betting he *will* run with this, but not in the way you'd want or expect. He'll start out by keeping it low key. He'll get Jeff Geiger to retrace our steps and ask questions. Lipinski doesn't want us to be right, so he'll concentrate on digging up counter-facts. What I mean is, he won't be looking for evidence that fits. He'll be looking for evidence that doesn't. If Geiger digs up enough to discredit our theory, Lipinski will stop right there and call Sam."

"And if he doesn't? If our theory stands up?"

"Then he and Geiger will make a house call."

"You mean . . . ?"

"Yes. They'll interview Tribe."

"That would screw everything!"

"Probably, but from Lipinski's point of view, there's no downside. The last thing he wants is to spend the next two months doing the kind of spade work you've been doing, reading his way through multiple boxes of evidence, looking for dots to connect, and trying to establish the movements of someone thirty years ago. The Ted Lipinski I knew was always looking for shortcuts. Because of that, he was next to useless on our task force. If Geiger finds any evidence that supports our theory, I guarantee Lipinski will wheel over to Tribe's house, push his way in, and confront the man with whatever he's got. Either Tribe will deny he's the killer or he'll confess. If he denies, we'll be dead in the water, which won't bother Lipinski one little bit. But if he confesses, Lipinski will get credit for the most dramatic arrest in the State of Florida since Ted Bundy."

I was silent. After a mile or so, I said, "Don't think I haven't noticed."

"Noticed what?"

"That you know too much."

He grinned. "Really? I thought I wasn't young enough to know everything."

"Very funny! Don't play with me, Marc! What have you got? Some secret source you're not telling me about?"

"You'll learn."

"When?"

"When you're younger."

I growled in frustration. I wasn't going to let him off this time. I grabbed his arm. "Listen! If you're so damned sure about what Lipinski is going to do, what are *we* doing? I mean, *what are we doing right now?*"

"Getting there first," he replied. He gently removed my hand from his arm, gave it an affectionate squeeze, and placed it back on the steering wheel.

21

Marc looked up from the Levy County map on his knee. He pointed. "That should be it."

I braked and swung the car off the gravel. We passed between two faded white stakes that had been driven into the leaf litter on either side of a double-rut driveway that wound into a forest of tall, spindly longleaf pines.

"It should be about a quarter of a mile," Marc said.

"Here we go again," I muttered uneasily as we moved into the forest. "I do the driving, but you're the one in the driver's seat."

"It only seems that way."

"What are we going to find here?"

"Only what we need to know."

"You're talking in riddles again!"

He didn't respond. I glanced over at him. His head was bowed, and he seemed to be lost in thought.

We followed the ruts at crawling speed. Eventually, the trees opened up and we were at the edge of a large clearing. I stopped the car. Directly ahead was a dilapidated breezeway-style cottage—what Southerners used to call a dogtrot, and today's green architects still do. The basic design consisted of two adjoining cabins with a narrow breezeway between them, all under a common roof. In this case, the front entry into the breezeway was sealed off by a door. A lopsided veranda extended across the front of the entire structure.

The place appeared uninhabited. There were no vehicles in sight, the corrugated iron roof was covered in rust, and the walls looked like they hadn't seen a coat of paint in twenty years.

Marc tossed the map onto the dash. "Let's take a look."

I eased my car across the clearing and stopped in front of the house. We got out. I scanned the ground. There was no sign of vehicle tracks other than our own.

I walked toward the cottage. As I got closer to the veranda, I noticed that vines from a line of bushes planted along the front had wound up, over, and around the railings. In a few places, they had crept all the way across the veranda floor.

Small, dark pods dangled from many of the branches. I picked one off and peeled it open.

Crab's eye peas spilled out into my hand.

"Marc!"

No answer. I turned.

Marc was gone.

Then I heard his voice. "Claire!"

I hurried toward the rear of the cottage. When I rounded the last corner, I stopped in my tracks. The back of the property consisted of a few sagging outbuildings and an overgrown stubble grass field that ran off toward the banks of the Suwannee River. In the distance, thick cypress trees lined the edge of the water.

But what riveted my attention was Marc. He was standing, almost transfixed, staring at the back of the cottage.

The rear wall of the building was completely overgrown with crab's eye vines. They covered the windows, much of the peeling door that closed off the rear end of the breezeway, and in several places, they reached as high as the eaves.

While I was still absorbing this sight, Marc came out of his trance. He strode over to the back door. He tested the handle. The door was unlocked. He began tearing away the vines that would hinder entry.

I couldn't believe my eyes. "Marc, don't! We need a warrant!"

He turned back to me. He'd been preternaturally calm when we got out of the car, but now he was sweating profusely. His shirt was mottled with dark, spreading stains. His face wore a haunted expression. "*You* might need a warrant. I'm a civilian."

"You're a state agent!"

"Based on what? Grayson ordered me off the case, and the cops won't listen to me! I'm a private citizen."

I rushed toward him. "I'm not a private citizen, and you're with me!"

"No, Claire. You're with me."

He pushed on the door. Its baseboard scraped and chattered for a few inches and then jammed.

"Breaking and entering is a felony!"

"Only when there's criminal intent."

"It's still criminal trespass!"

"So arrest me!"

He shouldered the door. It swung inward, hinges squealing. He shot me an apologetic look and stepped through the opening.

I stood frozen. Marc had just forced me to make a decision. I ran the known facts through my mind: the crab's eye pea in Jane Doe's locket; the toxin levels in Amanda Jordan's bone marrow; the possibility that Tribe had learned serial dilution from his sister's textbooks; the fact that he had lived here during the key time period; the location of this property in the red zone on Charlie McNabb's probability map.

I ran the odds. They were dead against us. It was one thing to drive onto the property and discover the crab's eye pea vines. It was quite another to enter the building without a warrant.

I was halfway back to the car when it hit me.

Looking back, I can only describe it as an overwhelming combination of recklessness, anger, and curiosity.

It stopped me in my tracks.

I took a deep breath, retraced my steps, and entered the cottage.

The dogtrot hallway was no more than four feet wide. The floor was bare plywood, swollen from moisture and blotched with mold. An open doorway on the left revealed a stripped-out kitchen. There were no appliances. A ragged pattern of holes and bent hardware on one wall stood as mute testimony to plundered cabinetry. A clutter of camp-style kitchenware gathered dust in a chipped enamel sink.

Thump!

The sound seemed to come from behind the kitchen wall. I hurried along the passageway. A door was open. I looked in.

The room was carpeted in wall-to-wall shag. Much of it was flattened with age and, in places, threadbare. Unworn sections near the walls were the color of pale urine. The fulvous wallpaper was equally unappealing. The sole sign of the room's previous use was a narrow cot jammed against one wall. There was no mattress, just a frame of angle iron rails with a sagging sleep surface of discolored cord and rusting wire.

Marc was kneeling near a small open closet. A wooden crate sat on the floor in front of him. The words OCEAN SPRAY were stenciled across one end. The crate appeared to be sealed, its top seated into the frame formed by the tops of the four sides.

"What the hell are you doing?" I demanded.

He didn't reply. He felt around with his fingers, located a gap, and pried the top loose. He set it aside. From where I stood in the doorway, I could see folded clothing.

Marc raised his head. "To answer your question . . . some psychos like to keep trophies." He reached for the top garment. He held it up. It was a woman's pleated skirt.

A familiar prickly sensation rippled down my spine.

No, please! Not now!

"Marc, right now would be a really good time for us to leave! Please!"

The back of my neck started to burn. I could feel perspiration starting on my forehead and upper lip.

Marc ignored me. He extracted another garment. He rose to his feet and shook it free of its folds.

It was a woman's dress.

He held it up, facing me, and seemed to be about to say something when he happened to glance down. Abruptly, he tossed the dress aside, dropped to his knees, and seized the next piece of clothing visible in the crate. Another dress . . . an older-style blue floral print.

He rocked back on his haunches, fingers fumbling, searching around the neckline.

"What is it?"

"Laura Ashley," he replied, reading the label.

"She was a designer! What's that got to do with anything?"

I was starting to feel very sick.

"Claire . . ."

"What?"

"It's Mandy's dress."

I backed out of the room and ran.

When he found me, I was leaning against a tree, retching my McDonald's breakfast into the shrubbery. He put a hand on my shoulder. I shrugged him off. I felt in my pockets for a tissue, gave up, and wiped my mouth on the sleeve of my windbreaker.

I could feel him watching me.

"Women's clothes," he said. "Old. Out of style."

"Tribe had a sister, remember?" I croaked.

"One skirt. One blouse. Three dresses. All different sizes."

I wheeled to face him. "What? No Denny's uniform with Ina's name tag still in place?" I asked. "No jogging shorts with Victoria's Social Security number stitched across the ass?"

"No. Just that blue dress." There was a catch in his voice.

"I read the reports, Marc, and I have a damned good memory! Amanda Jordan was last seen, quote: 'wearing a blue floral dress.' No mention of a Laura Ashley design!"

"It's her dress. I was with her when she bought it."

I let out a breath. "Secrets, secrets . . ."

"It was more than a year before she disappeared, and it was never a secret."

"Why wasn't the designer label mentioned in the reports?"

"It was."

"I would have remembered!"

"It's there. I'll show you when we get back."

I sighed, exasperated. "You had no right to go in there! Now we're screwed! You've destroyed our case!"

"I want you to come back inside."

"Did you not hear me?"

"I'm the one who did the searching, not you. I'm the one who will swear the affidavit for the warrant, not you."

"Do you actually believe that will make a difference?"

"I want you to see something. I want you to see this so you'll know you can't stop now."

He took me by the hand and led me back to the cottage.

In the hallway, Marc turned right through an open door. I had noticed the door when I first entered, but it had been closed. I followed him into the cottage's tiny living room, which was marked by a few pieces of decaying wagon-wheel furniture. In an adjoining dining area, a rotting area rug had been folded back, revealing a rectangular-shaped black void in the floor.

Nearby, a cross-braced section of wooden flooring leaned against the wall.

"A trapdoor?"

"Yes. Leading to a basement . . . with a dirt floor."

"You think—?"

"I know. Give me your cell. The battery died in mine."

"Who are you calling?"

"No one. I want to show you something."

I handed him my phone. "Come." He led me to the opening. He switched on the phone's flashlight feature and shone the light into the void. A set of rough wooden steps led downward. The light wasn't strong enough to reach the floor below.

Marc handed me my phone. "Go down eight steps and shine the light thirty degrees to your right."

I hesitated, staring at him. He encouraged me with a nod.

With a growing sense of dread, I did as he asked. He held my arm, then my hand, to steady me as I descended. I kept the light pointed at my feet and counted the steps. By the sixth step, Marc released my hand. By the eighth step, I was below the main floor level.

I pointed my cell phone's penlight to the right, as he had instructed. I played the beam right, swept it left, and then quickly back to the right. The pale light showed where runnels of intruding rainwater had spread a stain of black mold down the inside of the unpointed stonework foundation. Where the water had flowed onto the earthen floor, it had hollowed out a shallow depression.

Something white glinted in the bottom of the depression.

I steadied the light.

Bones.

The bones of a human hand.

22

The judge was a widower. The mid-level shelves on two walls of his otherwise packed personal library were lined with evidence of a long, and apparently blissful, marriage. Photographs of his departed wife on their many trips abroad were interspersed with curios and memorabilia collected on those wanderings. From where I was sitting, I could see exotic bird feathers, a matched set of brass Chinese guardian lions, and a blowgun.

Judge Evan O'Connor sat behind an antique desk that had a green tooled leather writing surface. If he hadn't been wearing faded sweats, he could have passed for a character in a Dickens novel. All that was missing from his round, kindly face was a set of muttonchop whiskers.

Marc and I sat silently while the judge sealed the jurat on the affidavit Marc had just sworn. When he finished, he said, "Thank you, sir. Wait outside, would you, please?"

"Of course, Your Honor." Marc stood up and looked at me. "I'll be in the car."

When the door closed behind him, Judge O'Connor said, "Claire, you look like hell!"

I took a deep breath before I replied. "Tough day, Your Honor."

"This could have waited till morning."

"It's Judge Barlow's week in chambers."

The judge scratched an ear. "I guess he'd be a problem." He caught himself and gave me a sharp look. "Not that I condone judge-shopping, young lady!"

I suppressed a smile. "Of course not, Your Honor. May I speak frankly?"

"I would hope you always would."

"Even during his chambers week, Judge Barlow can be . . ." I hesitated.

The judge finished for me. "Unapproachable?"

I nodded.

Judge O'Connor tapped his fingers, thinking. "I'm not happy with this prior entry. You, of all people!" He took a long breath. "I'll issue the warrant, but only because I've accepted your argument that I would have issued one in any event, just on the evidence already in your possession before the entry."

He passed the warrant across the desk to me.

"I'm stretching a point here. Please don't embarrass me!"

It was an hour past sundown and the Suwannee River property was ablaze with lights. Unmarked squad cars and Florida Highway Patrol cruisers sat parked at odd angles. The cottage's breezeway doors had been removed from their hinges, front and rear, and a cube van was positioned next to the front entrance.

Marc and I were standing near my car, which was parked outside the ring of police vehicles. To say we both felt completely drained would be an understatement. "Shattered" would be a more fitting description. We'd had only about six hours' sleep in the last two days, but we couldn't leave.

We had to know.

As we watched, two figures wearing protective suits slid a pallet bearing an almost flat body bag into the back of the van. A few seconds later, Lipinski, Geiger, and Terry Snead appeared in the doorway. Terry had removed his protective headgear, so I knew it was him. He conferred briefly with the two cops and then broke away and stepped up into the van.

Geiger started walking toward us. He was carrying a plastic evidence bag. As he approached, he was shaking his head. He looked at me. "I told him," he said. "I *told* that drunken ass you might be right!"

I tried to head off that line of discussion. "I counted seven body bags."

"Yup. Seven. All buried in the cellar."

"Then we have a problem."

"Yeah. Seven here, and two by the highway. One too many. Some girl never got reported."

"Tribe might help you with that. I just talked to Sam. He wants him picked up tonight." Lipinski joined us as I was speaking. His eyes were locked on Marc. "Did you hear that, Lieutenant?" I asked.

Lipinski grunted.

"Is that a yes?" I asked a little testily.

"Yes! Set it up, Jeff." He was still staring at Marc.

"Keep us informed," I said to Geiger.

"Us?" Now he glanced at Marc.

"Yes. Us."

"Okay. Leave your cell on," he replied.

"What's that?" I asked, nodding at the evidence bag.

"A gun. We found it under the cellar stairs, jammed behind the butt end of a floor joist. Found a slug, too. Dug it out of the floorboards next to the trapdoor."

I felt Marc shift from his position next to me. He leaned back against the car and asked in a careful tone, "What kind of gun?"

Geiger held up the bag. In the faint light, I made out the shape of a snub-nosed revolver. Geiger's answer confirmed my impression. "Colt .38 five-shot. Ted says it looks like a Third Series."

"Serial number?"

"Can't get at it. There's so much corrosion, the cylinder is welded tight. I'm going to drop it at the lab." He walked off and started talking to a pair of uniformed officers.

I started moving around my car, heading for the driver's side.

As Marc opened the passenger door, Lipinski grabbed him by the sleeve. "Explain it to me, Hastings!"

Marc pulled free. "Explain what?"

"How you knew that trapdoor was there?"

A second passed. Neither man blinked.

"Detective work, Ted." He got in the car, and then added through the open window, "You should try it sometime."

I got behind the wheel and started the engine. We pulled away. I could see Lipinski in my rearview mirror, staring after us.

Our headlights picked up the entrance to the double-rut driveway that led out through the pines. I headed for it.

"I've been wondering that myself," I said, keeping my eyes ahead. "About the trapdoor."

"I just followed the outline," he replied.

I looked at him. His face wore a strange expression.

"In the carpet," he explained.

Ten miles up the highway, Geiger's lit-up unmarked cruiser blew past us. I could see he was alone in the car. A few seconds later, my cell rang.

"Jeff?"

"Better put your foot down if you want to be there."

"And if I get pulled over?"

"You won't."

I tromped on it. Forty minutes later, we rounded a corner and I spotted a Gainesville PD cruiser, headlights on and light bar strobing, nosed at an angle to the curb. Beyond it I could see another marked car, also lit up. I parked, and Marc and I got out. A uniformed officer standing next to the nearest car moved to intercept us.

"Claire Talbot, State Attorney's Office," I said.

He recognized me. "Yes, ma'am. They're bringing him out now." He led us to the foot of the driveway.

The thirty-year-old ranch-style house sat in leafy seclusion under the spreading boughs of a pair of mature water oaks. An old Mercury Sable station wagon sat in the driveway, with Jeff Geiger's cruiser parked behind it. Judging from the drifts of dead leaves piled against the older vehicle's tires, it hadn't been moved for a while.

"Mind standing to one side, ma'am?" the cop asked. "The lights . . ."

His cruiser's high beams were pointing directly at the front door of the house, and we were blocking one of them. Marc and I moved into the shadows of a high hedge that ran next to the driveway.

At that second, the front door of the residence swung open. Geiger and two uniformed officers emerged, escorting a handcuffed prisoner.

Although I had little trouble recognizing him, the man I watched being led through the night appeared strikingly different from the image of Harlan Tribe that had lingered with me since I'd first studied the faded photograph in Anna Fenwick's album. Tonight he wore a stretched and faded T-shirt, dress slacks (no belt), and loafers (no socks). His body was still lean, though slightly stooped with age.

What really struck me were the shaven head, the sallow, skull-like face, and the patchy wisps of an uneven beard. He looked exactly like someone you'd see on some redneck reality show.

Marc must have been channeling my thoughts. "A jury will love this guy."

"The defense will clean him up."

"They can't clean up a mug shot."

"Or the video," the cop said, gesturing toward the cruiser's windshield. "The camera's running."

"What about the microphone?" I quickly replayed our remarks through my head as my eyes scanned his uniform for a wireless mike.

"No worries, ma'am. I left it in the car."

Tribe kept his eyes straight ahead as Geiger and the officers led him past our position and over to the second cruiser. They quickly loaded their prisoner in the rear compartment, and the two uniformed officers got in the front.

Marc and I stepped back into the light as the cruiser executed a two-point turn to change direction. I noticed Tribe peering out. He seemed to be looking in our direction. As the car pulled away, his head whipped around and he stared continuously through the rear window until the car was lost from view.

Through the murk of darkness, it was hard to be certain . . . but I could have sworn the man was staring directly at me.

23

Christmas fell on a Saturday. I had already planned to spend the holiday with my mother in Charleston, but I was too exhausted to risk six hours behind the wheel. I could have flown, but the idea of changing planes at the Atlanta airport in the middle of the holiday rush held no appeal for me. I wanted peace, and I wanted quiet. So on the Thursday before Christmas, I had a quick lunch with Marc and then drove to the Amtrak station in Palatka, forty miles to the east, and caught the northbound Silver Meteor.

Marc seemed quiet at lunch . . . but then, I guess we both were. I was going for multiple counts of first-degree murder against Harlan Tribe, which meant the case had to go to the grand jury. Sam had insisted on taking conduct of that hearing, and it was still under way. There was no doubt in anyone's mind that Tribe would be indicted. The thing was . . . neither of us knew if Sam would hand the file back to me after the indictment was unsealed.

"Aren't you the guy who always knows what's going to happen next?" I asked.

I received one of his typically cryptic replies. "Remember, we're relying on the judgment of others."

The one other thing I recall about our lunchtime conversation was a completely out-of-the-blue comment he made about train travel.

"There are certain dangers," he said.

"Dangers? That sounds a bit elitist. What? Like, getting mugged?"

"No. But there's a good reason why people use the phrase 'train wreck' to describe the disaster-prone lives of other people."

"Amtrak's disaster prone?"

"It has been said."

Despite the occasional sensational news report, I figured the odds were less than microscopic that the driver on my randomly selected train would be stoned out of his mind and slam us head-on into a southbound freight. But when I pressed Marc, he changed the subject.

Marc Hastings was a frustrating man to know.

The Charleston Amtrak station wasn't in Charleston at all. It was actually located in a run-down section of North Charleston, ten miles from the city center. The station's office-block design and utilitarian interior reminded me of photos I'd seen of 1950s Greyhound bus stations. I'd always found that a bit strange, considering Charleston's reputation for money and so-called Southern gentility. But, then again, the elegant money doesn't usually ride the rails—unless, of course, it's sipping Bollinger on the Orient Express.

My train arrived after nine that night. My mother was waiting inside the station, looking as spare and withdrawn and carefully collected as always. She was still young enough to attract male attention, but apparently damaged enough to be permanently on guard against that eventuality. I carried stark childhood memories of long, lacerating silences between her and my father. Then, when I was only five, he'd packed two bags and disappeared from our lives forever. After nearly three decades of absence, I could barely remember his face.

Mom gave me a wordless hug, and we walked out through the glass doors, past the row of newspaper boxes, and over to her car.

She lived in a rented second-floor walk-up apartment just off Interstate 26 in Midland Park. It was only a ten-minute drive from the station. Her bedroom overlooked a cemetery, which didn't bother her at all. She always said it was a good thing because I wouldn't have far to move her.

I rolled my suitcase into the spare room, unpacked the Christmas presents that I'd already wrapped, and headed to the living room.

I stopped and looked around, dumbfounded.

No tree.

"Mom?"

"I thought we could get one together."

I set the gifts on the sofa. "There won't be any left—at least, not any good ones!"

"They've still got some behind the gas station."

"Are they open?"

"We can go in the morning, dear. You must be—"

"Are they open, Mom?"

"Yes."

"Well, then? It's Christmas! The one time of the year when I still get to be a kid! I want to decorate the tree! Let's go!"

She gave me one of her trademark shrugs, and went for her coat.

As we went out the door, I playfully put my arm around her and kissed her on the cheek. "And I hope you bought me lots of presents!"

She was quiet for a second, and then she turned to look at me.

I had always preferred small kindnesses to big staged demonstrations, and that suited my mother. The trouble was . . . it had always suited her too well.

But this time, I saw the faint sign of a twinkle in her eye.

Maybe Christmas wouldn't be completely bleak after all.

Our scrawny Charlie Brown Christmas tree was drooping in the corner and I was lounging barefoot on Mom's recliner, reviewing my copy of the grand jury evidence binder. It was the Tuesday after Christmas, and I was planning an early night. Tomorrow's train back to Florida was scheduled to depart at 5:00 A.M.

Mom was watching some reality show stupidity on TV. At least, I thought she was. But when I looked up, I discovered she was watching me.

"What did you say his name was?"

"Who?"

"That killer."

"Harlan Tribe."

After a pause, she said, "He liked brunettes."

"You remember the case?"

"Yes. I remember thinking it was safe because we lived in Archer, and he was taking Gainesville girls. But then he took that girl in Newberry."

"Her name was Amanda Jordan."

She nodded. "It was the year before you were born. I always wondered if he'd been prowling Archer as well." She went quiet for a moment. "Has he confessed?"

"No. He hasn't said a word." I closed the binder, released the tilt on the recliner, and stood up. "I'd better get packed. Are you sure you don't mind driving me? I can always call a cab."

"My alarm is set. Do you think I have something better to do at four o'clock in the morning?"

"How about sleep?"

"I'll sleep when I'm dead. You're my daughter and I hardly ever see you."

There was no reproach in her tone, just a sort of hollow regret.

"Okay. Wake me when you get up." I bent to kiss her good night and turned to go.

"Cat . . ."

I turned back.

"This case . . . I want you to be very careful."

"Mom, Tribe is an old man. He can't hurt me."

"I know." She paused. "I just have this feeling."

"What feeling?"

"That something . . . something's out of balance."

I stared at her. "How long have you had that feeling, Mom?"

She sighed. "Since before you were born."

My mother woke me right on time the next morning. Half an hour later, I was waiting in the small entrance hallway, my pinned-back hair still damp from the shower, while she retrieved her keys from the peg board in the kitchen.

A dozen cut roses were sitting in a vase on the entranceway table. I had picked them up in a half-price deal during my Christmas Eve wanderings at a local mall.

I bent to smell them. When I touched a flower, the petals fell.

I heard a gasp.

I looked up. My mother was standing, keys in hand, with an ashen expression on her face..

I moved to her quickly. "Mom? What is it?"

She opened her mouth as if to speak, and then closed it. She looked at my face as if she were seeing it for the first time.

"Mom?"

She gave a long blink, and then answered slowly. "I'm sorry. Just then, you reminded me . . ."

"Of what?"

"Of . . . someone." She took a deep breath, slung her purse strap over her shoulder, and said, "Let's go."

As we drove out of the parking lot, I leaned closer and put my arm on the back of her seat. "Mom, your face went gray back there! What was that about?"

"It was a long time ago, dear."

"Mom?"

"Please let it go, Claire-Bear. I was just confused."

She might have been confused, but I was disconcerted. My mother hadn't called me Claire-Bear since my father left. That's what he had called me.

We drove to the station. Despite the hour, the waiting room was full of post-Christmas travelers. We found a couple of seats and Mom waited with me until the southbound Meteor pulled in.

When we stood, she kissed me and then hugged me tighter than she had in years. "I love you, Claire-Bear. Always remember that. Always re-member that your mother loves you." Her eyes were big and wet, and as soon as I heard those words, my vision blurred.

"I love you, too, Mom. I'll try to come more often." I wiped my eyes and reached for the handle of my suitcase.

"Claire . . ." Her face wore a strange expression. "I don't understand . . . how . . ." Words died in her throat. She seemed transfixed by a thought.

"How, what?"

She didn't respond.

"Mom? What is it?"

"Just . . . thank you. Thank you, sweetheart."

I puzzled over that as I walked to the train. She stood watching until I made my last turn to wave before I boarded.

24

When I rolled my suitcase up to my car in the parking lot outside the Palatka station, Marc Hastings was leaning on the trunk. Before I could open my mouth, he pulled me into a hug.

I was too startled to return the warmth of his welcome. "Thank you," I said, perhaps a bit severely, after he released me. I thumbed the remote to unlock my trunk. "Now, tell me why you're here."

"I have news," he replied, ignoring my coolness. He hefted my bag into the trunk.

"You could have phoned."

"Your phone's been turned off."

"You could have left a message."

"I wanted to see you."

I wasn't touching that line. I looked around. "How did you get here?"

"I got a ride."

"From?"

"A friend."

"You don't have any."

He smiled. He opened the passenger-side door and held it for me. He stood there, unfazed, until I surrendered and got in the car.

He went around the car and slid behind the wheel. He held out his hand for my keys. I gave them up.

"When do I get to meet her, this friend of yours?" I asked as we drove away.

He didn't reply.

"It is a 'her,' isn't it?"

"Sam got the indictment," he said.

"That's your news?"

"Yes. The grand jury returned nine counts."

"I thought they went into recess for Christmas!"

"They agreed to skip the after-Christmas sales and sit on Monday. And all week, if necessary." He paused. "It wasn't."

"Nine counts! So we kept Jane Doe!"

"Yes." His voice softened. "You kept Jane Doe."

We rode for a mile without speaking.

Finally, I asked, "Why didn't Sam phone me?"

"I told him I'd tell you."

I was about to say that I found that hard to believe, but Marc got there first. "Sam's attitude toward me has changed. I was the last witness he called. He was more than polite during our meetings before . . . and after."

"Tell me."

As we talked, the subject of his mysterious female friend slipped from my mind.

That evening, we ate at the Thai place on North Main that had replaced Tribe's former seafood restaurant.

"Did you find those missing pages?" I asked after our food arrived.

"Not yet."

As I lifted my chopsticks, his cell phone rang. He checked the display and then stood up. "Just be a minute."

"Your girlfriend?"

The phone rang again.

"No."

I shrugged and plucked a jumbo shrimp off my plate.

As he walked behind my chair, he trailed his fingertips across the nape of my neck. "My girlfriend's sitting right here," he whispered.

My shrimp froze in midair a few inches from my mouth.

The phone rang again. He answered in mid-ring, walking away. He didn't say hello or hi or give any kind of greeting. I heard only four words before he moved out of earshot: "I know it's hard."

For the next few minutes, I picked at my pad Thai, occasionally glancing at Marc. He was standing in the restaurant entrance lobby, facing determinedly away from our table, speaking in low tones.

I read somewhere that the sensation of being watched is triggered by a faculty of heightened awareness that is hardwired into our basal ganglia—otherwise known as our reptilian brain. I have no idea whether that is true. I only know that, as I watched Marc, I had an overwhelming feeling that someone was watching me. I swung my head, but no one in the restaurant was looking at me.

When my attention shifted back to Marc, he was snapping his phone shut.

I caught movement out of the corner of my eye. A figure in the shadows outside a window near our table was in motion.

The figure was turning away.

Turning away . . . and at the same time removing a phone from his—or her—ear.

The figure disappeared into the gloom.

Marc returned, grinned apologetically, and took his seat. As he picked up his chopsticks, I laid mine down.

He looked at me. "You're not eating?"

"I've lost my appetite."

"What's wrong."

"I'll tell you what's wrong! I'm sick of you and your secrets!" Smoldering anger drove me to my feet. I snatched my coat off the back of my chair and grabbed my purse. "You're a man with a past, and you're hiding something! You're also a witness in a murder case—*my* murder case! When I really analyze it, I should have nothing to do with you outside the courtroom!"

"You should, and you will," he said calmly.

Too calmly.

"Don't be an ass!" I snapped, raising my voice and turning heads at nearby tables. "You're twice my age! Give me my keys!" He handed them over. "Take a taxi home! Or call your girlfriend! And stay away from me until the trial!"

I felt every pair of eyes in the restaurant follow me as I strode out.

The drive home gave me plenty of time to regret my cruel words.

25

I was late getting into the office on Thursday. There was a handwritten message sitting on my chair: SEE ME!

I walked quickly to Sam's office.

As I entered, he was sitting behind his desk with his back to the door, staring out the window.

"I'm here."

He swung his chair. His expression was thunderous. "Where were you?"

"Sorry. I had a bad night." To avoid the next question, I kept talking. "I heard about the indictment. Nine counts! It's everything we wanted!"

He slid a sheaf of documents across his desk. "Tribe's attorney served a motion to suppress this morning."

"What? It's only been three days!"

"He managed to get a copy of the search warrant file."

"How?"

"Who knows? The Court Clerk's Office is a sieve. He'd get it on discovery anyway, but now we'll have to deal with it up front."

I picked up the documents and spent a few seconds flipping pages, scanning passages of formulaic text. "Standard language here, Sam."

He held out his hand. I passed the papers back.

"Paragraphs sixteen to twenty-one are not exactly 'standard language.'" He started reading passages aloud. "'. . . human remains found under cellar floor product of unwarranted prior search. . . . Defendant says the warrant judge was deliberately misled or erred in law . . . the conduct of the Assistant State Attorney and her agent was a flagrant violation of Defendant's rights,' et cetera, et cetera." He looked up. "He's made you a witness, Claire. He plans to flay you on the stand."

I wondered if the sudden strain I was feeling was etched on my face. "Will you take the hearing?" I asked, quietly hoping.

"Would you prefer Standish?"

"No!"

"Of course I'll take the hearing! And if we survive it, I guess I'll have to take the trial!"

"Sam, I want second chair."

"I'm not sure we can pull that off—not with this judge."

I had an awful premonition. "Who is it?" I asked.

"Barlow."

The jury box was empty. Any decisions made at this hearing would be made by the judge alone. And from my position next to Sam, I could see the bastard was relishing the prospect.

Marc and I had made up.

Well . . . sort of.

With the hearing date breathing down our necks, I had called Marc and apologized.

Well . . . sort of.

I'd told him that when I said, "Stay away from me until the trial," I actually meant, um, until the defense's suppression hearing.

"I know."

"You know? *I* didn't know! How the hell could you—?" I sucked in a breath and swallowed my frustration. "Never mind . . . we really need to meet."

"Come to the apartment."

"No. At the office. Sam wants to interview you."

"Figured."

"What?"

"That he would take it."

"He has to. The defense is forcing me to testify."

"Make sure he puts me on first. I'll make the ride easier for you." He sounded perfectly relaxed.

And that was exactly how he came across on the witness stand—cool and relaxed. Under Sam's careful questioning, Marc walked the court through every step in the process of reasoning that had led us to the cottage on the Suwannee, underlined the fact that he had acted independently and without notice to me when he entered the cabin, and wound up his direct examination by rattling off an executive summary of every shred of evidence already available to us at the moment of entry.

Well, almost every shred. He did manage to leave out the small matter of forty-one lever-arch binders stuffed with police reports that lined the shelves in his upstairs bedroom. And he diplomatically failed to mention the many hours he had spent sequestered in that room with a certain Assistant State Attorney named Claire Talbot.

But then again, he had failed to mention those little details to Sam Grayson as well.

After two hours, it was the defense's turn.

Harlan Tribe's attorney, Adrian Bannister, was fresh from a news-grabbing jury victory in Jacksonville. Goateed and ponytailed, with a baritone voice and a radioactive smile, he was as sleek as an otter in his tailored suit. The defendant, wearing a weedy sports jacket and open-necked shirt, sat in scrawny silence at his counsel's table, never once offering a single word of whispered instruction to his attorney. The only time he displayed any visible interest in the proceedings was when I was in the witness box. During that uncomfortable hour, Tribe never took his eyes off me, and he wore the confused look of a man who was struggling to remember something.

Bannister's bare-bones cross-examination of Marc and, later, of me, left the distinct impression of a lawyer more devoted to image and style than to meticulous preparation or legal acumen. In other words . . . a jury charmer. By the time the evidence phase was over, I was left with a lingering—and certainly startling—second impression. Tribe's attorney didn't really want his motion to succeed. He was hoping the case would go to trial. The jury charmer saw a chance to turn the decades-old murders of nine young women into a marketing opportunity.

Bannister and I were both about to see our neat little plans shot to hell.

The argument phase began after the lunch adjournment. Marc took a seat directly behind Sam to make it easier for us to maintain eye contact.

The tension between us had evaporated during the course of the hearing. Three rows back, Geiger and Lipinski sat side by side, stone-faced and staring. Technically, they were the lead investigators, but their evidence about recovery of the bodies at the cottage had been covered by an agreed stipulation of facts.

Otherwise, the courtroom was empty. The nature of the hearing required that it be heard in camera, and a bailiff stood ready outside the main doors to ensure that no one entered.

At Judge Barlow's nod, Sam rose to commence his final argument. Steadily and precisely, he stitched the facts together. Then he turned to the law.

Ninety minutes later, Bannister was in full flow, rocking on his feet, his notable voice—another marketing asset he was happy to deploy for the ubiquitous microphones on courthouse steps—swelling with righteousness as he read passages aloud from prior reported cases that were only marginally relevant.

But Judge Barlow wasn't looking at Bannister.

He wasn't looking at Sam, either.

His pale eyes were fixed on me.

I could barely keep still. I turned my pen over and over in my fingers, at the same time hating myself for displaying such compulsiveness under this despised judge's gaze.

"And, in conclusion, Judge—"

At last Barlow's attention shifted to the defense table.

"That's the third time you've said that, Mr. Bannister."

"My apologies, Your Honor. But never in my entire career have I encountered such a flagrant example of a defective warrant! Why, even my old friend, the distinguished law professor Morton—!"

"Forget your old friend!" Barlow interjected as his chalk eyes slid back to me. "*Miz Talbot*," he stated—laying equally disdainful emphasis on both the "Ms." and my surname—"repeatedly made it clear in her evidence that she fully disclosed the circumstances of the prior search to the issuing judge. Mr. Hastings's testimony supported her in this. Do you concede that the judge who issued the warrant was aware of the prior entry?"

"Yes, Your Honor, but—!"

"So, the warrant is prima facie sufficient on its face."

"Yes, but—"

"But . . . you're pressing a more fundamental point, are you not, Mr. Bannister?"

"Here it comes . . . ," Sam muttered to me.

"Yes, Your Honor!" Bannister replied. "You mean, of course . . . You mean the point that . . . that . . ." He trailed off.

"Yes, Mr. Bannister?"

"The prior evidence was, uh, was probably . . . insufficient."

Probably insufficient? Bannister's apparent reluctance to drive the point home confirmed my earlier impression that he didn't give a damn about winning this closed-door hearing. He had his eye on the bigger prize—a national television audience.

I was rooting for him.

But the judge wasn't letting him off the hook. "Exactly," Barlow resumed. "You are pressing the fundamental point that no search warrant could ever properly issue on the evidence available to *Miz Talbot*"—that emphasis again—"prior to the moment of entry *onto,* much less *into* your client's recreational premises."

Bannister's back straightened. "My very point, Judge." Victory was being forced upon him, and he decided to take it like a man. "If we ignore everything that was found during that initial search, the remaining evidence listed by Mr. Hastings does not reach the threshold of probable cause. Therefore, the search warrant must have been, uh . . . must have been . . ."

"Void ab initio, Mr. Bannister?"

Bannister flushed. "Er . . . yes, Your Honor. Void."

Barlow nodded slowly. "Thank you, sir. You may be seated."

Bannister hesitated, and then subsided into his chair.

Sam rose to his feet. "I'll say it again, Judge, and I ask you to pay close attention to this crucial point! No matter what your personal *hindsight* view might be on the grounds for the search warrant, the 'inevitable discovery' rule applies. At this hearing, we have demonstrated on a preponderance of evidence that normal police investigatory procedures would have inevitably led to the discovery of this evidence. In those circumstances, this evidence is clearly admissible!"

Barlow's eyes locked on me as he responded to Sam. "This wasn't just a perimeter search, Mr. Grayson! Nor is there any doubt that Mr. Hastings was acting as your Assistant State Attorney's agent on this occasion, and that she and Hastings were both trespassers on that property! The inevitable discovery exception has sometimes been held to apply to derivative evidence, but never to primary evidence!"

"With respect . . . Judge O'Connor himself specifically stated that he would have issued a warrant in any event, just on the evidence already in Ms. Talbot's possession before the entry was made."

"How do I know what he stated? He made no record of his reasons for issuing this warrant!" He leaned back in his chair. "That in itself I find extraordinary."

"Ms. Talbot related to you under oath what Judge O'Connor said. She gave you his exact words."

"Yes, she did." Barlow's mouth twisted. "And very conveniently this alleged assurance by Judge O'Connor was given out of the hearing of your only other witness. Therefore, I have only the word of the Assistant State Attorney that *your* office permitted her to conduct a freelance investigation, assisted by an obsessed retired policeman who—also very conveniently—appeared on the scene within hours of the discovery of the two bodies at Bronson."

Sam's expression darkened. "Judge, I find that comment—"

"Why the midnight visit to Judge O'Connor, Mr. Grayson? What dire emergency required *Miz Talbot* to get *that particular judge* out of bed during a week when another judicial officer—namely, me—was on call? What evidence was likely to be lost by waiting until morning?"

"Your Honor, decisions in both the Second and Eighth Circuits have held that the inevitable discovery exception applies to primary evidence where—!"

"I have read your memorandum, Mr. Grayson! Sit down!"

Sam remained on his feet. A second ticked by, then another. He looked like a man ready to risk a hearing before the state bar by firing back with a cutting reminder that the rules of courtroom civility applied to judges as well as attorneys.

Barlow sensed what was coming. "Permit me to restate that. *Please* sit down, Mr. Grayson."

Barlow was nothing if not a coward.

Sam resumed his seat.

"My decision is as follows. . . ." Barlow proceeded to enunciate his ruling through his teeth without glancing at his notes. "I find as a fact that Marcus Hastings was an agent of the State. I find his conduct, and the concurrent conduct of Assistant State Attorney Talbot here present, to have been reprehensible in the extreme. I am astounded by the conduct of this woman, who is an officer of the court. I am equally astounded that this warrant was issued by my brother judge. Perhaps his normally acute faculties were affected by being awakened in the middle of the night. I don't know, and I don't need to know. Whatever the reason, there was no legal basis for Judge O'Connor to grant this search warrant. I rule that none of the physical evidence recovered from the defendant's recreational property may be tendered before the jury! My written ruling, with full references to the governing legal authorities, will be filed on the case record within seven days." He banged his gavel, rose to his feet, barked "We are adjourned!" and strode out of the courtroom.

26

Sam finished a short discussion with Tribe's lawyer and stepped back to our table. Behind him, Bannister started packing his papers into a briefcase. He was speaking in low tones to his client, but the old man didn't seem to be listening.

Tribe was watching me, and he was still looking confused.

"He's moving for a fresh bail hearing," Sam said.

"No surprise there," I replied bitterly. I was feeling sick to my stomach.

"I told him we'd review our evidence and take a position."

"The case is screwed, Sam. Bannister's got to know you're stalling."

"I want to stall long enough to see Barlow's written ruling. His conduct was outrageous. He displayed personal animosity toward you, and—!"

"That won't show in the transcript, Sam! You know that."

"Maybe not, but he gave the game away with that swipe about you going to another judge during *his* chambers week."

"A revenge ruling? Nine women are dead! I know Barlow is petty, but this?"

Sam put his hand on my arm. "We've been down this road with the bastard before. He doesn't like me—I'm that Indian who whipped his ass too many times when he was an attorney and embarrassed him too many times in the appellate courts. I don't know why he doesn't like you, but it isn't hard to guess: You're a woman and you're smarter than he is. Together, we're a constant reproach to his delicate ego. Bottom line: Some of that poison will leak onto the pages of his ruling and bolster our grounds for an appeal."

I sighed. Every instinct told me the case was permanently lost, but I felt a glow of gratitude to the fine man standing in front of me. He'd questioned my judgment from the start and I'd gone against his specific instructions, but now the chips were down, and here he was, fighting for me and fighting for my case.

As Sam and I left the courtroom, a bailiff was leading Tribe away. He was still looking at me.

Marc was waiting outside the courthouse, standing out of the flow of foot traffic on the grass verge next to a lamppost. Sam said, "See you at the office," and kept going.

I walked over to Marc. I offered some stilted greeting, even though I actually wanted him to hug me.

"He'll get bail," Marc said.

"I know."

"Don't worry about it."

I stared at him. "Don't worry? That man murdered nine women!"

At that instant, Geiger and Lipinski walked past. Lipinski's face was flushed with anger. "Fuckin' stupid woman!" he muttered as he walked by.

Marc's explosive reaction took me by surprise. He had Lipinski by the throat and slammed up against the lamppost so quickly that not even Geiger—thirty years his junior—had time to react.

"You're a disgrace to the badge, Lipinski!" Marc hissed. He tightened his grip.

"*Let him go!*" Geiger pushed in and tried to break Marc's hold. He failed. He reached for his weapon.

"Marc," I said quietly. "Please."

Marc released Lipinski, who immediately bent double, wheezing and coughing.

Geiger threw an arm around Lipinski's shoulders. "I should arrest you for that, Hastings!"

"Do it, pretty boy!" Marc shot back. "A public trial will give me a chance to show the world what a pair of fuckups you two are!"

Geiger hesitated, and I seized the moment. "Come on, Marc. Sam wants to talk to us." I led him away.

After we were out of earshot from the two cops, I said, "Very chivalrous of you, old man."

"I come from a different generation."

"You come from the same one as Lipinski."

"He's an aberration."

"*Fuckups.* Is that one of those old-time expressions?"

He smiled. "You'd be surprised how we talked back then." We walked in silence for a few more seconds, and then he added, "I thought we were seeing Sam."

"I am. You're not. I just said that to get you out of there."

"Okay. But we're walking in the wrong direction."

"I know." I glanced at him. "I need a drink first."

When I walked into Sam's office, his phone was ringing. He waved me into a seat as he picked up the receiver.

"Yes?" He scowled as he listened. "Tell her I'll call her back! And don't put any more calls through! I'm in a meeting." He hung up and looked at me. "We have a problem! I've just been—" His cell phone started vibrating. He snatched it off the desk and checked the display. "It's Diana."

I started to get up. "I'll come back."

"No! Stay!" He thumbed a button and put the phone to his ear. "Hi, honey. . . . Yeah. No, she's with me now. I'll talk to you later, okay? Yes, I'll tell her. Okay, love. Bye." He put the phone down. "Diana sends her love."

"She knows?"

"She made me promise to call her when we had a ruling. I left her a voice mail."

"You mentioned a problem."

"Yeah."

"Did you mean a problem more serious than losing the evidence of seven buried bodies and a crate stuffed with murdered women's clothes?"

"Yes."

Somehow, I guessed from his tone what was coming. "No!"

"I need you to clean out your desk." His throat convulsed. "I feel sick about this. I'm sorry."

"Why? Why, Sam?"

"I just had a phone call from the AG's office."

I stared. I felt a cold chill. "Perry Standish! He made a call, didn't he?"

"Yes. He got that Whitman conviction, and now—"

"—and now he's riding high and figures he can take me out!"

"You got it."

"Sam! Whether I stay or go is *your* decision, not the Attorney General's!"

"You're right, but she boxed me in."

"How?"

"She also got a call from our favorite judge."

27

The next day, just before five o'clock in the afternoon, I slipped the key Marc had given me into the lock of his apartment door. I opened the door and walked in.

Music was playing. It was an old song—"Broken Hearted Me."

I shut the door quietly.

Marc was stretched out on the couch. As I approached, I saw that his eyes were closed. For a horrible second, I thought something was badly wrong. Then I saw the tear on his cheek. I felt a lump rise in my throat.

My shadow rippled across Marc's face. His eyes opened.

"Anne Murray," I said. "I haven't heard that in years."

"Number one on the charts in November '79." He sat up and wiped his cheek without any sign of embarrassment. "The same month you were born."

"I don't recall telling you when I was born."

He responded with an ironic look and I flashed on an earlier discussion in this room: my affair with a law school professor . . . a bottle of '83 Margaux . . .

I nodded in defeat. "Research."

"Right." He picked up a remote and killed the music. "I've been waiting."

"They're calling it an 'administrative suspension.'"

"It was on the news."

"There's a Channel 20 news crew camped outside my town house."

"I made up the spare room."

"Thanks." I sat down. "Barlow has filed two formal complaints against me—one with the Attorney General and another with the State Bar."

Marc reached for my hand. "It's just bluster, Claire."

"Sam's doing his best to protect me. He knows the press will try to crucify him, but he seems more worried about me. He's insisting on handling the appeal himself."

"I'm sorry. I knew better than to go in there. But I just . . ." He went quiet.

"C'mon! You would have gone there no matter what I said! All I had to do was stay home! Sam would have given you immunity on the burglary, Barlow could never have gotten away with ruling you were a State agent, and your evidence would have gone in." I could feel the tears coming as I spit out my next words. "All we needed was a decent, thoughtful judge, but instead we got stuck with that woman-hating egomaniac!"

The tears flowed. Marc slid an arm around me, and I collapsed against him.

For a long, warm minute, with my face pressed to his chest, it felt like I belonged there.

At least, until the defensive part of my brain pointed out that he was stroking my hair.

I sat up and straightened my top. "I need a drink."

"Beer? Wine? Scotch?"

"Anything."

He rose and padded into the kitchen. I heard a cupboard open, glasses and ice clinking. "Something to eat?" he called.

"Not hungry."

He reappeared with three tumblers enclosed in the clasp of both hands. One was filled with ice cubes, with a spoon standing in the ice. He lowered the three glasses to the table and then passed one to me. It was half-filled with scotch.

He grinned at me. "Last time you weren't hungry, you yelled at me and stormed off."

"How did you get home that night?"

"Took a cab." He sat next to me and spooned an ice cube into his drink.

I looked at him. "How can you be so calm? A serial killer just walked!"

He shrugged. "I said you would solve this case, and you did. The killer has been identified. And after all these years, any other suspects are finally eliminated."

"Other suspects?"

"You read the files upstairs."

"Okay, but . . ."

"The world now knows who and what Tribe is . . . including his neighbors. Take a look at O. J. Simpson's life after his acquittal."

"Simpson was a celebrity! The world knows him on sight. Tribe could move to another state—hell, he'd only have to move to Miami—and no one would know him from Adam!" I took a swallow of whisky. "I screwed up and I can't fix it!"

Marc wiped a tear off my cheek with his knuckle. "Dear, dear Claire. Maybe you already have."

"What?"

"Fixed it."

"Please, no more of your riddles!"

"The Chinese have a saying. . . ."

I groaned. "And what do the Chinese say?"

He answered, looking straight into my eyes. "Only the future is certain. The past is always changing."

I had no idea what that meant, and I was too upset to ask.

When I eventually fell asleep, with my head on a cushion and my bare feet on Marc's lap, my third glass of scotch was sitting untouched on the coffee table, right beside the half-eaten remains of a pizza we had ordered. I have a wispy memory of Marc gathering me into his arms and carrying me across the apartment.

After that . . . nothing.

When I woke up, the sun was high and I couldn't tell if it was morning or afternoon. I was lying on my back, under covers. I had one of those invidious headaches that hurts only when you move your head. A roll to the left ramped up the pain in my skull, but confirmed that I was alone in the bed. It was only then that I realized I was in my underwear. I did a quick check to make sure I wasn't wearing a thong. I wasn't, which was something of a relief, but still . . .

I sat up and surveyed my surroundings. My jeans and top were on separate hangers on the back of the door. A glass of water and a bottle of Tylenol sat waiting on the bedside table, along with a neatly folded terry bathrobe on an adjacent chair.

I swung my legs out of bed, shook two Tylenols out of the bottle, and gulped them down with a swallow of water. I stood up and pulled on the robe. I hadn't decided yet whether to be peeved or not about Marc's undressing me.

While I was making up my mind, things got suddenly strange.

There was a tap on the door, and Marc's voice called out: "Cat? Breakfast is ready!"

It took me a few seconds of shock to digest what I had just heard. By the time I opened the door, Marc, wearing oven mitts, was carrying plates from the kitchen to the adjoining dining area.

He set one plate down, circled the table, and then spotted me standing in the bedroom doorway. He must have noticed the expression on my face. "What's wrong?"

"'Cat'?" I asked sharply.

"Oh . . . uh . . . your initials. Just popped into my head, I guess."

I marched toward him, my bare heels thumping on the hardwood floor. "Only my mother calls me that! Have you been talking to her?"

He stood stock-still. "No."

I studied the plate on my side of the table . . . eggs, sunny-side up, weird-looking bacon, fried tomatoes, and wheat toast . . . cut into narrow strips.

"What's this?" I asked, pointing.

"Dippers. For your eggs."

He was still holding his own plate. I stared at his toast. It was unsliced.

I was spooked. My head was pounding, which made the tone of my next question sound more harsh than I had intended.

"How the hell did you know I like to dip my eggs?"

He set his plate down. "I guess . . . I guess I know quite a few things about you."

"More 'research'?" I glared at him. "And just why this burning interest in my personal preferences, Mr. Hastings?"

There was an uneasy moment, and then he said it.

"Because I'm in love with you."

I blinked at him. I remember that blink because it wasn't a sponta-neous blink. It was an act, because he had just admitted what I already knew. I had been ready for it, but I pretended that I wasn't. I pretended I was surprised.

But pretense is hard to sustain. What do you say next when you're totally at sea and confused about your own feelings? I couldn't think of a damned thing that wouldn't sound lame, so I sidestepped.

"Oh, hell!"

"Oh, hell . . . what?"

"Oh, hell . . . I'm hungry and it looks good!"

I sat down and so did he. For a few minutes, we ate in silence.

"What kind of bacon is this?" I asked. It was spicy and delicious.

"Pancetta. It's Italian."

"Hmm. You're just full of surprises, aren't you?"

By the end of the meal, my headache was gone.

28

Situational awareness.

Good cops have it, and if they want to stay alive, they keep it switched on all day, every day, on duty or off.

Most often, situational awareness just means seeing something that others miss: clothing or body language that doesn't fit; a light in the wrong window; an out-of-place sound. But sometimes it means the reverse. Sometimes, especially in police work, it means the well-honed skill of ensuring that other people don't see something.

For example: making sure that those other people *don't see you.*

After our breakfast together, and after a quiet discussion over coffee, I showered, dressed, and took my leave from Marc. I drove home. Thankfully, the news crew was gone.

But they'd been replaced.

A blue VW Jetta was parked in a visitor space three units up from mine. A man was sitting behind the wheel. When I noticed him, his head was down, his face obscured behind the peak of a ball cap.

But his window was open, and his left arm was resting in plain view. Even from sixty feet away, I instantly deduced his identity.

I entered my town house and bolted the door behind me. I waited ten minutes, then used my landline to call Marc's cell.

When he answered, I announced, "I'll be back in three hours."

"Okay."

"Just so you know."

"Okay."

"I'm being tested."

"I understand."

I disconnected, wondering if he had really got my message. Then I relaxed. Based on past performance, I was pretty certain he had.

I ran up the stairs to my bedroom. I stood a few feet back from the balcony window and watched the parking lot.

Sure enough, after a few minutes, the man in the Volkswagen took a call on a cell phone. Seconds later, he drove away.

I started packing a suitcase.

I parked on the street near the entrance to Marc's building. It took about three seconds to confirm my earlier impression. Either my stalkers' situational awareness skills were severely deficient, or they had an extremely low opinion of mine.

The car was parked on the opposite side of the street, halfway up the next block. This time they were using a full-sized American sedan, but they hadn't had the sense to tuck the nose of their car tight against the vehicle parked in front of it. With the setting sun dipping low behind me, the wigwag emergency lights mounted behind the car's front grille glowed like neon.

I left my suitcase in the car. Feigning oblivious confidence, I walked directly to the front entrance of Marc's building. I pushed the button on the console. Marc answered.

"I think you should come down to the lobby," I said.

"On my way," he replied, and buzzed me in.

Sixty seconds later, he was standing in front of me. "Let's go," he said, taking my hand.

"Where?"

"I'll explain on the way."

He led me out through the rear door into the alley. We walked two blocks east and then took a jog back to the main street. We crossed to the opposite sidewalk and strolled west, approaching the vehicle from behind. When we were one car length back, Marc stepped quickly into the street and strode toward the driver's door.

The man sitting behind the wheel must have spotted Marc in his side-view mirror. He opened his door, but before he could step out, Marc had him by the jacket. With the same strength and speed I'd seen him use on my assailant outside Sam's apartment building, he hauled Ted Lipinski out of the car and slammed him facedown on the asphalt.

Geiger was in the passenger seat. He was taken by surprise. He spilled coffee down his shirt, yelled with pain, and immediately tried to open his door. I kicked it shut. He gaped at me in shock and went for his gun.

I stared at him, daring him to pull it.

He seemed to shrink. His hand reappeared from under his jacket, empty.

Marc jerked the now-dazed Lipinski to his feet, disarmed him, and yelled at Geiger. "Give Claire your gun!"

"What the fuck! Are you both crazy?"

"Shut up! Lower your window and give her your gun!"

Geiger slowly removed his weapon from its holster. The window slid down. He passed his gun out to me.

Marc maneuvered Lipinski into position and shoved him headlong back into the car. His face landed on Geiger's crotch. The old cop scrambled to right himself. "Aggravated assault on the police!" he spluttered. "I'll have your ass, Hastings!" He swung his head to glare at me. "And yours, too, you bitch!"

"We'll welcome the charges, Lipinski! Not only will they give us a chance to expose your utter incompetence, but we look forward to hearing you explain to the feds what part of your *lawful* duties required you to stalk Claire Talbot and illegally tap her phone!"

"And," I added, yelling at the two red-faced cops, "you can expect a civil complaint against both of you for malfeasance! Get ready to lose your houses, your cars, and"—I stabbed a finger at the TAG Heuer on Geiger's wrist that had given him away—"your fancy watches!"

I straightened, heaved Geiger's gun over a chain-link fence into the empty lot next to the sidewalk, and walked away. Marc joined me, still carrying Lipinski's weapon. After a few steps, he dropped it into a storm drain.

"He'll have fun explaining that," I said.

He chuckled. "Nice performance."

"You, too."

"Are you really going to sue them?"

"Maybe," I replied. After a few seconds, I said, "Probably not."

"That's good. I don't think you'll have time. I'm planning on keeping you pretty busy."

"Oh, you are, are you?"

"Yes. I am." He studied my face, and broke into a grin.

At that moment, I realized that I had grinned first.

I took his arm, and we walked to his building.

When we reached the front door, I said, "I brought some clothes."

"I thought you might."

"Presumptuous of you."

"I figured you'd want to get away from the newshounds."

"Or idiot cops?"

He nodded and looked up the street. I followed his gaze. Lipinski and Geiger were down on their knees in the gutter. They had the storm grate pulled vertical. Lipinski was holding it while Geiger had one arm shoulder-deep in the drain.

"Get your suitcase." Marc instructed. "I'll meet you in the lobby."

The expression on his face sent me hurrying to my car.

As I rolled my suitcase back to the building, I spotted Lipinski walking determinedly toward me from the opposite direction. Geiger was trailing several feet behind him, walking slowly. Marc opened the lobby door. I entered and headed for the elevator. He put a hand on my arm. "No. We walk."

"The front door won't stop them! They'll get someone to open it!"

"Don't worry." He hefted my bag and led me up the stairs, taking them two at a time.

As we passed the last landing, I panted, "Are you doing this just to show off?"

"Sort of," he replied. "But not in the way you think." I was about to blurt some caustic remark when an alarm bell sounded.

Marc smiled at my confusion. "The elevator," he explained. "It jams between first and second floors."

"Since when?"

"Since three minutes ago."

I gaped at him. "How did you do that?"

"I know things."

"I've already gathered that! But how—?"

"Preplanning." He grinned and started up the last flight of steps. "Coming?"

29

Four hours later, we were sitting at Marc's dining room table, nursing the last drops of a very fine Montrachet. Empty plates and dishes were all that remained of a two-course dinner Marc had calmly prepared while the sounds of the elevator alarm and, later, the commotion caused by the fire department's rescue efforts, drifted up from floors below. Eventually, we'd watched from the dining room window as Lipinski and Geiger plodded away from the building in the direction of the police car.

"How did you know they wouldn't keep coming, pound on your door, and arrest us for assault?"

"Geiger isn't the smartest cop around, but he has a bit of common sense. I figured an hour or two in an elevator would give him enough time to convince Lipinski that he was playing with fire."

I was long past hiding my skepticism. I gave him a narrow look. "You're very good at guessing everybody's next move, aren't you?"

As usual, he didn't answer. He sipped his wine, waiting for me to change the subject.

And, as usual, I did.

"Who taught you to cook like that?" The main course Marc had prepared—salmon poached in a wine and blueberry sauce, served with a dish that he called Persian jeweled rice—had been exquisitely delicious.

"A beautiful young woman."

"Was she also intriguing?"

"Oh yes. Definitely."

"Did you love her?"

"Yes."

"Where is she now?"

His eyes were suddenly damp. "It's a long story."

I sighed. "They always are." I drained my glass.

"One day you'll understand."

Damn!

I already knew I was in love with this enigmatic man, but all this evasiveness about his past was pissing me off.

"For God's sake, Marc! How many years between us?"

"Too many."

"And how many years could we have together? Ten? Fifteen?"

"Too few."

"Right! And what about kids? What if we wanted children? You wouldn't be around to see them grow up!"

Marc's eyes filled. I saw his throat working. He rose slowly from his seat. "I think I'll get an early night. Leave the dishes. I'll clear them up in the morning." Before I could think of a response, he left the table and strode across the apartment to his bedroom. He entered and shut the door behind him.

Once again, my temper and my caustic tongue had left me silently kicking myself.

I got up and cleared the table. In the kitchen, I rinsed off the dishes and methodically loaded them in the dishwasher. I'd been told a hundred times that prerinsing before loading a dishwasher is a complete waste of energy, time, and water, but the mindless action was exactly what I needed at that moment.

It didn't work. My mind was in turmoil. I returned to the table. There was still an inch of wine left in the bottle. I lifted the bottle and poured the wine straight down my throat.

"Go to bed, you idiot!" I whispered to myself. "Just go to bed! And tomorrow, you apologize!"

I set the bottle on the table and walked straight across the apartment to Marc's bedroom. I opened the door and walked in. In the spill of light from the door, I could see Marc lying on his side, with his back to me. Somehow, I sensed he was awake. I stripped off all my clothes and slid in next to him.

"I'm sorry," I whispered.

But then . . . my nerve failed me. I didn't touch him. I just lay there, trembling like a schoolgirl. A long second passed. I was about to change my mind and flee when Marc rolled over and folded me into his arms. He kissed my eyes, my nose, my neck . . . my mouth. The kiss was long and soft, and I felt a rush of heat and desperate need.

I melted into him.

And then it came . . . an unbelievable lust that almost stopped my breath. It was a desire for this man and this man alone that seemed at once alien and familiar, known and unknown.

Can this be me? my reasoning mind asked in the single millisecond before I forgot everything and let myself go.

Marc Hastings devoured me.

And then I devoured him.

And then he cried.

It was long after midnight when we finally fell asleep.

When I awoke, the room was soaked in sunlight and I was sprawled on my stomach with the covers down around my thighs.

I felt Marc touching me.

Actually, I felt only his fingertip. It was tracing the outline of the butterfly tattoo that I'd had on the small of my back since I was a college student.

I murmured. "It's a blue morpho."

"First one I ever slept with."

"Butterfly?"

"No. Tattoo. I've slept with a few butterflies in my day."

I rolled over and stretched, giving my best imitation of feline contentment. "How did you know?"

"What?"

"How did you know exactly what I would . . . like?"

"Experience."

I snorted. "Oh, of course!" I reached over my head, grabbed my pillow, and whacked him with it. "The arrogance of the elderly!"

A broad grin spread across his face. "Elderly, huh?" He grabbed me and held me down. He really was surprisingly strong, and he kept grinning while I squirmed and bleated and giggled.

He hovered over me. "Elderly, huh?"

Ten seconds later, he didn't have to hold me, and I wasn't squirming or bleating or giggling.

I was savoring every second.

At the end—after the end—we lay in each other's arms.

I couldn't speak.

I couldn't speak because I was totally stunned.

Stunned by his tender lovemaking.

And . . . stunned at my own desperate passion for him.

After long minutes, Marc stirred. He stroked my face and whispered, "I knew this."

I felt my brow knit as I looked into his eyes. "Knew what?"

"That we would be here." He spoke so quietly, I almost missed the words. "And I still find it impossible to believe."

I kissed his hand and asked lightly, "And how long have you known this, my oh-so-very-handsome older man?"

He tried to smile, but I saw haunted eyes. In place of a reply, gentle lips touched mine. His kiss was long and filled with emotion.

He broke away and rose from the bed. Pulling on his shorts, he said, "I'll fix us some breakfast." He lifted my arm, kissed the inside of my wrist, and left the room.

I decided right then that I would get to the bottom of the mystery that Marc sometimes seemed to flaunt but more often seemed to wear like a mortifying hair shirt.

30

I didn't start out with the idea that my affair with a man who was twice my age couldn't last. All rational thinking, all critical awareness—and all my inbred wariness—were swept away by a torrent of emotion. I just drank in the passion, and lived minute to minute.

It was late on the fourth day before we left the apartment, and even that was just a quick trip to pick up some groceries. We cooked, we drank, we embarked on dozens of unfinished conversations, snuggled in front of the television, and made love in every room.

Eventually, we ventured out. We took my car, and after running through a few countersurveillance moves, went out for romantic dinners. On one of those evenings, Marc directed me to Laredo, a little Mexican restaurant in Starke, a town about twenty-five miles from Gainesville that I had seldom visited. After an unbelievably delicious meal, Marc suggested we stay the night.

I glanced around the almost empty restaurant. "Here?"

"I'll show you."

He paid for the meal. We left the restaurant and got into my car. He pointed north. "It's that way."

He directed me through a few turns into a residential cul-de-sac. The end of the street was dominated by a magnificent Craftsman house nestled among mature holly and magnolia trees. It looked at least a century old, but it had been meticulously maintained. A discreet sign at the end of the driveway read: ABERDEEN HOUSE B & B.

"How did you know this was here?" I asked suspiciously.

"I didn't. But there's this amazing thing . . ."

"What amazing thing?"

"It's called the Internet."

Marc had already reserved a room on the top floor. It had a huge bed and an en suite with a Jacuzzi. We soaked together in the tub, drank wine, and made love all night.

The next morning, we went out and bought a change of clothes and some bathroom stuff and stayed for two more days.

A week later, we ventured farther afield. We drove west, joined Route 98, and turned north. Five hours on the road put us in Mexico Beach, a community on the Panhandle coast that I had to admit I'd never heard of.

"What's here?" I asked. I eyed the long stretch of sugar-white sand beside the road and added, "I mean, apart from the long empty beach with no cover to hide our usual activities from a shocked public?"

"The Driftwood Motel."

"We drove five hours to stay in a motel?"

"Not just any motel."

We parked in front of a two-story white beachfront building with red doors, quirky gingerbread accents, and crossed palm trees above the main entrance. The sign said DRIFTWOOD INN—VACANCY.

We got out of the car. Marc stood back, taking in the building. "Well, this used to be a motel. Looks a lot different now."

"Marc?"

"Hmm?"

"Is this, by any chance, some kind of sentimental journey?"

"It is."

"Should I be feeling awkward?"

He kissed me. "Not at all. Just savor the moment. You won't be disappointed."

I accepted his advice, and I wasn't disappointed. We took a suite on the upper floor that came equipped with a full kitchen. We spent three idyllic days reading, walking the beach, whipping up improvised meals . . . and making love in a magnificent four-poster bed.

Only once during our stay did I feel particularly uneasy. We'd been lounging on a patio on the upper beach, surrounded by flowering plant boxes, *Alice in Wonderland* weathervanes, and a serpentine network of sand fences. I awoke from a doze, still holding the Agatha Christie paperback I'd picked up in the lobby, to discover that Marc was gone. I found him examining a collection of framed photographs hanging on the wall in one corner of the inn's breakfast room.

The photos showed the inn at various stages of its development, dating back to the 1950s. When I appeared at his side, Marc tapped an aerial photo showing a much-reduced version of the main building, surrounded by an undeveloped sea of white sand. There were a few 1970s-era cars parked in front. He slipped his arm around me and said, "That's the Driftwood I remember."

"She was very special, wasn't she?" I asked carefully.

"Yes, she was. There has never been anyone like her."

"I remind you of her, don't I?"

"Yes, you do."

"I understand."

He bent to kiss my forehead. "I don't think you do, but thank you."

At the time, I was blinded by love, but as I replay those days in my mind, as I have so many times, two things stand out:

First, this man who had spent twice as long on the planet as me had still revealed very little about his past life. Several stories from his childhood, a few anecdotes from his early years in the police, and occasional comments about his daughter, Rebecca, who had moved to Canada and seldom visited. That was all.

Apart from that one reference to lost love, not once did Marc speak about Rebecca's mother.

The second thing was that, with each passing day, Marc Hastings became quieter.

Quieter . . . and more distracted.

Distracted . . . but not distant. From time to time, I would catch him looking at me, and his eyes seemed to blaze into my soul. As the days passed, whenever we embraced, he seemed to press closer, to hold tighter. It was as if he was savoring every kiss, every touch, and every moment because they might be our last.

The end came on the day Harlan Tribe was released on bail. It was all over the news. We sat in Marc's living room, watching the coverage. I didn't need a goggle-eyed reporter to tell me the case would probably never go to trial. I could see it in Sam's expression when he left the court-house, brushing microphones aside, as he and Eddie Carlyle made their way to a waiting car.

Marc and I decided to leave town for a few days. But then my car refused to start. I thought it just needed a new battery until Marc pointed out that it was less than halfway through its warranty period. "It might be the alternator," he suggested. "If I can get it going, I'll take it to a shop and get it checked." He called a taxi to give it a jump start and then drove off to find a mechanic. I figured we weren't going anywhere until at least the next morning, so I got to work in the kitchen, hoping to impress Marc with my mother's recipe for shrimp creole. I was working pretty much from memory, but from the tastes and smells, I figured I'd nailed it.

I left the sauce to simmer and wandered into the living room, looking for something to read. There was a stack of old newspapers lying on the lower shelf of a side table. I'd noticed them before, and recalled vaguely wondering why Marc was keeping them. I pulled them out, sat on the sofa, and spread them across the coffee table.

It didn't take long to solve that little mystery. The papers were actually a collection of pages from several editions of *The Gainesville Sun*, with dates ranging back several months. Every one contained a story about one of my prosecutions or, in one case, about me personally. The paper had run a profile piece a few months before I was appointed to replace Roy Wells. The individual stories weren't marked or circled or otherwise highlighted on the page, but I was the only subject that each of the disparate sections had in common.

Finding them was not exactly a shock. Marc had made no secret of the fact that he had singled me out some time ago to work with him on the "Gainesville's Disappeared" file.

No, not a shock.

Flattering, actually.

I replaced the papers and got up to browse Marc's bookshelves. There were, I would guess, a few hundred books—novels, travel guides, biographies, a matched set of regional cookbooks—but to my eye, something didn't look right. They were arranged too perfectly on the shelves, with each spine exactly aligned with its neighbors and each shelf arranged so that all the spines of all the books on that shelf were the same height. I was reminded of the false-front Western towns people sometimes see on

Hollywood studio tours. I had a crazy, fleeting suspicion that they weren't books at all.

On an impulse, I pulled one out at random—I remember it was a biography of Alice Roosevelt, Theodore's famously outspoken daughter—opened the cover, and flipped through some pages.

Of course it was a real book. I snapped it shut and replaced it on the shelf, sighing at my own silliness. I browsed on and selected another book from the same shelf—this time one about Princess Diana, one of the dozens that were released after her death. When I opened the cover, I noticed a stamped inscription:

Clapton's Used Books
682B Rackham Avenue NE
Atlanta, GA

Something bothered me. I went back to the Roosevelt biography I'd just replaced.

The inside cover bore the same stamp.

I checked the book next to it . . . and the one next to it . . . and the next one.

I checked every book on that shelf.

They all bore the same stamp.

I checked half a dozen books on the next shelf down.

Same result.

I'd heard that some people—maybe to impress visitors, or maybe in a blitz of low-cost decorating—will find a used bookstore and buy up a few shelves of books. "Books by the yard," it's been called. It seemed Marc had acquired his library that way.

But why?

I felt a knot growing in the pit of my stomach.

Why?

Was this collection of books designed to impress someone? Certainly, the titles weren't likely to. Or was it just instant decorating—an attempt to make the place appear lived in?

Why do instant decorating?

I stepped back so my gaze could sweep in the entire wall. Directly in front of me were the bookshelves I'd just been examining. To my left was a flat-screen TV with remote speakers, each piece set into customized spaces provided in the wall unit entertainment center. Above the TV was another short row of books. I'd noticed them before—a row of five identical leather-bound volumes.

I moved closer and craned to read random titles.

Plutarch's Lives
Orations of Cicero
The Essays of Montaigne
The Decameron
Paradise Lost

I reached up and extracted the Plutarch volume. I opened the cover. The inside cover and its facing page were blank. I flipped pages.

They were all blank.

Puzzled, I pulled down *Orations of Cicero*.

Again, all the pages were blank.

I pulled down next two books. All blank pages.

Faux books.

Why?

Distracted and confused, I pulled down *Paradise Lost*.

I opened the cover.

The inside cover was blank, as was its facing page.

But behind the facing page, I found a photograph.

For a few seconds, I didn't recognize the girl.

Then I did.

It was the coat that did it. I'd worn a coat just like it my final year at law school.

The girl in the coat was me.

Someone had photographed me as I was crossing Harvard Yard, carrying an armload of books. I felt my jaw tighten. Experimentally, I flipped pages.

Paradise Lost was a photo album.

I went back to the beginning, and turned to the second page. Another picture of me . . . this time, alone at my favorite table in Café Pamplona on Bow Street, one hand wrapped around a cup of coffee, my eyes glued to an open textbook.

I flipped through the following pages. Each sheet bore a single photograph. They were all taken in and around Boston, and were apparently spread across all three years of my JD program. Two shots showed me in the arms of Robert Vance.

They were taken outdoors, and we were fully clothed, but still . . .

My face burned with anger. I turned the page . . . and suddenly I was younger.

I immediately recognized myself in the first photograph. I was standing in a row of girls. Each of us was wearing shorts and white T-shirts with a number pinned to the front. The photo was taken on the day of my one and only attempt to gain entry into my high school's in-crowd. I had tried out for the cheerleader squad. Judging from the angle of the shot, the photo must have been taken from high up in the bleachers.

My tryout had been an utter failure. "Come back when you're better coordinated," the cheerleader trainer had told me. She looked pointedly at my chest and added, "And better developed." Before I could think of a comeback, the bitch had walked away.

As quickly as that humiliating memory coursed through my mind it was forgotten, because now I was turning pages quickly, finding photo after photo as, younger and younger, the album pulled me deeper and deeper into my past. Here I was, walking to middle school . . . here, leaving elementary school . . . here, riding my bike, chasing my pet rabbit across our yard, cavorting in the surf at Melbourne Beach the summer after my eighth birthday . . . here . . . and here . . . and here!

Every photo had been taken from a distance with a long lens. And, although many pictures included other people, it was obvious that I was the primary subject.

In the last photos—on the back pages of the album—I was in the playground across the street from the house in Archer where I grew up.

I was no more than four or five years old.

My endlessly recurring dream about the watching man slashed across my consciousness.

A low moan started in my throat.

I dropped the book and staggered to the couch.

I was grabbing a few things from Marc's bathroom when he returned. I heard the door open and the jingling of keys.

"I was right, it was the alternator!" his voice called. "I picked up a rebuilt and had them install—"

I assumed he'd stopped in midsentence because he'd just spotted my suitcase sitting by the door. I left the bathroom and crossed his bedroom. I scooped the photo album off the bed, where I'd left it after painfully leafing through it a second time. My heels clicked on the hardwood floor as I emerged from the bedroom and marched toward him. His eyes flicked from my face to the book in my hand and back to my face. He stood stiffly, watching me approach.

"You're leaving," he said when I stopped in front of him. It was a statement, not a question.

"Yes, I am!" I didn't try to hide the raging hurt in my eyes. "I called my mother. I'm going to stay with her."

"Why?" He asked the question, but his tone told me he already knew the answer.

"You stalked me!" I slammed the photo album against his chest. A few loose photos fell out and fluttered to the floor. "What do they mean, Marc?"

"Claire, I—"

"Did you take these pictures?"

After a beat, he replied, "Yes."

"Explain them to me!"

A second passed, then another.

"I . . . I can't."

"You can't? You can't explain why you've been following me for my entire life?" I was shouting. "Why, Marc? *Why?*"

He didn't reply. He just looked forlorn.

"Give me my keys!"

He handed them over.

I pushed past him. He reached out.

"Don't touch me!"

I grabbed my suitcase and threw the door open so violently that it slammed into the baseboard stop and shuddered on its hinges.

As I stormed out of the apartment, Marc's sorrowful voice followed me. "Claire, I'm sorry! Soon you'll understand."

I wasn't listening.

I took the stairs in case he'd sabotaged the elevator.

31

Seconds after I claimed a pair of reclining seats against the bulkhead at the rear of the near-empty passenger car, the train gave a lurch. I shoved my bag onto the overhead rack, kicked off my heels, and collapsed.

Moving imperceptibly at first, and then with slowly gathering speed, the Silver Meteor pulled away from the DeLand station and started rolling north.

I had decided against boarding at Palatka. If Marc had taken it into his head to follow me—and for all I knew, he had—that's where he would have gone. Instead, I'd driven to DeLand, the nearest station to the south. I suppose it would have been smarter to drive north, to Jacksonville, but I was in no mood for freeways and city traffic.

I reclined my seat, and for several miles I lay completely still, watching the passing landscape but seeing nothing.

On the drive down from Gainesville, I had deliberately suppressed all thought and emotion for fear of causing a traffic accident. Now that I was on the train, the compulsion to turn over in my mind, again and again, the events of the last few months was overwhelming. I reexamined every step in my relationship with Marc, every remembered nuance of conduct and conversation, searching for something—anything—to reproach myself with. I set about this task with all the masochism that accompanies the 20/20 hindsight of the betrayed; and with all the despair that came with my struggle to deny that I had just lost the only man that, against all odds, I had truly loved.

My expedition into this slough of despond kept circling back to the bottle of '83 Margaux.

That was the moment, I decided.

The moment when Marc Hastings revealed he had researched my affair with my law school instructor . . . an affair that had ended nearly a decade before.

That was the moment, I decided, when I should have walked away.

But I still could not penetrate the reason, the motive—the sickness!—that had driven this man to single me out as a child and stalk me for half a lifetime.

Why?

It had to be connected somehow to the missing girls, but I couldn't fathom how. A horrifying question niggled on the margins of my consciousness.

What if Marc was the killer?

The thought made me feel physically ill. But it couldn't be right. The police files I'd studied clearly showed he was working and on shift when some of the abductions had taken place. I forced the suspicion from my mind.

While I was wrestling with all this, something registered in my peripheral vision.

It was just a slight movement, but for some reason it triggered that old situational awareness ganglion in my brain. It brought me back to the here and now and made me aware of a woman who was seated a few rows in front of me.

She had twisted in her seat, and she was staring directly at me.

She appeared to be in her fifties, maybe early sixties, a bit heavy in the face but still quite attractive. My first thought was—as Geiger had put it—"another dissatisfied customer." But I had no recollection of ever seeing her face at a courtroom defense table.

When my eyes locked on hers, the woman paled and turned away. I noticed her shoulders hunch together, as if she had felt a cold draft. I puzzled over her behavior for a few seconds, and then closed my eyes and went back to my ruminations about Marc.

A few minutes later I sensed someone in the aisle next to me. I opened my eyes. The woman was standing there. She looked frightened.

"Can I help you?"

"Is your name Claire?"

I stiffened. "Why?"

"Is it? Is it Claire?"

"How do you know that?"

"God! You don't look a day . . . !" She stared at me in wonder. "It's happening!"

"What?"

"I don't understand!"

"Neither do I." I kept my tone even. The woman was obviously a mental case. "What's the problem?"

"We've got to get off this train!"

"I don't."

"Okay, *I've* got to get off this train!"

"Okay." I suppressed the urge to roll my eyes. "I think there's a stop coming up."

The woman wheeled around and hustled back up the aisle. She tugged a bag out of the overhead rack and then called back at me. "Claire!"

"Yes?"

"Thank you!"

"You're welcome."

I didn't know what else to say.

The woman gave me a long look and then hurried up the aisle past the few other passengers, some of who had been watching her antics bemusedly. She got off the train at Palatka. A few seconds later, I spotted her on the small ground-level platform, staring at the railcar we had shared.

Then another person caught my attention. A dark-haired young woman crossed my field of view and grabbed the older woman by the arm. She appeared to speak to her in a hurried fashion. The older woman recoiled, but she didn't pull away; she just stood there, staring at the young woman's face. At first she appeared surprised, then shocked. After a brief exchange, she raised an arm and pointed at the window where I sat watching.

The train started to move. The young woman released her grip and started jogging along the platform, trying to keep pace with my window. Her eyes were big with emotion. She called out to me, but I couldn't hear what she said.

The train picked up speed and she fell behind.

Just before I lost sight of her, she dropped to her knees.

Her face had looked familiar.

Then I remembered: She was the woman who had stopped me outside the courthouse to ask directions to Starbucks.

The episode spooked me.

I got up from my seat and went searching for the lounge car. What I wanted more than anything was a drink. But as I made my way forward through the train, I felt unsettled.

Something wasn't right.

That damned sensation was back.

Something's going to happen.

I stamped down on the feeling.

You're too late! It's already happened!

Engineers and other science-minded people who study what some of them refer to as "the normal accident environment" often deploy technospeak phrases such as "congested complex networks," "subsystem linkages," and "cascading failures." I know that because I studied some of their reports and academic papers during our office's investigation of a bleacher collapse at a college game that killed three people. But what actually happened on that evening of March 1, 2011, on that Amtrak train, on that north–south route, I will never know.

I know only what happened to me.

I reached the train's lounge car, felt for the money in my jacket pocket and found a photograph.

Correction: It was only one side of a photograph, because it had been cut in half.

It was one of those photos from an old Polaroid Land Camera . . . the ones that used pack film. The picture was in color, but it was badly faded. The subject was a young woman sitting at bar with a drink in front of her. She was gazing with studied intensity at someone to her right. There must have been another person in the original photograph because, close to the picture's sliced right edge, there was another drink on the bar.

I turned the photo over. There was writing on the back, done in ball-point pen. I had seen enough of Marc's handwriting to recognize it instantly.

He had written: *Remember to tell me the truth.*

I puzzled over the words.

I flipped back to the picture and studied it closely.

The woman looked like me.

The woman *was me*.

But I didn't recognize the setting . . . or my hairstyle . . . or my clothes.

That's when I felt the first jolt.

The railcar began to shudder, and the cans and bottles in the tall cooler behind the bar started rattling and smashing. There was a horrendous sound. At first it groaned, and then rumbled, and finally ramped up to an earsplitting roar, followed immediately by the shriek of tearing, twisting metal. In uncanny slow motion, the floor of the car buckled upward, tilting and twisting. The windows crazed and bulged. I threw myself to the floor just as, one by one, they exploded in a shower of glass. The car began to roll on its axis. I struggled to a kneeling position in time to see the drink cooler topple to the floor, pinning the bar attendant. The car kept rolling and I watched in horror as the giant appliance ground the screaming man's legs to boneless mush. Now desperate to counter the car's deadly roll, I tried to crawl up the opposite wall. Pain ripped through me as I smashed a shin on a heating unit. I lunged for a handhold, felt my fingers grip . . . slip . . . grip again, and then, sickeningly, claw at empty space.

I fell straight through a window and into the night.

I plunged earthward.

I had a fleeting glimpse of black water below.

I fell . . .

I was weirdly aware that I wasn't screaming, that I was . . . calm.

I fell . . .

Time slowed.

I fell . . . into silence.

And all consciousness ended.

LIPINSKI

32

When Jeff Geiger burst into Lipinski's office, his boss was hunkered over a pile of paperwork. The lieutenant looked up in annoyance at Geiger's unannounced entry.

"Got something, boss!"

Lipinski's morose expression was not exactly calculated to encourage conversation. "Better be good."

"I think you'll like it. You know that .38 we found in Tribe's cabin?"

"Yeah."

"The lab freed up the cylinder so they could fire it. The bullet we dug out of the floor by the trapdoor definitely came from that gun."

"I saw that report. Old news."

"Maybe, but this isn't. The feds traced the serial number."

"I thought there was no record of it!"

"It was never added to their database, but one of their agents went back to basics and tracked down an old paper trail. Turns out the gun was stolen back in the '70s." Geiger dropped a thin, dog-eared file folder on the desk in front of Lipinski. "That's the original theft report."

Lipinski picked up the folder. "They sent us an original?"

"No. I got it from archives."

Lipinski stared at him. "You mean *our* archives?"

Geiger smirked. "Yeah. That gun was stolen from one of our detectives. Take a look."

Lipinski opened the file. He scanned the top page, quickly flipped through the two pages of typed and handwritten text behind it, and studied the signature on the final page. He lurched to his feet.

"We go . . . now!"

Geiger grinned. "Thought you'd like it."

Lipinski had insisted on taking the wheel. He wove through traffic, wigwags flashing, while Geiger used the yelper to clear the heavier knots of congestion. Lipinski slid the squad car to a halt in front of the building's main entrance, and then drove it up over the curb and onto the sidewalk. The maneuver placed the front end of the car within a few feet of the front door, scaring the daylights out of an older woman who was just in the act of exiting.

Lipinski jumped out, waving his badge. "Hold that door!"

The woman stared at him as if he were a madman and stumbled backwards into the foyer. Geiger sprinted for the door in time to catch it before it clicked shut. He held it open for Lipinski and then followed him in.

"What's the matter with you?" Lipinski barked at the woman. "Didn't you hear me?"

The woman's initial expression of shock hardened into anger. "What's the matter with *me*? What about you? You could have killed me! Do you think that badge gives you the right to drive like a lunatic?" Her voice was quivering with rage. "And why do you think you can just storm into a private building? Do you have a warrant?"

"We're on police business! And, anyway, this is a public area!"

"Really? I don't recall anyone buzzing you in."

Geiger intervened, trying to soothe. "Ma'am . . . we just need to find a person who lives in this building."

"C'mon, Jeff!" Lipinski said. "We've wasted enough time here!" He strode over to the stairs and started up.

Geiger was about to follow when the woman caught his sleeve.

"What is that man's name?"

"Lieutenant Lipinski, ma'am. Gainesville PD. And I'm sorry if we frightened you."

"You didn't frighten me, young man. He did. And you weren't rude to me. He was."

"Geiger!" Lipinski's voice echoed down the stairwell.

"I have to go. This really is police business."

"I'm sure it is. And I'm sure my brother will want to hear all about it."

"Your brother?"

"Yes, Mr. Geiger. My brother is the mayor."

Geiger sighed and headed up the stairs. After taking them two at a time, he caught up to Lipinski on the final landing. "I think you stepped in it, boss. That woman—"

"Tell me later." Lipinski exited the stairwell into the corridor, drew his weapon, and strode to the door of Marc's apartment. He pounded on the door. "Open up, Hastings! Police!"

Silence.

"This is Ted Lipinski, Hastings! Open this door now, or I'm coming in to get you!"

Dead air.

Lipinski stood back, ready to kick in the door.

Geiger stepped in front of him. "Boss! We need a warrant!"

"Out of my way, Jeff!"

"Boss!"

Lipinski stared at him. Geiger stood aside.

Lipinski kicked the door. The sound boomed through the narrow corridor. He kicked again . . . once . . . twice. It exploded inward.

Lipinski surged through the doorway. Geiger followed cautiously.

Lipinski yelled, "Hastings!"

His voice echoed through the empty living room and kitchen.

The cops pivoted, guns up.

"It's the wrong apartment!" Geiger blurted.

Lipinski rechecked the number on the door. "No, it isn't!" He pointed at the curving staircase. "Check up there!"

Geiger raced up the stairs.

Lipinski ducked into the kitchen. The double doors of the large stainless steel fridge stood half-ajar. Its interior was dark, and its shelves were empty. He checked a few cupboards. They were bare.

Doors banged upstairs. Lipinski stepped from the kitchen just as Geiger appeared at the top of the stairs. "Nothing up here, Lieutenant!"

"Furniture?"

"Not a stick." He started down the stairs.

"Knock on a few doors," Lipinski said. "See if anyone in the building knows—" His cell phone rang. He checked the display and answered. He listened for a second and then said, "Tell them we're coming." He disconnected and headed for the door. "Let's go!"

"Where?" Geiger hustled after him.

"We've got a homicide."

CLAIRE

33

I awakened to silence.

Not the silence of 3 A.M. in a quiet house on a quiet street. Not that silence, which really isn't silence at all.

This was a dense, moonless, impenetrable silence that deadened my senses.

More accurately, this silence hadn't simply deadened my senses—it had deleted them. I had no sense of physical existence. No sense of having a body.

No sense, in fact, that I'd ever had a body.

My first conscious thought was that I was dead. My second thought was that my first one was idiotic, because if I were dead, why was I thinking?

As I write this, I realize that I am not absolutely certain that those were my first two thoughts. I only know that they are the first ones I remember.

Then, after what seemed like an interminable time, I felt it.

Numbness.

Numbness was encouraging, because it signaled to my floating consciousness that something was attached to it that could feel numb.

My mind sighed, and I slept.

When I awoke, I had a body.

This welcome development was somewhat sullied by the fact that my body was lying facedown. The surface under the upper half of my body felt rough and uneven. In the same instant, I realized that the lower half of my body was wet.

I was partly immersed in water.

Then the silence was broken.

First I heard buzzing insects.

Then I heard a splash.

Much later, I learned that the splash was caused by the dip of an oar.

I tried to move, but my body refused to respond. Although it had dutifully telegraphed that it was attached to my consciousness, it was as yet unready to acknowledge that higher authority. I lay inert while my mind shouted orders and my body ignored them.

But my ears worked. I could hear more splashes, one upon the other, louder and louder, closer and closer. Belatedly, I remembered I had eyes. The uncomfortable pressure on my left cheek told me that my head was turned to one side. I tried to open my eyes. The lower eyelid seemed to be sealed shut, but the other one responded.

I saw mud. And sedge weed.

Then I saw a man's boot.

I felt strong hands lift me, and once again, the world went black.

When I woke up, I was in a hospital bed. I lay there for long minutes, willing myself back to life. Perhaps it was hours; I'm not sure. It felt as if every joule of energy had been methodically drained from me while I slept.

At least I was alert enough to be thankful I was still alive. I took inventory. One by one, I checked my limbs. I could move them, and when the effort didn't generate assaults of leaping pain, I concluded that they were intact. As for the rest of my body, there was no acute pain: just pervasive, debilitating exhaustion.

I tried to take in my surroundings. The window blinds next to my bed were pulled all the way down. From the absence of any light leaking in around the edges, I deduced it was nighttime. The room itself was dimly lit from a small light above the door, and I could see that the single bed opposite mine was unoccupied.

My left arm was hooked to an intravenous feed. I tracked the line upward. It was connected to an inverted glass bottle. I strained to read the label on the bottle, but the angle defeated me. I tried to sit up. Instantly, my head swam, and I felt nauseated. I dropped back on the pillow and waited for the sensation to pass.

There was an old visitor's chair next to my bed, its wheat-colored arms discolored by a thousand sweaty palms, the beading of its vinyl cushions ragged and cracked. Behind it, running under the window, a cast iron radiator ticked quietly, proving that my ears were still working.

I need a phone. . . .

I rolled my head. The top of the bedside table was bare.

Looking around again, I realized the room had an old-fashioned feel about it. I decided I must be in one of those old Catholic hospitals.

Meaning: no in-room telephones.

I felt about with my hands, hunting for a call button to summon a nurse. Finding nothing, I craned to check the wall above my bed, hoping to spot a lanyard to pull. No luck. The only thing mounted above me was a mercury manometer with a dangling blood pressure cuff.

I considered shouting, but I was so desperately tired, I couldn't find the breath to do it.

I fell asleep.

34

The deputy was sitting on the vinyl chair. He had pulled it closer so he could hear me. At that moment, he was chewing on the end of a pencil and looking confused.

I was eyeing him and thinking: *You're confused?*

Yes, I was groggy, and my speech was slurred—making me suspicious about what the medical staff might have been adding in my IV—but by now I was pretty confused myself.

The cop's name tag read TATTERSALL, and his shoulder patch told me he was from the Putnam County Sheriff's Office. When I woke up and found him sitting there, the first words out of my mouth were "Where am I?"

"Putnam Community Hospital, ma'am." He told me how two fishermen had found me half-drowned on the western shore of the St. Johns River, twelve miles north of Palatka.

"That would make sense," I slurred. "I was on that—" I coughed weakly. "I was in that train wreck on Tuesday. What day is it?"

His gun belt creaked as he leaned forward, craning to hear me. "What day is it?"

I nodded.

"Today's Saturday, ma'am." He scratched his ear. "What train wreck?"

"The Amtrak wreck! That train that fell in the river!"

"Ain't heard of a train wreck."

I stared at him.

His brow knitted.

Silently cursing, I sank back into my pillow. Just my luck to get saddled with the dumbest cop in Florida.

He took out a notebook. "Could you please tell me your full name, ma'am?"

"It's Claire Talbot. . . . Claire spelled C-l-a-i-r-e; Talbot, T-a-l-b-o-t."

"Miss or Mrs.?"

"Ms."

He looked up. "Like that magazine?"

I suppressed a sigh. "Yeah. Capital *m*, small *s*. Like the magazine."

"Any middle name?"

"Alexandra." I had to spell it for him.

"Address?"

I gave it.

"That's in Gainesville?"

"That's what I said!" I was getting impatient.

"Phone number?"

I gave it to him. He scratched his head for a second, asked me to repeat it, and wrote it down.

At that moment, the door hissed open and a pretty redheaded nurse appeared. She was wearing a starched white uniform, complete with cap.

Okay, I thought, maybe not a Catholic hospital, but definitely a traditional one.

"Time's up, Norm! The lady needs her rest."

The deputy rose slowly to his feet. His eyes lingered appreciatively on the nurse's tidy form for a second and then swung back to me. "I'll come back when you're feeling better, ma'am."

My irritable attempt at a contemptuous reply morphed into a coughing fit. The cop left hurriedly while the nurse busied herself settling me down and pouring a glass of water.

"You've given us quite a scare," the nurse said. Her name tag read: G. HOPKINS, R.N.

"Scared myself," I croaked.

She smiled gently. "I'm Gertie. What's your name, hon?"

"You don't know?"

"There was no identification . . . I mean, on your person."

"Oh . . . right. It's Claire. Claire Talbot. I really need to make a phone call."

"You'll have to wait until the doctor says you can get up. Is there somebody I can call for you?"

"Can't you just bring me a phone?"

She looked at me strangely.

"Okay, could you please call someone for me? Sam Grayson. He's the State Attorney in Gainesville."

"Sure." She felt in the pocket of her uniform. "I left my pen. I guess the number's in the book?"

"Yes. Just tell him where I am, and he'll come for me."

"Okay."

"Thanks. And now—" I made a face. "—I really have to pee."

She opened a drawer in the bedside table and pulled out a bedpan.

"I'd rather use the bathroom."

"I'm sorry, but the doctor was firm about you being confined to bed."

"Well, maybe you should call him."

She assessed me, weighing her response. "Okay. I'll do that. Then I'll phone your friend. Meanwhile . . ." She held up the bedpan.

I sighed and capitulated. She got me organized and stepped away. When I finished, she removed the bedpan and carried it to the bathroom. I heard the toilet flush, and she returned to my bedside.

"So, it's Mr. Grayson, right?"

"Yeah," I replied. "Sam Grayson." I examined her face. Something about it seemed familiar. "Gertie, can I ask a question?"

"Sure."

"Does your mother live in Florida?"

The question seemed to startle her. "My mom passed away three years ago."

"Oh, I'm sorry! I didn't mean . . . It's just . . ."

"What?"

"I met someone who looked a bit like you, but older."

"Where was that?"

"On the train."

"You talked about a train. In your sleep."

"Oh?"

"Actually, you were yelling," she said with a little half smile.

"Sorry."

She shrugged and started straightening my blankets. I moved my hand and caught one of hers. "Gertie, did anyone else survive?"

She looked at me warily. "Survive?"

"Survive the wreck."

"Nobody else was brought here," she said carefully. "To our hospital."

I could see she was trying to protect me from a shock, so I let it go. She checked my IV and then asked, "Are you hungry?"

"Starving!"

"That's a good sign. Okay, officially it's not mealtime, but I'll see what I can scare up."

"Thanks."

She turned to leave, but then stopped. "Miss Talbot . . ."

" 'Claire' is fine."

"Claire. Do you mind if I ask what kind of work you do?"

"I'm a lawyer. Why?"

"A lawyer? No kidding! Okay, well . . ." She hesitated, shook her head, and said, "Forget it."

Now I was curious. "Tell me."

"Um, okay. Did you ever . . ." Now she seemed thoroughly embarrassed. "Did you ever, uh . . . you know, work as one of those exotic dancers?"

"No." I suppressed a smile. "Why?"

"Oh. It's just . . . that tattoo on your back. I've never seen that before."

"Really?"

"Yeah. But, you know, I'd kinda like one myself."

She left me thinking about what a strange pair she and Deputy Tattersall were.

I didn't see the deputy again.

Instead, shortly after I downed a bowl of surprisingly tasty buttermilk soup, half a tuna sandwich (white bread; crusts removed), and a tumbler of pale apple juice, I received a new visitor.

Dr. Arthur Bland was just what his name implied—five foot nothing, with a flavorless personality, a colorless face, and eyes as pale as a mackerel. Moving at a snail-like pace, he checked my pulse and blood pressure, reviewed what I assumed was my chart—he had carried it in with him in a buff folder—and then stood perfectly still next to my bed, just looking at me.

I said, "I need to get out of this bed!"

"I'm sorry. I'm not your GP."

"Well, who is?"

"Dr. Weaver. He'll see you on rounds tomorrow morning."

"Then who are you?"

"A consultant. Dr. Weaver asked me to see you."

"What kind of a consultant?"

After a beat, he replied, "Psychiatric."

Warily, I asked the obvious question. "Because?"

"Dr. Weaver has expressed some concerns."

"Concerns? He's never bothered to speak to me about them! I've never met the man!"

"He's been speaking with Nurse Barnes."

"Gertie?"

"Yes. And with the police officer who visited you."

"That idiot!"

Dr. Bland cocked his head. "Idiot?"

"He didn't even know about the wreck!"

"Do you mean . . . the train wreck?"

"Yes! The Amtrak wreck! On Tuesday!"

"Miss Talbot . . ."

"What?"

"There hasn't been a train wreck."

"Are you crazy? I should know! I was in the lounge car when it happened! I was ejected out a window, which is probably what saved my life!"

Bland continued as if he hadn't heard me. "I've also been told that no one in the State Attorney's Office has heard of this Sam Grayson person."

I lay there, staring at the man's expressionless face. "Tell me please . . . where, *exactly*, am I?"

"You are in room number 202 in the Putnam Community Medical Center, in Palatka, Florida."

I let out an exasperated breath. "Let's start again. Forty miles west of here is the city of Gainesville." I looked at him sharply. "Are you with me so far?"

"Yes, Miss Talbot. I am aware of the city of Gainesville."

I spoke slowly, as if to a child. "In that city, at 120 West University Avenue, is the Office of the State Attorney. There, a truly resourceful investigator will have no trouble finding Mr. Sam—not Samuel, his birth certificate says 'Sam'—Grayson, State Attorney for the Eighth Judicial Circuit." I rattled off the telephone number. "Alternatively, if that task is too challenging, someone could easily contact the Gainesville Police Department and ask to speak with Detective Sergeant Jeff Geiger. That's spelled G-e-i-g-e-r. Sergeant Geiger and I did not part on the best of terms, but since I *was* one of Gainesville's leading prosecutors until about one month ago, he might be persuaded to admit that he knows me!"

Dr. Bland said, "I see." He lowered himself onto the vinyl chair, took out a pen, and began writing in my chart. Finally, he raised his eyes from the page. With a level gaze, he said, "Tell me about this train wreck."

When I was a teenager, I became addicted to a British television series called *The Prisoner.* The series had actually been produced in the late '60s, but it was shown on our local PBS affiliate during the '90s. After devotedly watching a dozen or so episodes, I discovered that only seventeen episodes had been filmed. I remember being infuriated because by then I was hooked. The main character in the series was a former British secret agent. When he resigned from his job, his employers arranged for him to be knocked out with some kind of drug and abducted to a mysterious, isolated village. Although he was given free run of the community, in fact he was a prisoner. Every time he tried to escape the village, the attempt was foiled.

The thing that had really stuck with me was that the village was populated with dozens—or maybe it was hundreds—of seemingly ordinary people whose primary aim was to fuck with his head.

My first thought, as I stared into the piscine eyes of the creepily bland Dr. Bland, was of that television show.

My second thought was less fanciful.

"What time is it?" I demanded.

Bland moved his arm. His unblinking gaze flicked away and returned. "Five forty-two P.M."

"Thank you. This discussion is over. Tell your invisible friend, Dr. Weaver, that I will be discharging myself at eight o'clock tomorrow morning. And please tell Gertie I'd like to see her."

"Anything else?"

The little bastard's condescending smirk set me off.

"Yes! Whether you believe it or not, I am an attorney! And a damned good one! If you try to put some bogus Baker Act hold on me—you're familiar with the Florida Mental Health Act of 1971, I trust?—I will sue your ass from here to the next century! Now, get out of this room!"

The smirk vanished. He closed the chart folder and stood up. "As you wish." He left without another word.

Gertie appeared a few minutes later. She was wide-eyed. "Dr. Bland was all red and angry when he came to my station. What on earth did you say to him?"

"I threatened to sue him."

She gawped. "Wow!"

"Gertie, did you tell him that no one's heard of Sam Grayson at the State Attorney's Office?"

"I'm sorry, Claire. I talked to two people! They said they didn't know him."

I studied her face. There was no sign of guile. She must have called the wrong office. I decided to let it go and focus on the present. I took a deep breath. "Okay, first off—" I lifted my arm and rattled the IV line. "—I want this thing out. No one's shoving any more drugs into me!"

"Oh! I'll have to call Dr. Weav—!"

"No, Gertie! As of this moment, I'm treating this intravenous line as an assault on my person. Please take it out of me now, or I'll tear it out!"

"Okay, just wait! I'll be right back." She hustled out of the room and reappeared in seconds with alcohol, a swab, and a bandage. She got to work.

"Thank you," I said when the job was complete. I sat up. "I would walk out of here right now, but I don't relish finding my way home in the dark. And, I suppose the hospital has a business office that will want my insurance details."

"Dr. Weaver asked them to leave you alone until you're better."

"Well, I'm officially better! I'll spend the night here and discharge myself first thing in the morning. I'll need my clothes."

"They're in here." She opened a small closet. I could see my jeans, top, and underwear neatly folded on a shelf. "They were all muddy. I sent them down to the laundry."

"Thank you. That's was very kind." I peered. "I had a jacket. . . ."

"Not when you were admitted."

"Damn! I must've lost it in the river." I settled back, feeling suddenly weary. "If you see the doctor—"

"You mean Dr. Weaver?"

"Yes. Tell him if he tries to put me back on an IV, or sends some nurse in here"—I looked her in the eye—"to give me a shot in the middle of the night, I'll have him charged with assault and battery." I paused. "What have you people been giving me, anyway?"

"Just a sedative. Diazepam."

It took me a second. "Wait a minute! Are you saying the doctor ordered a sedative for a drowning victim?"

"That's just the thing. . . ."

"What?"

"You were found on the riverbank, but you weren't a drowning victim. You were barely a Grade One."

"Which is . . . what?"

"The lowest classification for a near-drowning. Grade Ones almost never end up in the hospital. They usually recover at the scene. The fishermen who found you said you were breathing and there was no foam around your nose or mouth. When they brought you to the ER, your vitals were good and there was no fluid in your lungs. It's just that we couldn't wake you up! There was no sign of a head injury, but you kept thrashing and crying out like you were having a nightmare. After you pulled off your oxygen mask a few times, they intubated you. But then you pulled out the tube, so Dr. Weaver told us to just sedate you and keep you under observation."

It took me a second to absorb all this. "Okay," I replied. "It sounds like I was out of it. But as of this minute, I'm awake and alert and a bit pissed off. Please make sure Dr. Weaver gets the message: Any treatment without my written consent will result in a lawsuit."

Gertie grinned. "Got it!"

"And, Gertie, thank you for taking care of me."

"My job. Thanks for making it interesting. Want something else to eat?"

"You know what? I'd love a hamburger."

"We've got a McDonald's."

"In the hospital?"

"No. Across the street."

"One problem . . . Unless my purse is in that closet, I have no money."

"No purse. But I'll get you something."

"A Quarter Pounder?"

"Sure."

Gertie was as good as her word. I'd forgotten how terrific fast food can sometimes taste. Afterwards, I slept like a baby, undisturbed by skulking doctors and nurses, and awoke at first light.

As I washed up in the bathroom and got ready to meet the day, I was already ticking off the things I would need to do to get my life back on track: call my mother; start on the tedious process of replacing all my lost IDs; borrow a key from my landlord so I could get into my town house; find my spare car key; beg a lift back to DeLand to pick up my car . . . The list in my head kept getting longer.

35

It has been said that one of the marks of genius is the ability to explain complex ideas in simple language. Albert Einstein once summarized, in only ten words, the intersection between human perception and the true nature of matter, space, and time: "Reality is merely an illusion, albeit a very persistent one."

According to the clock on the wall in the hospital's admissions office, it was 8:46 A.M. when Gertie showed me in. Earlier, while getting dressed, I'd found my watch tucked in a pocket of my jeans. It had stopped at exactly one minute to seven—either the battery was dead or river water had gotten into it.

A woman in her forties was sitting behind a low counter. She watched us approach. Her shoulder-length bleached-blond hair, parted in the middle to frame her face, gave the immediate impression of someone desperate to forestall the aging process. But what caught my attention was her makeup. It looked like it had been applied with a palette knife. There might have been an attractive face under all the Max Factor enamel, but it was hard to tell.

"Sally, this is Claire Talbot," Gertie told her. "She's the patient I spoke to Mr. Aldridge about. The lady from 202."

"Uh-huh." The woman gave me a once-over. "Officer's on his way."

"What officer?" I asked.

"From Gainesville," she drawled. "They're sendin' a detective to pick y'all up."

"Great! Somebody must have got to Geiger."

"I guess. . . ." Gertie sounded a bit uncertain. "Well, I'd better get myself back to the ward. You take care of yourself, Claire."

"Thanks. You, too!" I gave her a hug, a move that seemed to startle both her and the enameled receptionist. Gertie squeezed my hand and left. In the corridor, she gave me a little wave before the door swung shut.

I turned my attention to Sally. "You must have some paperwork for me to fill out."

"Y'all the train-wreck lady, rahht?"

"Yes! I—"

"Officer's on his way."

"You said that. But what about my hospital charges?"

"Y'all could have a seat." She nodded to a chair sitting against the wall on my left. "Said he'd be here by nine."

Flummoxed, I sat down.

That's when I started to notice some strange things.

It began with an unfamiliar sound—a sort of muffled clacking noise. It was coming from somewhere behind Sally. I craned to look. Today was Sunday, so I wasn't surprised that most of the desks were unoccupied. But one lone secretary was working near the back wall. She was typing on one of those old electric typewriters . . . the one with the moving typeball.

I thought that was totally weird. I mean, who uses a Selectric in this day and age?

Then I noticed that all the desks had typewriters.

My mind tumbled back over the last few days. Vinyl-covered furniture, steam radiators, starched nurses' uniforms . . . now typewriters! This hospital was taking the traditional approach a bit too far. I began to wonder if it was an accredited facility. How would it ever pass muster with the state regulators?

I was about to get up and start cross-examining Sally when my eyes were drawn to a calendar on the wall above the reception counter. The picture depicted a typical Florida beach scene. The month of March was showing on the calendar page below. But the days were in the wrong place. Today was the first Sunday of the month. It should have been the sixth.

The calendar said it was the *fifth*.

Then I noticed the year.

1978.

What the—?

"Sally?"

She looked up.

"Why is that there?" I pointed.

"It's a calendar."

"I know it's a calendar! Why is it a 1978 calendar?"

"Why wouldn't it be?"

My mind flashed on *The Prisoner.* Was someone trying to screw with my mind?

If so . . . *why?*

I lurched to my feet. "Okay, what the *hell* is going on here?"

Sally and the secretary straightened in their chairs, startled by my raised voice. Behind me, the door from the corridor opened. Footsteps approached. I paid no attention. I stepped to the counter, my eyes fixed on Sally. "I asked a question!"

A male figure appeared to my right. Sally turned to him, eyes wide.

"I'm here to pick up a patient," the man said. "A Miss Talbot."

I froze at the sound of the voice.

Sally replied with a quick nod toward me.

Slowly, I turned my head.

The man was tall and fit. He was wearing a sports jacket, slacks, and an open-necked dress shirt.

I stared at him, openmouthed.

"You're Miss Talbot?" he asked.

My breathing became ragged. I felt my body sway. Obviously alarmed, the man reached out to steady me. I backed away and collapsed into the chair.

"Miss Talbot! What is it? Are you all right?"

Sally's voice drifted from the background. "Poor thing's bin like that, bless her heart. Doctor's sayin' she's confused. Laak, ya know . . . *confused?*"

I slowly raised my head. I was looking straight into the startling blue eyes of a thirty-something clone of Marc Hastings.

A voice said, "This can't happen."

I think it was my voice, but it sounded far away.

I must have blacked out, because the next thing I remember is waking up on a bed in a curtained-off cubicle. I was fully clothed. An oxygen mask covered my nose and mouth. It took me a second to deduce that I was in the ER. I yanked off the mask. I could see Gertie and the Marc Hastings clone standing just outside the partly drawn curtains. The clone noticed I was awake. He whispered to Gertie, and she came to me.

She sat on the edge of the bed. "You keep scaring us," she said gently.

"Well, now you people are scaring me," I replied. I struggled to sit up. "I want out of this place! Now!"

Gertie stood up and backed away. She looked faintly offended. "I'll check with the doctor."

"No doctors! I'm leaving now!"

Gertie stopped. She appeared uncertain.

Marc's clone intervened. "I'll take care of her." He opened a billfold, extracted a business card, and handed it to her. I caught the glint of a police badge. "Please ask your accounts department to send Miss Talbot's bill to our office."

Gertie took the card. "Okay. Good-bye again, Claire."

"Bye, Gertie. And thank you."

Gertie pulled back the curtain and left. As soon as she disappeared from view, I turned to the cop. "Tell me your name!"

"Detective Hastings, ma'am. I'm with the Gainesville police."

"First name! What's your first name?"

"Marcus."

"Sure it is! I don't know what you people are up to, but I'm not falling for it! Show me one of those cards of yours!"

He handed one to me. I studied it and felt a rising sense of panic. I shot him an accusing look. "He only mentioned a daughter!"

"What?"

"Your father! What's his name? It's Marcus, isn't it? Same as yours!"

He looked at me as if I were insane. "His name was Robert. Why?"

"'Was'?"

"He died several years ago. Did you know him?"

"What is going on here?" I was starting to lose it.

"I'm not sure how to answer that. I'm just here to take you back to Gainesville."

I slid off the bed. "Why would the Gainesville PD send an officer to pick me up?"

"I guess . . . because you were pulled out of the river with no ID. And because you claim you fell off a train and you gave a Gainesville address."

I decided not to get into the falling-off-a-train thing. Instead, I shot back with: "So, you think I'm either a victim of crime or some kind of nutcase, is that it?"

He was polite enough not to answer, but the tilt of his head told me I'd pretty well summed it up.

By now, my rational mind was shrieking: *Why are you going along with this charade? Get a grip!*

In my short life, I had found that the best way to deal with overwhelming pressure was to focus on small necessary tasks and execute them one by one. Such an approach was crucial when I was trying to get a handle on a big, legally complex prosecution file. I was definitely feeling overwhelmed, so I gave myself a hard mental slap and cast around for my shoes. I spotted them under the bedside table.

I leaned on the bed and slipped them on.

Left foot . . . good . . .

Now right foot . . .

Okay. Now check your pockets. . . .

Of course there was nothing in my pockets except my moribund watch. Everything else had been in my jacket and my purse.

I faced my cloned minder. "Okay, Junior. What now?"

He grinned, and it was the same grin I had come to love . . . back in the real world.

Not the grin of a killer.

Definitely not.

But then, I'd heard it said that Ted Bundy had a winning smile.

Stop it!

"Do you mind if I ask how old you are?" he asked.

"Thirty-one."

"In that case, I'll let you call me Junior."

"I'll bite. How old are you?"

"Thirty. But I'm working real hard on thirty-one. Shall we go?"

I was busy redoing the Marc math in my head that I had already done back . . . whenever that was. The numbers came out the same. That is, the numbers would be right if this were 1978—which it fucking well couldn't be!

"I'm sure your people have some new trick lined up," I said. "Let's see if they can pull it off."

"What trick?"

"Making me believe this is 1978! Isn't that your weird game here?"

His brow furrowed. "It is."

"Thought so!" I waved an arm at him. "The question is, *why?*"

"I meant . . . it is 1978."

I felt my jaw tighten. "Yeah? Well, here's your chance to prove it, Junior! Lead the way!"

Looking bemused, he escorted me out of the emergency ward. My eyes scanned left and right as we walked, taking in every detail: the glass IV bottles; the typewriter at the nursing station; the male orderly with the—was that a mullet haircut?; the wan faces peering at us from vinyl chairs in the ER waiting room . . .

The headline on a newspaper:

SOVIETS SET SPACE ENDURANCE RECORD

"Either you've hired a really good set designer," I told the Marc clone, "or this stupid hospital could use an upgrade! Where are you taking me, anyway? To some village where I'll never be able to escape? I mean, what's the point to all this?" I was babbling now, whistling in the dark to keep the rising horror at bay. I could no longer deny that something was wrong.

Seriously, seriously wrong.

Maybe I just need to wake up.

That's it, I thought. This just had to be—had to be!—some crazy extended dream. *Okay, Claire, just go with it. You'll wake up soon.*

Then I had another thought.

What if I'm dead? What if I really did die in that train wreck?

What if this was some kind of bizarre, undreamed-of afterlife? I once read about an African American woman who had nearly drowned. She'd been brought back from the brink of death by a lifeguard and an off-duty fireman. After she recovered, the woman related a strange tale about finding herself in an African marketplace, centuries before European contact, and being sold to an Arab slave trader.

Maybe the woman hadn't really been describing an afterlife. Maybe she was describing a *before-life* experience. An experience from an earlier lifetime.

The detective's voice jerked me back from my tortured speculations. "I'm sorry, miss, but I'm afraid you're not making a lot of sense."

I grabbed his sleeve. I was pretty fed up. Maybe a bit of controlled rage would end this nightmare. "Okay, how's this for making sense? After this little circus act is over, Sam Grayson will be filing criminal charges against all of you!"

Unfazed, he asked, "Who's Sam Grayson?"

"You'll find out soon enough!"

We exited the building through a set of double doors. I looked around. We were standing at the top of a flight of steps that led down to a walkway, which in turn led to a large fenced parking lot. The lot was almost completely full.

It was filled with row upon row of boxy bodies, waterfall grilles, landau roofs, two-toned paint . . .

Row upon row of 1960s and 1970s cars.

That was the moment when my illusion of reality, as Einstein described it, came completely loose from its moorings.

My knees turned to water.

The detective caught me in his arms just before I fell headfirst down the stairs.

He eased me down to the walkway. Fortunately, his car was parked nearby, because he was forced to half-carry me the entire way. My mind had gone numb, reminding me of those few moments of consciousness when I was lying on the riverbank.

As we stumbled along, his strong arms around me began triggering memories.

Memories of an older Marc—strong and capable and so deeply in love with me.

Memories of an older Marc—the man who had followed me for my entire life.

I was afraid to speak. We reached a big unmarked sedan. He opened the front passenger door. I sighed to myself, relieved that he wasn't confining me in the back. I saw a broad bench seat, and a radio and emergency equipment console mounted under the dash. I allowed him to lower me onto the seat, unready to give up his comforting arms.

He clicked my door shut and strode around the front of the car. My eyes tracked him, recognizing the confident gait, the confident bearing . . .

What are you doing?

I brought myself up short. Here I was in an advanced state of shock— imprisoned in some surrealist nightmare—and finding myself attracted to a young stranger.

Was he really a stranger? Or a thirty-year-old version of the most irresistible man I had ever known?

What the hell are you thinking?

With this new reality overwhelming my senses, the persistent remnants of my old reality kept clawing this way and that, stubbornly determined to find a rational answer.

Maybe I'm hallucinating. . . .

Maybe I had lost my mind. Maybe at this very second, my 2011 self— my real self—was locked in a seven-by-nine room at the Florida State Hospital. Maybe at this very second, I was under court-ordered psychiatric observation.

If that was it—if that was my *true* reality—how would I fix it? How far back would I have to go to identify the turning point? The microsecond in time when all reason failed and my sanity collapsed?

The train wreck?

Finding Marc's photo record of my entire life?

Finding the bodies in Tribe's cabin?

Noticing Marc in the back of my courtroom?

Farther back?

Young Marc got into the car. He slipped the key into the ignition.

"This is impossible," I stated dully.

"What is?"

I didn't know how to answer, so I backpedaled. "Why did they send you—I mean, *you* in particular—to pick me up? Why not . . . the deputy who came to see me?"

"Tattersall."

"Yeah. That one."

"He's County. Our office caught your file, and my lieutenant asked me to follow up. There are two reasons I'm here. First, we've been trying to make some sense out of the information you gave Tattersall." He reached into his jacket and pulled out a small notebook. "That street address . . ."

"What about it?"

"It's a plant nursery." He looked straight at me. "And your phone number doesn't exist."

I held his gaze for a second and then looked away. This sickening new reality was turning my world upside down and I wasn't ready yet.

"The deputy said that was the only information you gave him—name, address, phone number."

"I was barely conscious. Gertie made him leave."

"You told him you were in a train accident. Gertie mentioned that as well."

It occurred to me that this might be a setup engineered by the creepy Dr. Bland, so I stayed silent.

He continued. "Look, I'm sorry! It seems clear that you've been through some kind of trauma. But I do need to ask a few questions."

"Such as?"

"Such as your date of birth."

This should be interesting, I thought.

I went for it. "November fourth, 1979."

"Try again."

"That's when I was born! The first day of the Iran hostage crisis! And you know it! You followed me!"

"I know it? First of all, it's a ridiculous answer, and secondly, I've never seen you before in my life!"

Good, I thought. *Be irritated! You irritated me enough when you were . . . you were . . .*

Damn it!

"It's the only answer you're going to get!"

"The first day of the what?" he asked.

"What?"

"You said the first day of some crisis."

"Never mind!" I was born on the day the hostages were taken, but I was pretty certain that discussion wasn't going to take us anywhere.

He shifted in his seat, leaned back against the door, and stared at me in frustration. Now, at least, we were both confused. Of course, he was just perplexed and probably a bit annoyed. He had no inkling of the complete, utter, and monumental confusion he would face if this fantastical experience became *his* reality. But I wasn't ready to confront that directly. At least, not yet.

I needed to conduct an experiment.

I took the plunge. "I'm sorry. Of course you don't know me. This time around, everything is reversed. This time, I know you, but you don't know me. I don't expect you to understand that yet."

"That's good, because I don't."

I looked at him, and my own doubts began to erode. Against all natural laws, I was looking at Marc Hastings, aged thirty. Against all logic, I was looking at the same alternately bemused, indulgent, admiring, laughing, and loving face I had known three decades later in his life.

Later?

There was no other explanation. All the things Old Marc should never have known about me, but did . . . explained. Those things I'd forgotten, or had tried to forget, that he had seemed to know . . . explained.

The pieces dropped into place.

In 2011, my future lay in Marc's past.

In 1978, my past lay in Marc's future.

As insane as it sounded, my new reality in 1978 was just the logical extension of my old reality. Well, *logical* it certainly wasn't, but however I labeled it, the impossible was staring me straight in the face.

"I have a suggestion. Why don't you call me Claire, and I'll call you Marc?"

"Okay with me."

"You once told me to tell you the truth."

"I don't remember saying that, but the truth is always a good place to start."

"You wrote it on the back of a photograph. You said, 'Remember to tell me the truth.'"

His expression warned me that I needed to be careful. I couldn't afford to alienate him before . . .

Before what? Before I told him that I was visitor from the future?

"This is a test," I said.

"What is?"

"Be patient. This is a test for both of us. You believe we've never met before, am I correct?"

"Correct."

"So, would you agree that—?"

He interrupted. "I would *definitely* have remembered." I caught that same flash of admiration in his eyes I'd seen the first time I met Old Marc.

I deliberately ignored the implication so I could stay focused. "Do you agree that there is no way I could possibly know your middle name or your birthdate?"

"Unless you're a psychic. Or," he added with a smile, "unless my boss put you up to this act."

That remark startled me. "You think this is an act?"

"If it isn't, one of us is definitely crazy!"

"Okay. You be the judge of that. Your middle name is Daniel, and you were born on September sixth, 1948."

A second passed. Wonder mixed with suspicion on his face. "How did you—?"

"What you mean is, how *could* I know that? It's a long story, Marcus Hastings, and one you're not likely to believe . . . at least for a very long while."

"You saw my driver's license!"

"Think back. When did I see it?"

He sat staring at me.

It was all too much, and I felt a headache coming. I leaned my head against the cool of the passenger window. "My folks live in Archer," I said without looking at him. "Any chance you could drive me there?"

"You told the nurse—Gertie—that your father's dead and your mother lives up north."

I gritted my teeth and faced him. "Okay, Marc, am I under arrest? Is that how this starts?"

"No. You're not under arrest."

"Are there buses from Gainesville to Archer?"

"Yes, but—"

"Then just drop me at the bus station there."

"Do you have money?"

"I . . . uh . . . no." My resolve crumbled. "Could you lend me the fare? I'll get it back to you. I . . . just need time to, uh . . . get my bearings." This impossible new reality was crushing in on me again, and I could feel myself starting to unravel. I felt tears coming, so I turned away. A girl walked past. She was wearing a satin jacket, and her hair was done in a Farrah-do. She peered suspiciously at the police car and hurried on.

Marc's hand touched my arm. "I'll drive you."

36

Stuccoed bungalows, two-lane highways with narrow graveled shoulders, old cars that looked new, and a McDonald's sign that bragged OVER 24 BILLION SERVED.

"They gave up on that."

"Hmm?"

"McDonald's. Now the sign just says 'Billions and Billions.'"

"Yeah? Where did you see that?"

"Never mind." I kept watching for something modern, something telltale, but the world of Jimmy Carter's presidency just kept on rolling past my window. After a few miles—and after the surreal apparition of a giant Virginia Slims billboard proclaiming YOU'VE COME A LONG WAY, BABY!—I couldn't take anymore. I hunched in the corner of my seat and concentrated on Marc. He wasn't *my* Marc, strictly speaking, but resting my eyes on him helped me feel "grounded," as the rehab therapists love to say.

He must have felt my eyes on him. A puzzled smile flickered on his face. "What is it?" he asked.

I deflected. I read off the model name of the police car inscribed on the glove box. "'Matador' . . . What is this car?"

"A Matador."

"I can see that. I've never heard of it. Who makes it?"

He gave me a strange look. "American Motors."

At first I blanked on the company, but then I remembered it had something to do with making Jeeps and had eventually gone broke. I decided not to press that button. Listening to the rumbling V8, I ventured, "Bet it's hard on gas."

We passed a Mobil station. The sign read: REGULAR 0.64 PREMIUM 0.67.

"Forget what I just said."

"Okay."

After a few seconds, he looked over at me and said, "Do you know how completely weird you are?"

"Weird . . . but intriguing?"

The corner of his mouth lifted into a faint smile. "Maybe."

Time to change the subject. "You said there were two things."

"Two things?"

"Two reasons your boss sent you to pick me up."

"Yeah." He chewed his lip. "I'm sorry. Obviously, we were wrong. It's just that there's this case we've been working on. Disappearances . . . all young women. We think they've been abducted. We were hoping you might be a victim who got away. Someone who could give us a lead."

Instantly, I felt light-headed.

Of course!

"Marc, please pull over!"

He eased off on the accelerator. "Why? What's wrong?"

"Nothing's wrong . . . well, *a lot* is wrong! It's just that I don't think you should be driving while we have this discussion."

We were on Route 20, just west of Hawthorne. Marc signaled and turned into a side road. He swung the car onto a grassy field next to a row of mailboxes. A road sign said SE 199 ST. I happened to know the area, but it didn't look anything like I remembered. The only thing I recognized was an old shed on the opposite corner that was in much better shape than its collapsing 2011 counterpart.

Marc shifted the car into park but left the engine running. He fixed me with a skeptical look. "Is this going to be more crazy talk?" he asked bluntly.

"If I told you I was a passenger in a train in the year 2011 and the train derailed and I woke up in a hospital in 1978, would that sound crazy?"

"Certifiable."

"If I told you the first time you and I met, you were over sixty years old, would that sound crazy?"

"Do you have to ask?"

"And, if I said you and I worked together, thirty-three years from now, and solved this string of murders?"

"Murders? I didn't say anything about murders."

"These aren't just abductions, Marc! These girls are being killed!"

"You're probably right, but until we find a body—!"

"Just humor me for a minute, okay? Suspend your disbelief and listen. I knew a few things about *you*, didn't I? Things I shouldn't have known?"

"Yeah, maybe, but—"

"So pretend I'm a psychic if that works better for you."

"Let me be straight with you, Claire. *None* of what you're saying—"

In that instant, a horrifying thought crash-landed in my brain.

"—works for me."

I put up my hand. "I need you to be quiet for a second!"

"What?"

"I need to think, goddamn it!" I felt him recoil, but I didn't care. I was picking through the crash scene in my brain. Recognizing something in the wreckage . . .

A paradox.

The paradox of me.

It explained why Old Marc had forced me to repeat the entire investigation in the last six weeks of 2010. And it explained why he had invariably taken the lead.

Even on the one occasion when I had taken the lead—linking the crab's eye peas to Harlan Tribe, and engaging the analytical services of Charlie McNabb—I hadn't really been leading. I'd been following a trail I laid down for myself.

I could feel Young Marc watching me as my roiling thoughts searched for a way out. My immediate problem was that, knowing—or thinking that I knew—exactly where I came from, I wasn't sure how much I could say without changing history. It crossed my mind that I could be risking my own elimination.

But there was no way out.

I took a deep breath and went for it. "What you believe about me right now probably isn't important. Belief will come in time. Let's just say I know a thing or two about the future . . . including your future." The expression on his face stopped me. "This isn't helping, is it?"

He cocked his head. "I'm starting to wonder if I should have cuffed you and locked you in the back."

"Okay, let's do this: I'll tell you what has already happened in your case, and you tell me if I'm right."

"Try me."

I rattled off names and dates. "Ina Castaño, April second, 1977 . . . Constance Byrne, July eighth, 1977 . . . Catherine Brady, October twenty-eighth, 1977 . . . Patricia Chapman, Christmas Eve, 1977 . . . María Ruiz, February thirteenth, 1978."

He stared. "You'll have to do better than that. Every one of those cases has been reported in the press. Newspapers, TV, all over Florida and the Southeast."

"The press . . ." It hit me. "Lots of out-of-town reporters are covering the story, right?"

"Some."

"What's today? March sixth! There's one case you haven't made public!"

His eyes narrowed.

I drove the point home. "Pia Ostergaard. She's a *Miami Herald* reporter. She hasn't been seen since Wednesday night."

His face froze.

"Has she, Marc?"

He released a breath. "She doesn't fit the—"

"—profile! I know! She's blond and she's older than the others, and you guys aren't following your own instincts. You're letting the FBI run the show, telling you what to think."

"How could you know all this? Are you—?"

"—involved in law enforcement? I was, once upon a time." I read his face. "Oh, I see! You're wondering if I'm involved in the crimes!" I fixed him in my gaze. "Where was I on Wednesday night? Where have I been since last Tuesday?"

"In the hospital," he conceded a bit grudgingly.

"And drugged and unconscious most of the time! Look, what's happened to me is crazy! If you only knew *how* crazy! But my brain is intact and I'm perfectly sane—and, believe me, I know this case better than you do!" I shifted and faced forward in my seat. "I've said enough for now. Can we go?"

He took a long, deep breath . . . and then he surprised me. "I've got to say . . . you might sound pretty crazy, but you don't look crazy."

"Oh? What do crazy people look like?"

"Well . . ." He grinned. "Definitely not like you."

So . . . here's when it started.

Here's when we began the beguine.

"Drive on, Junior," I said.

37

The JCT 27 sign on Route 24, just before the turnoff to Archer, was in the same place, but nothing else was. There were no traffic lights at the intersection, the future Kangaroo gas station was a scrubby pasture, and the tire shop had reverted to being the single-pump corner store of earlier times. There was no escaping from the mind-numbing conclusion that when I was ejected from that railcar window, I had plunged through more than just space. Either I had landed on a muddy beach on the St. Johns River in the year 1978, or I was having some weird psychotic break.

I was hoping for psychosis.

With a faint heart, I directed Marc through the turns toward my childhood home on Mcdowell Street. I recognized some of the buildings along the way. I hadn't returned to Archer often as an adult, but just from memory, I knew that many of the residences we were passing had been torn down or modified in my lifetime.

But, no. Unless I was psychotic, I had it backwards. It wasn't "had been" torn down—it was "would be."

My past was now in the future.

It was all so damned confusing.

Then I saw the house. "Can you pull over here?"

The car slowed and drifted to the right, onto the grass next to the road. I sat perfectly still, staring in wonder at the house where I grew up. It appeared exactly the same as it did in my earliest, gauziest memories—the pale green clapboard siding, the white trim, the broad veranda, the power pole set unaccountably in the middle of the lawn, the row of hibiscus bushes along the road at the front . . . even the two creases in the roof gutter that I had once convinced myself were left there by the runners of Santa's sleigh.

Reluctantly, I shifted my gaze to the playground across the road.

The playground of my fragmented and recurrent dream.

"Your hands are shaking."

Marc's expression was part curiosity, part concern. Thinking back, there was a third element in that look—fascination. But I wasn't noticing. I couldn't speak. I locked my fingers together and shoved my hands between my legs. I took deep breaths. I felt like throwing up.

And then it happened. The door opened and a man appeared on the front veranda. He was carrying a small suitcase. He was young, maybe mid-twenties, with dark hair and a lean frame. He stopped at the top of the steps and set down the suitcase.

He looked familiar, but it still took me a few seconds.

It was my father.

My father!

I gasped—and then almost choked, because the woman who appeared beside him a second later was definitely, categorically, undeniably . . . my mother.

The mother I remembered from her wedding pictures.

I sat frozen as my parents kissed. My father picked up the suitcase, descended the stairs, and disappeared around the corner of the house. My mother stood waiting. A moment later, Dad's red '78 Bonneville convertible—the one he was still driving when he abandoned us in 1985—appeared from behind the house. It gleamed as I had never seen it gleam when I was a kid. With a wave to my mother, he drove onto the street, passed Marc's squad car without giving us a glance, and disappeared in the direction of the highway.

I watched my mother. I expected her to return to the house, but as soon as my father's car disappeared from view, she lowered herself to the top step and sat there, watching the street. For a few seconds, the surrealism of where I was—of *when* I was—vanished from my conscious thoughts. My hand inched toward the door handle.

Abruptly, she rose to her feet and went back in the house.

Marc's voice brought me back. "Attractive girl. Sister?"

"Mother," I replied dully.

He was silent. His cheek twitched. "She looks younger than you."

I didn't answer.

"Are you planning to get out here?" he asked.

"I can't."

"You said—"

"I know what I said! But I—I . . ." I let out a rattling breath and slumped against the door. "I don't know how to deal with this! It's so fucking crazy!"

"Nice language."

"Drop me on the highway! I'll figure something out."

"On the highway . . . with no money?"

No money.

Of course!

"That's right! I have no money . . . and no place to go!" I favored him with what must have seemed a spooky look. "But you must have done something about that."

"I must have done something? What does that mean?"

"Never mind. To quote you: 'One day you'll understand.' But just for right now, answer this: What do you do with lost girls after you take them into custody?"

"You're not in custody."

"Maybe I'm not in police custody, but I'm in your custody."

He couldn't help himself. His eyes flicked over my body. "Guess we could find you a meal and a bed."

I locked him with a cool gaze.

He stammered. "I—I mean . . . I didn't mean . . ."

"Of course you didn't."

"It's just that . . ."

"What?"

"You're right. You intrigue me." He gave a nervous laugh. "There. I said it!"

I laughed.

It was unbelievable. I had just fallen down a rabbit hole into 1978, and this man had made me laugh.

He flushed. He started the engine. As the police car reversed through a one-point turn, I had one last, lingering view of my childhood home. Then we drove away.

As we rolled back through Archer, I recalled my conversation with Old Marc, when he'd promised to find the missing pages from that Ostergaard binder—the pages that should have explained the subheading: PUTNAM COUNTY REPORT—WOMAN IN RIVER.

Pages he must have deliberately removed.

Pages about me.

"What will you tell him?" I asked as we pulled back onto the highway and headed east.

"Tell who?"

"Your boss. About me."

He kept his eyes on the road. "False lead. County cop got his facts wrong. I drove the lady home."

"And my hospital bill?"

"We'll work something out."

Yes, Claire, today is definitely when it all began. At least . . . for him.

"Where are we going?" I asked.

"I have a fishing camp on Lake Lochloosa."

I nodded to myself, remembering the night I'd followed Marc's taxi to Cross Creek. "I should have guessed."

"It's not a shack," he said quickly, and a bit defensively. "It's got power, running water . . . It's a nice little place."

"Is that where you live?"

"When I'm off shift. I have an apartment in town."

It was all coming together, whether I wanted it or not.

Let it happen. It's not like you have any choice.

I settled back in my seat.

38

"Letting it happen" was a more dramatic transition than my reeling imagination could have conceived. On the long return journey east through Gainesville, and then south to Cross Creek, I said as little as possible. I resolved to watch, listen, and stay alert for clues remembered from the future that might serve as cues I would need here in the past.

Here in the past?

It was unnerving to realize how little time it had taken for me to adapt to the insane concept that I was living in 1978.

Maybe I really was a mental case, locked away in a psychiatric ward somewhere.

I shoved the thought aside, which only made room for another—one that had been lurking in the wings for hours: the mounting sense of inevitability with Marc. In many ways, this was hardly a surprise. I hadn't missed his younger version's perplexed but clearly intrigued smile; I knew already that I was destined to end up in his bed three decades from now; and I remembered how his older version had made love to me with such uncanny familiarity. I realized—with an acute spasm of remorse over my conduct when we parted—that when Marc Hastings stepped into my courtroom on that first day, he was already in love with me. He had waited for that moment for over thirty years.

He had waited for me to grow up.

Watched over me . . . and waited.

The bottom dropped out of my stomach.

I had actually allowed myself to suspect that Marc was the killer.

I swallowed, barely controlling the wave of nausea that almost overcame me. I released my seat belt and moved close to him.

"What's wrong?"

"Just hold me. Please."

Without a word, he slid his arm around me. The bond between us was already there, even though he didn't understand it.

I laid my head against his shoulder and tried to empty my mind.

"Fishing camp" was not just a misnomer—it was completely misleading. A half mile south of Cross Creek, Marc turned into a narrow unmarked driveway. After a few hundred yards, the graveled surface decayed into a rutted track lined by ancient live oaks thick with Spanish moss, interspersed with sweet gum and hickory. Twisting limbs met overhead, creating a tunnel of foliage. Marc slowed the car to a crawl. A few minutes later, we debouched into a small clearing occupied by a rustic shake-roofed cottage nestled on the shore of a verdant cove.

Marc parked next to the front steps. He led me across the veranda and unlocked the door. A tour of the interior revealed a two-bedroom, one-bathroom affair, with beamed ceilings and tongue-and-groove pinewood floors. It had a galley kitchen with a banquette, a cozy lounge area complete with a native stone fireplace, and—as Marc proudly highlighted, swinging the bathroom door wide to prove this important point—full indoor plumbing.

When I admitted to being impressed, he reacted with almost boyish pleasure.

Eventually, I settled into the cushions of an old rocker on the veranda while Marc drove off to grab us a takeout supper from The Yearling. It was one of the few structures I'd noticed as we passed through Cross Creek that looked pretty much the same—at least on the outside—as it would thirty years from now.

Sitting in the rocker, gazing out over the cove and the lake beyond, I felt like I'd been catapulted back an extra forty years into a Marjorie Kinnan Rawlings novel.

The sun was sinking when Marc reappeared with containers of pub food and a six-pack of beer. The label on the cans read BILLY.

"'Billy'?"

"President Carter's brother." Marc paused, and then added, "He's a bit of an embarrassment."

"You mean, to the president?"

"Yeah."

I had a vague memory of reading somewhere that Jimmy Carter's brother had been a problem for him, but I'd never heard of "Billy" beer. In an odd way, that was at once comforting and disturbing. If I was crazy, how could my febrile brain dream up a brand of beer that I had never known existed?

It was evidence that I wasn't hallucinating.

But it was also evidence that I had, in fact, been catapulted into the past.

My lawyer's brain, always the heckler, butted in: *How is that evidence of anything? You dreamed up this cottage, didn't you?*

Ignoring the contentious voices in my head, I surrendered to the impossible proposition that I was breathing the air of 1978 and gratefully accepted a cold beer. There was nothing imaginary about its taste in my mouth.

We ate at a small table on the veranda. Marc deliberately steered away from asking the many disturbing questions that must have been tumbling through his mind. No doubt he sensed my emotional fragility. How could he not, after the bizarre day he had just spent with me? Somehow he managed to confine the conversation to birds, fish, and stories about some of the unique local characters he had come across since buying the property five years earlier.

In our quieter moments, he sat looking at me with an expression of bewitched wonder, as if I were some marvelous, unexpected present that had dropped into his life from the sky.

In a very real sense, I was.

After we finished eating, he told me he had to drive back to Gainesville to return the police car. "I've got three more shifts in this rotation, but I'll come back every night." He hesitated, then added, "That is, if you're planning to stay."

"I'll be waiting."

"Just like that? You'll stay?"

"Yes. You once told me I would understand. Now I do."

His brow knitted. From his point of view, I was talking in riddles. But it was obvious that he was afraid to delve too deeply, in case I changed my mind. So he let it go with a doubting nod. "Okay. I'll bring some fresh groceries. Meanwhile, you won't starve. You'll find sandwich fixings in the fridge, and there's lots of canned stuff in the cupboard."

He led me to the bathroom and found a new toothbrush that was still in its package.

"The guest room is yours. There's a bathrobe in the closet. What about a change of clothes?"

"Would be nice."

He rooted through the drawers in his bedroom and found me a couple of shirts and some sweatpants. "Best I can do right now, sorry."

"No apology needed. Thank you."

"Okay. See you tomorrow night." He gave me an awkward hug, and left.

I spent a dreamless night in a deliciously comfortable bed.

Three days later, my love affair with Marc Hastings began.

Again.

39

I heard Marc coming before I saw him. I was sitting on the veranda rocker, idly twirling a strand of my hair and watching a great blue heron stalking minnows in the shallows of the cove. I had showered late and slipped into one of the summer dresses Marc had bought for me. After seeing my hand-washed bra and panties dripping in the bathroom, he'd shown up the following evening with three shopping bags filled with new clothes.

I was frankly astonished. I started checking labels. "How did you get my size?"

"Looked for a salesgirl with your figure." He smiled and added, "Took a while."

I wasn't thrilled with some of the color choices, but everything fit perfectly.

Even the underwear.

Marc's Dodge pickup rumbled into view and parked in the usual spot. The first time I saw the truck, I'd been ready to laugh. I didn't have to. True to the understated personality I would come to know thirty years hence, Young Marc had spurned the usual Southern cracker yee-haw kit—oversized winch, vinyl seats, and obligatory gun rack. His canyon red pickup was factory standard, and surprisingly comfortable.

He stepped out of the truck and saw me. His eyes lit up.

He bounded up the steps and then stopped in his tracks when he noticed that I was staring at him, aghast.

"What's wrong?"

"What is that?" I demanded.

"What?

"That . . . thing you're wearing!"

He looked down at himself, puzzled. He plucked at the cloth of the dreadful shirt-jacket. "You mean this? It's a leisure suit! I thought I'd take you out for—"

"Wearing that?" I laughed. "Anyway, supper's made."

"No kidding?"

"I can cook! It's not *all* fast food where I come from. And I mixed a couple of martinis. If you value my company," I added with a sternness that was only partly simulated, "you'll get out of that getup! I mean . . . bell-bottoms? Are you kidding me?"

By now he was smiling. Apparently, my nagging-vixen routine amused him. "Okaaay! I'll change!" He ducked into the cabin.

The entire act was just a way of trying to bury my inner torment. I knew it wouldn't work for long. Over the past three days, I'd had plenty of time alone and plenty of time to think. It hadn't required much close analysis to calculate my extreme peril. I'd spent most of those days trying to work out an escape.

There wasn't one.

I was doomed, and I knew it.

Ten minutes later, Marc and I were sitting side by side on the veranda. He was infinitely more acceptable to my twenty-first-century eyes wearing jeans and polo shirt. We were sipping martinis from smoked-glass tumblers because, not surprisingly, it had never occurred to Marc to stock his "fishing camp" with stemware. Behind us, through the screen door, the kitchen radio was playing Gerry Rafferty's "Baker Street." I'd always liked that song, although where I came from, it was played on the oldies stations.

Marc swirled his martini, watching the olives bounce around the bottom of the glass. I hadn't been able to find any toothpicks.

"Gin," he commented.

"Yeah. Sorry. I'm not big on vodka martinis."

"I don't keep gin out here. Don't remember buying olives, either."

"The olives were jammed in the back of your fridge. The sell-by date is two years old, but they're fine."

"And the gin?"

"The Yearling."

"You walked all that way to buy gin?"

"I had that twenty you left me. I had a nice talk with the lady there . . . the bar manager."

"Nonie."

"Yeah. I like her."

"What did you tell her?" He sounded alarmed.

"I didn't mention your name. I just said I was staying at a friend's cabin on Lochloosa." I paused. "She offered me a job."

He looked unnerved.

"It's just three nights a week to start. Marc, I'm grateful that you've taken me in even though you think I'm a bit crazy, but I need to do something to contribute."

"Okay, but what about ID? You don't have any."

"I said I'd work for tips."

"You *told* her you have no ID?"

"No. I just said I wanted to stay off the grid."

"Which means?"

"Below the radar. Invisible."

"Do you know how that sounds? I'm a cop, remember?"

"Are you planning to turn me in?"

"No. It's not a crime to have no ID. I'm just wondering why you don't apply for replacements."

"Marc, I'd need to start with a birth certificate, and I can't get one!"

"Because you aren't born yet. Claire, really . . ." He sipped from his drink and stared out over the lake.

Then, unaccountably, he switched subjects.

"What do you know about Cross Creek?"

"I've been here a few times."

The last time I was here, I was following you.

"Have you noticed that white house with the screened porch across from where we turn in?"

"Yes."

"Know who lives there?

"*Lived.* Marjorie Rawlings died in 1953."

"Read any of her books?"

"*The Yearling.* A long time ago. I think, in high school."

"Did you go to college?"

"Boston U, then Harvard Law." I gave him a laser look. He was trying to steer the conversation, and I could see where it was going, so I laid a marker down. "What's with the twenty questions, Marc? Yes, my past is bigger than a bread box, and no, you won't find any record of me at either of those schools."

He drew a long breath. "I know I won't. That young couple in Archer . . . Gregory and Margaret Talbot?"

"Yes."

"They have no children."

"Not yet."

"C'mon, Claire! Who are you, really? Is Claire even your name?"

"Claire Alexandra Talbot. That's my name, Marc. It's not some secret identity."

"I've been doing some checking."

"You're not ready for this, Marc."

"The labels in your clothes—the ones you were wearing when I picked you up. I made some calls. No one's heard of those brand names."

"That would be right."

He reached into a pocket and brought out my watch. He handed it to me. "I took that to be fixed."

"Thanks!" I was surprised. But then I saw the watch face. The hands were frozen in the same place.

"I took it to a guy I know. Really good . . . trained at a special school in Switzerland. He didn't know how to fix it. He'd never seen one like it."

"Okay," I mused, "for one thing, it isn't a Swiss watch. It's Japanese." Then it dawned on me. "And it's an Eco-Drive. It runs off solar power."

"I've never heard of that."

"I'm not surprised."

"I don't get any of this, Claire! Should I be talking to the feds about you? I'm working with a few of them, you know!"

"The feds? Why?"

Abruptly, he switched to a foreign language. The intonations sounded vaguely familiar, but I couldn't identify the specific language until he said, "Brezhnev."

"'Brezhnev'?" He flushed when I started laughing. "So now I'm . . . what? A Russian spy?"

"You're living 'off the grid,' as you call it. You've got some kind of high-tech watch. You're too young and too smart to be a seasoned criminal, so what does that leave? You're either working for the Russians . . . or you're one of ours. Which is it? KGB or CIA?"

"Neither. And if you really believed that, you'd never have trusted me enough to leave me alone out here. You wouldn't have bought me new clothes."

"You talk like a lawyer."

"I am a lawyer." I changed the subject. "I didn't know you spoke Russian."

"Picked up a bit in the navy."

"You never told me."

"That's another thing! Why do you keep saying you know me?"

"Because I do."

He shook his head in frustration.

"As I said, you're not ready for this." I drained my drink, stood up, and set the empty glass on the porch railing. "But rest assured, Marc Hastings, I know you much better than you think."

He remained seated. I could see the conflict on his face. He'd been thinking and brooding while he was away from me, and his brain and his heart were pulling in different directions. At least I had the advantage of knowing which one would win in the end. I glided toward the door. "For example," I tossed back at him, "I know you're hiding me out here so your bosses won't find out."

"There'd be a hell of a lot of questions if they did!"

"I suppose. I also know that you paid my hospital bill." I had seen the receipt on his dresser when I was hunting for an extra towel.

"I had to! Otherwise, there'd have been more questions!"

I opened the screen door and dropped the bomb I'd been planning all day. "I also know you're aching to make love to me, but you're too scared to try."

I heard him twist in his chair a second before the door banged shut behind me. "Scared?" I watched through the screen as he jumped to his feet. He crossed the veranda in three strides. "Cat! Listen to me, girl! I'm not scared!" I stepped closer to the door. He saw me.

" 'Cat,' " I said evenly. "Only my mother calls me that."

"Your initials . . ." He tugged the screen door open. "It just came into my head." We were inches apart. I stood perfectly still, looking into his fathomless blue eyes. He bent toward me. "You're right," he whispered. "You scare the hell out of me." He tried to say something else, but his voice caught. I slid my arms around him, and suddenly he was kissing me . . . my lips, my cheeks, my neck.

All my studied restraint evaporated and something deep inside me let go. Tears burned my eyes. "All those years! Oh, Marc, I'm sorry! I'm so, so sorry!"

He lifted me into his arms and carried me to his bedroom. He laid me on the bed. I saw the swirling confusion on his face as he lay down beside me. I pressed my fingers to his lips.

"Don't say anything. Don't ask anything. Just . . . make love to me."

Twenty minutes later, we melded into one.

40

A baneful fate was slouching toward me like William Butler Yeats's rough beast. The clock was ticking; I knew it, but Marc didn't. I was clinging to the idea that at least one of us should be allowed to remain innocent for a while longer. Old Marc had protected me from my truth, but I wasn't sure how long I could protect Young Marc from his.

Wednesday was Marc's first day off in a scheduled rotation. We spent most of that day in bed. The sex was spectacular, and the tender hours between were ineffable, but the loom of crisis was never far from my consciousness.

By some unspoken understanding, Marc avoided cross-examining me any further about my enigmatic provenance. But the reprieve didn't prevent the occasional collision between us as I attempted to adjust to a less well-informed decade than the one I had left behind.

The first incident began with my lame attempt at comedy. It ended on a more somber note. On Thursday morning, Marc made breakfast while I showered. When I heard his voice call, "Cat! Breakfast is ready!"—the exact words he would use on a different morning, thirty years from now—I swallowed the lump in my throat and forced myself to focus on a mini-mission of cross-generational education. I wrapped myself in my bathrobe and marched into the kitchen.

The kitchen banquette was neatly set, and Marc was in the process of deploying plates loaded with bacon and eggs and toast.

"You know," I began, "a few things around here will have to change."

"Yeah? What?"

I dipped my hand into the pocket of my robe and retrieved the red plastic bottle I'd found in the shower. I held it under his nose. The multi-hued label shouted: "GEE, YOUR HAIR SMELLS TERRIFIC."

"My shampoo? What about it?"

"Forgive me for pointing out that your hair does *not* smell terrific! It smells like you spent the night in a Turkish bordello!"

He assessed me carefully. "You don't look Turkish." His eyebrows danced. "But I have to admit, you do have certain bordello skills."

"You ain't seen nothing yet."

"You promise?"

I kissed him. "Promise." I dropped the shampoo bottle into the trash bin and slid into my seat. "Another thing . . ."

"What?"

"I checked some of the junk food packages you've been hoarding." I pointed toward one of the kitchen cupboards behind him. "Bad news!"

"Meaning?"

"Meaning chemical additives! Are you in the habit of eating plastic bags?"

"Of course not!"

"Same ingredients! After breakfast, we're going shopping." I surveyed the food arrayed on my plate—eggs sunny-side up, wheat toast, fried tomatoes, and . . . "Well, what do we have here?" I exclaimed. "Pancetta bacon!"

"Not many people would know that."

"Learned it from you."

"When was that?" Mark was standing over me.

Oh hell . . .

"Just now," I answered, deflecting. I tasted the bacon. "Perfect!" I looked up. "Aren't you joining me?"

He sat.

"There's another thing. . . ."

"What?" Now he was on the defensive.

"I threw away your leisure suit. You'll thank me one day."

He blinked, but said nothing.

I cut my toast into strips, and then dipped a piece into a yolk. I popped it in my mouth.

Marc ate slowly, watching me.

"Watch closely. This is part of your education," I said, mopping up more yolk. I was trying to keep the mood light . . . trying to make the best of the disorienting surrealism of living in a prequel to my own life.

"You're talking in riddles."

"Now you understand how I felt."

He laid down his fork. One look at his face, and my brief foray into chatty superficiality cratered. I reached over and took his hand. "I'm in love with you, Marc. That's all you need to understand right now. More will come, I promise, but right now, I just need your trust."

"I love you, too, Claire. I do. But it's like being under a spell. I know there's something much bigger going on here, but I don't understand it. The strange thing is . . . it's making me afraid for both of us."

I flashed on a memory: the ornate living room . . . the clear-eyed old lady . . . the quiet warning.

"A lovely old lady once warned me to prepare myself. 'Ready yourself for the sorrows to come,' she said. I think she meant both of us."

Two more girls were going to die.

Very soon.

We would have to decide if we could save them.

Decide if we could change their history, and ours . . . and survive.

I didn't know how to tell him.

The Yearling's interior décor hadn't changed much. The dining room I'd seen on the evening I followed Old Marc was a screened-in porch, but otherwise, the place looked pretty much the same in 1978 as I knew it would three decades later.

It didn't take me long to adapt. I had worked tables in restaurants and bars all through my high school and undergrad years, so mixing drinks and slinging beer were no mystery to me. Nonie Friedrichsen, the bar manager, was the same woman who had been tending bar on the night of the brawl. This earlier version of her wasn't much older than me, but already her hair was flecked with gray and her face was showing the miles she'd traveled. She definitely had her rough edges, but I liked her, and I admired the cool way she handled men twice her size when they became insulting or raucous.

Marc had written his schedule on a calendar for me, and I had planned to coordinate my part-time duties with his shifts. But it didn't work out that way. While we were ravishing each other after I seduced him, the news blackout on the missing *Herald* reporter was lifted. On Friday morning, he was called back to work. He spent the next few nights at his apartment in town, leaving me to fend for myself at the cabin. To keep myself sane—perhaps an unusual concept for someone claiming to be a time traveler—I offered to work extra shifts at The Yearling. Marc and I tried to stay in touch, but the cabin's old rotary-dial phone had no answering machine, and voice mail was a marvel yet to be invented, so our contacts were pretty much hit-and-miss while he was in Gainesville.

When I next saw him, late on Sunday, he told me he had to go back in on Tuesday. A string of severe thunderstorms had blown through—"old cacklers," Nonie called them—and it was a cold night, so I had the fireplace going when he arrived. We sat on the couch in the lounge. He started talking about the frustrating dead ends the task force was encountering. Of course, having read all the reports, I could have predicted their next disappointment. But I stayed quiet. I waited for Marc to bring up our conversation on the first day, at the side of the road near Hawthorne, when I had spooked him with my knowledge of Pia Ostergaard's unannounced disappearance.

He didn't, so I decided to give him a nudge.

"Collect dental records."

"What?"

"Track down the missing girls' dentists and get copies of their charts."

He hesitated. "I think someone's doing that."

He didn't sound certain.

"Make sure, Marc. It's important."

"Good point. I will." He leaned back and regarded me with interest. "Lawyer, huh?"

I didn't reply. I could see that he still wasn't ready for the truth. We were almost there, but if this slow waltz was ever to end, I needed to hand him irrefutable evidence.

I decided to start with a parlor trick.

I'd never been much of a fan of memorizing dates just for the sake of pleasing pedantic history instructors, but one specific date in 1978 was etched in my memory. When I was in third-year law, I had written a term paper analyzing the long-running lawsuit brought in U.S. Federal Court by the Government of France against the Amoco Oil Company of Illinois. The suit had been launched after the infamous grounding of the supertanker *Amoco Cadiz,* a catastrophe that spilled more than 200,000 tons of crude oil into the North Sea and polluted nearly two hundred miles of the French coastline. The case finally reached the Seventh Circuit, where, after thirteen years of litigation, the Court's award for prejudgment interest ended up being more than double its award for damages.

The *Amoco Cadiz* ran aground just before ten in the evening on Thursday, March 16, 1978. Twelve hours later, the ship broke in two and spilled its entire cargo. I had read and reread the law reports on the case at least a dozen times, and I knew the facts by heart. It was a turning-point disaster that led to the adoption of tough new maritime inspection standards for all ships operating in the North Atlantic Basin.

I was certain I couldn't possibly change all that history, but at least I could use it for effect.

Marc kept an old flat-bottomed cypress-plank boat with a ten-horse kicker in a shed behind the cabin. On Monday, we went out on the lake, jigged for bass at Allen Point, and then went for a long cruise. It was late afternoon when we returned to the cabin. Neither of us felt much like cooking, so Marc made a run to The Yearling for takeout. As soon as he drove off, I went directly to the desk in the spare room, where I'd earlier noticed some notepads and envelopes. I filled one side of a sheet of legal-sized notepaper with writing, folded the sheet in four, and sealed it in an envelope. I left it in the desk.

That night, we ate pub food, drank wine . . . and made love.

Later, exhausted, I lay beside Marc with my eyes half-shut, savoring the afterglow. I felt him shift on the bed.

"Amazing!" he whispered.

"Yeah," I replied. "And just think," I added naughtily, remembering my first night with Old Marc, "you'll get even better."

I felt his finger tracing the tattoo on the small of my back. "I meant this."

I bit my lip.

"I've never seen a tattoo on a woman's body before."

I sighed. "One day they'll be all the rage." I opened my eyes and glared. "And by the way, Mr. Man . . . exactly how many naked women *have* you seen?"

"A few." His eyes ran down my body. "But none as beautiful as you, or . . ."

"Or, what?"

His eyes locked on mine. "Or . . . as intriguing."

I kissed him. "Good answer."

41

Early the next morning, while Marc was showering, I ducked into the spare room and retrieved the envelope. As he was getting ready to leave, I handed it to him.

"What's this?"

"You're a police detective."

"Okay . . ." He waited.

"You must have a personal locker at work . . . one where only you have access."

"I have an exhibit drawer. It's secured with a steel bar and a padlock. Why?"

I tapped the envelope in his hand. "Lock that in your drawer and don't open it until Friday. Where will you be on Friday? Here or there?"

"There during the day. I'll probably be working late, but I've got the weekend off. I'll try to get back here before midnight."

"Does your squad room have a TV?"

"There's one in the conference room."

"Okay. When you get to the office on Friday morning, open that envelope. Inside you'll find one sheet of paper. Read what I wrote on it and then turn on CNN."

"What's CNN?"

Dumb girl!

"Right. Sorry. Just turn on the news, any news."

"What's this about, Claire?"

"It's about me getting your full attention."

He shook his head in puzzlement, kissed me, and left.

Cross Creek was a tiny community. To deter gossip, Marc and I had agreed we should never be in the bar at the same time. But Nonie was no fool, and with me negotiating my shifts to suit Marc's, I figured it wouldn't be long before she concluded I was either involved in an illicit affair or hiding from the police. My refusal to be drawn into a discussion of my background, and my quick put-downs when one of the regulars tried to pick me up, could only reinforce that impression. Whatever her suspicions, Nonie never voiced them to me, and she refrained from asking questions—even when I lied and said there was no phone at the cabin where I was staying. She seemed happy to have an extra body available on a tips-only basis, and she was happy to work out my roster as we went along.

I walked to The Yearling late Tuesday morning, but the place was pretty dead during the lunch hour, so Nonie and I agreed that I'd work straight evenings until Friday. For the rest of the week, I spent part of each day out on the lake, or hiking the rustic trails behind the lakeshore, but mainly I sat on the porch reading.

I had found a pile of books stacked behind the couch in the lounge. This time—unlike my experience in Marc's loft apartment of the distant future—there was no evidence of decorating artifice. After spending a fascinating afternoon lost in Kipling's *Rewards and Fairies*, I found a copy of Alvin Toffler's *Future Shock*. I was surprised Marc had it. The verso page reminded me that it had been published in 1970, and I recalled the book had become a bestseller, but I had never read it. Flipping through the chapters, I was struck by some of the author's predictions. Runaway technology, homeschooling, digitally enhanced instant celebrities, superficial personal relationships, and the widespread use of drugs to treat stress—it was all there. But, then, so were underwater cities and family spaceships, which made me pretty sure I could have done a better job writing the book.

Of course, given my specialized knowledge, I'd have had a bit of an advantage.

I waited for Saturday.

But, for me, Saturday never came.

•   •   •

It started on Thursday morning. I woke up feeling shaky, and the sheets were damp from sweat. I made some coffee and tried to shrug it off. I took the boat out on the lake, but returned after half an hour. I couldn't get interested in reading, so I dozed on the bed, trying to fight off what I was sure was just a cold. But after going to the bathroom a few times, I knew I was in trouble. Peeing was painful, and my urine smelled foul.

I had a bladder infection.

I rummaged through the bathroom cabinets and Marc's dresser, hoping to find an unfinished prescription of antibiotics—*any* antibiotics— that might hold this thing off until Marc got home on Friday night and we could figure out what to do.

No luck.

The walk to The Yearling at five o'clock nearly destroyed me. I'd felt nauseated for most of the day and hadn't eaten. I was desperately tired, and a dull pain had developed on the left side of my lower back. But it was a busy night, and for Nonie's sake, I was determined to see it through. I'd heard once that cranberry juice is good if you have a bladder infection. I drank as much as I could force down while I worked, but as the evening wore on, I only felt worse. It didn't help that a couple of boors at the bar were getting on my nerves. Eventually one of them started making ignorant comments about "pussy," with his eyes fixed firmly on me. Nonie intervened as I was about to rearrange the drunk's face with a beer pitcher.

Fifteen minutes later, it struck.

I was upending a bucket of ice into the reservoir when my knees buckled. I dropped the bucket, and a mini-glacier of diced ice splayed across the floor. I made it to the restroom just in time to throw up in the sink.

Days later, I learned what happened after that. Nonie found me in a restroom cubicle, burning with fever, with my jeans around my ankles and the toilet red with blood. Her first thought was that I'd had a miscarriage. She phoned for an ambulance. The following morning, Marc called the cabin. He wanted to tell me he'd opened the envelope and watched the news, and, yes, for fuck's sake, I had his full attention. When I didn't answer the phone, he wasn't too concerned. He was used to me missing his calls.

He arrived at the cabin around eleven that night. He was disappointed that I wasn't waiting, but he still didn't worry. He figured I was working at the bar and I'd show up after closing.

By the next morning, he was frantic.

42

Munroe Memorial Hospital was in Ocala, twenty-five miles south of Cross Creek. I have hazy memories of the ambulance ride and of white-clad forms hovering over me, but nothing that I can fit into any logical continuum. When I eventually came to my senses, I was sweating in a malodorous, fully occupied eight-bed ward with an IV running into my arm and a catheter draining my bladder. *Christ!* For most of my life, I hadn't seen the inside of a hospital except as a visitor, but since landing in 1978 less than three weeks ago, I'd been hospitalized twice. Harboring dark thoughts, I roused enough strength to press a call button mounted on the bed rail, and eventually a nurse came into the room. She was an older lady with kindly eyes. Her name tag read: D. BOWLES, LPN.

"What's wrong with me?" I croaked at her.

"Nice to meet you, too, young lady! Welcome back!" Her voice was soft and comforting, like velvet. She checked my pulse. She stuck a thermometer under my tongue, disappeared into the bathroom, and returned with a wet facecloth. She gently wiped my burning forehead. She checked the thermometer. I couldn't tell if her sigh was from relief or alarm.

"I thought I just had a bladder infection," I said, trying to sound more polite.

"It's much more serious than that, dear. The doctor says you have a kidney infection."

I groaned. My imagination immediately ran wild with dread thoughts: Do these people have an antibiotic that will work? Did I transport a strain of bacteria from the future they can't deal with . . . some flesh-eating superbug that will turn my insides into suppurating mush and trigger a pandemic?

Nurse Bowles offered a soothing answer to my unarticulated fears. "The doctor thinks the antibiotics are starting to work. He told us the latest lab results showed quite amazing improvement. But your fever was dangerously high."

"Was?"

"It's coming down. It was topping a hundred and four when you were admitted. What with the infection and the sedatives, you've been pretty much out of it, my dear."

"Wait a minute! How long have I been here?"

"You were brought to Emergency on Thursday. You've been here on the ward since Friday."

My stomach tightened. "What day is it now?"

"Sunday."

"Sunday? What time is it . . . please?"

The sudden note of terror in my voice startled her. She checked the watch that was clipped to her uniform. "Just before ten, dear. What is it?"

"Oh, God!" I tried to get up. She stopped me. "You don't understand! I have to—!"

"What is it, dear? What's wrong?"

I couldn't talk.

"Is there someone I can call?"

I gasped out Marc's name.

"What's the number?"

"He's a police detective in Gainesville. I need to tell him something! Please!"

"Okay, you calm yourself! I'll find him!" She hurried off.

I started to weep.

I had failed.

Marc showed up at one thirty.

He had waited at the cabin until late Saturday morning, and then decided to break our private protocol. He'd driven to The Yearling and stormed in, looking for Nonie. The dayshift bartender told him she wasn't due on until four, so he flashed his shield and questioned the guy about me.

He made it sound like I was the subject of an investigation, a ploy that got quick results. He learned that I'd collapsed at work on Thursday night and been taken away in an ambulance. Not unexpectedly, my collapse had generated gossipy interest among the staff, but no one could tell him which hospital I was in. The bartender called Nonie's home, but there was no answer.

On the assumption I'd been taken to the nearest community with medical services, Marc drove to his office and started calling all the hospitals in Gainesville that had an ambulance service. There weren't many, and he soon determined that I wasn't there. He was about to start calling hospitals in Ocala when a robbery at a pawnshop turned into a shoot-out. The proprietor was dead, the wounded robber on the run, and Marc was ordered to join the investigation.

Marc hadn't personally taken the call from Nurse Bowles, but when he finally made it back to his office late Sunday morning, a message slip was waiting on his desk.

I didn't learn any of this until after I'd left the hospital. When Marc appeared at my bedside, I moaned with relief and threw my arms around his neck. I hugged him so hard, I nearly ripped out my IV.

But when he started to recount how he found me, I cut him off. "It's today, Marc! It's probably too late, but you have to do something! Her name is Victoria Chan!"

"What?"

"Did you open that envelope?"

He lowered one of my bedrails and sat next to me. "You knew the exact time that ship would go aground," he whispered. "We need to talk. I want to know how—"

"You know how. I've told you enough times. You're just in denial. But we can talk about that later. You have to get back to Gainesville!"

"Why?"

"Because another girl will be taken today! No, she's already been taken! But maybe it's not too . . . Oh, damn!" I was crying.

He wiped my tears. "Tell me, Claire! Tell me now!"

"Her name is Victoria Chan. She's a student at the university. She lives off campus. She went running this morning—on that path that circles Lake Alice. It was early this morning! He's probably taken her!"

"Do you know her address?"

"No! Yes! I mean . . . I knew it, but I just . . . I can't think!" I raked through my memory. "Somewhere on Third . . . Southwest Third!"

"Street or Avenue?"

"Avenue!"

Marc's face hardened. He straightened. "I'll make a call!"

"No! No calls! Just go yourself! Don't waste time trying to find her apartment. Go straight to Lake Alice! Search the running path!"

"I have to call the office! They can get there faster!"

"Maybe, but if you do . . ."

How can I tell him this?

"What? Tell me!"

"Her disappearance hasn't been reported." I took a breath. "Victoria Chan won't be reported missing until seven o'clock tonight. If you make that call, you'll eventually have to explain how you knew five hours earlier. Who's going to believe a psychic told you, much less a woman from the future! Where were you between six and eight this morning?"

"Asleep at the apartment. We worked till nearly four this morning."

"You could end up being a suspect!"

He stared at me. I watched realization dawn. I thought he was going to be sick. After a few seconds, he stood up. "I'll go myself. But I'll be back tonight."

"No, you won't. You'll be working straight through. After the report comes in tonight, you and a cop named Lipinski and an FBI agent will go to her apartment." I paused. "I know what you think of Lipinski, by the way, and you're right." Marc cocked his head in surprise. Before he could respond, I pressed on. "Tomorrow, an engineering student named Matthews will come forward. He'll tell you he passed an Asian girl while he was running the Alice Lake loop this morning. They were running in opposite directions, so he got a good look at her face. He'll take you to the spot where he saw her. The FBI will waste a whole bunch of time running a background check on him, but it's not him, and he has an alibi for almost every other disappearance."

"You know all this." His words were framed as a question, but sounded like a statement.

"Yes, Marc. I do."

"I'm starting to believe that." He leaned over me, his hands on my pillow, and whispered. "You didn't even give me a chance to ask why you're in here."

"Kidney infection." I smiled. "Probably from too much sex."

He chuckled. "You get better, young lady! I need you!"

"I need you, too. And, don't worry . . . I will get better. This isn't over."

"I'll call the nursing station every day. When they tell me you're being discharged, I'll come for you."

"Okay."

His kiss was long and soft. "If I didn't love you so much," he whispered, "I'd have you committed."

"If I didn't love *you* so much," I replied, "I'd commit myself. Now, go!"

Marc left quickly, but I knew we had lost.

All I'd managed to achieve—at the cost of a young woman's life—was credibility with Marc. I had planned to tell him everything on Friday night, after shocking him with my *Amoco Cadiz* prediction. I had set out on the sheet of paper every detail I could remember from the first forty-eight hours of the disaster, even—as Marc had pointed out—the exact time the tanker had gone permanently aground (it had grounded twice). I had planned to convince Marc to save Victoria Chan's life. If he was successful, I was going to tell him about Harlan Tribe and save Amanda Jordan's life as well. I'd been ready to change the past and take my chances, even if that meant amputating myself from the future.

But, I kept thinking, *I'm still here, in the past. I'm thirty-one, flesh and blood, and living in 1978 with all my memories intact. Which means: I must have lived in the future.* Would I vanish from existence if I saved two lives and changed history? Or would I live on, in some new life—in a new "time line," as one physicist had described it in a speculative article I once read?

A time line with a different set of memories.

I kept coming back to the same question. The question I couldn't face, and couldn't avoid.

Could there be two of me?

I'd been trying to think it through, but then I got sick and my grand plan to save Victoria Chan failed.

So, maybe I wasn't meant to save her.

Or Amanda Jordan.

But then . . . why the hell was I here?

43

That evening, Nurse Bowles showed up at my bedside. She had a young orderly in tow.

"Your policeman friend must have some pull with our Admin Department."

"What do you mean?"

"He wants you off this ward." She wrinkled her nose. "I can't say I blame him. We've been asked to move you."

They rolled my bed out of the room and down the corridor to a private room.

Before Nurse Bowles left, I asked if Marc had left any messages. He hadn't.

But a few hours later, another nurse came to see me. "I just received a call from a police officer in Gainesville."

"Detective Hastings?"

"Yes. He asked me to give you a message. He said to tell you they were still searching. He said you would understand."

I had expected this, but it was still a shock. I let out a rattling breath.

"Can I get you anything? Are you comfortable?"

"I don't think I'll ever be comfortable."

She eyed me curiously. "You're not talking about your health, are you?"

"No."

"Do you need someone to talk to?"

"Why?"

"You're . . . different from most patients. When you were sick, you said some things. Some of the nurses think there's something else going on with you."

Here we go again . . .

"You mean something psychological."

But she surprised me. "Not really. Just some of the things you were saying. We wondered if you're not, you know, from here. I mean, you sound American, but . . ."

I played it straight. "Actually, I grew up not far from here . . . over in Archer." And to head off any further conversation, I added, "You know, I really need to sleep."

She gave me a long look, then proceeded to dim the lights and leave the room.

Of course, I didn't sleep. I was awake most of the night.

By Wednesday, my temperature was back to normal. The IV was gone and I was on oral antibiotics. I had a bit of lingering abdominal pain, but as far as I was concerned, I was ready to go home.

My doctor thought otherwise.

Dr. LaPierre was a six-foot-four giant with hands like suitcases. Every time he visited me on his rounds, I was worried he would announce that he needed to do a pelvic. That never happened—at least during my compos mentis period after Sunday—but on Wednesday morning, he told me he wanted me to stay one more day.

"Why?"

"For observation."

"Could you be more specific?"

"You had a serious run-in with bilateral pyelonephritis, Claire. You're very lucky the infection didn't spread to your bloodstream. I'm worried about permanent damage."

My heart sank. "You mean, damage to my kidneys?"

"Yes. The hospital has just installed a new B-mode scanner. I'd like to run you through a test."

"Are you talking about ultrasound?"

"Yes." He looked intrigued. "You've heard about that?"

Uh-oh . . . be careful.

"I . . . read something. It uses some kind of a sound wave for medical imaging."

"Congratulations! You're the first patient I've ever met who has even heard of it. I'll book it for later today. I'll come back to see you when I have the results."

"When will that be?"

"By tonight."

He was as good as his word. Just before six, he reappeared at my bedside. He stood there silently, just looking at my face. It was a bit unnerving. I steeled myself for bad news.

"You're an interesting patient."

I blinked. "I hope that's a good thing."

"Well, before I get into the ultrasound results, you haven't provided us with any background information, Claire. Who's your regular doctor?"

For lack of a better answer, I said, "I don't have one."

"You must have seen a doctor sometime. It would be helpful if we could get a clear picture of your medical history."

"I've never been sick."

"I think you have."

"Why do you say that?"

"Because you have no appendix."

I groaned inwardly. I'd had an acute attack of appendicitis when I was twenty-six and been hospitalized for two days.

"Oh, yeah, I forgot," I replied lamely.

"But that's not what makes you interesting. What makes you interesting is that you have no surgical scar."

"Yes, I do."

"You have four tiny scars on your abdomen, Claire. Two of them are almost invisible."

"They did it with a laparoscope."

He raised an eyebrow. "Even more interesting."

"What is?"

"May I ask where this surgery was performed?"

The correct answer was Gainesville, but I knew I couldn't tell him that. Then I remembered something Sam had always said: *When Americans run out of good ideas, they steal from the Europeans.*

I picked a country with a reputation for precision. "In Switzerland. I was on vacation."

"Hmm."

"Hmm, what?"

"I read the literature, Claire. I'm very diligent about that. As far as I know, no one has ever done a laparoscopic appendectomy."

He had me. I fabricated quickly.

"I think, uh, the technique might have been experimental. I was pretty much out of it. My father dealt with the doctors."

Intelligent eyes locked on mine. "Ultrasound, laparoscopy . . . you seem to know a lot about cutting-edge medical equipment for someone who's never been sick."

Yeah, pal, and I'm not even a doctor. I tried to adjust the topic. "Speaking of ultrasound, you were going to tell me the results."

"It looks okay, but the blood flow is not perfect. I'm going to let you out of here, but I want to see you for a follow-up in three weeks. Call my office and make an appointment." He looked at me curiously. "In the meantime, I'll do some research. When I see you, I'd like to hear more about this operation."

Time to find another doctor . . .

Marc picked me up on the following morning. He had already settled my bill when he came to my room. I offered to contribute all my earnings from the bar, but he wouldn't hear of it.

On the drive back to Cross Creek, he told me what had happened on Sunday after he left the hospital. A highway patrol trooper had clocked his pickup going over ninety on I-75. He'd lost fifteen minutes talking his way out of the ticket. He'd parked on Mowry Road and walked the entire length of the loop trail around Lake Alice. Finding nothing, he realized he was stuck with what I'd told him. So he'd gone back to his office, worked at his desk until just before seven, and then taken the elevator down to the police department's main reception area. He stood there with a sheaf of paperwork in his hand, pretending he was waiting for someone—and feeling like a fool. That feeling evaporated at exactly six minutes after seven, when a young coed walked in and asked to file a missing person report. The sergeant on reception had just launched into the standard line about waiting twenty-four hours when Marc intervened.

"The girl's name was Cynthia Bascombe. She told me her best friend was missing. They were roommates and she hadn't seen her since she went out for a run at seven o'clock that morning. The missing girl's name was Victoria Chan."

Marc had kept his eyes firmly on the road while he was talking, but now he turned to me. "You were right. About everything. We found Miss Chan's car parked on Memorial Road." He turned back to the road. I could see his jaw muscles working. "I'm sorry I doubted you, but it's still hard to take in."

"For me, too."

We didn't speak for the rest of the drive.

When we got back to the cabin, Marc made me go straight to bed. I didn't argue. I wasn't just feeling weak. I was desolate.

Marc brought me a cup of peppermint tea and sat on the edge of the bed. "I told my boss I needed some time off for a family matter. I'm here until Wednesday."

I took his hand. "Family matter, huh?"

"Absolutely." He kissed me on the nose. "I'll take care of the meals; you just get well."

"Sounds good."

"I wanted the time for something else as well."

"I think you're ready now."

"This is going to make me crazy, isn't it?"

"Just as crazy as it made me."

"Okay. We'll start when you're feeling up to it."

"We'd better start tonight. You're going to need time."

"For what?"

"To think."

44

I dropped *Future Shock* on Marc's lap. "Did you ever read that?"

"Started it. Never finished."

"You won't need to. The future ain't what it used to be."

"I have a feeling 'impossible' ain't what it used to be, either."

He wasn't smiling.

It took us two days.

Two days of me talking almost nonstop and Marc listening.

The skepticism was gone. I was amazed at how quickly he adapted to the ludicrous proposition that the woman sitting next to him had lived most of her life in the future. The *Amoco Cadiz* may have been the tipping point, but my predictions about the Victoria Chan case had closed the deal.

He couldn't believe it when I told him that nearly forty years after Apollo 17 left the moon, America still hadn't returned there, and neither had any other country; that Russia was capitalist; and that, in place of our Cold War adversaries, America's number one enemy was a shadowy network of Muslim fanatics.

At times he was captivated by my descriptions of the world to come— cell phones, the Internet, an African-American president—and at other times he was visibly appalled. He couldn't comprehend mindless obsessions like social media. "Instead of colonies on Mars," he raged, "we get 'Twitter'? What the fuck?"

It was the first time I'd heard him swear . . . at least, as Young Marc.

"So, did you have one of these Twitter accounts?"

"No."

"Facepage?"

"Facebook. And, no."

"Why?"

"Too many people posting lame jokes and photos of their latest restaurant meal." I sighed, struggling to find the right words. "I don't know how to explain it—it's like really annoying background noise. I just thought I had better things to do with my time."

"Like . . . traveling through it."

All I could do was nod bleakly.

The long narrative of my own life was easy: my father's disappearance just before my sixth birthday; my mother's remoteness—and her abiding strength—my years in school and college; my doomed relationship with a lecherous law school teacher; my climb up the greasy pole at the State Attorney's Office; my abiding love and respect for Sam Grayson, who had always looked out for me and had never once given me a reason to doubt his motives. I laid it all out for him, unadorned and unvarnished.

But those two days were spent covering only what I *could* tell him.

By Saturday night, my narrative had reached that pivotal scene when Marc's older and infinitely wiser self reentered my life. Our first encounter in the courthouse lobby was limpid in my memory, and I recited our conversation word for word. It was almost hilarious to see Young Marc's expression as I recounted my snarky exchange with his older self.

"'Intriguing and beautiful'?" he gawped. "I said that to a girl half my age, a girl I didn't . . . didn't even . . . ?" He trailed off, confused.

I finished the thought for him. "Didn't even know?" I took his hand. "But you did! You knew me because we're together now! You're going to say those words to me in thirty years *when I don't know you!*"

His face went ashen. "If you don't know me thirty years from now, where are *you* going to be? *You* . . . the girl I'm talking to right now."

I felt sick. I knew it would come to this. I had just hoped it wouldn't be . . . so soon.

I was direct. I had to be, even if I sounded cruel.

"Where do you think I'll be, Marc? I'm not born yet. What do you think will happen on the day I'm conceived?"

I had told him my birthdate on that first day, sitting in his police car.

Then, he'd thought I was either playing games or deranged. Now I sat watching him trying to do the calculations.

He gave up.

"How long do we have?"

"Until March," I said. "The fourth, to be exact."

"Less than a year?"

"Yes. I was premature."

"How do you know? How could you know that? *How?*" I saw the man I loved crumble before my eyes. I had just dragged him into the psychological wasteland I had been struggling through from the moment I accepted my new reality.

"When I was seventeen, my mom and I had one of those mother-daughter moments. They were very rare with her. I knew from comments she'd made over the years—and from an overheard conversation with my aunt Bev, her sister—that her marriage to my father had been in trouble even before I was born. I was a typical know-it-all teenager, and my mom and I had gotten into an argument about my snippy attitude, and it just escalated. "Why was I even born?" "You never loved my dad." "Why did you get pregnant if you didn't love him?" That sort of thing. When all the yelling and sobbing was over, and we'd both calmed down, Mom made us some tea and told me about their marriage. I won't get into it now, but basically it was the old story—she loved not wisely, but too well. Dad was a rep for a building supply chain and he was on the road a lot. At first he didn't like being away from her, but over time, that seemed to change. She started to get the sense that he looked forward to his trips. And the separations started to get longer."

"Claire . . ." Marc was pale, impatient, hanging on my words.

"I'm getting to it."

"Okay."

"Now we're in early 1979. My father had been away on business a lot since Christmas, but even when he was home, he was quiet and distant. Aunt Bev was telling Mom she should get a divorce, and Mom had even spoken to a lawyer. But one morning she got up and found my dad sleeping on the couch. He told her he'd come in after midnight and didn't want to wake her.

"They had breakfast and spent the day together. They drove to Cedar Key, did some shopping, and walked on the pier. Everywhere they went, he held her hand. She said he seemed different. They bought some fresh shrimp from a fisherman and came back to the house and she made shrimp creole. They made love that night, for the first time in a long time. She told me that was when I was conceived."

"But how could she be sure? He was home! It could have been that night, or the next night, or a week later! How could she know the exact date?" His voice was a deathly rasp as he clutched at straws.

"It could have been another date. If he had stayed. But he left for Atlanta the following day. He was gone for over a month."

The air went out of him. "No! No! Not after all this! No!" He wrapped me in his arms. We sank to the floor.

"We have to face it, my love. *You* have to face it!"

His face seemed ripped open, distorted by a level of anguish beyond all imagination. All imagination except mine.

I kissed him. "I love you. We're together now. And one thing is certain: We'll be together again."

He looked at me.

"Your future . . . my memories," I whispered.

An unearthly moan came from deep in his chest. He pulled me close and hung on for dear life.

As far as I knew, I had another year to live.

But part of me died right then.

On Sunday, by tacit agreement, we didn't return to that subject.

Over the morning and into the early afternoon, I walked Marc through the events of my final months in the future. In other words, the time I had spent with him. But now I had to be selective, and the accounts I gave became more and more like thin slices of Swiss cheese. I told him about the missing person files he delivered to my office. I snared his attention when I related how I'd been warned to steer clear of him. That took us into a long sidebar about Lipinski. He wasn't in the least surprised at the man's oafish incompetence—he'd seen all the signs already—but he was disgusted to learn that he was destined for promotion to lieutenant. I told him about the attack on me in the parking lot, about his timely and decisive intervention, and about my visit with Lipinski and Geiger in the squad room. I told him about following him to The Yearling, and the brawl in the bar.

"Eight fourteen P.M.," I said. "You have to remember that."

He nodded, his eyes locked on mine.

But, overall, more and more of the story had to be told with fewer and fewer details. I could tell him about his visit to the morgue to deliver dental records, but not whose records, because Amanda Jordan's was among them. I couldn't mention his examination of Amanda's skeletal remains—or Jane Doe's, for that matter. I told him about my visits to his loft apartment, and about his mirror version of the police investigation file—I had to tell him that so he would get started—but I could only summarize the events that followed. How we found the bodies, how many there were, the identity of the killer . . . I couldn't tell him any of that. I couldn't tell him what he really needed to know as a working detective in 1978, because if he and I were destined to solve these crimes together in thirty years' time, he couldn't be allowed to solve them now.

I now believed that if I told him everything I knew, and he acted on the knowledge, the future would be indelibly changed. If I told him Amanda Jordan was next, he'd do everything in his power to save her. If he succeeded—if Amanda survived, and Tribe was caught, and the bodies were found—then our joint investigation in the future would never have happened.

My memories of our months together would be erased . . .

I would never have boarded that train . . .

I would never have plummeted into the past.

This Claire Talbot—the only one I knew, the one Marc loved—would never have existed.

So I faced an agonizing choice: sacrifice my own life now, or let Amanda Jordan die.

It was a lead weight in my heart.

I finished my narrative with an account of our idyllic weeks together after my disgrace, culminating in my discovery of the photograph album he had kept and storming off to meet my fate on the train.

The photograph album brought us back to the fraught emotional subject we had been carefully avoiding. Marc's eyes were filled with hurt and fear and helpless anger. He'd been forced to confront, in just three days, what had taken me far longer to comprehend.

"So this is my destiny? To lose you, and go through years of torture, watching you grow up? To shadow you all your life, taking pictures for that album, until the day I walk into that courthouse . . . and then to lose you again!"

"Just as my destiny was to be here with you. To have these months."

"It's not fair!" He was crying out, not at me, but at fate, or at the heavens, or maybe at God himself . . . at whatever or whoever was responsible for this onslaught of agony and confusion.

I tried to answer calmly. "Not much is, my love."

"It also makes no sense! It has no purpose! You tell me the missing girls are already dead—all victims of a single killer! But I can't arrest the sick bastard because that might change our history together, and even eliminate you—or even both of us—from existence!"

"Me, probably. At least, *this* me. Not you."

"And yet, thirty years from now, you and I will work together to track the killer down and bring him to trial?"

"Yes." I knew what was coming.

"But, even then, he still walks free! So what's the point, Claire? What's the point?"

"I don't know. But there must be a reason. It just isn't clear to us yet."

"How can we wait? How can *I* wait? I'm a cop. There's a monster out there, as bad as Bundy, and I'm not allowed to stop him!"

"If we don't wait, my past with you didn't happen, and your future with me never will. Maybe the whole point of my life *is* to change the future! But if that's true, and if we decide today to change history, logic says I will no longer exist. At least I will no longer exist here and now with you. Maybe another version of me will be born next year and live a life entirely different from the one I remember. Maybe I'll disappear into some parallel existence. I don't know. But your memories of me will surely disappear. How could they not? You'd have no reason to have them! You solved the case in 1978! Why would you watch over me as I grow up? Why would you follow me through school? Why would you even know I existed?"

"Because we're together right now, and I can touch you, and that memory is permanent. You will write a long letter to yourself, in your own handwriting, describing every minute we've had together. We'll include some photographs. When you're grown, I'll show you the letter. I'll make you love me again."

I steeled myself and said what had to be said: "If you're right, we might be together again . . . one day. If you're not, your memories will be gone, and the letter and even the photographs—if they continue to exist, which I doubt—will be meaningless to you. Are you willing to take that chance? I will, if you will. I'll write that letter, we'll take some Polaroid photographs, and then I will tell you everything."

He was silent for long, tortured seconds. Finally, with a gasp of pain, he capitulated to his doubts. "No. I'm too afraid to be wrong." He took me in his arms and spoke quietly in my ear. "But . . ."

"Yes?"

"You are certain another woman will die?"

"Yes."

"Then I will always hate myself."

Marc didn't speak for the rest of the day. I left him alone. He sat on the veranda for a while, and then went for a long boat ride on the lake. We ate a quiet supper and retired to bed early. The doctor had forbidden sex until a follow-up urine sample was cleared by the lab, but sex was the furthest thing from our minds. I lay there wrapped in Marc's arms, and after an eternity, I fell asleep.

I woke up once in the night and heard him weeping. I slipped my arms around him and he stopped. He'd been crying for us—and perhaps for himself, humiliated that I seemed to be the strong one.

But he was the strong one, not me. I knew that because I had seen the man he would become.

Marcus Daniel Hastings would bear a devastating, unthinkable burden for more than thirty years and never lose his sanity.

45

The English word "scheduled" normally conveys a fairly innocuous and businesslike concept. For death row inmates, of course, the word carries a rather more pitiless connotation—one that is anything but innocuous. As the days ticked by, the only difference between those luckless prisoners and Amanda Jordan was the fact that Harlan Tribe's last victim had no inkling of her impending fate.

Amanda was scheduled to be abducted on April 22, and she was scheduled to die, I surmised, very soon thereafter.

And I was going to let it happen.

But then something changed.

In the wake of the last two disappearances, Marc was spending long hours at work. He didn't want to be there. He was still reeling from my revelations and his experience on the Chan case. He knew his task force would never solve the crimes, and he just wanted to be with me.

He just wanted to spend every waking and sleeping minute with me and shut the world out of our lives.

I wasn't in good shape myself, psychologically or physically, and it was several days before I could bring myself to return to The Yearling. When I eventually showed up, Nonie welcomed me back, asked enough questions to satisfy herself that I had recovered enough to work, and then left me to get on with it. With Marc gone for days at a time, I ended up working ten straight days without a break. The disciplined schedule helped take my mind off my intractable dilemma—at least for a part of each day—and as time went by, I began to feel better physically. Even my appetite was returning.

On Monday, April 17, Marc drove me to Ocala for my scheduled follow-up visit with Dr. LaPierre. While Marc went off with our grocery list, I submitted to another ultrasound. Fifteen minutes later, Dr. LaPierre entered the consulting room.

Seeing the tension in my face, he quickly set me at ease. "Relax, Claire. It's good news."

I relaxed.

"Blood and urine results are fine, and the sonogram showed no anomalies. You'll be peeing just fine well into old age." He paused. "There is one thing, though."

My heart sank. "Is this about that old surgery?"

"Not exactly . . ."

He sat down.

I was a coward.

I was a coward because all the way home, I didn't say a word to Marc about what Dr. LaPierre had discovered. I just said I'd been given a clean bill of health and suggested we go home and make love.

But that was just a distraction.

I had to tell him.

The next morning, it was my turn to make breakfast. I went all out and produced what my mother used to call a "logger's breakfast"—sausages, bacon, eggs, hash browns, pancakes, and toast. When I set the plates on the table, Marc blinked.

I sat down, grinned at him, and started in.

"This is a lot of food," he observed.

"I guess it is." I poured maple syrup over the pancakes, sliced into the stack, and slid a triangle of sweetness into my mouth.

"I've never seen you eat that much."

"I've been sick, remember? All those antibiotics didn't help my appetite. I'm just getting it back."

"It seems more like you got somebody else's appetite back."

Tell him!

I set down my fork. "Marc."

"What?"

"I'm eating for two."

He leaned forward. "Are you saying you're pregnant?"

"No. But that's what the doctor is saying."

A grin started spreading across his face.

"I didn't even notice I'd missed my period. The ultrasound tipped them off, but it's too early to see much. The blood test was positive."

Tell him the other part!

"How far along are you?"

Bingo . . .

"They're not sure yet. Best guess is I'm due in November."

It didn't take a genius to count backwards. Marc's face registered uncertainty. "Claire, is this baby mine?"

Got it in one . . .

I sighed. "One way or another, this baby is yours."

"One way or another?" He swallowed. "Wait a minute, are you're saying—?"

"Yes. That's what I'm saying."

"You're saying I made love to you in 2011, and you're having our baby in 1978?"

"That depends on her date of birth. If it's in early November, then Old Marc is probably the father. Late November, probably you. Where the cutoff would be is anybody's guess. But either way, you're Dad."

He stared at me, speechless.

I picked a stray piece of bacon off my plate and nibbled at it. "You're not talking, Marc."

"Did you just say 'her date of birth'?"

"Her name is Rebecca."

"How could you know that?"

"You told me you had a daughter named Rebecca."

Marc looked sick. "This means . . ." He trailed off.

"For one thing," I said, trying to distract him with a bit of offbeat humor, "it means our daughter will be a year older than her mother, which has to be a first."

My ploy didn't work. Marc replied tonelessly, "It also means I'm going to be a single dad."

"Yes, it does."

I could see his mind working. "Claire . . ."

"Yes?"

"Your theory is that two of you can't exist in the same time period. That's why you think you'll cease to exist as an adult after your date of conception next March."

"That's right."

"But if you're right about that," he continued, speaking slowly, "and if Rebecca was conceived in the future *before* you stormed out of my life and boarded that train, she will cease to exist as an adult at the age of thirty-two."

The shock hit me.

I got up and left the kitchen. I stumbled out to the veranda. I vomited my breakfast over the railing. I leaned there, staring at the ground. I felt like dying.

I felt Marc's hands on my shoulders. "Morning sickness, or despair?"

I wiped my tears with my sleeve. "At this moment, I'm not sure there's a difference."

"Marry me."

"Wh-what?"

He turned me around and took my face in his hands. "Marry me!"

"How can I?"

"We're having a baby."

"That's very traditional of you, and I'd marry you in an instant, but—"

"But, what?"

"I have no ID."

"I can solve that."

"You're a police officer. You'd be breaking the law!"

"Yes. But it has to be done. Not for us . . . for Rebecca."

It took me a few seconds. "She needs a birth certificate!"

"Correct. You were hospitalized twice even though you had no ID. That wasn't a problem, because all any hospital cares about is getting its bills paid, and I took care of that. This time we're dealing with the state government. A 'father unknown' entry on a birth record isn't that uncommon. But . . . 'mother unknown'? I don't think so."

"You'd be risking your career."

"No choice. You're going to need a birth certificate and a Social Security number. Better have a driver's license, too, just in case. There's a guy I know. He owes me."

"In that case, get him to marry us."

"Huh?"

"It's just a piece of paper . . . isn't that what people say? So let's skip the ceremony and go straight to the piece of paper. Ask him for a marriage certificate. I want to be Claire Alexandra Hastings."

46

I walked into The Yearling just before five on Thursday afternoon. The first person I saw was a slim young woman in a blue print dress. She was perched on a stool at the far end of the bar, talking to Nonie.

She had her back to the door.

As I approached, a snatch of conversation drifted my way.

". . . mentioned some mysterious girlfriend. He said nobody's ever met her."

My step faltered.

Nonie spotted me. "Claire!" The young woman turned. She gave me a friendly smile.

I froze where I stood.

I looked at the young woman's face . . . at her dress with its distinctive blue pattern . . . back at her face . . .

Recognition hit me like a punch in the stomach.

"This lady is trying to track down Marc Hastings," Nonie said. "He's a cop in Gainesville . . . sort of a regular here. He used to come in every week or so. Owns a camp somewhere on one of the lakes." Nonie stopped. She fixed me with one of her perceptive looks. "But maybe you know all that," she finished.

I didn't answer.

"Reminds me of something I was going to tell you," Nonie continued. "Hastings came in here a day or two after you took sick. Teddy was on the bar. He says the guy was kinda persistent." Nonie glanced at Amanda and then fixed me in her sights. "He made it sound like police business."

I gave in. "He was looking for me, but not for that reason."

"That's good to hear."

Amanda had been listening quietly. Now she interposed, holding out her hand. "I'm Mandy Jordan, by the way."

"Claire . . . Claire Talbot." Her cool touch was like a jolt of electricity.

"Marc and I are old friends. I've been trying to reach him."

Since the cat was out of the bag, I said, "I'm staying at his place on Lochloosa."

"Great! Maybe you can help me? I left messages at his office, but he didn't call me back. I phoned his apartment in town a few times, but no answer. I want to ask him to my wedding." My mind was reeling as she continued in a confessional tone. "The thing is . . . Marc and I used to go out. So I didn't want to just drop the invitation at his office. I didn't want him to think I was, you know, leaving it just to slap him in the face. I'm not like that. I wanted to ask him in person. One of the detectives told me he's been spending a lot of time in Cross Creek. I remembered him telling me he had a camp out here somewhere. I figured this was the main bar in town, so I took a chance someone might know him."

Nonie interjected. "Actually, we're the only bar."

I was starting to feel light-headed. This was cutting too close. I managed to conjure a lame smile, and in the steadiest tone I could muster, I said, "I'm the mysterious girlfriend you were talking about."

Amanda's cheeks went pink. She put a hand on my arm. My eyes locked on it.

She was wearing the ring.

The ring with the cushion-cut topaz.

The one the police found in her grave.

"Oh! No, hey, that's great! I'm not here to stir up trouble! I'm really glad he found someone!" She took her hand away and prattled on. "He was always good to me! We just weren't . . . meant to be. I wanted to ask him in person, so he knows the invitation isn't just, you know"—she finished in a small voice—"me trying to be mean."

Somehow, I couldn't picture this sweet girl ever being mean.

By now my emotions were a heaving landscape of despair. I needed to end this conversation. "Mandy, that's really kind of you. I'll tell Marc you were looking for him, and I'll tell him what you said. Can he call you?"

She beamed. "Sure! In fact, would you give him this?" She took out a sealed envelope out of her purse. "My phone number is printed right on the invitation. I'm staying at my mom's right now." I was about to take the envelope when she said, "Wait! Let me just make this little change. . . ." She pulled out a pen and wrote something on the face of the envelope and then handed it to me.

Under the addressee's preprinted name, M. MARCUS HASTINGS, Amanda had added & Mlle. Claire Talbot.

I looked at it quizzically.

"My mom's French. She was studying over here when she met my dad. We have lots of relatives in France, so the invitations are in both languages."

"Are any of your French relatives coming over for the wedding?"

"Yes! Some of them I've never even met! It's going to be so great!"

I felt sick after Amanda Jordan left us, but I couldn't show it.

And now I had another problem.

"Want to tell me about it?" Nonie asked.

"About what?"

"Let's start with . . . Is 'Claire Talbot' your real name?"

" 'Claire' is," I conceded. No point in confusing things with extra bits of truth.

"I'm waiting," Nonie said quietly.

I didn't want to lie to her, but clearly I couldn't tell her the truth. So I spun the tale that Marc and I had agreed on in case of emergency: I had been a witness for the prosecution in a serious case. My life had been threatened, and Marc had been one of the detectives guarding me. I'd fallen for him—and he for me—but, of course, he couldn't let his bosses know, even after the trial ended. So I was living "incognita" at his place on the lake, and he was spending his free days with me there.

In other words, I was a kept woman, and in circumstances that could impair a certain police detective's chances for promotion.

Nonie didn't need me to spell it out.

"Don't worry about the other staff," she said, patting me on the arm. "I'll take care of it." And I knew she would.

That short interview with Nonie was a breeze compared with the one I was having with myself. I worked a full shift, and Nonie was kind enough to drive me home after we closed. But when I walked into the cabin, I couldn't remember a single thing I had said or done for the last eight hours.

There was only one thing on my mind: Amanda Jordan.

I went straight to bed, but sleep eluded me. I got up and opened a bottle of wine. I was about to drink myself senseless when I remembered . . .

You're pregnant.

A stray thought sliced across my mind, telling me that what I was planning now meant that my pregnancy didn't matter, but I still couldn't bring myself to drink, so I put the bottle away. The sun was lifting over the horizon before I finally fell asleep.

I woke at noon. As if to remind me of my condition, I immediately got sick. I didn't know whether it was morning sickness or the result of self-flagellation, but in a perverse way, I embraced my punishment.

After my stomach settled, I dressed and went for a walk.

A long walk.

It was nearly four in the afternoon when I returned to the cabin. I hadn't eaten in twenty-four hours, but the thought of food nauseated me. For my baby's sake, I forced down some soda crackers and a glass of milk.

I showered and went to work.

The next two days were hell. On Saturday morning, I capitulated and phoned Marc. For the first time since I had taken up residence in his life, I called him at the office. The switchboard put me through to the Joint Task Force.

A male voice answered. "Lipinski!"

Just my luck . . .

His voice wasn't as raspy as I remembered, but its familiar tone of off-hand negligence came through loud and clear. I gripped the receiver tighter, suppressed my disdain, and said, "Detective Hastings, please."

"Who's callin'?"

It wasn't hard to imagine how a timid witness might react to this slug's red carpet reception. It occurred to me that Lipinski might have been the reason the case was never solved.

"My name is Marjorie Rawlings. I'm with the phone company," I replied coolly.

There was a pause, and I heard a muffled "Hey, Hastings! Line three! Lady named Rawlings from the phone company. Maybe you should pay your bill!" followed by a coarse guffaw. The line went dead, and then Marc came on.

"Marc Hastings speaking."

"I was hoping you'd catch on."

"I did. Just a second . . ." I heard the creaking of a chair. "Okay," he said in a low voice. "What's wrong?"

"When will you be back?"

"Not sure. It looks like tomorrow night."

"I need you back, *today*."

"You mean . . . ?"

"Yes. I think we should talk."

"We already have."

"Marc! We can't ignore this! It's selfish and it's wrong!"

He was quiet for a second.

"How much time do we have?"

"It's tonight."

A pause. "I'll be there. I'll think of something."

47

Marc called just after three. I was lying on the couch. The ringing telephone roused me from a fitful stupor, awash in crimson dreams of violence.

"I'm leaving now," he said.

"God! Look at the time!"

"The lieutenant pulled me into a witness interview. I couldn't get away!"

"Hurry!"

There was another cold front moving through. I brewed a mug of tea, slipped on the jacket Marc had bought me, and waited in the rocking chair on the veranda.

He showed up forty minutes later.

He kissed me. "What's in the mug?"

"Tea."

"I think I want something stronger. Right back . . ."

"Marc!" But the screen door slammed and he was gone.

Somewhere a clock was ticking. I sat there listening to the trill of some unidentifiable songbird, trying desperately not to think.

Not to feel.

Marc reappeared with a shot of whisky. He dropped into the lounge chair next to me. Before I could say a word, he said, "Funny thing . . . after we talked, I was told we'll be working a lot of overtime for the next couple of weeks. The feds are saying this guy will hit again very soon. The abductions are getting closer together. The chief canceled everybody's leave—uniform, plainclothes, even the civilian staff."

"When are you due back at the office?"

"Tomorrow morning, eight sharp. But I have a feeling I won't be getting much sleep tonight."

"Neither of us will."

"Tell me."

"If they don't arrest the killer today, they never will! Four months from now, the FBI will pull out. Next spring, the task force will disband."

"You told me all this. I thought we'd made a decision. I thought we agreed we have no choice!"

"You sound like you don't want to know."

"I don't! I don't want to lose you!"

"I wasn't being fair to you. I should never have asked you to choose." My voice was shaking.

Marc set aside his drink. He pulled his chair closer. He took my hand. "You were just being fair to yourself! And most of all, to our baby! I get it! I do! I hate it, and I know you hate it, too, but I accept it. We'll win in the end."

"We can't be sure of that! Nothing I saw in the future pointed to that." I felt tears starting. I rubbed them away. "I'm beginning to think . . ."

"What?"

"That I'm really not here to preserve the future. That I'm here to change it. I'm here to save a life that needs to be saved."

"No! Listen! It's the future. We can't change it, and we shouldn't try! There's a higher purpose for you being here. There must be!"

"I met her."

"What?"

"On Wednesday. She came to The Yearling."

He stared at me. "You met the next victim?"

"Yes. And you know her."

"I know her?" He looked shaken.

"You told me from the beginning that you knew her. You told me when we were drinking that bottle of Margaux in your file room. Sometime later, Lipinski said there'd been talk that you and this girl had dated. Eventually you admitted to me she'd been your girlfriend. You said the relationship ended a year before she disappeared. But there wasn't a hint about any of that in your files. You must have edited it out."

"A year?" Marc was dumbfounded. "Are we talking about Mandy Jordan?"

I pulled the wedding invitation out of my jacket. "We've been invited to her wedding."

He blinked at the inscription on the envelope and then tore it open. He opened the card and quickly scanned the flowing script printed inside. His face went pale.

"Unless you and I do something," I said quietly, "your friend Mandy will die tonight."

The card dropped from Marc's hand. He shot out of his chair so quickly that, for a terrified second, I thought he was going to hit me. He lurched toward the railing, but before he reached it, he sank to his knees.

I went to him. I knelt and held him. "I've racked my brain," I whispered, "trying to understand why you tried to keep it from me—why you delayed telling me until the day we broke the case."

"Maybe," he croaked, "I didn't want you to start thinking I was the killer. *Her* killer."

"You mean, a copycat?"

"It's not unheard of . . . using a serial killer's modus to cover a targeted murder."

"But then there was this conversation."

He looked at me blankly.

"*This* conversation, Marc! The one we're having right now! There must have been a reference somewhere in the Amanda Jordan file to your previous relationship with her. But I never saw it mentioned. So did you edit it out *because* we had this conversation today? Or are we having this conversation today because you edited the files?"

He let out an explosive breath.

I continued. "I've just told you I met Amanda, so you—as Old Marc—knew that. You also knew I had revealed to you *ahead of time* that Amanda would be the next victim, because I've just done that. So the question is: Why did she die? Why didn't you save her?"

"Either I tried, and failed, or—"

"—*or you didn't try at all!*"

He was silent. He looked almost shamefaced.

"We need to make a choice, and we need to make it now! I can give you the information you need to save her! Do we save Mandy's life, and risk annihilating mine, along with Rebecca's, or do we allow her to be killed and spend our lives in guilt and torment? I can't make this decision, Marc. Only you can."

"Me?"

"If we stick to our original agreement and let Amanda Jordan die, you're the one who will be forced to carry the memory of that decision. I only have a year left. Next March I will be gone, and nine months later I will be born. I will have no conscious knowledge of any of this. Neither will Rebecca—assuming she is ever born. Of the three of us, only you will suffer the burden of guilt every waking moment of your life."

"But if we save her," he replied, his voice thick with emotion, "you never read a police file about her, the investigation will be forever altered, and even if you don't vanish completely from history, you and I might never meet in our altered lives. In that case, why does this feel so right?" He sobbed. "You and me, Claire! Why do we feel so right? Why?"

My heart was breaking, but I knew I had to be strong. I had been thinking about this for three days, and I thought I had an answer. It was a precarious, uncertain answer, but it was a plausible one. "After the killer's trial collapsed and I was suspended from my job, I was in despair. A killer had gone free and I couldn't fix it. I couldn't understand why you were calm. You said something strange. You told me I had *already* fixed it! You quoted a Chinese proverb to me. It was as if you wanted me to remember it. You said, 'Only the future is certain . . . the past is always changing.' "

"What did I mean?"

"You must have meant that I could change the past, and the future would survive. Now I'm here, in the past. If you stop Amanda from walking those few blocks to her girlfriend's house, and I don't tell you the abductor's name, there will still be seven missing women. There will still be an open investigation. You will still wait for me and help me solve the case."

I hadn't told him about the extra body. I didn't know if Jane Doe's death predated or postdated Amanda Jordan's, and I didn't see any value in complicating the discussion.

I could see Marc processing what I'd just said. I pressed the point. "My love, I think we can save Amanda and still go on. I'm willing to take that chance. Are you?"

His body stiffened. I saw new determination in his eyes. "Just time and place . . . that's all I need to know!"

"She's staying with her mother. Do you know where that is?"

"I've been there. It's near the high school in Newberry."

"One of Amanda's girlfriends is throwing a bridal shower for her. The girlfriend lives nearby, so Amanda will decide to walk. She'll never arrive. You need to save her without catching this monster in the act. All you need to do is drop by to see her. It's just a social call. Use the wedding invitation as an excuse. Tell her you wanted to RSVP in person, since she went to so much trouble to find you. Just make sure you drive her to her friend's house!"

"What time will she leave the house?"

"A little before seven."

Marc checked his watch. "It's nearly five already! How exact is that time?"

"The shower was set to start at seven. Her mother told the investigators she left the house just before that."

Marc took my face in his hands. "Will you be here when I get back?"

"I don't know. Maybe not."

"If you're not . . ."

"You'll have to wait for me, Marc. You'll have to wait until I'm thirty-one."

Tears rolled down his face. He folded me into his arms. He kissed my face, my lips. I wanted to die. He released me. He rose to his feet, picked up the wedding invitation, and walked out to his truck. He didn't look back.

Watching Marc Hastings drive away was the hardest thing I had ever done.

But it wasn't the last thing I ever did, because at six fifteen, the phone rang.

"The time . . . it was wrong." His voice was desolate.

"What are you saying?"

"She left the house at quarter to six."

"Her mother said seven! The police file said—!"

"You mean *my* file, Claire?"

"You changed it? You changed the time in the file!" I shouted at him in my confusion. "What were you thinking?"

"I don't know yet! How can I know now? I must have had a reason! Something important hasn't happened yet! What else can it be?"

"Marc! That beautiful girl is about to die!" I sobbed. "Look for a carpet! A rolled-up carpet! That's where she was taken. It's lying next to the road near her house. That's the spot. And set up a roadblock on the high-way to Cedar Key! The man you're looking for is driving a—!" The phone went dead.

Marc had hung up. He didn't want to know.

I must have fainted. I was still lying by the phone when Marc found me later that night. He lifted me off the floor and carried me to bed. I lay in his arms and wondered how long it would take before both of us went insane.

When I woke up on Sunday morning, Marc was gone, but he'd left a note.

The FBI guys want to talk to me. Mandy's mother told them about my visit. Don't worry. I'll show them the wedding invitation. Then I'll suggest we use a tracking dog. It might lead us to that carpet so I won't have to pretend I had a hunch. I love you, Claire. I will always love you. M.

48

"Keys are under the mat."

Nonie and I were standing in the doorway of the rear entrance to the kitchen. She had just agreed to lend me her car in return for a full tank of gas.

"It's a standard. Know how to drive one?"

"Yeah, no problem. How's the clutch?"

"Smooth as silk."

"Okay. Thanks. I'll be back in a few hours."

I believed the promise when I made it.

"If you don't mind me asking . . . where are you going?"

"Archer."

"Oh." She looked puzzled, but she didn't pursue it.

I couldn't tell her why I was going to Archer.

I couldn't tell her that when I woke up that morning, three days after Mandy Jordan's abduction, I just wanted to see my mother.

Maybe I needed to see her for comfort.

Or, maybe just to keep myself sane.

I don't know. I just knew I had to see her.

Nonie's '65 Chevelle was a basic six-cylinder model. The body had a few dents, but the engine had been well maintained and it ticked over smoothly. It took me longer to get from Cross Creek to Archer than I'd planned, mainly because the route I would have taken through Gainesville in 2011 was not continuous in 1978, which meant I had to make two detours along the way.

I parked a few hundred yards short of my destination and walked the rest of the way. The playground was empty. I sat on a swing and watched the green clapboard house across the road.

After a while, my mother appeared. She came around the corner of the house, carrying a short rake and a five-gallon bucket. She was wearing the old pair of Helly Hansen waterproof pants she had always used for gardening.

I watched as she began working her way along the hibiscus hedge, clearing detritus from under the bushes. The bushes were in bloom, alternating in white, red, and yellow, which was how my parents had planted them when they first bought the house.

It was surreal.

I was watching my mother working in her garden a year and a half before I was born. She didn't know I existed. She didn't know I would ever exist. She didn't know she would get pregnant just when she was thinking about divorcing my father. She didn't know she'd stay with him for my sake. She didn't know he would eventually leave us and never return.

She didn't know anything.

I almost wept.

I felt conspicuous where I was sitting, so I moved into a nearby grove of trees. Settling on the cool grass, I was about to resume my surveillance of my mother when I saw it.

It wasn't the car itself that first caught my attention; it was the way it was being driven. It was creeping along the shoulder of 174th Street toward the corner where the road bends and becomes Mcdowell. Its wheels moved soundlessly on the grass. It stopped a hundred feet or so to my left. I squinted at it through the afternoon glare. The driver was definitely male, but he was slouched low and I couldn't make out facial features.

The car was a gray four-door Plymouth.

I felt a prickling sensation on the back of my neck.

With rising horror, I leapt to my feet and ran.

I made it back to Nonie's car in less than a minute. Praying I wouldn't be too late, I started the engine, peeled out, and drove straight toward my mother's house. I slowed, peering for my father's car. It was nowhere to be seen. I swung the wheel hard, drove into the driveway, and stopped.

As I stepped out of the car, my mother rose to her feet. I swallowed hard and strolled toward her.

"Hi, there!"

"Hello. Can I help you?"

"Yes, I—" My voice stopped in my throat. I coughed nervously and then blurted the first thing I could think of. "I . . . I'm sorry to bother you. I think I'm lost. I'm trying to get to . . . Newberry."

"Oh! You've taken a few wrong turns, I'm afraid. You'll need Route 45. If you drive down this way"—she pointed down 173rd—"that will take you back to Route 24. Turn right and look for the sign for Route 45. Turn left there and it will take you right into Newberry."

I was enthralled to hear my mother's voice, still young and textured with hope. At the same time, I was afraid. I peered past her shoulder. From where I was standing, the house blocked the gray car from my view. I needed the driver to see me. I needed him to know my mother wasn't alone, so I kept moving closer to her as she spoke.

When she finished, I thanked her. "Could you tell me how far it is? To Newberry."

"Oh, I'd say about ten miles. It shouldn't take long once you're on Route 45."

Now I could see the gray car. I needed to stretch out our conversation. "This is an amazing hedge!" I gushed. "What are these bushes? They're gorgeous!"

My mother flushed with pride, and I wanted to hug her.

"They're hibiscus."

"Of course! I always get them mixed up with . . . what are those other flowers?"

"Bougainvillea?"

"That's it! These are beautiful! I just love the way you've alternated the colors!"

My mother's answering smile was the one I had always loved. It was a rare smile, reserved for almost no one. It washed over me like a warm evening breeze, and I nearly broke down. Desperate to distract myself, I singled out a prominent red bloom on the bush next to me and stooped to smell it. I knew hibiscus had no discernible scent, but I needed the misdirection so she wouldn't see the tears in my eyes.

When I touched the blossom, it broke off and dropped to the ground.

I straightened. My mother was staring. Her face wore a strange expression.

"I'm sorry. It just fell when I touched it."

"It's okay." She hesitated. "It's odd, but you seem familiar."

I am, Mom. I am. Then a memory from our last Christmas together came back with a shock.

She will always remember this moment.

At last, I understood.

Behind her, I saw the gray Plymouth speed past. I began to back away. "Good-bye, Margaret."

Her eyes widened. "You know my name?"

"Yes. And I want you to remember something."

"What?"

"This moment."

I got into the Chevelle and started the engine. I reversed into the street. My mother and I exchanged one long look.

She gave me a puzzled little wave as I drove away.

Ahead, the Plymouth sped toward Route 24. Struggling to catch my breath after the flood of emotions, I followed. I had almost caught up to it when it reached the main highway.

It turned left.

So did I.

At last, I understood why I was here.

I was here to protect my own mother.

The highway was almost die-straight. Traffic was light, and for long stretches there were no vehicles between us. I hung back, but never let the Plymouth out of my sight. I still had no wristwatch, but according to the clock on the dash, it took us fifty minutes to reach Cedar Key.

Fifty minutes to plan my next moves.

Despite my efforts, by the time I crossed the bridges over the marshlands separating Cedar Key from the mainland, the Plymouth had vanished. I found myself facing a looping wood-decked pier and, beyond, the waters of the Gulf of Mexico. I knew the central part of the town was fairly small—and I could see it was much less built-up than I remembered—so I backtracked and drove a grid, working my way back to the shoreline.

I didn't expect to find the Plymouth. I was just eliminating possibilities.

I parked and walked onto the pier. I thought of it as a pier, but in reality it was a raised roadway sweeping out over the shore of the Gulf. In years to come, it would undergo a series of kitsch renovations and transform itself into a tourist attraction, but today it supported perhaps a dozen weatherworn structures and had the ramshackle atmosphere of a fishing village that had seen better days.

I picked my way down a bouncing ramp to a floating wharf. An old man was perched on the stern deck of a battered Hatteras, cleaning fish. An attentive audience of gulls and pelicans had gathered around, patiently eyeballing his every move. As I approached, a pair of pelicans moved politely aside so I could join the crowd. I tried to engage the fisherman in idle conversation. His initial responses were laconic and uninterested, but he became slightly more voluble when he raised his head and saw he was speaking with a young woman.

I got to the point. "I'm looking for a man named Harlan Tribe."

The old man scowled. "Ever heard of The Crab's Eye, young lady?"

His question caught me off guard. I answered cautiously. "I think so."

"Well, that's where you'll find the bastard!" He jabbed a gloved finger toward a point in space over my shoulder.

I turned. Behind me, a row of weathered buildings squatted on a forest of creosoted pilings. A sign on the structure at the far left read:

THE CRAB'S EYE

SEAFOOD SPECIALS DAILY

I entered through a set of double doors. The interior was an incongruous aggregation of driftwood paneling, red linoleum flooring, and black Formica-topped tables. Dim overhead fixtures combined with the spill of dirty gray light from salt-rimed windows to provide marginal illumination. The restaurant section was empty, but there were a few customers in the bar area. They were all male, and every one of them gave me his full attention when I entered.

I was carrying a newspaper that I'd fished out of a trash bin. I walked up to the bar.

A gum-chewing, overweight barman looked me up and down as I approached. "Ma'am?"

"I'll have whatever's on tap."

"Don't get many single women in here," he stated pointedly.

"Oh, haven't you heard?" I asked.

"Heard what?"

"About women's lib. It's all the rage up north."

He snapped his gum. "You mean them hippie women, burning their bras 'n' shit?"

"You're very astute."

"'A-stoot'?"

"Yes. It means 'smart.'"

"Guess I can hold my own."

I leaned forward conspiratorially. "You know what those women are saying?"

"What?"

"They're saying they want to be equal to men. But you know what *I* say?"

"What?"

"I say they lack ambition."

He gave me a blank look. I decided I'd rather have my drink than spar with an unarmed man, so I offered a suggestion. "Why don't we just say I'm meeting a guy here, and I'll have that beer while I wait?"

He chewed on that for a second. "Pabst okay?"

"Sure."

He drew a glass for me. "Buck 'n' a half."

I dropped two dollars on the bar. "Keep it."

He looked confounded, as if tip-leaving women were an unsettling novelty in his microscopic world. I picked up the glass and moved to a booth in the back. I sat down, ignoring the stares, and opened my newspaper. I pretended to read while I waited.

Forty minutes later, the door behind the bar swung open and Harlan Tribe walked in.

He was unmistakable. He was even dressed the same, in stovepipe slacks and a white dress shirt, as the man in Anna Fenwick's photo album. The only thing missing was the thin tie. He muttered something to the barman, and I heard the guy reply, "Yessir. He'll be in at six."

Tribe nodded and slid into the booth closest to the bar. Earlier I had noticed an old crank-style adding machine sitting on the table, along with a scattering of papers.

Tribe was positioned facing me, so I slipped lower in my seat. After a few minutes, I heard him cranking the adding machine.

By now, some of the earlier drinkers had decamped and the stragglers had lost interest in ogling me. I took advantage of their inattention, slid out of the booth, and left.

I walked back to my car and retraced my route across the marshes to the mainland. Nothing looked the same as I remembered, but I found the turnoff on the second try. After that, I had no trouble. The driveway's white marker stakes were in exactly the same place, but now they were freshly painted. I kept going and parked in a cleared area around the next blind curve.

I set out on foot through the pines.

I reached the clearing and stood stock-still, staring numbly. Tribe's cottage was brightly painted in white and sea green. The corrugated iron roof glinted in the sun, revealing not a hint of rust. The surrounding lawn was trimmed and neatly bordered. Flowers bloomed from beds set around the base of every tree within fifty feet of the residence. The overall effect was nothing like the one that had met my eyes on that fateful future day when Marc and I emerged from the rutted driveway into this same clearing. On that day, the dilapidated shell had hidden a barbarous secret. I knew it held the same secret today, but in this pristine condition, it no longer looked the part.

I stepped out of the woods and walked directly to the veranda. I checked the front door. It was locked. I walked around to the back door.

Locked.

I returned to the front. The crab's eye vines were in bloom, a riot of red and purple flowers. I knelt down and searched the ground below, but it had been swept clean. I craned, scanning the sterile area under the raised porch.

There!

Straining to reach, my fingers closed on a dried seedpod. I stood up, took one last shuddering look at the cottage, and retraced my steps back to the car.

There was one piece missing, but I had an ominous feeling it would find me.

49

It was nearly dark when Nonie dropped me at the cabin. I had kept her waiting two hours beyond the end of her shift, but she forgave me. "Count yourself lucky!" she replied after I handed over her keys and apologized.

"Why?"

"'Cause while I was waitin', I picked up twenty bucks in tips."

Marc was sitting on the veranda. He came down the steps to meet me, waved to Nonie, and gave me a hug. "I was a bit worried. Where were you?"

"Just went for a drive."

"With Nonie?"

"No. I borrowed her car. I wanted to visit a few places." I grinned at him, trying to give some propulsion to the lie. "I wanted to see how they looked thirty years ago."

"Very funny. What places?"

I rattled off a list of the places I had quickly driven by on my way back from Cedar Key, including my high school (it looked the same), my town house development (a plant nursery, just as Marc had said), the State Attorney's Offices (I found them in an old bank building), and the Criminal Justice Center (restaurants and a bicycle repair shop).

We made drinks and sat on the veranda.

"I need to be sure of something, Claire."

I sensed what was coming.

"I need to be absolutely sure that Amanda was the last one."

I took his hand and said, "I'm certain she was. There were no other missing girls in your files."

He let out a long, pent-up sigh.

Technically, I had spoken the truth . . . but I was lying. I was lying to the man whose devotion to me had spanned decades. I was lying to the man who waited thirty years just to spend a few final months with me before I was torn from his arms forever.

I was lying to him because I loved him, but the sickness I felt inside threatened to drive me insane.

That night, as I stood at the dresser brushing my hair, Marc appeared behind me. He kissed my neck. "I want you to have something." He slipped a chain around my neck. "It was my mother's, and her mother's before that. I want you to have it, no matter what happens."

My heart sank.

The final piece had found me, as I knew it would.

Marc fumbled with the clasp. "If it disappears with you next year, at least I will know you had it. I will know you carried something of me with you at the end, when you went on to make a new beginning."

My fingers felt the locket. I held it up to my eyes. It had a cobalt blue enameled cover, embossed with a white Tudor rose.

Marc felt my shudder. "What's wrong?"

"It's just that, for us, nothing can be ordinary. Nothing can be what I deserve or you deserve, and it's killing me." I turned into his arms and buried my face in his chest. "Thank you for the locket, my love. Now, take me to bed."

At five o'clock in the morning on April 26, 1978, I decided to change the past.

MARCUS

50

There was no mistaking the distinctive sound.

The cranking Mopar starter jerked him from a deep sleep. He heard the engine catch and tires rolling on gravel. He leapt from the bed and stumbled to the window . . . in time to see his pickup's taillights disappear into the trees.

He wheeled around.

The bed was empty.

"Claire!" he yelled, hoping against fading hope that his truck had been stolen.

No reply.

He ran naked from the bedroom to the bathroom to the kitchen.

He found the note.

My dear love,

Your future self once told me the past is always changing. I have come to believe you were giving me a message. You were telling me I would change the past.

If I succeed, you will forget me. Every trace of me—even this note I'm writing now—will cease to exist. I can only hope that one day, against all odds, you will find me again, and we will have a different future together . . . a better future, without the endless tyranny of pain we are facing today.

Just know that I love you more than life, and I am doing this for us.

Claire

Thirty seconds later, he discovered that his service revolver was missing.

It took him until noon to find Nonie Friedrichsen.

It was a six-mile walk from his camp to the rented house Nonie shared with her on-again, off-again truck driver boyfriend. He stopped at The Yearling on the way, but it was locked up tight and the parking lot was empty. When he reached Nonie's house, her car was gone and no one answered his knock. He waited on the porch for two hours, and then hiked back to The Yearling. Teddy was behind the bar. He said Nonie was due on at twelve.

Marc was standing in the parking lot when she drove up.

She got out of her car and walked quickly toward him, alarm on her face. "It's Claire, isn't it?"

"I went to your house."

"I was at the dentist. What's happened?"

"She's gone. She took my truck."

Claire's note stayed in his pocket. It would be impossible to explain its contents.

"Archer," Nonie stated flatly.

"How do you know?"

"I don't. But that's where she went last time, when she borrowed my car."

"Did she tell you why?"

Nonie answered warily. "No, and I didn't ask."

"Will you lend me your car?"

"No."

"Why?"

"Claire might need a witness."

He looked at her appraisingly. "You think she's seeing someone else. You're afraid I'll hurt her."

"Something like that."

"I wouldn't hurt her, Nonie. Not in a thousand lifetimes. Would you drive me?"

She didn't hesitate. "I'll tell Teddy." Nonie hurried into the bar and reappeared in less than a minute. She handed her car keys to Marc. "In case we break a few speed limits. You're the one with the badge."

They got in the car, wheeled out of the lot, and headed north.

"Route 346 is shorter. Not by much, but maybe less traffic."

"I know." He made the turn.

Nonie looked over at him. He was staring intently ahead, his eyes damp with suppressed emotion, his knuckles white on the wheel.

"Is there?" she asked quietly.

"Is there what?"

"Is there someone else?"

He took a deep breath. "Yes. But not like that. In fact, not in any way you could possibly imagine."

He drove on while Nonie pondered his cryptic answer.

And while Marc Hastings wondered if he and Nonie would find Claire Talbot before both of them forgot she existed.

Ninety minutes later, when they found his truck, he still remembered Claire.

He just wasn't sure how long the memory would last.

CLAIRE

51

It was still dark outside. Sunrise was an hour away and Marc was asleep. I got dressed in the kitchen—jeans, T-shirt, runners, and one of Marc's zip-up windbreakers. I slid his gun into my pocket, left a note on the counter, grabbed his truck keys, and slipped silently out of the cabin.

Above, wisps of cloud moved like wraiths across a crystalline sky, and the air smelled of jasmine. But I barely noticed. I was an automaton. I got in the truck, snicked the door shut as quietly as I could, and turned the key. When the engine caught, I backed away fast, spun a 180, and made for the highway. I bounced and banged at breakneck speed along the bush road, hit the asphalt with a squeal of rubber, and headed north.

I was driving like a woman possessed, but I didn't care.

This time, I didn't take the long way through Gainesville. I had mapped out a shorter route, using County Road 346. It saved only six or seven miles, but I figured there'd be fewer traffic cops—especially at five thirty in the morning—and I was right. I made it to Archer in thirty-five minutes.

I drove past our house. The windows were dark, and as I expected, my father's car wasn't there. I circled to the far side of the playing field that adjoined the playground. I parked near the base of the water tower, where Marc's truck would be screened behind a row of gum trees.

I took the locket off my neck and opened it. I cracked the seedpod I'd taken from Tribe's cottage. Crab's eye peas spilled out. I put one in the locket, snapped it shut, and then slid the locket and chain into my pocket.

The clock on the dash said 6:10 A.M.

I checked Marc's gun. It was fully loaded, as I'd known it would be. I left the truck keys in the ashtray, got out, and walked across the field to the grove of trees near the playground. During my visit the day before, I had noticed a well-concealed observation point just inside the fence.

I sat down and waited.

By ten o'clock, the only sign of life I'd seen was my mother. She was working her way around the inside of the house, washing windows.

I had already decided that if Tribe didn't appear by noon, I'd hunt him down.

But then he showed up.

I almost missed him because this time he was parked facing the wrong way on the left shoulder of 173rd. Thick brush had screened his arrival. I have no idea how long he had been there before the sound of the Plymouth's idling engine penetrated my consciousness. I crept slowly toward the car until I found cover about twenty feet away.

Tribe had a newspaper propped on his steering wheel, but he wasn't reading it. His eyes were locked in feral intensity on my mother's house.

Seconds later, my mother appeared in the front yard, tugging a garden hose.

In horrifying slow motion, I watched Tribe lay aside his newspaper.

He's going for her!

By the time his right hand reached the gearshift, I had already covered most of the distance that separated us. I vaulted the fence on pure adrenaline and reached the driver's-side rear door just as the Plymouth thumped into gear. I wrenched the door open and dived into the rear compartment.

The car stopped rolling. Tribe craned behind him. I drove my fist into his face. He cried out and scratched at me like a cat, clawing air.

I jammed Marc's .38 into his cheek. He froze and went pale.

"Drive!" I barked.

"What is this?" he whined.

I pressed the muzzle hard against his cheekbone. "Drive, you bastard, or die right here!"

He corkscrewed away, pawing for the door latch. I clocked him on the side of the head with the gun. He bleated.

"You don't get it, do you? I said drive!"

He probed at his scalp with his fingertips. They came away covered in blood. His whimper gave me a sudden rush of pleasure. "Now, Tribe!" He hunched in defeat and put his hands on the wheel. The car pulled onto the pavement. I knelt behind him, with the revolver pressed against his neck.

"Route 24!"

As we rolled past our house, I saw my mother standing in her yard. She was staring at the Plymouth. Then she spotted me. I saw her take an uncertain step forward. Then she was swept from my view.

"Left here," I ordered when we reached the highway.

Tribe tried to turn his head. I prodded him with the gun. "Eyes on the road, Tribe!"

"What the fuck is this?"

"A kidnapping! You're familiar with the concept, I believe."

"How do you know my name?"

"Where I come from, you're notorious." There was no traffic visible in either direction. "Go!"

"You won't get away with this!"

"I already have! Just shut up and drive!"

"Where?"

"To your pretty little cottage on the river . . . where else?"

"How do you—?"

"I know everything, Tribe! From here on, you and I are just playing roles."

"Woman, you're crazy!"

I jabbed him with the gun. "And that means I'm dangerous! Not another word! Get moving!" The car picked up speed.

With a killer at the wheel, we rolled down the highway toward Cedar Key.

The Plymouth coasted to a stop in front of the cottage.

"Stay where you are!" I ordered. I got out of the car and positioned myself. I trained the gun on Tribe. "Now, get out!"

He opened the door slowly and stepped out.

"Back door!"

He started walking. I followed, staying five feet behind him. We passed the front corner of the veranda and started down the side of the building. Tribe walked slowly, hugging the wall. I kept my eyes locked on him. As we approached the rear corner of the building, I saw his shoulders tense. I knew instantly what he would do. I looped wide, keeping my steps silent on the lawn.

At the corner, Tribe ducked left and bolted.

In one step, I was clear of the corner. I took careful aim and shot him in the right leg. Tribe pitched sideways, straight into a crab's eye bush, and lay there, tangled in vines, yipping like a kicked puppy. I strode over.

"You shot me!" he bawled.

"Yes, I did. Get up!"

"I can't! You shot me!"

"You already said that. I put the slug in your thigh. The bone's not broken." I pointed the gun at his head. "Get up, or die right here!"

Whining and grimacing, he struggled out of the bush, got to his knees, and finally to his feet. He stood there, swaying and whimpering.

"Move!"

Groaning, he limped and hopped to the back door. He stood there, looking stupid.

"Open it!"

He made a show of patting at his pockets and then looked at me. "Keys are in the car."

I swung the gun up. Tribe scrambled backwards, tripped, and fell on his ass.

I fired. The lock disintegrated.

"Jesus!" Tribe yelled.

I pointed the gun at him. "He's no friend of yours! *Up!*"

He rolled on his side, pushed himself to his knees, and crawled to the door. He used the handle to pull himself to his feet. He nudged the door open.

We entered.

The cottage was as tidy and pristine inside as it was outside. It was nothing like the decaying shell Marc and I had entered on our ill-starred warrantless search. The dogtrot hallway was laid in glazed tile. One wall was papered with a damask design; the ceiling and opposite wall were painted white. The kitchen, immediately to the left, was clean and fully equipped.

"I gotta stop this bleeding!"

I nodded. Tribe hopped into the kitchen. As if to dramatize the gravity of his wound, he came down hard on each hop, making the floor shake. The effect seemed deliberate.

He pulled a tea towel out of a drawer and bound his leg. He glared me. "So, what're we doin' here?"

I jerked my thumb, pointing behind me. "In there!" I stepped back.

He limped past me, into the living room. I followed.

The wagon-wheel furniture I'd seen on my last visit now looked like it had just been delivered from the factory. I pointed at the rug in the small dining area.

"Pull it back!"

"What?"

"You heard me!"

He stared at me.

"Now, Tribe!"

"The table . . ."

"Move it!"

Slowly, moving from side to side, he shifted the table into a corner so its legs were clear of the edge of the rug. He stooped and pulled the rug away.

The trapdoor was there, with an inset ring to lift it.

I gestured with the gun. Tribe grabbed the ring and swung the door up. Instead of lowering it to the floor, he let it go. It dropped with a loud bang.

"You first," I said.

He scowled. "You won't get away with this!"

I fired a slug into the floor between his feet. He yelped and staggered back.

"I will, Tribe!" I yelled. "I definitely will!"

He scuttled forward, gulping breaths, put his foot on the top step, leaned on the floor, and started down.

"Turn on the light!"

He pawed under the floorboards. I heard a click.

"When you get to the bottom, stand away!"

I stood above the opening as he hobbled his way down. When he reached the bottom, he stepped away as I had ordered.

I started down. I could still see his feet. I kept my eyes on them as I descended.

When I was two steps from the bottom, he lunged for my legs. His feet had already given him away, so I was ready. I shot him through the arm. He yelled and fell backwards, out of my view. When I reached the bottom step, Tribe was folded up on the dank earthen floor like a pesticide-sprayed spider, clutching his bleeding arm and glowering.

"You stinkin'—!" he rasped.

"Shut up!"

"What now? What do you want?"

"To start with, a confession."

"What the fuck you talkin' about?"

"Let's start with where you're sitting! Three feet below your scrawny ass is Constance Byrne! She was number two. She was hitchhiking to Cedar Key when you grabbed her. Right there—" I pointed at the ground to his right. "—is María Ruiz. She was number five! There"—pointing again— "Ina Castaño! She was the first, wasn't she? Bet you scared yourself. But then it got easier, didn't it? Over in that corner, Patricia Chapman!"

Tribe stared at me in shock.

"Where is Amanda Jordan?" I hissed.

Tribe didn't answer. He just stared at me and then looked to his right. I swung my head. A beat-up old mattress lay on the floor, pushed up tight against the wall. I kept my gun trained on Tribe as I backed over to take a closer look. The mattress was stained and filthy.

I strode back over to him and shoved Marc's gun in his face. *"Where is she?"* I yelled.

His jawline tightened. His expression hardened.

"So . . . she's already dead!"

I hadn't expected to save Mandy, but I had nurtured a lingering hope that I would find her alive. I knew the consequences, but I'd come ready for them.

I had come prepared to change the past, and even her death wasn't going to deter me.

"I don't get it, Tribe."

"Get what?"

"Why you didn't bury her here, with your other . . . girlfriends."

He sneered. "How do you know I didn't?"

I cocked the hammer of the gun.

Tribe's eyes burned. "Ran outta room."

I studied him. "Psychos like you usually start younger. So either you're a late bloomer, or you killed women we don't know about. How many? How many have you killed?"

"'We'? Who's we?"

"I asked you . . . how many?"

"Eight."

So . . . I'm right.

I am Jane Doe.

I examined my own skeleton.

There can be two of me . . . but one of me has to be dead.

"Why crab's eyes?"

His cheek twitched. "They die a piece at a time."

My mind recoiled, but before this ended, I wanted answers.

"Is there a point to that? Other than sick sadism?"

"They'll do anything for the antidote."

"There isn't one."

Tribe ignored me. He clutched at his arm. "I need a doctor!"

"What made you so sick, Tribe?"

"It's not me." He licked his lips. "You fixin' to kill me?"

"And bury you in this cellar? Now, wouldn't that be justice?"

His gaze shifted to the stairs behind me, then back to me. He straightened his back. "I don't know where ya came from, bitch, or why yer here or how ya found me, but I know one fuckin' thing—you ain't got the nerve to kill me!"

An eerie calm washed over me.

It was time.

"You don't understand, do you?" I cocked the gun.

Tribe shrank back, his eyes wide. "Understand what?"

I aimed between his eyes. "Only the future is certain. The past can be changed."

52

The blow came from behind. A split second before I was hit, an unholy animal screech shattered the cellar. The gun flew from my hand as I landed in a sprawl on the cellar floor, my head an inch from the cottage's stonework foundation.

I was half-stunned, but my instincts kicked in just in time. I rolled to see a wild-haired woman launching herself at me. I kicked at her. My foot caught her in the stomach, but she kept coming. I had a flashing glimpse of Tribe, crawling toward us on his hands and knees, his eyes bright with malevolent glee. Then the shrieking woman was swarming over me, ripping at my face and neck with her fingernails. We rolled and wrestled until she was on top of me with her fingers around my throat. I twisted in vain to get away. She had me pinned. But my left arm was free. I grabbed a handful of dirt and threw it in her eyes. When she reared back, I punched her. It was a weak blow, and she shrugged it off. She attacked again with her claws.

I had been ready to die, but I wasn't ready to lose a fight. I grabbed the woman's ear and ripped it off.

She howled like a demon from hell and tore at my throat.

I caught movement to my left. Tribe had Marc's gun. He stretched out his arm, aiming at my head.

So this is how it ended, I thought hazily.

And then my brain shrieked at me:

CLAIRE! YOU'RE NOT JANE DOE!

Frantically, I seized Tribe's wrist and twisted.

BOOM!

The gunshot was deafening.

Time seemed to dilate . . . slow . . . stop.

The woman toppled sideways.

I rolled to my left and snatched the gun out of Tribe's now slack fingers. I kicked the woman's legs off my own and rose unsteadily to my feet. My right knee throbbed.

My attacker lay motionless in the dirt. A trickle of blood oozed from a bullet hole near her right temple.

Tribe crawled to her. "Doris? Doris!" He touched her cheek and started moaning. "No . . . No . . . No!"

"Tribe?" He ignored me. I left him to blubber while I took inventory. I had no broken bones, but I was bleeding from a dozen scratches and lacerations on my face, throat, and upper body. My shirt was covered in the other woman's blood; most of it, I guessed, from her torn ear rather than from the gunshot wound.

Tribe was hunched like a ghoul over the woman's corpse, his spidery fingers stroking her matted hair.

I prodded him with my foot. "Look at me!"

He raised his head. His face was a mess of tears and snot.

"Is this your sister?"

"Yes!" He spit the word at me.

"So, it was a lie. She didn't die in India." I answered his shocked expression. "Yes. We know that, too. But what we don't know is why. Why, Tribe, *why?*"

His jaw started working, as if he was about to hurl himself at me. I pointed the gun at his face. *"Answer me!"* I yelled.

"Yeah, I took them girls, 'n', yeah, I screwed 'em! We both did! But I never killed 'em! Not one of 'em! It was her!"

"She killed them?"

"Yeah. After she finished."

"Finished what?"

"Her experimentin'. When she was done, she'd just up their dose."

I felt my gorge rise. Less than ten percent of serial killers are female, and almost all of them kill for money or power. A woman who kills for sadistic pleasure is extremely rare.

But . . . one who employs a willing partner?

It beggared belief.

"How did you do it? No witnesses! How did you make them vanish?"

His eyes went cold. "Nobody notices a girl talkin' to a girl. I just drove the car."

"You were alone! *Today!* Stalking my . . . Stalking that woman!"

"Doris was coming with me tomorrow."

My mind sighed relief.

That's why you're here, Claire. To save your mother.

I leaned down. "Why? Why did you help her?"

"She was my sister!" he wailed.

I stared into Harlan Tribe's uncomprehending eyes for a few seconds and then turned away. I limped over to the stairs. As I reached the bottom step, a cramp hit me. The pain started low in my abdomen, and then sliced like a hot knife into my lower back.

I gasped.

No!

I grabbed for the stair railing. I waited. It hit me again. I doubled. I waited.

Slowly, interminably, it eased.

I waited for another.

It didn't come.

I looked at Tribe. He hadn't noticed. He was still sniveling over his sister's body.

"One more question, Tribe . . ."

"Ain't ya gonna kill me?"

I wanted to.

I wanted to end this vermin's existence. One bullet through his head, and I would permanently eliminate myself from this time line. In eighteen months, I would be born. I would grow to become a different Claire Talbot. I would have no consciousness of all the young lives Harlan Tribe had destroyed.

My failure to save Victoria Chan and Mandy Jordan was like a garrote around my throat.

It would take only one bullet.

But now I knew I wasn't Jane Doe.

Now I knew I had a daughter to protect.

"Not today," I said.

Tribe glowered at me. "You said you got a question."

"Who got Doris pregnant?"

He didn't reply. He didn't have to. His eyes told me everything I needed to know. I took the locket out of my pocket and tossed it over to him. It landed in the dirt next to him.

"That belongs to your sister."

He stared at it, uncomprehending.

I dropped the gun on the floor. "There's one bullet left. I suggest you use it on yourself." I started up the steps. "I'll know if you don't."

53

I was back in Archer by late afternoon. I rolled past my mother's house and worked my way south to 147th Street. A sign warned: NO EXIT. I drove to the end of the road and stopped at a cemetery beside a small church. The road's unpaved extension followed the south edge of the graveyard and terminated in dense brush.

I had a table knife and a grocery bag with me, taken from Tribe's kitchen when I left. I used the knife as a screwdriver and removed the car's license plates. Next I pried the VIN plate off the dash and scraped the build sheet off the doorpost. From my work on the Martínez case, I knew where to look for the second VIN plate. I lifted the hood. It was right where I'd expected, riveted to the top of the driver's-side fender. I pried it off. There was still a derivative number stamped into one of the radiator supports, but I couldn't do much about that. I cleaned out the glove box and searched the rest of the car, grabbing anything that might identify the owner. I dumped everything into the grocery bag and set it on the floor. Then I got behind the wheel and stomped on the accelerator. I was doing nearly fifty when I ran out of road. The Plymouth punched through a hundred feet of scrub before it high-centered and stalled.

I grabbed the bag, climbed out of the car, and started walking. With my bad knee, it took me nearly an hour. Along the way, I tossed Tribe's license plates and keys into the bush at intervals along the roadside and dropped the rest into the playground trash can.

Tribe would have to explain his gunshot wounds. I remembered that when Annie had run Tribe's name during our investigation, his only record was as a victim who had been shot during a robbery. He'd probably tell them some perp shot him and stole his car. Next, he'd require surgery to remove the bullets. The slug in his leg was still there; the one in his arm might have gone through.

Until he obtained another vehicle and his wounds healed enough to lift a body into the trunk, he'd be forced to stash his sister's putrefying corpse in the cellar.

It would take only one anonymous tip to send him to death row.

But Marc and I had only eleven months left, and we had a baby on the way.

As I crossed the playing field, I saw Nonie's Chevelle parked behind Marc's truck. The car's doors swung open, and Marc and Nonie stepped out.

Marc took one look at my bleeding face and rushed toward me. He reached me just as my knee gave out. He lunged and managed to break my fall. He hoisted me into his arms and carried me to the truck. Nonie pulled the passenger door open so he could lift me onto the seat.

"How did you know I'd be here?"

"I didn't. But you told Nonie where you went when you borrowed her car."

The terrible strain of the day had visibly aged him. His eyes were rimmed with red. I felt sick with shame.

He reached behind the seat and yanked out a first aid kit.

"I have things to tell you," I whispered.

"Later." He opened the kit. "First we need to take care of that bleeding!"

I grabbed his hand. "Marc, I made a mistake!"

Nonie sensed she was intruding. She eased away from us and stood by her car.

"More than one, I'd say," Marc said as he ripped open a gauze pack.

"I was so fixed on changing the past, I forgot the future is certain."

He stopped what he was doing. "Meaning?"

"Meaning . . . no matter what I do, you and I will be together in the future."

"I've already figured that out."

"How?"

"Because whatever you tried today didn't work. When I saw you walking across that field, I still remembered you."

"I'm sorry!" I started to cry.

"I'm just thankful to have you back. Your note almost killed me." He dabbed at a wound on my neck. "I need to know what's coming, Claire. Please!"

"You will. I promise."

"You've always held back. What's changed?"

"What's changed is that I now know what I didn't know twelve hours ago. There *are* three of us. In the future."

"Three of us? You mean Rebecca?"

"She's part of our story, and I nearly lost her today."

"Lost her? How?"

"Two ways . . ." I rubbed away my tears. "I'll tell you the first part later. Right now, I need to see a doctor."

"No kidding." He showed me the gauze in his hand. It was red with blood.

"No, not that." I told him about the cramping attacks that had almost felled me.

"Do you have cramps now?"

"No."

Marc wasted no time. He called Nonie. She joined us. I reached out and took her hand. "Thank you for bringing him. And I'm sorry."

"Least I could do, girl," Nonie answered with mock gruffness. "You and your secrets! Have 'em from me if you want, but not from your man!"

If you only knew, dear Nonie . . .

It wasn't difficult for me to look seriously chastened. "He's about to hear all my secrets," I told her.

"Good! Now, get moving and find a hospital!"

"On our way!" Marc replied. He hugged her and then circled the truck to the driver's door.

"See you back at the Creek," Nonie said as she shut the door.

We drove at high speed to Ocala. Knowing we'd need a feasible story to account for my torn flesh and multiple bruises, we concocted a fable that I'd been attacked at work by a jealous female barfly who thought I was making a play for her boyfriend.

It was after dark when we reached the ER at Munroe. Dr. LaPierre was on call. A nurse cleaned and dressed my wounds, and then I had to endure a physical while Marc paced outside the curtain.

The doctor's enormous hands hadn't gotten any smaller. When he snapped on the surgical gloves, I cringed.

"Any bleeding?" he asked.

"A bit of spotting. Nothing to speak of."

"Let me be the judge of that. How long have you been spotting?"

"Just for a day, then it stopped."

"Tissue or clots?"

"No."

While he conducted the exam, he peppered me with more questions—was I having any backache, were my breasts sore, was I having morning sickness? To my relief, his touch was gentle.

"You've lost weight since I saw you last. That's a bit worrying. You should be gaining weight."

"I've been under a lot of stress. But that's over."

"What's over?"

"The stress."

"Care to talk about it?"

"No."

"Your friend there . . ." He jerked his thumb toward the curtain. "Is he honorable?"

I suppressed a smile. "Yes. Don't worry. We both want this baby."

He sighed and peeled off the gloves. "Okay, baby's probably okay. Have you seen the ob-gyn I referred you to?"

"Not yet."

He didn't look happy. "I want you to start seeing Dr. Frost. I'll make the arrangements. No arguments! In the meantime, call me right away if you have any of the symptoms I just asked you about. You have one job, Claire—carrying your baby to term."

And don't I know it . . .

"Her name is Rebecca."

"We don't know the gender yet. We probably won't know for several weeks." He smiled. "So I hope you have an alternative name for a boy."

"No. She's definitely a girl."

He stared at me. "I'd like to know where you get your information."

"There are certain things I just know, Doc. This is one of them. Am I good to go?"

"'Good to go'? Now, there's a space-age expression. Yes." He paused, regarding me appraisingly. "May I offer a word of advice?"

This time, I smiled. "You will anyway."

"This is your first pregnancy and we don't know how your body will handle it. You need to take better care of yourself. If you must work, I recommend you find a job that's less . . . boisterous. Consider finding something where you can use your brain."

"Care to tell me what's really on your mind?"

"You're clearly an educated woman. I don't know why you've exiled yourself to Cross Creek of all places, and I guess that's your business. But you shouldn't be working in a low-life tavern where you risk being assaulted. You owe it to your baby to be more careful."

I didn't think he'd appreciate me telling him that I'd started the day intending to erase both our lives, so I just nodded and tried to appear suitably chastened.

"Based on the nature of the fight you were in, I'm ordering a tetanus shot. It won't harm the fetus." He was about to yank the curtain back.

I stopped him. "Before you go . . ."

"Yes?"

"Could you pass me my jacket? I have something for you."

Puzzled, he plucked my jacket off the chair next to the bed. I dug in a pocket and found my watch. I handed it to him.

"A watch?"

"Not just any watch. It's like my appendectomy."

"I don't follow."

"It's the only one on the planet. Keep it to remember me."

He stared at me, then examined the watch. "It's not running."

"Maybe you'll get it fixed one day."

He looked perplexed. "Thanks, I think." He yanked back the curtain. Marc was standing there. "Claire will be getting a shot," the doctor told him. "After that, she's all yours. But for God's sake, young man, take better care of this girl!"

"I will, if she'll let me," Marc replied.

Dr. LaPierre shook his head and left. I saw him examining my watch as he walked away.

Marc moved to my side. "I heard that. You gave him your watch. Why?"

"I'm a mystery to him. I thought I'd give him a new puzzle to solve."

"That watch will drive him crazy."

"If he keeps it for twenty years, he'll be able to get it fixed."

"Which will make him even crazier."

"At least he'll remember me."

Marc understood. He stroked my hair, kissed me, and helped me get dressed.

54

"How could you think you were Jane Doe?"

We'd been sitting in our usual places on the veranda since we got back from the hospital. Now, hours later, the eastern sky was brightening with another dawn. Those hours had been filled with a monologue from me . . . long, emotional, and utterly necessary. We were both drained and ready for bed, but neither of us was ready to surrender.

"She was pregnant, and I'm pregnant. Your mother's locket was found in her grave. The crab's eye pea inside the locket was obviously a clue. It only made sense if it was a clue I'd left for myself, because it was that clue that led us to the killer. It all pointed to one conclusion: I was Jane Doe."

"But you stood in that morgue with Terry Snead and examined her body! How could it be *your* skeleton if you were looking at it? That would mean two of you would be existing at the same time. You've already convinced me that that's impossible!"

"Not *exactly* two of me."

"What do you mean?"

"Something I remembered from high school biology . . . the human body is constantly replacing itself. The person you are today is not identical to the person you were yesterday. Your body replaces around two million cells every day. It happens at different rates. Some cells are replaced every few days. Blood cells, every few months. Bone cells take years."

"Years? How does that—?"

"Those are just rough replacement rates. It's a constant process. I figured the skeleton I viewed in the morgue was just a *later* version of me—at least at the cellular level. It would have been about six months older than my living skeleton. Most of the bone cells would be the same, but millions of them would be newer. I thought Jane was me, just not the *same* me that stood there looking at her."

Hope flashed across Marc's face. "So you're saying there can be two of you?"

"It was just a theory. She wasn't me. She was Doris."

"A theory that almost got you killed."

"Yeah."

Marc went quiet. Then he asked the question I'd been expecting: "Okay, what changed your mind? In that basement."

"The entry wound on Jane's skull was close to her right temple. Tribe was about to shoot me in the *left* side of my head."

He was thoughtful. "So . . . the future actually saved you."

"Or I saved it. What about your gun? What will you tell them?"

"That it was stolen from the cabin while I was out fishing. I'll make the report to the state police and give a copy to my boss. He'll give me hell, and they'll issue me a new weapon."

I was quiet.

"What are you thinking?" Marc asked.

"We need to plan. We have less than a year."

"I wish you'd stop reminding me of that."

"We both need to be strong, but you need to be stronger. For a long time."

"I know." His voice sounded steady, but I knew it was a struggle.

"Have you started copying files?"

"I've filled a Bankers Box. It's in my apartment."

"Has anyone noticed?"

"Not yet. I'll take my time. You said I've got a year."

"You told me you resigned in April of '79, but because of accumulated leave time, you actually left the job sometime in March. You didn't tell me the date."

"I'm still trying to get used to the way you talk. You say I told you something that I haven't told you yet, and I'm supposed to nod wisely and file that away so I can remember to tell you thirty years from now."

"All I know is that it did happen, so it will happen."

"I think you should write it down. All of it. Not just for me. For Rebecca. How will I ever explain it to her? She'll think I'm deluded!"

He was right, but he didn't know I was one step ahead of him.

"I already have."

"What?"

"The manuscript's in your desk."

He looked shaken.

"I'll keep writing," I added. "You're going to need it."

He let out a breath. "Because I'm going to need a script."

I kissed him. "Yes, my love. You're going to need a script."

"Make sure it's all there. From the beginning."

"Which beginning?"

"The courtroom one, when I dropped into your life."

"Instead of the hospital one, when I crash-landed in yours?"

He managed a desolate smile.

"Rebecca will need time. Time to take it all in. Time to adjust to the impossible. You'll need to prepare her long before you come to sit in the back of my courtroom."

"Why?"

"Because she'll be driving you around in a white SUV."

"A what?"

"A 'sport-utility vehicle'—like a Bronco, or a Blazer. Pretty soon there'll be one in every driveway." I hesitated, distracted. Something was lurking on the ragged edges of my memory.

Realization slammed home.

"Oh God!"

"What?"

"One day Rebecca will stop me outside the courthouse and ask for directions. I didn't know her!" I felt my throat constrict. "Marc! I didn't know my own daughter!"

He took me in his arms.

"She was beautiful! She was beautiful and she didn't even know it."

"That's the best kind. She'll be just like her mother." He held me tight for long seconds.

But when he released me, I could see something was bothering him. "What is it?"

"Where will Rebecca be while I—" His voice caught. "—while I watch you grow up?"

"You'll just be visiting. Maybe she'll be with a nanny. Or your wife."

"I *have* a wife. And I'll soon have the papers to prove it."

"Thirty years is a long time."

"There won't be another wife." His voice was adamant.

"Okay," I said. "Then, what about money?"

"I've been meaning to ask you about that."

"Let's analyze it. You quit the police and moved away so you could raise Rebecca somewhere where no one knows you. If you stayed here, people might start asking questions. But raising a child will cost money. According to Lipinski, you quit before your pension locked in. You never mentioned where you went or what you did for a living. All I know is that when you showed up in my life, money wasn't a problem."

"Then I must have found another job."

I thought for a moment. "The answer is staring us in the face."

"What do you mean?"

"Where am I from?"

His eyes narrowed. "The future. Two thousand and—"

"—eleven! Right! Do you own any stocks?"

"No."

"There are certain names you should know. I'll write them down for you."

"What kind of names?"

"Names like Steve Jobs . . . Bill Gates . . . Warren Buffet. Geniuses who made themselves and a lot of other people very rich. I'll start racking my memory, and you start learning about investing."

55

I gave birth to Rebecca Claire Hastings on November 28, 1978.
Which meant she was almost a year older than me.

Marc and I had obtained a backdated certificate of marriage, and I
had a wallet full of ID. Everyone in The Yearling knew, or thought they
knew, that I had been Marc's "top secret wife"—as Nonie put it—since
October 1977.

Before my pregnancy began to show, I arranged for one of my workmates at The Yearling to take a Polaroid photograph of Marc and me
sitting at the bar. That night, I dutifully cut the photo in half and explained to him what use he would make of my side of the picture in the
future.

Around the same time, I persuaded Marc to take some time off and
drive us to Mexico Beach. With its red board-and-batten siding, pine furniture, and cedar paneling, the Driftwood looked a lot different from its
successor hostelry of later decades, but we spent an idyllic time reading,
walking the beach, and making love—just as we had on our first visit.

At least . . . on my first visit.

By the time Rebecca was born, strikes and demonstrations were para-
lyzing Iran. The revolution had begun—and Marc and I were the only two
people in the world who knew exactly what would happen at the U.S.
Embassy in Tehran on my birthday eleven months later. It was painful
knowledge that I regretted sharing with him, because in the end, as we
both knew, he could do nothing. I told him only because he remembered

what I'd said in the police car on our first day, and he had questioned me about it.

By then, we had already agreed that he and Rebecca would leave the country after I was gone, and Marc had quietly bought a house in British Columbia's Fraser Valley, not far from Vancouver.

And by then, I had persuaded him to take me to see Gertie Hopkins.

I was heavily pregnant when we made the trip back to Palatka in late September. I had forced myself to wait until then because I wanted my condition to be glaringly noticeable. I was tying up a loose end, but I was also being prudent.

I wanted to deter retaliation.

We parked near the side entrance to Putnam Community Hospital. It seemed like a lifetime ago that Marc had driven me out of this parking lot.

I asked him to wait in the car.

"Why?"

"I don't want any witnesses. Especially police witnesses."

"Are you planning to commit a crime?"

"Yes."

He blinked.

I kissed him. "Don't worry. It'll never go to trial."

"Will I need to bail you out?"

"I'm not sure. If a sheriff's car arrives before I return, come looking."

I got out and walked into the hospital.

I had called ahead, without giving a name, so I knew Gertie was on shift. It wasn't hard to find her. She was rushing out of a patient's room on the medical ward and almost ran me over.

"Oh! I'm so sorry!" She stopped and stared at my face. "Butterfly tattoo!"

"That's not my name, Gertie."

"Right, right, right! Claire . . . Claire Talbot! How are you doing?" She gaped. "Look at you! When are you due?"

"In two months."

"Wow! What a comeback!"

"Yeah . . . I was pretty messed up back then. Do you have a minute? I need to talk to you. In private."

"Well, I'm due for my break soon, but first I've got to take care of something for a patient."

"I can wait."

She pointed. "There's a playroom down the end, on the right. There are no kids on the ward right now. There's a couch."

"I'll see you there."

I waited in the playroom. I was standing in front of the couch when Gertie showed up five minutes later.

"Gosh, Claire! You're allowed to sit down!"

I checked for witnesses. There was no one in sight.

I slapped Gertie across the face as hard as I could. She stumbled back and landed on the couch. She stared up at me in utter shock.

"I thought I'd wait for *you* to sit first," I said as I settled beside her. "I hope that didn't leave a mark."

"What was that for?" Her voice was a high-pitched squeak, and her eyes were big with tears.

I took her by the hand. She yanked it away and tried to get up. I held her by the arm. "I slapped you so you would always remember this conversation."

"What conversation? I'm not having one with you! You're crazy! I'm calling the police!"

"He's waiting outside."

"Who?"

"The detective who came for me that day."

"You came to assault me, and you brought a policeman with you?"

"He's my husband."

"What? What is this?"

"Gertie, please listen to me, and never forget what I'm about to tell you. Your life depends on it."

She gingerly felt her cheek, which was still red where I'd hit her. Her face hardened. "My life? What are you talking about?"

"How old are you?"

"I'll be thirty next month. What's that got to do with—?"

I held up my hand. She shut up. "Two things: First of all, you will live to the age of sixty-two. Second, you will not live *past* the age of sixty-two unless you do exactly as I say!"

"I don't believe in horoscopes!"

I ignored her and kept going. "A few months after your sixty-second birthday, you will get on a train. And on that train you will see me. When you do, you will remember the day I came here and slapped your face. And then you will remember what I told you."

"You haven't told me anything! You're talking in riddles!" She tried to get up again.

I sank my fingers into her arm.

She winced. "You're hurting me!"

"I'm hurting you so you will remember I told you to get off that train!"

"Get off the train? Why?"

"Because if you don't, you will die."

I released her arm. I stood up. "I'm sorry I hit you. Just remember what I said. I'll see you in thirty years."

I could feel her eyes boring into my back as I left the room.

I had paid my dues.

56

Soon I will be gone.

Becky sleeps in the crook of my arm while I attempt these final lines. In a few days, I will lose my little angel forever.

It is more than I can bear.

Across the room, Marc tosses and moans. The remorseless torment that has dogged our paths all these months never grants him a moment's rest. He knows what is coming. He tries to prepare himself, but I know his soul is filled with dread.

I have managed to keep my sanity. Marc never stops reminding me of this apparent miracle. But for me it has only been a year, and there were times, as he and I both know, when I barely held on.

As the final days have slouched toward us, Marc has tried to keep the talk hopeful. But hope is not the same thing as optimism, and just as I am dying, so is he. And, just as Old Marc did during my final weeks in the future, Young Marc has become quieter.

And quieter . . .

It is a cruel thing to know the date of my death. But it is a crueler thing still for the man who loves me beyond all reasoning, and who would gladly barter away his life for mine, to know that date as well.

He holds me. He prays. He weeps until he's exhausted.

But I can offer no solace.

•   •   •

My dear husband—

The thought of what you now face torments me. My life has been short, but my fate more merciful, and that is the cruelest twist of all.

Watch over me and love me until our day returns, and I can love you again.

This is my testament.

And your guide.

REBECCA

57

The detectives were on their way to interview a witness, but a dropped 911 call from a screaming child trumps last week's jewelry heist every time.

"Delta Five, you're the closest unit!"

Mattis responded. "Delta Five. Repeat that address!" His partner wrote it down. When his hand reached for the console, she grabbed his sleeve.

"Silent approach, John!"

He gave a quick nod. His partner had a sixth sense, and she was usually right. He braked and took the cutoff onto Grange Street. They cleared traffic with their lights and the occasional quick burp on the yelper. The Crown Vic burned down Grange and took the corner at Barker in a four-wheel slide. Mattis was ex–Unit B Traffic and it showed. He handled the big car like it was part of his body.

His partner already had the map up on her screen. She pointed. "It's the gray one!"

They were angled to the curb and out of the car in seconds.

The house was a run-down leftover from the 1940s, with asphalt siding and a daylight basement. "Check the back!" Mattis whispered as he double-timed for the steps leading up to the front door.

She wove past a pair of garbage cans, ducked under the boughs of a mature cedar, and stepped onto a strip of weed-choked lawn. Halfway along the side of the house, she came to a door with an overhanging porch light. The door was ajar a few inches.

She saw the back of someone's head on the floor inside the door.

She heard Mattis knock on the upstairs door and call, "Police!"

She drew her weapon.

Cautiously, she pushed on the door. The gap widened, revealing a ground-floor apartment.

The head belonged to a woman. But there was no body attached.

She took a horrified step back. After a few seconds of frozen shock, her training kicked in. "John!" she yelled. "Down here!"

Then she heard it.

A cry.

It was a child's voice.

She pushed the door open and stepped into a scene from hell.

The woman's body lay in a spreading lake of blood a few feet from her head. Next to it was an overturned coffee table, and beyond that, on a ratty couch, lay the body of a young girl. She was maybe ten or eleven years old. She was sprawled like a rag doll, and her throat was a gaping, bloody mess.

The cry came again. It rose to a wail and then ended, cut off abruptly.

She ran, clearing every doorway, every room, as she went. She reached the final bedroom. The door was shut. She kicked it open and came in low.

A wild-eyed, unshaven man was squatting in a corner with the child's small body positioned directly in front of him. He held a bloody hand across the girl's mouth and a vicious, blood-streaked blade pressed to her throat.

"*Let her go!*"

"She's coming with me!" he hissed. "We're a family!"

She looked into the little girl's eyes and saw terror in its purest form.

"*Release her! NOW!*"

"No!"

She saw his elbow rise.

She saw the blade change angle.

RCMP Sergeant Rebecca Hastings shot Wayde Patrick Elgin, estranged husband of Jacqueline Anne Elgin and father of two, in the precise center in his labium superius oris, one millimeter below his nose. The 147-grain hollow-point slug tore through his head, destroyed his brain stem, and blasted gore and bone fragments across the wallpaper behind him.

The knife dropped from boneless fingers, and the girl ran shrieking into Rebecca's arms.

When Mattis found her, she was still cradling a horrified six-year-old. He took in the scene at a glance. He put a gentle hand on Rebecca's shoulder. "At least you saved one."

Tears coursed down Rebecca's face as she caressed the shuddering child.

"I'm not sure I did," she replied.

Three months later, Rebecca was sitting in a witness box at the provincial courthouse in Vancouver. All seven members of a coroner's jury were leaning forward in their seats, rapt with horror, as she described those final moments in that basement suite. Two jurors and a number of members of the packed public gallery were in tears.

The coroner held up a hand, interrupting her testimony. "Excuse me . . . a moment, please." The coroner faced the jury. She spoke in a gentle tone. "Mr. Foreman, does the jury need a break?"

The man swiveled in his seat, scanning faces. Almost in unison, the panel members shook their heads. One of the more visibly distraught jurors replied in a loud whisper: "No! Please just let her finish."

The foreman rose to his feet. "Madam Coroner, the jury would like to continue."

"All right. Thank you." She turned to Rebecca. "Please continue, Sergeant."

Rebecca resumed her testimony. A few minutes later, the public entrance opened and a tall man stepped into the courtroom. At first she didn't notice him. But as a row of spectators shifted to make room for the latecomer, the rustling sound drew her attention.

Rebecca watched her father take his seat. When he saw her looking at him, he gave an imperceptible nod and sat very, very still.

Thirty-five minutes later, she found him waiting in the lobby.

•　　　•　　　•

November 28, 2008
Cross Creek, Florida

She experienced the near death of too much knowledge.

She wept. She raged.

But she finally understood.

She finally understood why her father had insisted she accompany him to Florida for her thirtieth birthday. Why he'd refused to take no for an answer. Why he'd visited her unit while she was off-shift and leaned hard on the OIC until the man agreed to reschedule her leave.

Her father had wanted her isolated.

Her father had wanted complete control, so he could manage the fallout.

That morning, he'd brought her breakfast in bed. Along with the eggs and toast and coffee and orange juice came a dog-eared manuscript. Most of it was typed, but the final pages were written in a looping natural hand.

In thirty years, not once had her father mentioned the manuscript's existence.

While she spent the day, propped by pillows, reading her mother's impossible story of her impossible life, her father had left her alone. He lay on his bed, as motionless as a stone effigy on a tomb . . . and waited.

The story was beyond belief, beyond logic, beyond comprehension, but it explained so much:

Why she had been raised in Canada by a single American father . . .

Why her father had never remarried . . .

Why she'd never seen a photograph of her mother . . .

Why her father had told her that her mother's parents were both dead . . .

Why there had always been so much mystery about her mother's death . . .

And it explained her father's impenetrable silences. Silences that had eventually driven them apart.

He found her on the bathroom floor. He carried her to his bed. He held her for hours. He talked to her softly. He sat up all night, watching her sleep.

By morning, she was shaky but ready to talk. He brought her coffee on the veranda. She was sitting in the old rocker. It had been her mother's favorite chair. She desperately wanted to feel a physical connection, but it was just an old chair. The story was the connection. She had never believed in out-of-body experiences, but now she was living one. Her body was here, but some other part of her was . . . somewhere else.

Wandering and confused.

"What happened?" her physical self asked. "What happened at the end?"

Her father was very still.

Her hand found his. "Dad?"

He wiped his eyes. "Our last day was a Sunday. Just before dark, I opened a bottle of Margaux. A month earlier, I had called every wine merchant in Gainesville until I tracked one down. It was a '68—not a great year I later learned, but that wasn't important. I wanted it to be a Margaux. I brought the bottle and two glasses out here. Your mother was sitting in that chair." He went quiet for a second. "She must have felt it."

"Felt what?"

"Something . . . a warning. I remember the screen door banging shut behind me. I remember the panic on her face. She said my name. She reached for me . . . and then the chair was empty." He looked at her bleakly. "I have never known such despair. I took your mother's place in that chair and drank the bottle of wine. If it wasn't for you, I would have taken my own life that night."

"Me?"

"You were three months old, and you were asleep in our bedroom."

"All those trips you took when I was growing up," she said. "You were coming here."

"I watched you both grow up."

They were quiet for long minutes.

He was remembering. . . .

Remembering three days in his car in a parking lot, listening to Anne Murray's heartbreaking chart-topper play over and over on the radio, waiting for Margaret Talbot to carry her infant daughter from the hospital.

Remembering the playgrounds and the schools and the colleges and the summer jobs.

Remembering the girlfriends and the boyfriends, the betraying lovers and the lovers betrayed.

Remembering three decades of grief, of madness, of unremitting sorrow.

Rebecca's voice rescued him from his sink of memory and pain.

"And now, Dad . . . what?"

"Soon it will be time for me to reenter her life. I will need your help."

"Do I look like her?"

"Yes. And you have her toughness, which is good. You're going to need it."

"I want to see her."

He handed her a folded section of newspaper. "She's running an extortion prosecution this week."

She read the brief account eagerly, her hands trembling, her eyes racing down the column, lingering over the quotes . . . and then she read it again, slowly, sentence by sentence. He watched the wonder and the fear in her eyes.

"You can see her today," he said. "She won't be aware of us for two more years."

Rebecca's eyes drifted to their rental car, parked in front of the steps. It was a metallic blue Malibu.

"She kept seeing a white SUV."

"I bought it a few months ago. It's in storage in Jacksonville. I'll install the taillights on my next trip."

"You mean *our* next trip."

"I was hoping you'd say that."

"Who's the registered owner?"

"You, but with a different name."

"Which means I'll need ID."

"Just a driver's license. Don't worry. I know a guy."

"He must be dead by now!"

"His son isn't."

That afternoon they drove to Gainesville. They parked at a diner on South Main, across from the courthouse entrance. They went in, took a table by the window, and ordered a late lunch. They lingered, killing time, barely touching their food. Just before four, they returned to the car.

They waited.

At four forty-five, Marc squeezed Rebecca's hand.

Rebecca's throat constricted as she watched a young white woman descend the courthouse steps accompanied by a tall middle-aged black man. In that instant, Rebecca knew it was all true. The angles of the woman's face . . . her figure . . . the way she moved . . .

It was as if she were watching a slightly altered version of herself.

"The man is Edward Carlyle," her father said. "He's the State Attorney's Chief Investigator."

"I remember . . . from the Hauser case."

Claire Talbot and Edward Carlyle crossed the street and turned north. They passed in front of the parked Malibu. Carlyle seemed to sense their presence. He gave Marc the once-over. His gaze lingered a little longer on Rebecca, and then he looked away. Claire was lost in thought and didn't notice.

Rebecca reached for her door handle.

"Becks!"

"I just want to hear her voice! I'll make something up! I'll . . . I'll ask for directions!"

"Please, sweetheart! This isn't the time. You know that."

"Dad! Please!" She grabbed at his wrists. "Why can't we stop this? Why can't we just fix it?"

"Fix it?"

"Why can't we just keep her off that train? We can do that! She might be running from you by then, but I could help! I could find a way to stop her from getting on the train, and then we could tell her the whole story, and"—in her fervor, her nails sank into his arm—"we can prove it to her!"

"Prove it? How?"

"With DNA! My DNA. It will prove I'm her daughter! She'll have to believe us!"

"Rebecca . . ."

"What?"

"Your mom and I had this conversation."

"You did? You mean . . . *that's the plan?*"

"No."

"Why not? It's so simple!" Now she was frantic.

"My love, it's the farthest thing from simple. Think it through . . . if your mother doesn't go into the past, she can't save her own mother from Harlan Tribe. If she doesn't save her, she'll never be born. And neither will you." He waited while his daughter processed his words. He could sense her resistance—her mind searching, searching for a way out . . . for any way out.

Searching for a solution where there wasn't one.

"You're forgetting something else."

"What?"

"'Only the future is certain,' and your mother's future is in the past." He was trying to keep his voice calm, but it was a plainly a struggle. "If our future—yours and mine—is to stop her from getting on that train, how could you be sitting here now? And how could I even know she exists? *That* future would cancel *this* present."

Rebecca's fortitude suddenly deserted her. She collapsed against her father, her body shuddering with sobs. Marc Hastings wrapped his daughter in his arms and waited for her to cry herself out.

He held Rebecca's hand as he drove, but they didn't speak for most of the trip home.

As they rolled through the last mile into Cross Creek, she heaved a long, rattling sigh and broke the wall of silence between them. "Harrison Ford, huh?"

He forced a smile. "Guess I'd better get in shape."

"Definitely."

"What does that mean?" he asked, feigning mild offense.

"It means if you think you're going to keep that wall-to-wall sex thing going with a woman half your age, you'd better join a gym!"

"See here, young lady! That's no way to talk to your father."

She laughed, and then he did.

They looked at each other in wonder, shocked that they could laugh at all.

They crossed the bridge over the creek.

"Do you ever stop at The Yearling when you come here?"

"Once in a while."

"Is Nonie still there?"

"Yes. She thinks your mom died in a car accident."

"So did I."

"I'm sorry, Becks."

"Does Nonie know about me?"

"Sure does. I told her you're one of those legendary red-coated Mounties in the Great White North. She was impressed."

"Let's stop!"

He slowed the car. "Are you sure?"

"She knew my mother. I want to meet her."

"You'll have to be careful what you say."

"I will, but I'm not worried."

"Why?"

"Because Mom said Nonie never pries."

Marc swung the Malibu into The Yearling's lot. When they entered the building, he led her past the bar, directly to the table closest to the rear exit door.

"Is this the table where you stopped that beer glass?"

"Yes."

"Who were you with, Dad? Who left the table and went out that door just before Mom came in?"

"It hasn't happened yet, remember?"

"Okay. Who *will* it be?"

"You, sweetheart. It will be you."

As Rebecca grappled with her father's reply, a gravelly female voice growled, "About time, Marc Hastings! Where have you been?"

Rebecca swung around. A white-haired woman was embracing her father.

"Are you Nonie?" Rebecca asked.

"I am." The woman turned to Rebecca. Her jaw dropped. "You must be . . . Sweet Jesus, you look just like your mother!"

Before Nonie could react, Rebecca pulled her into a hug. "Thank you," Rebecca whispered. "Thank you for being her friend."

Nonie stepped back. Her eyes were damp. "It was a long time ago, but I still miss her. There was something about her." Her mind seemed to drift off for a second. Then she wiped an eye and grinned at them. "Let's get you some drinks. First round's on me!"

They stayed for dinner.

The following afternoon, as they waited in the small business terminal at Ocala Regional Airport, Rebecca asked her father the Question.

The Question. The one that had haunted him for thirty years.

"Dad?"

"Mmm?" He looked up from his newspaper.

"What about Tribe?"

She watched her father's eyes turn to chalk. "That's something we need to discuss."

"I may not be here to help you. I mean, if you get Mom pregnant before she goes . . . back." Rebecca didn't elaborate. She didn't have to.

"You'll be here. You were definitely conceived back then."

"How do you know?"

"Your Mom saw you . . . from the train."

"But . . . her manuscript! She didn't know me!"

"Not then. But before she was gone, she realized it must have been you."

"She said that?"

"She asked me to tell you. She hoped that, maybe—knowing that—it won't hurt as much when you see that train leave."

Rebecca watched her father. Something wasn't right.

"You're not sure. You would have told me sooner."

He sighed. "No, I'm not sure. I'm counting on a mother's intuition. But it's *your* mother's intuition, so I'd bet my life on it."

"And my life?"

"Yes, dear Becks." He touched her cheek. "And your life."

The pilot of their chartered jet appeared at the security desk. He signed some paperwork and then nodded to them.

Rebecca rose and picked up her bag. "That's good enough for me," she said, and started walking to the plane.

March 1, 2011
Palatka, Florida

It was her second visit. The first one, ten days ago, had been to get her bearings.

Not that those bearings were needed. The Amtrak Rail Station at Palatka was not much larger than a house in suburbia. The covered portion of the ground-level platform was a twenty-by-fifty rectangle of worn and cracked concrete under split sections of tiled roof supported by four metal uprights. The uncovered portion consisted of a narrow asphalt sidewalk that yielded to a level road crossing a few hundred feet to the south and gave way to roadbed gravel and patchy grass a hundred feet to the north.

She took a position on the grass near the northwest corner of the station.

She ticked off the minutes in her mind, waiting.

There it was.

The distant sound of a train's horn. Two short blasts, then a long one. Ten seconds . . . twenty . . . then a distant light . . . *clang, clang,* as the barriers lowered at the level crossing . . . *clang, clang,* as the sleek engine rolled past her position . . . a second engine . . . a baggage car . . . sliding past the platform, braking, squealing . . . the long shimmer of the passenger cars slowing, slowing . . .

The train stopped.

Seconds passed. A minute, then another.

A family disembarked . . . mother and father lugging suitcases, two mop-headed boys.

Next, a man, twenty-something, alone, T-shirt, cargo pants, slinging a knapsack.

Then, from the next car down, an older woman, fifties, maybe sixties, with a small wheeled bag and an agitated expression.

Rebecca moved fast, marching across the platform, double-timing down the asphalt extension. She seized the woman by the arm.

"Are you Gertie Hopkins?"

The woman recoiled, startled. Her brow knitted. "That was my maiden name. How did—?" She fixed on Rebecca's face, and her eyes widened. "My goodness, you look like—!"

"—Claire Talbot. I know. Show me where she's sitting!"

"Why?"

"Show me!"

"What are you going to do?"

"Please . . . just show me."

The woman pointed at a window in the car next to them. It was about twenty feet away. Rebecca's eyes took a millisecond to focus, and then she saw her mother watching them through the darkened glass. In that same instant, the train started to move.

Rebecca released her grip on the woman's arm and started jogging, trying desperately to keep pace.

Her eyes locked on her mother's eyes. Her mother looked puzzled, then . . . disturbed.

All the anguish and longing that Rebecca Hastings had kept sealed off deep at the center of her being finally welled up and overwhelmed her.

"Mommy!" she cried. "I love you!"

The train departed on its final journey.

Rebecca fell to her knees.

Gertie Hopkins approached. She stood off a few paces, silent and respectful.

Rebecca rose to her feet. She faced the old nurse. "Claire Talbot just saved your life." Her voice was flat, hollow, empty.

"How do you know that?"

"Because she told me she would." She rubbed away her tears. "She saved mine, too."

"Who are you?"

"Her daughter."

"But . . . that's impossible!"

"I know."

Rebecca turned and walked away.

March 2, 2011
Gainesville, Florida

Tribe checked the street as he drove toward his house. There were no vehicles that didn't belong. He swung into his driveway and nosed the car up to the garage door. When he got out, he glanced around warily. With luck, the media hounds had moved on to the next big story, and the driveway ambushes were over.

Maybe, at last, he could get back to his life.

He scuttled to the rear of his station wagon and dropped the tailgate. As he lifted out the bags of groceries, he congratulated himself on his brains and his luck. Brains because the cops hadn't found the photographs, and luck because that young prosecutor and her ex-cop pal had done such a flawless job of tainting the evidence.

Young prosecutor . . .

That one made no sense. . . .

It made no fucking sense at all!

He pushed the perplexing thoughts away.

His attorney had told him the search of his residence at the time of his arrest would have been tougher to challenge. "Search incident to arrest," Bannister had called it. When he'd admitted, obliquely, that there might be some evidence in the house connecting him to the missing girls, he'd been confident that attorney–client privilege would prevent Bannister from ever repeating that to anyone. The lawyer had told him—through clenched teeth—that if the cops had found that evidence, he would definitely be facing a jury.

The cops were diligent, but not one of them had been smart enough to wonder why every single interior door in Tribe's house had a hollow-core design. Every door was adorned with an identical decorative panel. All someone had to do was remove the panel on his bedroom door, and he would have found an envelope filled with Polaroid photographs, each one featuring one of the girls lying naked on a bare mattress on a dirt floor.

Naked . . . and terrified.

Luckily, none of the cops had been clever enough to notice that the only modern feature in Tribe's forty-year-old house was its interior doors.

Earlier this morning, he'd pried the panel off. He'd spent an hour lingering over the pictures, wallowing in the memories. But he hadn't retrieved the envelope just for titillation. The time had come. The photos had to be destroyed. As soon as he put the groceries away, he would burn every one of them and flush the ashes.

It was something he should have done a long time ago.

He slammed the tailgate and carried the groceries into the house. He set them on the kitchen counter. He tugged a folded newspaper from one of the bags. He leaned on the counter, studying the front page story.

There was a rustling noise behind him.

"Hello, Tribe." A woman's voice, silky and calm.

He spun around.

"You should have listened," the voice continued.

Tribe stared, uncomprehending.

"Listened to what?" He stared at her. "You look like that woman!" His jaw contorted. "I don't understand!"

A gloved hand raised a matte black nine-millimeter pistol. It was mounted with a silencer. "Do you understand this?"

Tribe went pale. "Yes."

"I saw the photographs. I laid them out on your dresser so the police will find them."

Tribe let out a resigned breath.

She fired. The slug tore into his chest. He flew back, caromed off the counter, and crashed to the floor. A grocery bag toppled, spilling fruit and canned goods over his twitching form.

Rebecca Hastings knelt in front of him. She looked straight into the dying man's eyes. "My mother left you a bullet. Maybe you should have used it." She pressed the muzzle of the pistol against his nose and pulled the trigger.

The bullet ripped through his skull. Blood and brains tattooed the floor and cupboard behind him.

She rose. She picked the newspaper off the counter. She studied the headline:

AMTRAK DISASTER!
27 CONFIRMED DEAD; 1 MISSING

An aerial photo showed wrecked railcars lying zigzag in shallows next to the base of a damaged trestle.

Embedded in the article's text was another photograph.

A photograph of her mother, Claire Alexandra Talbot.

The caption read:

CONTROVERSIAL GAINESVILLE PROSECUTOR CLAIRE TALBOT MISSING IN AMTRAK WRECK

Rebecca folded the newspaper. She knelt down. She lifted Harlan Tribe's bloodless right hand and placed the newspaper under it.

She left the house.

Just before sunrise on the day Marc and Rebecca Hastings would leave Florida forever, they parked their U-Haul van in the breakdown lane on US 17, just south of the bridge over the St. Johns River. They walked slowly out onto the span. Three hundred yards downstream, a crane car sat on an undamaged section of a railway trestle, heaving and groaning. Thick steel cables sang like giant bowstrings as the crane strained to raise shattered railcars from the murky waters below.

Marc and Rebecca stood next to the railing, watching the recovery operation.

Behind them, cars and trucks whipped past, engines straining, tires clacking and rattling on the uneven bridge surface.

But they heard nothing.

Time stood still.

Rebecca clutched her father's arm.

He sagged against the railing.

She held him while he wept.